Cooner's Bench

John S. Hall

D1402857

ISBN: 1492122157
ISBN 13: 9781492122159

To Stuart, Louisa, Margaret, and Richard,
and their families.

Acknowledgments

Cooner's Bench would not have been possible without the day to day encouragement of my wife, Donna, during the three years while writing this book.

Thanks to my editor, Christopher Noel, for organizing and editing the manuscript.

Cherie Staples and Dawn Shaw did a great job proofing *Cooner's Bench,* as did Pat Belding, author, poet, and proofreader. She also gave guidance in the final review.

Thanks to Mary Hall, my sister-in-law, and Margaret Gladstone, my daughter, who have been huge supporters of my work; also for additional reviews by my brother, Phil, Betsy Parah, Linda Hall, and my daughter, Louisa Driscoll.

Thanks also to those providing valuable information: Bob Jarvis, Dr. Stuart Williams, Arthur Zorn, Mary Tebbetts, Bryan Pfeiffer, Alban Richey, Susan Turner, Al Martin, my sons, Stuart and Richard Hall, Art and Jo Chickering, Scott Maguire, Mark Jones, Fletcher Manley, Jim Young, and Keith Cushman.

Cooner Clapton

As I sit waitin' for breakfast on this wooden bench just outside the kitchen door, I'm thinkin' about those kids, Jason and Ruth Murray. Ya might's well say I raised them. 'Course, their mom, Maggie, made the meals and Marcus, their dad, helped when he was home nights, but most days I had the care of them. There wan't no need for me to step in and watch over them, but I'm mighty glad I was asked. Ya see both Marcus and Maggie were left plenty of money, but bein' from an old Vermont Yankee family, brought up scratchin' each day for the next cent, they were driven ta work.

I'm eighty-five years old, and have been a hired man at the Murray Farm here in Huntersville, Vermont, since I was fifteen. Through all those years a lot of water's gone over the dam. But in 1995 the dam broke for Ruth and Jason. Troubles gushed through a short stretch of time, changin' their lives forever.

Ruth was twenty-four in the spring of '95. She was as beautiful on the inside as she showed on the outside with her honey-blond hair, a sunny smile, and sky-blue eyes. Golly, she warmed the cockles of my heart. That year she did the financial stuff for the family businesses and helped on the farm.

Her brother, Jason, was twenty-two at the time, a handsome fellow—tall, broad shoulders, short blond hair, a serious sort, but decent at the same time. He'd graduated a year before from Vermont's agricultural school. He was home, takin' over the farm.

Of all the joys in my life, it just puffs me up when I think of the part I had in raisin' them two. What great folks they grew to be. During that terrible time dealin' with the tangles of life, they also struggled with young love, but that wan't surprisin'. In puttin' together two horses, it takes a few tries before ya get a good team.

Well, I'll let Ruth and Jason tell ya their story. I've got to go ta breakfast. I'm smellin' some good cookin'.

one

Jason

After feeding the cows and bedding them, I'd finished morning chores. The sound of contented cows munching on sweet smelling hay, and the scent of pine sawdust hung in the air. I admired the row of my Holsteins and felt a rush of pride that Dad and I had bred and raised every one of them. I slipped a bird book in my back pocket and left the barn.

Just then, a beat-up Ford pulled in the yard. The white car, fenders peppered with rust spots, looked as if it had been hit by a pellet gun. Steven Iverson got out, shut the car door, and came toward me to shake hands. He looked at me with his droopy brown eyes while stroking his iron gray hair. "Well, well, Jason, how are you doing?" His greeting sounded like a tired line he probably used a hundred times a day.

After shaking his soft hand, I returned a straight-face nod. He was Huntersville's representative to the Vermont legislature, a farmer but first and foremost a politician. He was always on the move, seen at all the chicken pie suppers, funerals, and rummage sales. Gilda's Forget Me Not restaurant was his late-night hang-out where he rubbed elbows with all the locals.

As we met, he pulled his pants up over his gut, tucking in his shirt. A knotted tie hung below an open collar. He hunched his shoulders while pulling on the edges of his off-white coat that didn't quite cover his paunch.

"How's it going?" He looked toward the barn, seeming not to care for an answer.

"What's up?" Half turning in my tracks, I wanted to move on with my morning plans.

He stepped back and leaned against the fender of his car as if we had all day. "I've been thinking about you."

"Me?" I stiffened immediately. What did he really want? I doubted Steven Iverson ever gave me a second's thought except during the election when he wanted my vote.

He hesitated and studied me. "Well…well, we could join farms. Hell, we could milk three or four hundred head at my place."

"Why would I want to do that?"

He frowed at me as if I'd just asked a stupid question. "To be more efficient, of course."

I turned. "Sorry, that doesn't interest me." I started to walk away. "And it never will, Steven."

"Wait." Iverson opened a squeaking rear door to reach in his car. "I have some paper work to show you."

I drew a deep breath, uptight inside, waiting. I wanted to take an hour or so to walk to the ridge in back of the barn. Since it was nearly May, I was anxious to plan for a spring tour of our woods, put on by the Huntersville Booster Club. They wanted to hold it here at the farm and have me point out the interesting plant life of spring.

Iverson returned with a bunch of disorderly papers. He leaned against his fender again, slightly rocking the car as he shifted his weight. The lines deepened between his eyes. "Well, you're good with cows." His forehead furrowed. "I have here the blueprints and financial plan for a new dairy." He thrust them toward me.

I backed away. "Large-scale dairying isn't my bag."

Of course I've always been with dairy cows. I've enjoyed the challenge of breeding outstanding Holsteins. Our herd had been analyzed for their strengths and weaknesses and mated to the bulls of my choice, or they carried embryos from outstanding females. A dairy of fifty cows was barely enough to make a living, but I had a plan of selling valuable stock as a second income to justify my small herd.

Iverson continued to act edgy, scuffing the gravel. "I want you to give my offer some thought. You know…" He fingered the fold beneath his chin. "Why don't you think about it?"

I hadn't talked directly to Steven Iverson for some time, but now I saw that he'd slipped—something wasn't right. His history of failed crops up the road swirled in my head. What I'd seen and heard around town was that he'd flopped as a farmer. I imagined the ramifications: sick cows, dead calves, bad milk, unpaid bills, and a looming bank foreclosure. Whatever his mission, I sensed desperation. Maybe his mother, Shirley Iverson, had stopped propping him up. Or Emily Ann Gray, the president of the bank, the woman who had practically raised him, had put her foot down. Whatever the case, under his fake politician's smile, he cried out for help. I knew Iverson coming to me wasn't anything I should get dragged into, nor would I want to. I tried to brush him off. "I'm into quality cattle."

Iverson scowled. He raised his voice in a pleading tone. "You could have both, quality cattle and a large herd at my place."

"No, your place isn't this place." I backed further away, thinking of my walk and that in a few days I'd have a bunch of people here depending on me for a tour. "Thanks anyway, but forget it."

Iverson didn't budge. "I want you to think about it."

I got antsy and blunt. "Forget it." I looked at the field that lay before us; our fifty acres connected to his fifty acres. His land had a matted dead appearance. "Sell us the meadow and raise some cash."

His eyelids lifted, his cheeks reddened. "I'm never selling the meadow!" He turned in disgust and opened his door. "Give my offer some thought. I'll be back."

After he left, I headed for the ridge to plan the upcoming event. The nature tour was sponsored by the Huntersville Bank and was the brainchild of Eve Hebert, a loan officer and vice president of the Booster Club. The club was made up of mostly merchants and organizations in and around Huntersville. Eve had known me since we were kids and knew I was capable of leading an interesting tour. She'd planned to have a picnic lunch at the ridge with a sampling of edible plants we identified during the morning: mushrooms, cowslips, wild onions, watercress, and mint.

Gilda Pierce, owner of Gilda's Forget Me Not Restaurant, would donate the food. She included her deep-dish apple pie in the menu— the first-place winner five years running in the annual Booster Club's pie contest. I'm sure some would come just to enjoy the luncheon and Gilda's pie.

Whatever the case, I wanted to plan the points of interest we were to see, such as the bog, wild flowers in bloom, animal signs, plus any birds I could identify.

I'd filled the feeder at the Hideaway—a little room up in a big maple. Previously, I'd gone there to check out the birds other than the common blue jays, crows, and chickadees that had sponged off my feeder all winter. I usually sat and watched the birds that visited the feeder placed just outside the window, hoping to identify unusual ones like the purple finch seen a few days earlier. I especially wanted to identify the white-throated sparrow and wondered if it had returned yet for the summer, but the last time I looked, I hadn't seen one.

My buddy, Jack Hebert, and I built the tree house when we were in high school. A flight of stairs led to the eight-foot-square space. It had an air-tight stove that kept a fire for a day. I went there several times a week to write in my log book while enjoying the warmth of the room. I'd recorded changes in the seasons, birds identified, when plants like the lady slipper poked out of the ground and, of course, wildlife I'd seen.

From the Hideaway's large bay window, I could see over the spires of the fir mixed in among the maples, beeches, and birches. Down below, the Blue River bordered the hundred-acre meadow in the shape of a crescent moon. It was the time of year when the river broke from its bond of ice, rushing and splashing over bedrock on its way from its source, a small pond just below the peak of Hardhack Mountain.

As I walked, scuffing through last fall's matted leaves and stirring the freshness of spring, I thought of Iverson. I was mystified by his offer and wondered why he acted so desperate.

two

Ruth

I could feel the 747 losing altitude as it came in for a landing at Boston's Logan Airport, the end of my flight from Atlanta, Georgia. I watched through my window and saw the outboard and inboard flaps on the wings slide down. The grass at the edge of the runway flashed by in a blur. In moments the tires squawked as they hit the tarmac. The jet engines roared, slowing the craft.

While the plane taxied to the gate, I brushed my hair and tied it into a pony tail and reached in my bag for a mirror to check my appearance. My face, tanned a walnut brown, looked unusual for a Vermonter who usually doesn't see much sun all winter and spring. I pinched and pulled on the front of my shirt for a more baggy appearance. Born and raised a farm girl, I was the outdoors type, more comfortable in jeans and a loose shirt than in frilly dresses, revealing tops, and tight pants.

I was heading home to Huntersville, Vermont, at the end of two years with Volunteers in Service to America. After graduating from the University of Vermont in 1993 with an economics degree, the thought of contributing and making a difference had excited me. Born into a prosperous farm family, I felt a desire to share my good fortune.

I was assigned to a community center in Piedmont, Georgia, deep in the south not far from the Gulf of Mexico. My work, providing counseling and one-on-one tutoring, was both rewarding and heart-wrenching. The children were sweet but so needy—the poverty was overwhelming. Part of my time, among numerous emergency situations, was spent seeking financing from the Elias M. Cole Foundation. With the Foundation's help, we were able to buy food and clothing and hire a recent college graduate to tutor and teach the children. Sara, a black woman, had grown up in the south. Frieda Angrish, the center's director, was especially excited that with Sara's help the children's education would be improved.

Looking through the plane's window, I watched workers wearing ear-protectors, directing us toward the gate—waving wands as if beckoning me home.

I would soon be in Huntersville where I faced a new challenge—discovering what would be next in my life. Dad and Mom wanted me home to manage the finances of the farm and florist shop, but that didn't interest me. They also wanted me to do farm chores with Jason, but I didn't see that as much of a future.

I stood and straightened my polo shirt and jeans. I slipped on the straps of my backpack and pulled my carry-on off the plane.

After leaving the gate, I looked for Jason. I searched the crowd, eagerly wanting to see him. Fellow passengers met with reunion hugs and laughter. Children chattered to a returning parent. But there was no Jason. The crowd thinned as travelers headed toward the baggage claim.

I turned, watching people entering security. Maybe I'd missed him at the gate or he'd become confused and was waiting at another location. Stumped and disappointed, I headed to get my luggage. The hallway cleared. I was the only one trudging along, wondering, concerned over miscommunication. Then in the distance, I recognized him, a tall guy, muscular but trim, running toward me. I yelled, "Jason!"

"Ruth!"

We hugged. I felt his shoulders and strong arms scoop me against his broad chest. Like a mother who'd rejoined a lost son, I looked into his deeply set eyes and at his clean-shaven face. "Jason, how are you?"

"Right now, I'm just happy to be with you. I got tied up in heavy traffic. The city and this place scares me." He lowered his arms and smiled. "How have you been?"

"It's been wonderful, but I'm happy to get home to be with you, the folks, and Cooner." I took his hand. "Let's go to the baggage claim."

After locating my bag on the clanking turnstile, we headed toward the parking garage and entered the first level packed with a sea of vehicles. He yelled, "Damn, I forgot where I parked!"

His edgy voice echoed as if we were standing in an underground cavern. Panicked, he started to run, carrying my bag. It was heavy and bumped against his leg. "I should've remembered!"

"Jason, come back here! Let's calm down." I reached and firmly grabbed him by the arm. "Did you walk down stairs or use the elevator when you came to the gate?"

"No!" He pointed at the cement. "I was right here!"

"Then let's look on this level. Same truck?"

"Yes—yes. My red '90 Chevy half-ton."

"We'll find it." I let go of him. "Just relax." We looked up and down the rows of cars and trucks. In the darkened space of the parking garage, we passed vehicle after vehicle, searching among several rows. Within minutes, I turned to him and laughed. "There it is! Shiny red, as always."

"Phew. Cities and me don't agree." He chuckled. "Now, if that had been red trillium, growing in some far-off place in the woods, I could have walked right to it."

"You're just a country boy." I laughed. "A modern-day Thoreau, feeling at home in your cabin."

"I guess. I can't stand this city."

After paying the parking fee, we were in heavy traffic on I-93. His white-knuckled hands gripped the wheel. He sat ramrod straight, locked on the view, going fifty-five. Cars whizzed by. I could see heavy traffic sent him into a panic. I casually asked, "How are things?"

His mouth barely opened as he clipped his words. "Nothing's changed." With the AC on high, beads of sweat rolled down his face. "I don't like this kind of driving."

"Jason, let's stop at the first rest area."

"Why? We just got on the road."

"I need to use the bathroom." In minutes, we came to a rest area. I suggested, "Why don't you get out and relax on that bench? I'll be right back."

He scowled. "Don't you want to get home?"

"Sure, but there's no hurry."

"Oh…okay." He reluctantly left the truck as I walked away.

When I came back, he was seated, looking down at the grass. The benches and tables were secluded by a trimmed row of bushes. Red berries the size of dried currants made for a showy hedge. The shriveled fruit had survived the winter.

I took a seat beside him. "It's great to see you!" I slid my arm over his shoulders.

He looked up, turning toward me with a slight smile. "I'm happy you're home."

With my hand on his back, I felt the tenseness leave. "What's going on?"

"As I said, nothing's changed since you left. Dad still wants me to sell the cows." He rubbed his forehead. "He's into the turf farming idea."

"Mom told me. How do you feel about that?" I watched for his reaction.

"Well, I'm not interested!" He clenched his jaw.

"Mom says the cows aren't making any money." I tucked loose hair behind my ear. "What comes in goes out in paid bills."

He sighed. "Dad and Mom, they're into showing a profit."

"Well, Jason, after all, making a profit, isn't that the general idea?"

"Yeah, but what I do isn't all about money."

"Jason, as kids Cooner told us why Dad and Mom are so driven to make a profit. We'd sit on his bench and he'd tell us how things use to be."

Jason smiled. "I know; on his bench, his memory would kick in and he'd turn back the clock. I can hear him now telling us that Dad was left an orphan as a baby—the awful day when the town drunk hit our grandfather's truck head-on, killing our grandparents instantly."

I nodded. "Yeah, they were on their egg route when the drunkard's car struck. Raw eggs, blood, glass, and carnage were splattered from here to kingdom come. Dad was on the seat, sleeping in his basket. He wasn't hurt. State folks brought Dad to Grandpa Thad, asking him to raise his grandson."

Jason smiled. "As kids, we'd sit either side, leaning into Cooner while he'd put an arm around us. We never tried to stop him from telling the same story over and over again."

I continued. "Cooner's wife, Addie, was all excited to have a baby in the house." I turned to Jason. "You'd rest your head against Cooner's warm coveralls and fall asleep, but he'd ramble on."

Jason added, "Yeah, I guess Addie made most of Dad's clothes, because Grandpa Thad hated spending money, grumbling at the cost of raising Dad. Meanwhile, Grandpa was saving money for the next great depression that never came."

"You remember, Jason, Mom never talked much about her childhood. Cooner was the one that first told us that she lived just up the road at the Murray Homestead. She was adopted by Uncle Bill, Grandpa Thad's brother, and Bill's wife, Rosie. Rosie died soon after. Uncle Bill, as a single dad, raised Mom, but his alcoholic days drove him and the farm into poverty."

Jason continued, "Yeah, then Uncle Bill died of cancer, and as a teenager, Mom came to live with Grandpa Thad, Cooner, Addie, and Dad."

While Jason left for the bathroom, I continued thinking; as adults, my folks were wealthy by anyone's standard. Both inherited substantially from family—my dad from Grandpa Thad's estate. Mom inherited from her mother's estate—a mother who mostly had ignored her daughter during her childhood. Mom's mother, Zelda O'Neil, as a pregnant teenager, had given her up for adoption to Uncle Bill and his wife. Zelda, then later in life, went on to become successful in the florist business.

Because Dad and Mom had grown up in poverty, they had the motivation to heap wealth upon wealth. In the back of their minds there was always that worry that markets could crash and financial systems could crumble, returning them to their impoverished childhood days. A few years back, I estimated that they were worth over five million dollars, including land, buildings, and financial portfolios.

After Jason returned, I continued, "It's easy to understand why Mom and Dad are driven to make money." I pulled my hair back and retied my ponytail. "Just the same, we have to be ourselves."

Jason agreed. "I enjoy life the way it is. I hate to admit it, but unlike Dad and Mom, making money isn't that important." He paused for a thought. "Maybe in the future I'll sell breeding stock to make enough to keep going."

"Isn't that a long shot?"

"Hey, whose side are you on, anyway?" He slumped and dropped his head in his hands. "Joining VISTA wasn't exactly a world-class moneymaker."

"Okay, tit-for-tat. Let's face it, neither one of us is a driven capitalist."

"Right." Jason turned to me. "There's a possible new wrinkle. Steven Iverson wants me to join his farm."

"Really!"

"Yeah, Iverson acted desperate." Jason scowled. "He says we could milk three to four hundred cows."

"Why don't you consider it?"

"No, thank you!" He sat up, raising his voice. "Hey, I'm satisfied. Why invite misery?"

"Okay, okay. Just asking."

"Let's change the subject." He sat back, seeming more relaxed. "Hey, look at that bird in the bush."

"Isn't he looking proud?"

"That's the white-throated sparrow." He touched my arm for me to listen closely.

Sooo seeeeee dididi dididi dididi

"Wow, Ruth, hear that pitch and tone?"

I smiled, agreeing.

"Of all the bird songs, that's my favorite." Jason's voice rose in enthusiasm. "Some nights at dusk, I sit on the stairs leading to the Hideaway and wait for his whistle. His song echoes from the ridge, filling the quiet air down to the river and through the valley. It's a mountain top moment—hearing that sound."

"That's special, Jason." I looked at him. "You always were one to find excitement in the sights and sounds of the wild."

"Yeah, those sweet clear notes, sung during twilight in the woodsy space, are sure thrilling." He turned to me. "I've been asked to lead a nature tour in May."

"Gee. Really?" I glanced at him. "Who for?"

"Eve. She's vice president of the Booster Club."

"Good for her." I laughed. "Remember when Eve and Jack and you and I spent nights at the Hideaway?"

"How could I forget?" Jason smirked. "Eve usually brought the beer."

I laughed. "She'd get a buzz on and show us her version of hard rock."

"Yeah, and the Hideaway shook so much we all thought it would fall out of the tree." He nodded. "And that was no joke."

"Eve's always been sweet on you."

"I know." He looked down at the grass. "I've never encouraged it."

"Why?"

"Oh, I don't know. She's too…too out there…forward." He paused. "Right now she's living with Charlie Brack."

"Charlie Brack. Gosh, he's been around or rather chased around a number of women."

"When it comes to Eve, all I can say is better Charlie than me."

We sat in silence for a moment, soaking in the warmth of the spring day. Then we walked toward the truck. On the way, I recalled my own varied affairs of the heart. Thus far I seemed to be drawn to warriors or wimps. I had yet to strike middle ground.

First, there was Sven from Wall Street, where I worked as an intern during the summer before my college junior year. Sven the stock broker—he was in his early twenties and a bit of a milquetoast. I considered him a guy-friend, expecting our friendship might lead to romance. He seemed promising, but when the market surged, he was high. When stocks dipped, he was low. I learned early on to watch the big board of the Dow so as to plan the upcoming evening. It would either be a night out with filet mignon, or a glum night at home with peanut butter sandwiches and warm milk. I breathed a big sigh of relief at the end of the summer, ditching the financial numbers and Sven as well.

Then at college, I fell for Alex. He was handsome, athletic and everyone thought him a great guy. We made a handsome couple. I was falling in love with him. But Alex had his dark side. One night when we were alone at my apartment, he turned into a completely different person. He kissed me aggressively while fondling my breast. His strong hands hurt as he tore at my blouse, sliding his rough hand under the band of my panties.

I was dumbfounded and pushed him away. "Stop!"

He lunged, shoving me toward my bedroom. "I know you want it!" He laughed at my resistance. "I've seen the looks you give guys."

"Alex…please! You're crazy!" With my back to him and my feet planted on the floor, I struck an elbow blow to his gut.

"Ahhhh." He bent over. "You bitch!" He straightened and kept coming.

I turned and grabbed a stoneware vase, slugging it at his face. It struck with force, falling to the floor with a crash, smashing into shards.

He reeled, covering his eye and mouth. Blood poured into his hand. He cried, "Look!" and turned ashen, seeing blood.

I shoved him. He blubbered like a baby. I opened the door and out he went. "Good riddance!"

I learned a lot from Alex, realizing that many guys have two suitcases. The first represents his every-day persona. For some, what you see is what you get. But others carry a second suitcase, and it takes time to discover what it holds. After finding out the real Alex, I vowed that I wasn't about to be batted around by the likes of someone who felt date rape was okay.

We reached the truck. Because we were away from heavy traffic, Jason relaxed, started his truck, and we headed for home.

I thought about my last attempt at love. I'd met Wentworth while at the Piedmont Center in Georgia. On days away from the center, he and I would relax over a meal or we'd go for rides in the Center's van. He was a nervous, slender guy, unsure of himself, forever willing for me to take the lead. On first meeting him, I enjoyed his company, but as time passed he opened his second suitcase. He showed an angry side, endlessly railing about US foreign policy and the evils of our society. Our relationship hit the rocks when I discovered he was the beneficiary of a large trust fund. An argument ensued with me calling him a hypocrite. That was the end of my romantic feelings toward Wentworth.

At this time, riding home to the farm, I was satisfied to put close relationships on the back burner. Anyway, the prospects in Huntersville were nearly nil. All the good ones had left.

Soon we were traveling in New Hampshire, passing wooded areas at the roadside. Jason's Chevy hummed along. After a pause, looking at the scenery, I asked, "Speaking of Cooner, how's he doing?"

"He's just the same. After Mom feeds him his breakfast, he usually gets in his truck and goes to Butson's to get the news."

"Gosh, still. I've missed him and all his wisdom."

"He's misses you, too."

"Remember, Jason, when you had just turned ten and Cooner let me teach you how to drive our old truck in the hayfield."

Jason chuckled, "My feet could hardly reach the pedals."

"We were always asking him to take us coon hunting. He'd say something like, 'Can't do that. I sold my guns, and I ain't got no dog'."

Jason joined in, "We'd jump up and down and beg. 'We just want to see some raccoons'."

"Yeah, we could get him to do most anything, if we teased enough." I paused. "You know, Jason, Cooner really raised us when we were kids."

"Yeah...Mom and Dad were always too busy."

By afternoon, we'd traveled for nearly three hours, reaching Huntersville's Main Street and business district with its brick fronts lining the sidewalk. It's a small town with a variety of commercial businesses. There's accuracy in the local joke, '*If you blink, you'll miss it*'.

Continuing on, we passed a cluster of turn-of-the-century homes with their shade trees, manicured hedges, and trimmed lawns. On the outskirts of town, we slowed when coming to Murray's Florist Shop. Across the street stood a three-story Victorian-style house we'd always known as the Murray homestead, Uncle Bill's old place. Electrician's, plumber's, and carpenter's trucks were parked in the yard.

I was surprised, seeing all the activity. "What's going on?"

Jason looked at the old house. "Mom's idea. She wants to live where she grew up."

"So they're moving."

"That's the plan, since you're home."

We pulled into the paved yard of Murray's Florist Shop and found a vacant parking spot in a row of several cars. Bold black lettering on a sign stood out on a field of white. The storefront was freshly painted. At least six greenhouses covered in white plastic were in back of the main brick building. Next to the business, a group of five field workers were hoeing between the plants. Row upon row of plants such as shrubs, sapling trees, evergreens, and perennials covered nearly ten acres.

It occurred to me how much my folks had planned for my life to be like a picture-book garden. With guidance, I grew and learned in a neat, sequential pattern. Reaching my twenties, I was a valuable asset to the family businesses.

Introduced to finance in eighth grade, I was soon balancing the checkbooks of both the farm and the florist shop. In high school, I worked as an intern for a local accounting firm, and in my senior year I interned at the Huntersville National Bank under its president, Emily Ann Gray. During my college years, I honed my ability to study the infinite details of finance: the ins and outs of the stock market, the analysis of spreadsheets, profit margins, enterprise gains and losses, taxation, and estate planning.

I graduated with honors. Dad and especially Mom had accomplished their goal—an educated wizard to add to their financial quiver, one to enhance their already successful businesses.

After college, I saw no need to return home to improve my folks' wealth. I had a different idea—volunteering for VISTA. Mom was beside herself with disappointment. "Don't you want to stay in Huntersville?"

"Please, not for now, Mom. I want to do this."

My view of the world had changed when, as a senior in college, I took an elective, studying world hunger. My introduction to a subject other than finance changed my life. To be honest, I also reacted to being too controlled by Mom and felt the need to break away. VISTA was a perfect fit.

Dad and Mom always expected Jason to be a dairy farmer. He worked with Dad and seemed to fit my parents' planned role. But now, even Jason was faced with an uncertain future. Dad was intrigued with turf farming— growing a lawn on cropland, harvesting small squares of sod for instant grass to be used by house builders and municipalities.

As we sat in the parking lot, I glanced at the florist shop. "Gosh, since I've been gone, Mom's grown this business. She in the shop?"

"No, taking the afternoon off. You know, planning a welcome home party."

"Wow, time off!" I smiled. "That's rare for her!"

"Right," Jason nodded. "Cooner remembers we were just minutes away from being born in the greenhouse."

"Bless Cooner. I can't wait to see him."

"Well then, let's go."

I hesitated. "Not yet. I want to take in my surroundings. You know, ease the shock of reentry." I looked toward the ridge in back of the meadow and beyond the Blue River—at the pine grove Marcus Murray, our great-great-grandfather, planted over a hundred years ago. "I forgot how spectacular the pines are, standing there for loggers to drool over."

Jason raised his voice. "And for all of us to admire."

The pines, rugged centurions, hugged the land with their huge roots—standing timeless through decades of strong winds, blizzards, and pounding rain. A huge white cloud settled just above the tops of the towering trees. With their enormous trunks spaced evenly across the ridge, they looked like pillars of the earth, supporting the white cloud hanging over them.

Jason backed the truck and pulled onto the road. As we traveled toward the farm, I noticed the meadow. Dead weeds matted by snow showed a grey sheen covering the Iverson parcel.

Jason commented, "There's Iverson's sickly corn field."

"How can he keep farming?"

Jason shrugged. "Thank God that's not my problem."

After passing Iverson's share of the meadow, we came to our half—rippling greens of alfalfa and grassland soon to be cut for the first time this season. Next we passed the fallow corn land ready for planting. In a wavy pattern, threads of steam rose from the warming soil. Soil that had grown bumper crops since the first Marcus Murray started farming.

On the far ridge, west of the pines, a blanket of green pasture spread for some distance, sloping sharply toward the Blue River below. The pasture hadn't always been as green and lush as today.

"Remember, Jason, when we were kids, helping to create this beauty—cutting brush on the ridge with Cooner and Dad in the late fall? When a large area was cleared, the tractor hauled in a trailer-load of ground limestone and parked it on an old logging road. The land was too steep to be spread with equipment."

Jason turned my way. "I remember. You had more fun spreading that stuff than I did."

"Maybe so." I recalled those days. "I can see Dad and Cooner strapping on a portable spreader with a spinner. The spinner sent great clouds of white dust over the ground. Dad was determined to bring the pasture back as it was when great-great-grandpa Marcus farmed it."

Jason looked toward the ridge. "I remember sticking my hands in the cold powder, having it blow back in my face. I scooped fistfuls into a small pail. When it was full, I'd walk to where it was needed, tipped the pail and raked the powder with my spread fingers. With a swing of my arm, the lime was sent into a puff of white dust, settling onto the cut-over stubble. At the end of the day we both were covered in white, looking like Halloween characters."

"Yeah, Dad kept clearing every fall until the whole ridge lay open. Then in a few years, when the snow melted and the spring rains came, the ridge turned a beautiful green."

Jason continued, "It makes a great pasture for the heifers."

As we came to the farm, the open ridge ended and woods of mostly maples grew. From a distance, the old trees were showing a light green of new leaves. "Gosh, there's the Hideaway over there, looking sturdy as ever." The square box structure built in a large maple stood out amid the background of green. I turned to Jason. "You still go there?"

"As much as I can."

He slowed the truck and turned into our farmstead. The red barn with its white trim was beautifully kept. A cement silo fifty feet tall towered at the end of the two-hundred-foot-long barn. The lawn in front was freshly mowed. He stopped the truck beside the sign, *The Murray Homestead*.

The two-story white farmhouse was neatly landscaped. My great-grandfather, Thad, had cobbled it together from parts of old dismantled homes around town. Although kept in good condition, the house remained architecturally odd. The huge dormer windows, jutting out on the second floor, caused it to look as if it could tip forward.

Jason parked and we heard the house door slam. Mom and Dad came running to meet me.

I threw out my arms and hugged them. "It's great to be home!"

All smiles, we walked arm in arm toward the house. With a bank of yellow daffodils in bloom, our farmyard sparkled in the freshness of spring. Cooner's wooden bench, with a worn path leading to it, was placed near the door. Flowers grew around the inviting seat. Mom had taped a "*Welcome Home*" sign on the door. She'd also pinned a small bouquet of purple violets at the top of the sign.

"Wow, the place looks beautiful!" I smiled. "And, Mom, you are clever with the sign—and flowers."

"Thanks, you noticed. Your dad just mowed the lawn for the first time this spring."

Dad opened the door for us. "We wanted the place in tip-top shape for our girl."

Jason followed behind us.

Dad and Mom, in their mid-forties, looked to be in their thirties. Mom could even pass as my sister. She wore her wavy blond hair at shoulder length. Her fair complexion showed no age lines. She nearly always beamed a pleasant smile, and seemed innocent and easy-going; but in reality, she was driven to succeed. Her summer wardrobe of sneakers, jeans, and a sports shirt suggested that she was casual, but in the florist business she was knowledgeable, well organized, and energetic. She'd learned the trade from my grandmother, Zelda O'Neil, and inherited the florist shop when Grandma died of lung cancer.

I've always seen Dad as the quiet leader of our family. He was tall and slim, with short blond hair. Most days he wore jeans and a colored t-shirt, making him look especially youthful. He's been the driving force in establishing the Murray Farm as a recognized source of top-quality registered Holsteins.

I walked into the kitchen, the walls a soft yellow. The cherry cabinets and matching table and chairs were polished. The late afternoon sun flowed through the window. Over the kitchen sink were two pots of purple African violets. The beige linoleum flooring looked as fresh as if it had been newly laid. As I stood absorbing the country-style décor, I noticed that the painting of grazing cattle and a 1908 De Laval Calendar of a comely milkmaid in period dress still hung on the wall. The mirror in back of the kitchen sink was there where I used to stand before school started, checking my hair. I felt fortunate to reconnect to the warm place where I grew up. "Mom, you've always kept a neat house—a homey home."

"Thanks, Ruth. Since you've been gone, I've been so busy at the shop, I've hired a cleaning woman."

"Anyone I know?"

"Yeah, Bertha Bean."

"Oh, my gosh, Bertha!" I turned to Mom. "She has the inside scoop on everybody."

Mom grinned. "You know, she and Cooner love to swap stories."

"I'll bet. What one doesn't know—the other fills in the details." I took a deep breath. "Mmm, smells good. What do you have in the oven?"

"Turkey and a casserole—a welcome home for our long-lost daughter."

"Maybe lost as far as you are concerned." I turned toward the living room. "But at the Piedmont Center I was busy almost every waking minute."

Mom motioned. "Marcus, you visit with the kids, I've got to make some phone calls."

We went from the kitchen through the archway into the living room. Jason sat at the side of the room.

Dad took an over-stuffed chair. "You mentioned being busy—what was going on?"

"Well, I've told you a lot in calls and letters, but really all kinds of stuff: families split, alcohol, drugs, teen pregnancies, crime, jail time. Young children are left with grandma or a relative who can't cope, and the Center is there to lend support. The contrast between Piedmont and Huntersville is beyond belief."

Dad settled into his chair eager to hear more. "We have similar crime and dysfunction going on here."

"Oh, but not the unemployment. That makes a huge difference."

Dad nodded. "Yeah, it would."

"When Frieda Angrish, the Piedmont Community director, came to the airport to pick me up, she wore a short-sleeved print dress. Her round face beamed a big smile when we met, 'Welcome to Georgia.'

"She put me at ease with her welcoming smile as she wiped her brow. 'Girl, you is in hot country.'

"The humidity was intense. The temperature must have been in the nineties. She led me to her beat-up van, and repeated, 'Ya, hot black country.'

"Dad, I'll tell you, hearing *black* threw me. Of course we've never lived where color was a factor. Me, a light blonde with a milky complexion, must have looked unusual to Frieda, bringing a white face to her all-black Piedmont Community.

"Frieda in her southern drawl made it clear on the way to the Center that she was an American, not an African-American. She told me, 'It's black and white down here, with the whites wantin' their thumb on us, pushin' folks down. I ain't takin' it. Nooo more. I ain't takin' it. We is risin' up, fightin' our way to the top.'

"I sat not knowing what to say, but I knew I figured in her plan for the Community Center—to work with the children, helping them make it to what she called 'the top.' Since the vehicle's air conditioner didn't work, I rolled down the window."

Dad shook his head. "I don't know if I could stand the southern heat and humidity."

"It was intense." I paused. "Frieda then continued my informal orientation.

"'My ancestors as slaves were forced to work the fields generations ago. Even after slavery, my grandma was expected at ten years old to pick cotton. No schoolin' at cotton-pickin' time. The schoolin' she did git was outta ratty torn books the white schools threw away'."

Dad leaned back in his chair. "Can that be true?"

"From what I heard and saw, I'm afraid it was. I can understand Frieda's bitterness and why she fights so hard for equality.

"As she talked, beads of sweat formed above her upper lip. Even with the windows down, it was hot. But Dad, you would have loved to see the country."

He nodded. "I know I would. I've never been outside of New England."

Tucking hair behind my ear, I continued, "In rural southern Georgia we traveled through what looked to me to be rich farmland. I saw neat orchards of pecan trees with mowed grass between the rows. Further along, combines were harvesting wheat. Next came row upon row of three-foot-high cotton, soon followed by acres of peanuts, growing on deep red soil without a weed in sight.

"You'd drool over the size of the cropland we were passing—field after field was at least a hundred or two hundred acres."

Dad raised an eyebrow. "No kidding, really?"

"Yeah, really. Row crops were irrigated with tripods, reminding me of giant daddy-long-legs. Motorized rows of irrigation on wheels moved at a snail's pace across the red soil."

"Irrigation. I *would* like to see that."

"The first small community we passed through looked deserted, except for two Baptist churches and a Quick Stop. Dale Cotton Exchange in faded letters was written across the front of a series of vacant buildings. We passed shells of structures that were once a grain co-op. Several tall rusted silos stood like giant Greek columns. Weeds and grass filled in the area around them."

Dad commented, "A deserted town?"

"It sure looked that way."

Jason asked, "Where did everybody go?"

"Lots of folks went to the northern cities like Chicago.

"Frieda told me, 'Wasn't too long ago this little town was bustlin' with activity, givin' jobs ta the locals. Farmers and share-croppers lugged their harvested crops here by horse-drawn wagons and small tractors. It's all different now. Big trucks and big machines took it all over.

'Folks moved north for jobs—away from Jim Crow laws, leavin' behind the old, the sick, women and kids. Those left behind depended on money bein' sent from the north.'

"Down the road, we passed several small houses lining a short street with shells of deserted cars. Old black men huddled around the raised hood of a junk truck.

"The cropland we had just passed was in contrast to the poor villages. Dad, it sure wasn't anything like you'd see up here. Golly, I found it depressing, seeing all the poverty.

"Frieda made it clear. 'The whites own all the cropland. We've been pushed off the land'."

Dad shifted in his seat, "Why so?"

"The banks and the government wouldn't give loans to black farmers."

"Really! That's a problem."

"We passed a peach orchard, beautifully kept, that seemed to stretch forever.

"Frieda continued her story, as she drove to the center. 'See all this we is passin'? My granddaddy owned here. The whites ran the seed and fertilizer stores, the banks, and the government's loanin'. He had no seed, no fertilizer, no money he could borrow.' With Kleenex in her hand, she wiped the sweat. 'He had no choice... had to sell.'

"Dad, I learned later that Frieda's story was the same across the rural south. Generations of white families control the land."

Dad scowled shaking his head. "Up north here, we never realized."

"I agree. In my studies, discrimination was never mentioned.

"Frieda and I reached Piedmont by late afternoon. She briefly filled me in on the local government. I told Mom over the phone that she's had an ongoing battle with the mostly white Piedmont City Council."

Dad nodded. "Yeah, I heard about the guy that runs the place. What's his name?"

"Wilfred Plumley. He's president of the City Council."

"That's the name." Dad looked my way. "What's going on with him?"

"He's a farmer, and the largest land owner in the county. In the past, Wilfred's grandfather made money off the backs of slaves. Now, Wilfred keeps pushing the blacks down by denying a permit to start a school at the Piedmont Community Center. Also, the Council sold Piedmont's public playground to an all-white Baptist church in town, denying black sports teams a chance to play in the local schedule. Frieda's at odds with Plumley and the Council over these issues with scant success."

Dad said, "Golly, that's mean."

"She hopes to eventually elect a majority of black Council members, but that hasn't happened."

Jason got up to leave. He glanced through the archway at the clock over the kitchen sink. "Ruth, I'd like to hear more, but it's chore time."

Dad got up. "After chores you can tell us some more."

I headed for my bedroom. Except for short stays, I hadn't been here for over two years. I looked at my surroundings and the pictures: one at the head of my bed of Mother Teresa and, near my closet door, one of Madonna and child. There was also a large group picture of children I visited while in El Salvador—another above my desk of Jason and me taken on a skiing trip to Colorado. Jason was great fun to be with. Jack and his sister, Eve Hebert, went with us. Eve and I often watched in awe as Jack and Jason flew over moguls with reckless abandon to see who would fall first.

After partially unpacking, I showered and changed my clothes and joined Mom. "What can I do to help?"

"I'm ready for dinner." She pulled out a chair. "Coffee?"

"Yeah, sure." I looked closely at a creamer on the table. "Gee, Mom, cute." I held it up by the handle. Decorated with blue blossoms, it was lettered "*Forget Me Not*" on a white ceramic background.

"Cooner brought it home from Gilda's—a promotional for her restaurant."

"What a neat idea." I poured some cream in my coffee.

"Yeah, it holds just enough for two cups." Mom took a chair. "I've been able to do chores in the barn, but now that spring's here, I don't have the time. Scoop has helped some when he's available."

"Scoop!…Scoop LaQuine?" I was surprised. "He's out of prison?"

"Yeah, got out last winter." Mom sipped her coffee. "He's good help…sober. If he starts drinking, he'll be sent back."

"Gosh, Scoop's been drinking since he was a kid." I reached for my cup. "He'd come to school half drunk."

"He's on the wagon now." Mom added in a hopeful tone, "Studying to become an electrician—wired our new greenhouse, and did a good job, too."

"He's smart enough, but as a kid he was always in trouble." I placed my cup on the table. "Remember when he got caught at the Vermont Fish Hatchery, scooping trout into a five-gallon pail?"

"Yeah. That's how he got the name Scoop," Mom recalled. "Eddie taught his boy how to drink and how to break the law."

"Eddie still in the repair business?" I asked.

"Yeah. Scoop does most of it, working for his dad."

"Well, there's no need to hire Scoop now that I'm home. I'll work with Jason until I decide what I want to do with my life."

Mom became especially attentive. "What are you thinking?"

"Oh, I don't know. I already miss the kids." Thinking, I looked across the room. "Maybe I could start a literacy program in the deep south."

"Ruth!" She started winding her shoulder-length hair on her index finger—a nervous habit I'd grown accustomed to ever since I was a kid. She frowned. "Aren't you home to stay? Haven't you done enough of this feel-good stuff?"

"Mom, it's all about the less fortunate." I finished my coffee.

"Well…whatever." Her finger was wrapped in hair. "Your dad and I have spent thousands on your education."

"Mom, I'm grateful to you and Dad, but I'm not wired the same. I want to make a difference—help the disadvantaged."

"Oh, dear!" She pulled her finger from her hair, leaving a ringlet. "I was expecting more than that." She left the table with dishes. "Why can't you settle in Huntersville?"

"Don't worry, I'll be home this summer." I got up and took my cup to the sink. "I'll do the finances and bookwork while I'm here."

Mom sighed, "Thanks. What a relief. This time of year I get way behind paying the bills and entering data for the monthly spreadsheets."

"I'll take care of it."

She stood by me at the sink. "Your dad has turned the dairy over to Jason. Papers haven't been signed yet. We're waiting to see if you want to be included."

"Pass the necessary legalities to Jason for now. I don't want to commit to the farm." I pushed my hair back and retied my ponytail. "Jason tells me you and Dad want to move to the old homestead with Cooner."

"We do. Your dad likes growing trees for resale." Mom checked the oven. "He's more interested in selling a finger-size maple sapling for fifty dollars than making a pittance or losing money on a hundred pounds of milk."

"He's always liked the cows."

"Right. But lately he'd rather work with the soil and get paid for his efforts. In fact he's talking about starting a turf business if Steven Iverson would ever sell his share of the meadow."

"Growing turf. Jason told me."

We moved to the living room to sit.

She continued, "There's a big demand down-country. But to grow turf you need flat productive land and enough of it to pay for the harvesting equipment." Mom looked out the window toward the meadow. "Like the Iverson acreage."

"Sounds interesting." I asked, "What's Iverson's land worth?"

"For development, the sky's the limit, but on the last appraisal, the town had it valued at twenty-five hundred an acre."

"Seems reasonable, a hundred and twenty-five thousand for fifty acres."

"Your dad would pay that in a heartbeat. He grieves the fact that half the meadow left the family." She sighed. "Now, it will never sell for crop land."

"Probably not." I glanced her way. "When do you plan to move?"

"Oh, late fall. When the house is ready." She sat back and resettled herself. "Tell me more about your job."

I was surprised she was interested. "The kids are so special. Just young enough to be cute and innocent."

"Really?"

I glanced toward the kitchen, recalling, "The children were playing in the yard. When they saw the community van pull in, they came running, but they slowed, seeing I was white."

Mom asked, "White is that significant?"

"Oh, yes. Whites and blacks don't mix. Ironically, on Sunday, the church is the most segregated place in the South." I turned to Mom. "Frieda introduced me to the kids in her southern dialect. 'You's all, dis is Ms. Murray, you's teacher'.

"Kids surrounded me as I sat on my suitcase. A lovely preschool child came to me. She had red barrettes in her tightly braided hair. I reached for her hand. She hesitantly touched me, running her tiny fingers over my face and nose. 'You's skin is white and soft as butter.'

"The kids laughed. I smiled. 'Your name?'

"She pulled away and shyly giggled. Everyone around me answered for her, 'Anadeepa.'

"After that day, Anadeepa and I became close." My emotions surfaced, and I reached in my pocket for a Kleenex. "Wow... sorry."

Mom's eyebrow arched.

I saw her disappointment in my emotional attachment to an unfamiliar face hundreds of miles away. I took a deep breath, but paused when I heard a truck rumble into the yard. A flash of gray crossed the living room window. "There's Cooner. I want to see him."

"Do that. He's missed you."

I slammed the door and ran toward his old gray Chevy pickup. He turned off the engine.

I grasped the edge of the open truck window and excitedly said, "Cooner, it's great to see you!"

"Well…well, same here!" His craggy weathered face equaled his eighty-five years, but those years hadn't dimmed the twinkle in his eyes. He chuckled with a smile. "Golly, ya've made my day—seein' my favorite girl."

"Well, you're my favorite guy." I got a whiff of the Beechnut Chewing Tobacco he carried in his shirt pocket. I've always liked the sweet aroma. It was definitely Cooner.

He opened his door and reached for his leverwood cane. "Let me get a good look atcha."

"Mom says your arthritis is bothering you."

"Yup, first my hips, now it's my knees. They hurt like thunder." He leaned on his cane and looked me up and down.

We hugged.

He stepped back. "You've slimmed down, lookin'… well, lookin' as sleek as a race horse."

I chuckled. "I don't know as I've ever been compared to a horse."

"Yuh." He sniffed. "Sayin' it like that, it don't sound good."

"Thanks anyway." I held his arm as we headed toward the house.

Cooner laboriously scuffed toward the door with his eye on his wooden bench. "Let's sit a minute and look off at Hardhack Mountain."

I stared at the high peak, seeing nothing unusual. "The mountain looks sort of misty-gray with no leaves on the trees."

"Well, it's only this time of year, just a few days before the leaves come and the snows melt, that ya can see the headwaters of the Blue River." He pointed. "See down from the peak that small dot of light blue?"

"Yeah, barely." I squinted. "You always tried to show me when I was a kid."

"Well, I ain't never been there, but I'm told that a giant spring runs into a pond that feeds the Blue River." He pointed with his cane. "After World War I, a small band of Germans settled there. When I was a kid, folks around town called the place Wunderland."

"Yeah, you've mentioned that."

"Well, most folks were leery of the Germans after World War I, so this small group of immigrants went where they wan't bothered." He popped a small pinch of Beechnut in his mouth.

I turned to him. "How come you've never been there?"

"Huh." He spat. "I'm told it'd take a day's hike."

I strained to see the small light area. "It doesn't look that far."

"Well, it tis." He swept the width of the mountain with his cane. "Ya can't hike straight to it. Ya got to go cross-lots." He pointed again. "See that gray line some distance across the mountain?"

"Yeah."

"Well that's a ledge more than a hundred feet high, makin' Wunderland a hard place ta reach."

"So much for Wunderland. I'm ready for something to eat. I guess I'll never go there."

He spat again. "All the folks that hated the Germans are now six foot under."

"Yeah, you've said." I held his arm. "You ready to go?"

"Sure." He held back. "You've been with my boy?"

"Yeah, it was great to see him again."

"Your dad hates him takin' so much time in the woods, checkin' birds and stuff like that." Cooner exhaled a gust of air to stand. "He also thinks fifty cows ain't much of a future."

"I gathered as much." We headed toward the house. "In time, Jason'll come to realize that."

Cooner reached for the door. "Well, Bertha says makin' the next generation do as you want is like pushin' a chain uphill."

three

Jason

On my way to the barn at 4:30 in the morning, I looked for a break from the long winter. The night was frosty even though it was early May. I saw only cold, gray clouds with shafts of sunlight just beginning to shine behind Hardhack Mountain. The yellow daffodils by the back door drooped from the burden of frost. My red truck looked to have been spray painted with white crystals. The barn fan, midway down the two-hundred-foot barn, hummed, blowing warm stable air. The grass below the outside shroud showed a green patch the circumference of a fifty-five-gallon drum. Surrounding the circle, the lawn looked to be covered with white frosting. The rising sun would soon melt everything to dew-drops by the time I headed for breakfast.

When I turned the lights on in the barn, most of the cows stood, jangling their neck chains. They faced inward toward a five-foot-wide feed alley. I took a broom and swept in the hay they couldn't reach. Next, I threw sawdust under each cow to freshen their beds.

Precious, the first cow seen when entering the barn was the foundation of my herd. She was evenly marked black and white with a white triangle on her head. She had deep body ribbing, a broad rump, and a tightly attached fore and rear udder. She stood tall with a top line even with my chest. An exceptional brood cow, with outstanding daughters, she was sired by SWD Valiant, a bull that had added a lot of dairy quality to his daughters—cows with flat-boned legs, showing dairyness, as opposed to round, coarse-boned legs as seen in beef cows. Many of the

Valiants lacked durable udders, but Precious was an exception. On a visit to the farm, a classifier from the Holstein Association gave her a score of 93. I was excited at such a high evaluation, knowing she could even score higher in subsequent visits from the Holstein Association. I knew Precious was exceptional, especially since less than two percent of the breed ever achieves such a high score.

In my college genetics class, I learned that the law of regression is at play in breeding dairy animals. In other words, daughters of outstanding females tend to regress toward breed average. In the event a cow produced daughters equal to her level or higher, you owned an outstanding cow. Precious was just that sort of animal.

Peaches, her first daughter, stood next to her. Sired by Tomar Blackstar, Peaches scored excellent at 90 points and produced milk way above her herdmates. The third cow in line was a younger daughter of Precious, also by Blackstar, scoring 86 points on her first classification. She was also an excellent producer.

Using only the best bulls of the breed, I knew that these three females would eventually, in all likelihood, give me a string of outstanding dairy cows—especially if I bore the expense of harvesting fertilized embryos from the Precious family and transferring them to others in my herd.

Dad was opposed to spending money on the process of super-ovulation. Depending on the number of embryos produced in what is known as a flush, it would cost hundreds of dollars and there was no guarantee of success.

My insistence on this relatively new technology in dairy cows hurried Dad's exit from the business. He was already just breaking even on the herd, so he couldn't imagine going in debt over something that didn't have surefire success.

By providing clean housing, good roughage, and quality care, I knew from my college experience that I was onto something big. My cattle from the Precious family could bring thousands of dollars. I only had to be patient and wait. And anyway it wasn't the money, but the satisfaction in knowing that I'd bred an exceptional line of cattle. I also knew with even stronger resolve that Iverson's offer of a commercial dairy in no way interested me.

The cows were now mine. They weren't a gift. I bought them for a thousand a piece, which was much less than they were worth. But Dad and Mom's Yankee background was counter to an outright gift. In March, I began making monthly cow payments. I hoped Ruth would join me, but it was too early to know her plans.

When I told Dad about the Iverson visit, he was disgusted that I had so firmly turned down the opportunity. "You should at least explore the offer." He shook his head. "It might be a chance to eventually own the entire meadow."

"But I don't want to leave here and milk more cows. I have a plan and it isn't commercial dairying."

I knew how Dad felt. He wished I'd sell the cows and convert the meadow to a turf farm, eventually including the fifty-acre Iverson land. But I wasn't as passionate about owning the whole meadow as he was, and I wanted to continue using our land for corn and hay.

Ruth came to the barn at five o'clock for the first time since returning home. "Morning, Jason." She stood beside Precious and ran her hand over her top line. "Jason, she's beautiful—so soft and smooth!"

I smiled. "She's the best."

Precious turned her head and lapped at Ruth's pant leg.

I stood behind the cow, ready to begin morning milking. "It's great to have your help, Ruth." I had a washcloth in hand for Precious's udder. "Now Dad can go off and do his own thing."

"I understand there's been a little tension between you two."

"Yeah, not so much in words, but in his cold stony glances. You know how he is when he doesn't agree. Lately, it hasn't been much fun working around him."

"Well, I wouldn't lose much sleep over it." Ruth stepped into the aisle. "You two just don't think alike."

"That's for sure!"

The chore routine hadn't changed since Ruth left two years ago. She first fed corn silage—two heaping forkfuls to each cow. They loved the feed, lurching forward eager for a mouthful that wafted a sweet pungent odor. She followed with a topping of mixed grains, ground and formulated for dairy cows. Bales of soft barn-dried hay were thrown from the mow to be fed as the cows' final three-course diet. Ruth finished her chores, feeding six calves their milk and cleaning their pens.

Ruth and I were a better fit working together. She always let me take the lead and never second-guessed what I wanted done.

When we left the barn at seven, the sun had risen over Hardhack Mountain. All the frost had melted. A layer of mist rose off the plowed ground—land I had planned for an alfalfa seeding. "The forecast's calling for rain tonight." I turned to Ruth. "So right after breakfast you could start harrowing. You should have time to seed that fifteen acres by chore time."

While we walked toward the house, Ruth took off her bandana she wore in the barn. "What are you planning to do?"

"I need to check the fence on the ridge. Tomorrow I hope we can turn out the heifers."

After hanging up our barn clothes in the entry, we entered a quiet kitchen. Cooner and Dad were still at the table, which was unusual for Dad. He normally ate and left. I sensed it was all about me.

Ruth raised her hand. "Good morning."

I headed past the table to the bathroom. Dad sat looking straight ahead, acting as if I didn't exist.

As a family we worked out our problems in near silence. I learned early in life that there is more power in silence and facial expressions than in words—especially with Dad. He often left me second-guessing as to what he was really thinking–except I got the message that I needed to mend my ways. Maybe that was why I always felt more at ease around Cooner. He always let me know what he had on his mind.

Mom had all the food ready: bacon and eggs, toast, jelly, dry cereal. All five of us were seated around the table, starting to eat. Cooner sat at one end and Dad at the other. The silence was eerie. Then Cooner cleared his throat. "I'm headed to Butson's." He groaned to stand. In silence, the thump of his cane resonated off the floor. The door shut behind him.

I sank in my chair. Dad was shooting glances at me. I turned the box of corn flakes. It blocked the view of his angry expression. Although I was twenty-two, his glare reminded me of times as a kid. I was disgusted when I realized I was hiding from him. I sat up in my chair and shoved the box toward the center of the table.

Mom sat winding strands of hair around her finger. Her face grew taut as she stared at her food. Times like these were so infrequent that at the moment I recalled most of them; one was when I was a first grader on the playground and Eve Hebert called me a queer. I didn't know what it meant except she said it as an insult. Having played a lot with Scoop, I'd picked up a few choice words. I yelled so everyone on the playground could hear, "You're a goddamned whore."

All the kids stopped in their tracks. The supervising teacher froze. My words spread through the school like a stink-bomb. That night I faced an angry dad with a cold stare that could kill.

Now, at breakfast, Mom continued winding hair, and Dad continued to give me that stony glare. Ruth tried to ease the tension. "Did anyone see the movie *Forrest Gump?*"

Silence.

Mom shook her head.

I thought: nice try, Ruth, but it won't work.

I started eating my cornflakes but they tasted like sawdust. It occurred to me that we were acting like kids. So I blurted out to cut the raw silence. "So what's the big problem?"

Dad snapped, "You!"

His anger was like a blow to the gut. I saw no need to hold back. "Oh, as if I didn't know!"

Mom's index finger was all hair by now. "Come on you two! Let's be civil!"

I bluntly said, "Okay, Dad, spit it out!"

His stern glare searched me. "Iverson stopped by the shop yesterday."

"Yeah, and why don't *you* milk his goddamned cows!" I leaned forward to stare down Dad, while raising my voice. "Iverson's looking for a big sugar daddy to bail him out!"

"Jason!" Mom pulled her finger, unraveling hair.

Dad's brow lifted and his eyes widened. "I don't have time to roam the woods and look for birds."

Pounding my fists, I rattled the dishes. "So that's what this is all about! Work, work, work, that's...that's all *you* know!"

Dad said sarcastically, "I...I never had the luxury of sitting in a tree house, writing a journal!" He stood and paced to the kitchen counter for a second cup of coffee.

Mom started a second hair wind but suddenly stopped. "This is enough!"

Ruth stared toward Mom.

She continued, "Jason, you know how much that meadow means to your dad. It's strange to you. Just as strange as your love of wildlife is to him."

Ruth joined in, "Yeah, let's have a civil discussion."

Dad cooled down as he sat. "Jason, if you go for Iverson's deal, we might be able to get back the meadow. The land I wish our family never lost."

"I'm not willing to change my whole life's plan for that meadow." I looked at Dad's worried expression.

He ran his spread fingers through his hair. "It makes me sick to think that those fifty acres might grow houses." He scowled. "Iverson says he wants a half million."

"Well, pay it and start your turf business." I knew Dad was torn inside and would never part with that amount.

"Five hundred thousand? That's crazy!" He looked at me calmly. "Could you at least give him the time of day and listen to his proposal?"

"I'll think about it." I stood and grabbed some toast with jelly. "Ruth, we've got work to do."

four

Ruth

The morning after Jason and Dad, as Cooner would say, 'cleared the air' I met briefly with Stanley "The Judge" Crabtree to review our insurance coverage. After retiring from the bench, he ran a small agency in town. Since I was responsible for the financial accounting of the florist and farm businesses, I was the one to meet with him. He had been directed by the insurance company to raise our coverage, approaching the replacement value. After he left around ten, I changed into some summer clothes and headed for the field.

In a t-shirt, shorts, and celebrity-size sun-glasses, my looks defied the fact that I was a farm girl—seeming more like a movie star, soaking in the sun on a luxury beach, on a beautiful spring day.

I enjoyed the work as the John Deere 2940 purred along, seeming to hardly labor, pulling the rolling disks and smoothing shanks. The twelve-foot path the harrows left behind looked as level as Murray's Flats. The soil was being prepared for the alfalfa seeding Jason had planned.

When turning, hearing the disk knife through the soil, heading away from the road and toward the ridge, I noticed the Hideaway. During the hours I drove, I remembered the times that Eve Herbert and I spent there with our brothers.

Eve, the wild one, usually brought the beer. Back then, we thought it was real cool to play poker and feel the buzz. But it wasn't cool the night Dad stormed in on us. He didn't say anything, just grabbed the beer and slammed the door. I could feel the room rock as he rumbled down the stairs. We sat stunned. Eve never brought beer again.

Driving back and forth across the field, I was reminded of the contrast between Vermont and Georgia. Vermont and its four seasons had plenty of challenges but seldom a shortage of rainy weather. Georgia's climate needed irrigation to get a good crop. I also thought, as I constantly did, about the Center, Frieda, the kids, and especially Anadeepa. I was wishing that all of the children could have the opportunities I had had growing up. But my concern lessened, knowing that at least they had Sara to tutor them.

I noticed Cooner brought the alfalfa seed from Butson's. I'd be planting until late afternoon to get ahead of the rain due late that night. At twelve o'clock, I finished harrowing and pulled into the yard, stopping in front of the equipment shed.

Cooner sat on the tailgate of his old Chevy pickup parked by the seeder. With a twinkle in his eye, he leaned on his leverwood cane. "Well, well, my girl has sure grown up." He chuckled. "Stoppin' traffic on Murray's Flats."

I blushed. "Cooner, don't exaggerate."

"I ain't. Clyde Shanks came into Butson's, reportin' he saw ya."

"Nothing gets by old Clyde."

"Yup, 'specially a good-lookin' woman."

I glanced in his truck. "You've brought the seed?"

"Yup. I'd load the seeder, but...." He nervously tapped his cane.

"Cooner, I'll carry the bags."

"You aimin' ta seed that fifteen acres before chores?"

"I hope so." I slipped my sunglasses onto the neck of my t-shirt.

He groaned as he slid off the tailgate.

I pulled a fifty-pound bag from the truck and carried it to the seeder and opened it. Green-coated seeds, twice the size of a pin-head, flowed into the first seed hopper.

Cooner stuffed a wad of Beechnut in his mouth. "Folks about town are talkin' about the tour Jason's givin'."

"All budding naturalists?" I chuckled, carrying the second bag from the truck.

"Not really. They're after Gilda's free lunch and a piece of her apple pie." Cooner leaned on the machine. "They ain't so wild about edible plants, though." He raised the cover of the second hopper. "'Specially mushrooms."

"Your buddies afraid they'll drop dead from mushroom poisoning?" I ran my hand over the seeds, leveling the hopper. They flowed in place like grains of sand.

"Well, maybe somethin' like that. Havin' ta eat bitter cowslips ain't too pop'lar either!"

"Gilda's free food might come at a cost."

"I guess." Cooner watched the seeds flow like water into the second hopper. "Scoop has offered ta drive the tractor and wagon up ta the ridge ta give us old duffers a ride."

"Gee, a good idea." I shut the covers.

"Yup, the new preacher in town is comin' too." He shifted his weight on his cane, with a twinkle in his eye.

"Really? What's his name?"

"Chris Ball." Cooner gimped toward his truck. "Bertha says he's a real nice guy." He continued his wry smile. "Single—of course."

"You old matchmaker."

He got in his truck, facing the meadow toward the Iverson property. "Seein' that failed corn crop reminds me, Bertha says Iverson and Gilda have a thing goin'."

"How would she know?" I asked, heading toward the seeder, not caring for an answer.

"Bertha cleans the restaurant nights."

"Poor Gilda." I got on the tractor. "She's better than Steven Iverson."

Cooner tapped the end of his cane. "Well it's a little like eatin' a mouthful of cowslips...bitter as all get-out, but ya take what's handy."

I stopped at the house for a sandwich and water then drove back to the field. I lowered the steel rollers that rang a soft resonating clank, and began seeding in a six-foot-wide pattern of packed soil. I finished the seeding by late afternoon.

Jason came to the barn, having fixed the fence on the ridge. He sat in back of Precious. "Phew, I'm not used to this spring's work." He pushed his cap toward the back of his head. "The new seeding looks good."

"Yeah, I had just enough." I sat beside him. "We're supposed to hit a rainy spell. Let's take a break and eat at Gilda's tomorrow night. Eve can meet us there."

"Eve!" Jason pulled on the bill of his cap. "Geez! Why did I let her talk me into that tour?"

"A weak moment." I put my hand on his forearm. "Your tour will be fun."

Jason looked down at the sawdust on the floor. "Yeah, but I don't know when I'll have time to get ready for it."

"I'll help you."

That night, I lay in bed hearing the rain pound on the roof outside my window. I felt satisfied and happy to have squeezed in the time to complete the seeding. I also lay thinking I was in limbo not having a plan for my future. But I resolved not to worry about it while I worked with Jason until fall, when all the crops would be stored for winter.

I woke at four a.m. All was quiet in the house. In the distance, I could hear the snarls of raccoons fighting in the Blue River. Their high-pitched chatters and growls rang out in the early morning. I figured they were fighting over a frog they'd found. There would always be winners and losers regardless of where you landed in the animal kingdom.

The south was ever present on my mind, folks like Frieda who were aware of who was and who wasn't on the top, as she called it.

Going downstairs, I started to leave the house when opening the door a blast of cool air backed me up. I slipped on Jason's winter jacket that hung in the entry, plus a wool ski hat.

Adjusting to the frosty morning, I took a quick breath and continued on, reaching the pasture gate and stopping. The gate's metal tubing, caked with white crystals, was ready to be opened for the coming pasturing season. I remembered Cooner saying, "Pasturin' time for the milkers is May 15, no sooner, no later—regular as the singin' peepers in spring."

Today the heifers would be turned out on the ridge. It was early because the snow left early on the south slope. The grass was also lush because Dad fed it plenty of fertilizer. The green ridge was sort of his trophy, a section of land that he admired—just as important to him as a hunter's ten-pointer, hanging on the wall.

I stood looking over the gate through the early morning light, seeing the expanse of green that was starting to grow, since the snow was nearly gone. But some still lingered under the huge willows that grew on my right, bordering the Blue River. Dad had told me that Great-Great-Grandpa Marcus planted the trees in the early 1900s to hold the riverbank during the rush of high water.

Marcus Murray had always been held in high esteem in my family—a successful farmer and one of the early conservationists. Long after his passing, the memory of him continues to be a model for the current generation.

I had no idea how long I stood by the gate, thinking of my ancestral place. As a young girl in summer, I'd walk through the pasture at this same time of day—always the first to get up, Cooner called me "Early Girl"—early to bed and early to rise.

I loved the quietness of morning, going out to get the cows for Dad, following the cow path in near darkness just before the sun poured on its morning light—barely seeing the lounging cows through the mist and feeble light. They looked like oblong blobs—manatees I'd seen in Florida —sea cows floating on the misty fog. I seldom had to speak. The cows' internal clocks told them it was milking time. They'd slowly stand and amble along the path toward the barn. Most knew their stalls. I'd have them all tied up by the time Dad and Jason came to the barn.

Now, standing by the gate with hands deep in my jacket pockets, I felt a moment of sadness. Times had changed. The business of the small dairy farm wasn't so romantic. While studying milk pricing in college, I discovered that net income on farms with fifty cows and less was most often nonexistent. I really agreed with Dad. It was time to move on. But Jason had his own plan for financial survival. I hoped it would work.

Lights from the barn flashed through the frosty air. He had come to start milking.

After milking and after breakfast, Jason went to rent a cattle trailer while I was in the barn, running the gutter cleaner that filled a manure spreader parked outside the barn. Then I bedded the stalls.

Scoop was due soon to help us load the heifers. His noisy van, with tools rattling against the tin sides, pulled into the yard. He entered the barn, stroking his closely trimmed beard. He was, as Cooner would say, 'a rough-shod guy.' "Well, bless me, Jesus, the princess of Murray's Flats has returned."

"Hi, Scoop. Thanks for your help." I placed a milk stool next to the wall in back of the cows. "Have a seat. Jason should be here soon." I turned my back to him, self-consciously pulling the front of my work shirt. I sat on a second stool a comfortable distance from him.

Scoop was scanning me with his wandering eyes. "Goddamn, you're a good-lookin' woman." He reached in my direction.

I quickly stood, looking down at him as I leaned on the wall. "How are you doing, anyway?"

"Well, I ain't had a drink since gettin' out of the poky two months ago." He dropped his head, staring at the floor. Suddenly, he raised his voice and jumped to his feet. "Son-of-a-bitch it ain't easy!" He clenched his fists and flung his arms. "I have to check in with my parole officer, go to AA, go to electrician classes, and afterward, go straight home. Usually, my old man sits watchin' TV…poundin' down beers." Scoop hit the barn wall with his fist. "Bastard, it's hard!" Whitewash flakes fell onto the sawdust floor, looking like bits of snow.

"Hey!" I caught his attention.

He stopped in mid-air, relaxing his fist.

"You're going to be an electrician, and someday settle down."

"What!" He slumped and mumbled. "With some welfare queen… divorced with kids."

"Depends on the queen." I looked out the window, wishing for Jason.

"None of the beauties visitin' guys at prison ain't turned me on none."

"Well, aim high." I checked the window again. "Give yourself a chance."

"Ya know who I'd aim high for?" He glanced my way. "Besides you."

"Who?" I shivered at the thought.

"Ellen Pierce."

"Gilda's sister? She's in nurse's training." He stepped toward me. I inched away.

"Hell, but Ellen ain't interested in no goddamn jail bird." He smoothed his mustache with his thumb and forefinger. "Besides, her looks don't amount to nothin' more than window dressin'." He glanced out onto the lawn with his arms and elbows resting on the sill. "She's always been into her germs. I remember on the playground as a kid, layin' a hand on her." He frowned. "You'd think I was a piece of shit."

Jason drove in the yard with the trailer. I drew a big sigh. Prison time hadn't improved Scoop. But I felt sorry for him. He never had a chance since the day he was born, growing up with a drunkard for a father.

Loading the eight heifers was no easy job—especially animals that had been penned up all winter. Even though the rig was backed tight to the door, with only a slight step up into the trailer, they balked, bracing their feet. They turned several times and charged back toward their pen. All the yelling, slapping, and pushing seemed at first to have no affect on the thousand-pound beasts. Soon six or seven ran onto the trailer, but turned and headed back out. No amount of arm waving stopped them. They dug in their hind feet and charged. We either had to step aside and let them go or get run over in a stampede. Finally, we turned them and pushed on their butts for what seemed like a hopeless effort. After a half hour or so, we got the last one to jump on board. We slammed the trailer door.

Scoop wiped his brow. "The last time I worked this hard, I had myself a nice cold one."

"Well, let's hope that was the last one." I left for the front of the barn, fixing my bandana and tying my ponytail as I went.

I could hear Jason from a distance. "Thanks for your help, Scoop. I'll settle with you during haying."

"Hell, forget it. Call anytime."

I watched the old van rattle out of the yard. Hand-painted black lettering on the side panel read:

LaQuine and Son
We Fix Anything

With the John Deere, Jason pulled the trailer around to the front of the barn.

He called out from the tractor seat. "Bring a bucket of salt."

After filling a small pail, I followed as we headed toward the ridge. He drove the tractor cautiously when coming to the bridge that crossed the Blue River. The rear tractor tires were within inches of the edge on both sides. There were no railings. The river was high. Mini geysers sprayed up through the boarding as the heavy load sagged the bridge. I held my breath, hoping that the supporting timbers would hold. I watched as the bridge sprang back in place. The decking momentarily held water as I sloshed in my pack boots to reach the other side.

Off the bridge, we went through the bar-way of the day pasture and followed a field road next to the fence line. A second gateway opened onto a wood's road leading to the ridge. We traveled next to an old fence line along a stone wall that was no longer in use. Here and there, weathered posts leaned in all directions; sagging strands of century-old wire hung from rusty staple to rusty staple. Frost and tree roots had caused what was once a straight wall to be crooked, with stones being moved through decades of seasons.

We reached the pasture's barbed-wire gate. I set the salt pail at my feet and lifted the smooth wire that looped around the top of the gate post. Jason drove into the pasture as I hitched the gate. When I opened the trailer door, the heifers nearest the door stood, bracing with stiff legs, unsure of their new surroundings. None of them had been on pasture before. Finally, with urging, they jumped out, charging off for a considerable distance. We watched, waiting to see if the four-strand barbed wire would hold them. They charged at the fence but stopped when they felt the sharp barbs.

Jason poured the salt into a trough he'd used for several seasons. They came charging back. One sniffed the salt and others followed. "Cattle love this stuff." He held the pail while we watched. The eight eagerly shoved to reach the trough, blowing salt from their flared nostrils, wanting to get at the white granules.

"Gee, Jason, they're beautiful—and huge!"

"They should be. Dad and I've been using the best bulls for years." He stood admiring them. "They're the fanciest heifers we've ever bred. He ran his hand over their broad rumps, reciting each one's sire and dam. "These mostly black heifers are daughters from a Precious embryo flush that I personally paid the cost. They're sired by Domoneer, a bull with the red factor."

"Golly, Jason, all three look alike."

"There're small differences." He stood by the closest heifer. "She's a bit taller. Her name's Penny." He pointed. "This one has more white in her tail. She's Posey and this one with the white diamond on her head is Popsey."

"Of course you know their names." I looked at them more closely. "Why red and white?"

"Red coloring in Holsteins is a big deal." He turned to me. "I bred them to the best red and white of the breed. If one of them has a bull calf, I've been promised a Canadian contract for five thousand."

"Wow, impressive!" I turned to him. "Does Dad know?"

"No. He won't until I can show him the check." He rubbed his forehead. "There're a lot of contingencies."

"Oh." I didn't want to question his good news too much, having him list the reasons a bull calf wouldn't be accepted.

We watched the heifers lapping the salt for a while until it was all gone. Some remembered their freedom and dashed off through the lush green. We looked across the ridge. Here and there dandelions were beginning to bloom. "Now, there's a picture. This pasture only stays this soft green for a few days in spring."

"We've never had a good camera." I paused, thinking. "We ought to buy one so we can keep the memory of spring alive."

"I wish I could do more with photography." He paused in thought. "Several nights recently, I have heard the yowl of a bobcat." He started for the tractor. "Someday I want to take the time to track one. Better yet, it would be awesome to get a picture. I've been told that it's rare to see one in the wild."

"Well, that would be something!"

"Yeah, you're right." He stopped by the tractor. "Listen! That's the white-throated sparrow."

"I remember." I looked up into the trees. "It's a beautiful song."

Jason smiled. "I love that sound."

I held my hand above my eyes. "Too bad we can't see it."

"It's difficult. They like to nest in the evergreens." He jumped on the tractor.

"Do you ever see them at the feeder?" I asked, still searching the trees in the direction of the birdsong.

"Sometimes."

"I want to get you a camera." I continued, trying to locate the bird hidden in the boughs of the spruce and fir. "You're missing out on some great wildlife photography, though, as the saying goes, 'The best pictures are never taken'."

"Right." He started the tractor. "Someday, I want to own a good camera."

five

Jason

That night after turning the heifers out to pasture and after chores, we headed to Gilda's. I slowed my Chevy truck when we approached a roadside sign:

Gilda's Forget Me Not Restaurant
Where good friends and good food meet

Ruth looked toward the restaurant. "Gilda still trade stuff?"

"That's what Cooner says." I shrugged. "I don't know. I haven't been here in years."

"She might have a camera."

"Maybe." I found a place in the crowded parking lot, turned off the truck, and waited for Ruth to lead the way.

Cooner had told me about Gilda. Many thought that at thirty-five, she was the grand matron of Huntersville. The oldest of ten children, she'd earned her reputation by Yankee ingenuity and hard work. In eighth grade, she started to help cook for the hot lunch program. After classes, when all the kids had left for home, Gilda was testing recipes in the school's kitchen. The kids loved her cooking. By her eighth-grade graduation, she had become a culinary marvel. Among her best dishes were Gilda's Chicken and Dumplings, Gilda's Hodge-podge Soup, and Gilda's Deep Dish Apple Pie, all her own secret recipes.

Gilda's dad, Hiram Pierce, worked at Butson's Feed and Farm Supply—a job that didn't pay a whole lot. Much of the family needs were met through what he called "tradin" —goods for services. The services came from his kids, stacking wood, mowing lawns, shoveling snow, and babysitting. Gilda grew up poor and vowed as a young teenager that she would never follow in her mother's footsteps—married with a lot of kids.

I recalled Cooner saying that, even before her graduation from high school, Gilda bought the old town hall to turn it into a restaurant. Her father signed the papers, and she talked the selectmen into giving her a mortgage—paying for the former town hall over time. What Gilda didn't have in beauty, she compensated in charm. Young Steven Iverson, then a member of the Board, was willing to swing a deal—that was over twenty years ago. At the March town meeting the year of the sale, the selectmen reported that they gave fifteen-year-old Gilda a generous offer. They wanted to keep the enterprising girl in town.

Bertha Bean grumbled, "Huh, we all know Gilda. She probably sashayed into the selectmen's meeting, wearing tight jeans and a sexy top, flashing those big brown eyes. With her come-on smile, the selectmen took one look at her and couldn't wait to sign the papers."

Whatever the real truth was, Gilda, with help from her dad and three brothers, remodeled the old town hall, turning it into a popular place to get a genuine home-cooked meal. Rumor had it that the state inspector sat down to a generous serving of Gilda's Hodge-podge Soup and a piece of her Deep Dish Apple Pie. Her dangling earrings and shoulder-length ringlets, plus her vintage smile, melted the guy right to his chair. He never left his seat, just pulled out his inspection report and gave her a temporary permit to open for business.

Gilda was off and running. Her excellent meals gave her instant success—along with the tradition of tradin'. She traded her good cooking for supplies, services, and valuable items. She wouldn't take junk.

A few years ago she totally remodeled her restaurant, adding a room with an overhead apartment for herself. The room was filled with clothing and worthy items locals brought to her in exchange for a good meal or meals. Even with her tradin', Gilda had plenty of paying customers.

Before Ruth and I entered the restaurant, we noticed Hiram Pierce, Gilda's dad, spreading bark mulch around a row of Japanese yews growing in front of the building. Ruth pulled open a big red door and entered.

Gilda met us near the entrance with a wide friendly smile. "Ruth! You're home!" Her brown eyes widened and glowed with enthusiasm on greeting us.

With open hands, Ruth spread her arms. "I'm here all safe and happy to be back."

"Gee, you look good! And who's this handsome stranger?"

"Hi, Gilda." I grinned.

If not for her winning personality, some might consider her to be rather plain-looking. The deep brown penciling and eye shadow drew attention away from a large Roman nose. Her brunette ringlets were held by sequined barrettes above each ear.

Ruth reached for Gilda's arm. "Eve Hebert will be joining us."

With three menus in hand, Gilda led us by the crowded counter to a booth.

After I sat, she caught my attention. "We've got to get together and talk about this upcoming tour."

"Yeah, I know." I swallowed hard, realizing a walking tour of the woods was turning into a bigger deal than I'd ever imagined. "Anything in mind?"

"Well, yeah." Gilda's cheerful personality turned all business. "Eve wants to offer samples of edible plants. They should be included in the menu."

"Really, I wasn't thinking..."

"Well, why not? Ellen has the week off. I'll send her to collect samples." She asserted, "I want these edible plants to taste good."

"Well, oh...okay." All the spring's work I had to do ran through my mind. "Gosh, I got corn to plant and fences to fix."

"How about tomorrow morning?" Ruth suggested. "I'll work the corn land, get it ready, and Cooner can plant."

"Okay." I thought about places along the Blue and in our woods. "I can easily collect mint, watercress, fiddleheads, wild onions, cowslips, dandelions, and maybe mushrooms."

"Let's see." Gilda paused. "Maybe a sample of a green salad would work, or soup, mint tea and sides of dandelions and a few fiddleheads." She continued concentrating. "Let's wait and see what you find."

I chuckled. "I'm sure Cooner and his buddies were only thinking of your popular egg salad sandwiches and apple pie."

Gilda grinned. "We'll surprise them." She placed the menus in front of us. "Ellen will take your order."

When Ruth and I took our seats the place was crowded, but the atmosphere was calm and quiet. Pleasant smells poured from the kitchen. Gilda played mostly country music for her patrons. John Denver softly crooned, *"Take me Home, Country Roads."*

All the counter seats were taken—probably most of those customers had made a deal with Gilda. I recognized Floyd Campbell. He plowed her yard in winter, probably in exchange for a few free meals. Next to him, Perry Green, the oilman, no doubt delivered at cost—then Judge Crabtree. He grew the biggest garden in town and kept Gilda supplied with potatoes, carrots, onions, beets, and corn. He ate most of his meals at Gilda's. The sheriff, Jasper Krads, sat next to the judge. On Friday and Saturday nights he was on duty, probably in exchange for free meals at the counter.

Steven Iverson ate most of his meals at Gilda's. Bertha claimed he traded a bunch of stuff for a steady meal ticket. She also enjoyed eating at Gilda's. After hours, Bertha cleaned the restaurant. She told Cooner that most nights near eleven o'clock, when all was quiet except for the mop sliding over the floor, she would hear footsteps on the apartment stairs. Under the security lights in the parking lot, she could see Iverson walking toward his farm that was located diagonally across the road.

Ellen, Gilda's sister, was a willowy blond with a shingle cut. She came carrying a tray and three water glasses. Her blue eyes and fair complexion glowed. "Oh my gosh, Jason and Ruth Murray!" She set the water glasses at our places.

"Hi, Ellen." we said in unison. "Eve will be here soon."

Ruth glanced up at Ellen. "Your sister tells us you're at school."

"I am. I work here part-time."

She'd matured since high school, not nearly as shy. I was struck by her delicate beauty.

Ellen smiled as she turned to me. "Remember the senior party?"

"I do. That seems ages ago."

"We danced." She pulled an order pad from her red apron. "The heart-throb of Huntersville High danced with me—whoa!"

"I don't remember that." My face reddened. I turned to the menu, then glanced up. "Gilda said you'd be out tomorrow morning to collect edible plants."

"She did?" Ellen's eyes widened.

"Yeah, about ten. Wear boots and old clothes."

"That will be exciting!" She warmly smiled. "An adventure!"

I noticed her white sneakers, the ruler-edge crease in her slacks, her robin's-egg-blue sweater with a gold turtle pin. I couldn't imagine her mucking through a swamp and over the woods floor collecting plants.

Ruth studied her menu. "We'll wait for Eve before we order."

Ellen left. Ruth looked up at me. "Wow, she's turned into a beauty."

I didn't comment, but silently agreed that she was about the most beautiful girl I'd seen, and disgusted that I couldn't cover my emotions while feeling the heat around my collar and high color in my face.

Watching me glow, Ruth laughed.

Moments later, Eve breezed in, making sure everyone in the place knew she'd arrived. She was loud, with a husky voice, "Hi, everyone!"

Eve, who was Ruth's age, had done well at the bank as a loan officer—basically because she could speak French. The bank drew a large French-speaking clientele. At twenty-four, she'd added weight. Men in particular would say weight in all the right places. And she loved to show it. Tonight was no exception.

She came bouncing toward our booth in tight slacks and a yellow sweater that clung like sticky paper. Her large breasts jiggled as she slid in next to Ruth. We exchanged glances. She excitedly grabbed my hand. "This tour I planned is turning out to be a great idea!"

I dropped my head. "Oh, don't tell me!"

"It's going to put the Booster Club on the map!"

I suddenly lost my appetite. "Well, I…I wasn't…"

"Well, nothing. I'll bet it'll draw a hundred people."

"Oh, really!" I said with alarm. "Gosh, limit it to twenty-five. You're making too big a deal out of this!"

"I guess not! The success of this tour will put me right into the presidency of the Booster Club."

"What a goal!" I said with a lot of sarcasm, imagining a hundred people tramping through our bog, woods, and wetlands, with folks getting stuck up to their hips in the spring mud. "I only want twenty-five on the tour."

"Is that all?" Eve turned glum.

"Yeah, twenty-five." I firmly said. "Interested folks."

"Well, okay," she said, resigned.

Ellen came for our order. Eve blurted, "Three beers. The drinks are on me."

Even a group of twenty-five people challenged me. I felt unprepared, anxiously pondering my inadequacy. Eve and Ruth ordered sirloin steak. All I ordered was soup and saltines.

Ellen sweetly smiled at me. "Is that all?" Her words came out in a soft purr.

I nodded. "Yes." I looked away, not covering my feelings as they raced from tour thoughts to a beautiful discovery—Ellen.

While writing on the order pad, she pressed her pen too hard. It popped out of her slender hand and flew onto the table.

Eve picked it up and passed it back. She blurted loudly, "Careful there, girl. You might hurt Prince Charming."

"Sorry!" Ellen turned instantly red like the blink of a stop light.

I glanced at a flustered Ellen as she completed our order. "Don't pay any attention to Eve."

In a while our food arrived. We ate in silence. Eve had drained her first glass of beer and was well into her second. I watched the crowd. Steven Iverson came through the door and huddled with Gilda at her receptionist station. He had his arm around her, whispering in her ear. She broke into an uproarious laugh. He pulled her closer, but she pushed him away.

He had on the same grubby clothes as when I'd seen him last. Pulling on the bottom edges of his off-white coat, he left Gilda's side and began working the crowd, heading toward our booth—doing what he did best, glad-handing his constituents.

Eve was on her third beer while I ate a small dish of vanilla ice cream—worry over the tour was ruining my night.

Iverson slowly came our way. I watched his jaunty exchanges. He knew everybody, eventually getting to our booth. "Oh, my gosh, Ruth Murray! You're home! And Eve!" He reached for her hand. "How are you, darling?"

"Feeling good." She pulled him down to reach for a kiss. In the time it took for him to get to our booth, she'd ordered a fourth glass. Her eyes were getting blurry.

"Mind if I sit?" He slid in next to me.

I knew what he was after.

He turned to me. "How's the best farmer in town doing?"

"Okay." It annoyed me, him trying to butter me up.

While Iverson's knitted fingers rested on the table, his thumbs were in constant motion.

I watched his long dirty thumbnails rotating like a fly-wheel. He stopped the action and reached for an empty Forget Me Not creamer, rolling it like a worry stone. "You Murrays make a hell of a team." He nervously shifted in his seat. "Ruth, the financial whiz and Jason, the cowman." He stopped momentarily and stared at the creamer. "Yeah, a hell of a team."

I had nothing to say.

Ruth gave him a glance. "What's the point?"

"We should join our farms. I have a modern dairy and you two have the brains."

I blurted, "Why don't you have an auction and sell?"

Squeezing the creamer with his fingers, his knuckles turned white. "I can't."

Eve's head was slightly swaying. "You're right! You're at the end…" She abruptly stopped.

I turned to him. "I've got better things to do than to milk a bunch of cows. As I just said, have an auction."

"I can't and I don't want to." He rolled the creamer.

"Hell!" Eve slurred. "He's up to his ass in alligators."

Iverson snapped, "Shut your mouth!" His double chin turned red, eyes bulged, and cheeks swelled. Wildly swinging his arms, he looked like he could explode. The creamer slipped from his hand and crashed to the floor, shattering into pieces.

Everyone stopped eating and looked our way. Gilda came running. "What's going on?" she demanded.

"Get Eve out of here!" Iverson pushed her arm off the table. "I want to talk business!"

Eve broke into tears, blubbering, "I'm sorry."

Grabbing a fistful of yellow sweater, Ruth held her. "Eve's staying right here. We're taking her home."

Iverson calmed. "Well, I guess we're okay."

Gilda stepped over the broken pottery and said frostily, "I won't allow rowdiness in my restaurant!"

A guy from the kitchen hurriedly cleaned the floor as Gilda left.

Eve wiped tears and dropped her head in her hands.

Iverson stared at her. "Now, let's talk."

Ruth offered, "The next rainy day, show us a proposal along with your financials and we'll listen." She glanced at me, narrowing her eyes, gesturing for me to accept her offer.

I scowled. "Yeah…okay, if…if I'm not too busy."

Iverson stared at me. "What are you so busy about on a rainy day?"

"Other interests." The guy continued to irritate me.

"Like?" He asked.

Ruth could see I was put off by him. "He's interested in nature." She quickly continued, "I'd like him to get a good camera."

"Oh, photography!" Iverson nodded. "I traded a hell of nice camera to Gilda last month…one Ma gave me for Christmas."

Surprised, Ruth said, "You did?"

"Yup, you stay right here and I'll get it for you."

I sat in disbelief. He even traded his mother's gift. I watched him hurry past the counter toward Gilda. They talked for a minute, and then he went toward a room on the far side of the restaurant.

Eve lifted her head. "The guy's broke. He'll be living in a cardboard box by fall."

Returning, Iverson carried the camera, case, and owner's manual. He slid in beside me, pulling the camera from the case.

I read the owner's manual for Ruth's benefit. "A Nikon N-90S, with a telescopic lens, automatic focus, automatic film advance, and a light-metering sensor." I reached for the camera and studied it closely.

"Sounds expensive," Ruth said.

Iverson added, "It was. But, hell, I'll never use it. I gave it to Gilda."

"Yeah," Eve said in a drunken grump. "For three squares a day."

Iverson glared at Eve then turned to me. "Ma loaded it with film. We took three or four pictures in my kitchen just to see how it worked."

I continued looking closely at the camera.

Ruth saw my interest. "Jason, I'd like to buy it for you."

"Thanks." I again looked at the cover of the manual. "It will be interesting to see what I can get for pictures."

"Good; see Gilda. You can own it." Iverson stood to leave. "Remember, next rainy day, we'll get together."

six

Ruth

After a morning call to the Center, I felt satisfied to hear that Sara was doing well tutoring the kids. Frieda in an amazed tone said, "Sakes alive, that girl has the kids writin' stories. I ain't believin' how good they do!"

Anadeepa came to the phone. "Hear my story."

"Sure, read it to me, Honey."

"I have a friend. Her name is Ruth. I love her lots. She lives far far away. By Anadeepa."

"That's wonderful!" I sniffed. "I love you, too." A lump stayed in my throat.

It comforted me to know Sara was a perfect role model for the kids—a teacher who'd risen from poverty, a black girl who had, as Frieda would say, 'Made it to the top'.

Frieda also reported that she'd just received the monthly payments from the Elias M. Cole Foundation that covered Sara's salary and necessary living expenses for most of the kids.

That morning, while Jason was collecting wild edible samples with Ellen, Cooner and I had plans to plant corn.

As I left the house, I looked at him sitting on his bench. "You ready to go to work?"

He groaned, "Golly, you folks are hard up for help." He leaned on his cane. "I ain't planted corn for several years."

"I'll load the planter." I held his arm as we walked toward the shed. "All you'll have to do is sit, steer, and pull levers."

"I'm happy to help, but this is still pushin' me a mite." In the shed, he sat on the frame of the planter. "Seems this tour is bumpin' right into spring's work."

"We'll manage." I rested a full seed bag on the edge of a hopper and turned to Cooner. "I sure hope the tour goes well for Jason."

"Yup, I agree."

"He has an interest in the natural world most of us take for granted."

"I will say when it comes ta what grows in those woods and swamp-land," he rattled his cane, "that boy knows his stuff."

"We'll see where this tour takes him." I placed the covers on the hoppers. "Who knows, he might want to study more and become a naturalist."

Cooner rubbed his chin. "Leave Murray's Flats?" He spat. "It'd kill him."

I pondered the thought. "You never know."

I drove the John Deere, pulling the harrows to smooth the soil for planting. Cooner drove an older Massey-Ferguson tractor, planting over the prepared soil. He did okay, hydraulically raising and lowering the machine, following the marker line for the next four-row pass. By late afternoon, I'd finished harrowing the field, so took over planting for him. It was early in May to have corn in the ground, but during the next week we had to fix the fences before we turned out the milkers by the 15th. The tour was planned for Saturday, May 14th.

While Jason was spending time in the woods, Cooner and I were fixing fence.

Friday was warm with a clear blue sky. The black flies were out in force. Cooner drove, bumping along in first gear as I checked the electric fence line, replacing broken insulators and twisting wire breaks together when needed.

After we completed our perusal of the electric fences, Cooner stopped his truck. He looked out over the field of mixed alfalfa and grass. "First cuttin' will be ready as soon as the dandy-lions die back."

"Yeah, haying will be next week if we get the weather."

I loaded some more supplies, staples, a half-used roll of barbed wire, and a few cedar posts in the truck. We were off to fix the barbed wire fence across the Blue. As we reached the bridge, the water roared over the riverbed. Cooner hugged the wheel of his truck. "This always scares me a mite, lookin' off the edge, thinkin' my truck could flip and we'd be suckin' mountain water."

I laughed. "That *would* be dramatic."

He inched across the bridge in first. "Phew, we made it."

The barbed wire fence needed little repair, having survived the snows of winter in good condition.

After fixing fence, I met Jason and Ellen in the yard. Her face was covered with red bites. She rubbed on some cream. "The black flies are fierce but we had fun. We found plenty of edibles, even a few shaggymane mushrooms." While reporting, Ellen held up plastic bags filled with watercress, cowslips, dandelions, wild onions, and mint.

When she left, Jason seemed relaxed, all smiles, satisfied he could lead an interesting walking tour. "Ellen and I figured how we can serve hot mint tea on the stove in the Hideaway. We'll drive the heifers to the cows' day pasture and park the food wagon on the ridge."

"How was your time with Ellen?"

"She's a lot of help." He grinned. "We had a good time planning for Saturday."

He reported finding wild flowers in bloom such as the lady slipper and red trillium, as well as orchids and pitcher plants in the bog. He also located several beds of bluets in bloom.

When he was walking in a grove of beech trees toward the ridge, he saw five evenly spaced scratches about six to eight inches long on the gray beech bark. He said the marks showed that last fall a bear had been climbing the trees to feed on beechnuts. He added the marks to his points of interest for the tour.

Saturday morning the weather was muggy and warm. The gray sky and heavy air had the telltale signs that a storm was on its way. At ten, the crowd started gathering. Scoop had the tractor and flatbed wagon ready for the pots and pans of food, with space for the older folks that wanted only the lunch and didn't feel up to the tour. Ellen rode on the wagon to get ready for the picnic.

Some older folks such as Shirley and Joe Iverson, Bertha Bean, and Judge Crabtree opted for the tour and not the wagon ride.

Eve Hebert was in her glory, wearing a red cap and a daring V-neck shirt. She introduced the program: "For our spring event this year, the Booster Club's planning committee decided to feature a little-known authority on the plants and wildlife of this area…"

Jason stood with his new camera over his shoulder, scuffing his feet on the gravel drive.

She acknowledged the Huntersville Bank as the tour sponsor and Gilda's Forget Me Not Restaurant for the picnic. Emily Ann Gray was introduced as president of the bank. She greeted the crowd and expressed her thanks to Jason. Everyone clapped.

After the introduction, Jason seemed relaxed. He wore a John Deere cap shading his broad forehead, alert blue eyes and tanned, chiseled face. He stood tall in his khaki field jacket and pants. He smiled. "Welcome to the Murray Farm. I don't pretend to be a fully informed naturalist, but I've become familiar with what we'll see during our walk. I hope you've all brought bug repellant. With no breeze this morning, the black flies are terrible."

There were at least twenty-five of us on the tour. Eve led with Jason. I followed last in line. A fellow I didn't know dropped back to walk with me as we headed toward the bridge. He was about my age. With a friendly smile, he spoke to me. "I'm Chris Ball, the new minister in town."

"Oh, nice to meet you. I'm Ruth, Jason's sister." Chris had a firm handshake.

At first glance, he didn't fit the character I imagined of a minister—a man of sophistication, carefully dressed with neatly combed hair. Instead, he was not a "strike'em-dead" sort of guy, but rather plain in fact. His medium-length curly hair had no combed pattern. His large brown eyes peered through horn-rimmed glasses. The glasses were his most distinguishing characteristic—definitely a 60's style. He seemed at ease as we moved along. "I've been told you've just come back from a stint with VISTA."

"Yes, I'm home for a while to help Jason." We continued to follow the group when we reached the bridge.

"I'd like to hear about your work sometime." We were sloshing through the water on the bridge.

"Come out tomorrow for Sunday dinner?" I looked at him. "Could you do that?"

"Sure, I'd like that." He left my side.

I smiled, watching his gawky stride as he moved ahead of me.

He visited with Mildred Butson, a staunch member of the Huntersville Community Church.

We all stopped on the bridge and faced upstream. The quantity of the water was spectacular as it came rushing toward us, buffeting against large boulders, shooting fans of spray high above the riverbed.

Jason explained that the Blue River was coming from the Hardhack Mountain watershed. "At this time of year, if we've had a decent snowfall, water charges over its granite bedrock with the force we see today. During dry spells the river only flows at a trickle."

He led us a short distance toward a bog. We moved along a beaten path as the ground shook beneath our feet. Jason faced the group. "This bog is an accumulation of decaying mosses that have formed peat deep enough to support us on this path."

"What is the purplish-red flower that looks like a cup?" Bertha asked.

"That's a pitcher plant," Jason explained, "It collects bugs in its blossom cup and digests them for its food. The other flowering plants you see here are in the orchid family."

He pointed to his right. "The beautiful white flower out there a few yards is the rare showy orchis. It sends off a beautiful odor similar to an exotic perfume."

"I want to take a whiff." Bertha, without hesitation, stepped off the path.

Several yelled, "Don't!"

Jason charged forward, catching Bertha by the arm, pulling her back on the path. One boot sucked free from deep muck. "Please stay on the path!"

"Sorry, I didn't realize."

Jason nodded, never losing his composure, and continued, "The turtles you see scurrying into hiding are mostly the wood turtle. The frogs are mainly the green frog, bull frog, and peepers. Peepers stop chirping when they hear noise such as our voices." We continued along the winding path. "Note the frog eggs. These wetland creatures provide food for the coons, bear, coyotes, and water animals such as the muskrats and mink."

We stopped to admire all the wild flowers in bloom. In a grove of maples a large quantity of broad-leafed, eight-inch-high green plants grew up through a mat of dried leaves. Jason pointed. "The plants you see are wild onion or leeks." He bent down, driving his field knife next to the plant. He pulled the stem, showing a white bulb the size and shape of a large pea. "The whole plant can be used in salads and soups. Ellen will have a sample for us to try at the picnic."

We walked on for nearly an hour, reaching the wagon and ending the tour. Judge Crabtree spoke for the group. "I never dreamed what we could learn from Jason in such a short time."

Everyone clapped.

The morning ended none too soon as storm clouds were rapidly coming our way. Chris Ball stepped next to me. "Your brother is quite the book of knowledge."

"He is." We picked up plates to serve ourselves. "I hope farm responsibilities won't keep him from building on his interest."

We hurried to eat before the storm hit. The meal, smorgasbord style, included samples of edibles, plus egg-salad sandwiches and Gilda's apple pie. Most tried the cowslips, wild onions, fiddleheads, and a salad made up of wild plants that she had prepared with a vinaigrette dressing. Clyde Shanks made a face when he started eating cowslips. "These are mighty bitter." He spit them on the ground. "I need some of that mint tea to wash out my mouth."

Folks laughed at Clyde, but most tried the samples anyway. All Gilda's sandwiches and apple pie were quickly taken. Even with the storm threatening, people sat along the ridge, enjoying the picnic while overlooking the valley. Jason helped Ellen bring pots of mint tea from the Hideaway to serve those seated on the ridge. But there was urgency while eating, especially when it started to sprinkle. Jason, Ellen, Eve and I hurried to gather up the dishes. We collected the paper plates and tableware in a garbage bag. Scoop yelled, "Everyone aboard or we're gonna get dumped on."

He had no sooner announced the boarding of the wagon when the skies opened up. We all couldn't fit, so Jason, Ellen, Eve, Bertha, Chris,

Shirley, Joe, and I ran for the Hideaway. The little eight-by-eight room had never been tested for such weight. It was hot inside from the stove. We were standing shoulder to shoulder. Jason's face was inches from Ellen's hair. The smell of steaming mint tea overpowered us. The air-space of the tiny room was mint filled, saturated as a dripping sponge.

"Open the window!" someone yelled.

A bolt of lightning cracked. The sky opened up even more, dumping quantities of rain on the roof. The wind roared, causing the branches of the old maple to sway, moving the Hideaway with the motion of the limbs. The room started to squawk as rusty nails pulled from the ply-wood. The nailed wood started separating at the seams as spikes holding it to the tree inched from their setting. I felt the floor tip forward. There was a collective gasp. Thankfully, the tipping stopped as the room rested on a limb.

Crash! Jason opened the door. We looked off into space. The stairs had left the Hideaway and fallen to the ground. He glumly announced, "We're stranded!"

Several moved on the slanted floor toward the window. Looking at the slope below, I realized it was at least fifteen feet to the ground.

A whimper rippled through the crowd as another crack of lighting buckled Eve's knees. She crossed herself. "Holy Mary, Mother of God!"

Bertha pleaded, "Lord, save us!"

Jason and I pushed toward the door. He yelled, "I hear a tractor coming!"

The storm had passed, turning to a light rain, but I could still hear thunder in the distance.

Shirley fanned her face with Jason's log book. "I can hardly get a breath."

Eve coughed. "I feel like I'm gargling a mouth full of mint."

The tractor stopped by the open door of the Hideaway. "Holy shit!" Scoop yelled, "You folks stranded?"

"Yeah, back the wagon to the end of the stairs," Jason ordered. "Lift the stairs to rest on the flatbed and shove them onto the wagon."

"Jason, these stairs are heavy," Scoop groaned.

He backed the tractor as the other end hit a tree, shoving the stairs onto the wagon.

Jason turned to Joe. "You and Ruth hold my feet." He hung out the door to help Scoop bring the stairs into place.

Scoop grunted, lifting them to rest on the floor of the Hideaway.

Jason ordered, "I'll hold this end. Scoop, use your feet and hands to hold the other end."

Joe went through the opening. "I'll reach and hold the hand of those that follow me."

He helped Ellen to the bottom step. Scoop put his arms out to catch her, but she turned and jumped. He shrugged after her rejection but continued to hold the stairs.

With Joe's help, the others walked out without a hitch.

"This was scary!" Chris carefully climbed down the stairs. "Jason, thankfully you were here."

"I'm just sorry it happened."

I followed and Jason was the last to leave. He had his log book in hand.

Chris walked with me to the farm. "I admire your brother. I couldn't have handled that situation."

"He's always been a leader." We continued on, following the group.

I looked back toward the Hideaway, cockeyed and split at the seams. Jason built it as a kid, but now he'd moved beyond those carefree days. I hoped he could repair the damage and continue to use it to study his passion. But with the demands of the farm, like chores, haying, and corn cutting, I wondered when and if he'd take the time.

seven

Jason

By Sunday morning, May 15th, there was plenty of grass to begin the grazing season. Ruth and I let out the cows for the first time. As usual, they tore around the field, checking the fence line, not touching it, knowing from past experience that it was hot from the sound of the line's intermittent electrical pulse. Ruth and I leaned on the gate, watching them. "Jason, they're a beautiful herd. Not a scrub in the bunch."

"Yeah, we can give Dad a lot of the credit." I tipped back the visor of my cap. "Buying Pride, when he was a boy, gave us the foundation."

"Now, her granddaughter, Precious, leads the herd." She came running up to me and sniffed my hand. "Yeah, you're the queen of the herd." I reached to touch her head. She turned and charged off, kicking her hind legs. We both laughed.

When we walked toward the house, the weather still hadn't cleared. The skies were overcast with a light misty rain in the air, but when I looked toward the mountains, it seemed as if the sun would be out soon. I glanced toward the shed. "I need to check and grease the mower this morning before it clears." I glanced at the western sky. "By noon I might be mowing."

Cooner sat on his bench, leaning on his cane. "Well, well, you two have done half a day's work already."

"You'll get your chance in a couple of days." Jason smiled. "Bailing hay."

"Good!" Cooner spat. "Looks ta be clearin'." He wiped the tobacco juice from his mouth. "I checked and the corn's germinated, ready ta peek through the ground." He shook his head. "Iverson ain't even touched his land."

"I know." I nodded in disbelief.

Cooner lifted himself to his feet. "Looks ta me as if the man's given up."

I shrugged. "Maybe so."

Ruth took Cooner's arm. "Let's get something to eat." She held the door. "After breakfast, I need to do some data entry on the computer." She followed him. "Then I'm going to church."

At breakfast Dad told me, "I'm sorry your Mom and I couldn't be on the tour." He passed the toast around. "We're swamped at the shop, getting ready for Memorial Day."

Mom had a cup in her hand. "Judge Crabtree stopped in. He said, Jason, that you have all the makings of becoming a full-time naturalist."

"Well, thanks." I chewed on a piece of bacon. "But I'm satisfied with my life the way it is right now."

An awkward silence passed over the table. Dad glanced at me. "Since it's been raining, Steven Iverson may be due…"

"So…?" I yanked toast off the plate.

"Milking fifty cows isn't practical." Dad bore down. "You're passing up an opportunity not to seriously listen to Iverson."

Cooner fumbled with his package of Beechnut. "There's somethin' brewin' with the guy." He slipped the tobacco in his shirt pocket. "Somebody's puttin' the screws ta him."

"Well, that's not my problem!" I pushed back from the table. "If he shows today, I'll tell him we're too busy."

"Tomorrow." Dad stared at me. "Tell him we'll meet tomorrow."

"I'm mowing if it clears." I headed for the door.

Dad raised his voice. "Tomorrow, Jason! Tomorrow!"

"Okay." I was almost out the door. I faced Dad. "If you want the meadow so badly, buy it yourself."

"Not for half a million."

For one of the first times in my life, I felt I was being used. Dad wanted me to sacrifice my future plans so he could, in some way, end up owning the meadow.

As the day progressed, I was relieved that Iverson never came. But my conflict with Dad put me in a sour mood. After night chores, I decided to go to Gilda's for my supper. I lucked out. Ellen was there, finishing her shift. She joined me at my booth. With her across from me, Gilda's hodge-podge soup, homemade bread, and apple pie melted in my mouth. Ellen's delicate beauty, coupled with the twinkle in her eye and easy conversation, captivated me.

When she talked, she slid her hand over the paper placemat at her place setting. Her slender fingers were soft and pink as a baby's cheek. The half-moon crescent of each fingernail was milky white with nails neatly manicured, perfectly trimmed.

I clenched my fists, pulling them to the edge of the table, careful not to show the palms of my hand. Having worked on the mower that afternoon, I didn't want to show my grease-stained hands. Even though I'd washed them, they were far from lily-white.

I watched her align the paper placemat with the edge of the table. She spread her fingers, examining them, sliding them over the ads on the mat: Butson's Feed and Farm Supply, The Huntersville National Bank, Murray's Florist Shop. She continued casually chatting, while I watched her. I became nearly breathless, noticing with each word the triangle of her throat move above the neckline of her spotless white blouse. "I love my classes...everything at the hospital...working side by side with medical *professionals*."

Hearing "professionals" caught me off guard. I didn't think of myself as anywhere near a professional.

"The doctors are so nice."

A pang of jealousy grabbed me. All of a sudden the supper felt heavy in my stomach. "The doctors..." I stopped in mid-sentence, not wanting to show I cared in the least if she gave doctors a second look.

"Gosh, they're handsome in their white coats." She ran her finger along the table's edge again.

"Oh, handsome?"

"Right, handsome." Her hand touched my plate. "I really like guys who amount to something." Looking up at me, she blushed. The tips of her fingers dropped next to my plate. The overhead light caused her nails to glisten like pearls. "You know, guys like..."

"Like?" I wanted to reach for her hand and would have if mine weren't so ugly. I wanted her to say, "Like you." But she stopped. I figured she probably thought it would sound too forward. I let it pass. At this point she could have said almost anything and it would have been okay.

She looked at me with a smile. "I could already be certified as a *professional* phlebotomist."

Probably she expected me to be impressed with her having emphasized professional. I was impressed, but I didn't have the foggiest understanding of the word phlebotomist. "Oh, really!" I must have had a blank expression.

"A phlebotomist draws blood, but being an RN pays more."

"I guess you'd have to move out of town to be a certified professional." I really wanted to know her plans.

Her index finger rose off the table to again slowly trace over the edge of my plate. Her hand was so close I could smell the blossom scent of her hand cream. Did she realize, or didn't she, that her finger was tantalizing me.

At any rate, I clamped my fists tighter, beginning to feel light-headed. Her blue, blue eyes widened as she smiled. Her lips were moist. She bent forward—her breath was sweet. "I could always commute." She reached for my hand.

The feel of her touch ignited my fire. "Yeah, commute?" My pulse rate must have been off the charts.

"I wouldn't be interested in a dirt-poor man, scraping along like my folks." Her finger left my hand and continued tracing the edge of the pie plate. "I want to be able to buy clothes, do things, travel to romantic places." She smiled, continuing that twinkle in her eye. "Sun myself on some lonely beach, while basking in a Caribbean breeze."

Her words struck me like a Mack truck. I'd never thought about providing for a wife and family. Suddenly, a great dawning came over me. Maybe there *was* no future in milking fifty cows. What if my plan of breeding quality cattle didn't work? In an instant, Ellen's words were like a bomb, blowing my very orderly plan to the winds. I was now in uncharted territory, dumbstruck with infatuation. I conceded I should at least listen to Iverson—because there wasn't a thing about Ellen not to like. Even though I hadn't kissed the girl, I'd fallen hard.

At that instant, I sat speechless. However, the yearning for her overwhelmed me. I'd never dated a girl so desirable. I wondered if she had dated all that much. "I'll…I'll bet you've gone with lots of guys."

"No." She blushed. "I…I guess in school, I…I was too shy."

"Oh, not at all!"

"Well, you never looked at me, and you didn't even remember dancing with me!" She lowered her voice, saying in a mumble, "I guess I wasn't sexy enough."

"That's… that's not true." My voice cracked. I did a lousy job of lying. I took a deep breath. "Anyway…you're…you're cute."

"Oh…cute." She looked down at her hands. "Little girls are cute."

"Cute's the wrong word. You're *not* a little girl."

She smiled. "Thank you."

Our conversation was going nowhere. I had an urge to kiss her, to hold her and tell her that she was about the most beautiful girl I'd ever met. But in Gilda's setting, I couldn't. I mustered the courage to ask, hoping she'd accept. "Can…can I take you for a ride?"

She brightened and reached for my hand. "Sure!"

I was weak all over. When I slid from the booth and stood, my legs were jelly, a sensation I'd never felt before. I gulped, which I'd been doing a lot, and followed Ellen out the door.

The night was warm with a cloudless sky and an almost full moon. Although it was getting dark, my truck was easy to see. "It's the bright red one near the yard light."

Ellen slowed down. "I know. I've seen you around town, acting all business. You never knew I existed."

"Well…I'm…I'm sorry I missed seeing you." I gulped again. I had my hand on the passenger door handle.

She stopped, ready to jump in. "This should be fun." She followed with a chuckle. "A ride in Jason Murray's jazzy red truck."

"Everyone knows my truck." At this point, I didn't think a recognizable truck was all that great.

My heart was doing flips, imagining Ellen in my arms. When I got in behind the wheel, I reached for her. From the yard light, I could see a smile wrinkle the edges of her mouth. She slid next to me and gave me a peck on the cheek. That was all I needed for sort of a come on. When

I held her, I forgot all about the grease stains. Her lips felt dainty and tender when we traded kisses.

I was breathless. The yard light showed that her flared skirt had slipped above her knees. I shuddered, looking at her shapely legs. Words left my mouth in a near stutter, "Le...let's go."

"Okay...where?" She straightened her skirt.

"I'll surprise you."

Traveling on Murray Flats, I pulled onto the Iverson land. I stayed parallel to the road until coming to our recently planted corn field. The pale green corn was just spiking out of the ground, showing two leaves. The truck's headlights picked up the line of green growing in the brown soil. The smooth ground and straight rows allowed me to drive across the corn field in second gear without hurting the plants.

Ellen sat erect on the edge of the seat. "What are you doing?" Her voice was tense.

"You'll see."

Shortly, we came to the end of the corn rows. I drove the truck across some grass and parked under a giant willow with its huge spreading limbs. I cut the lights and shut off the truck. It was nearly pitch black. Only the moon gave us light.

The river had slowed in the last few days, having lost its spring's rush. We could hear a soft-sounding ripple of water not far from the truck. The cold mountain stream was sending off a mist mixing with the warm night air. A cloud of fog hovered over the water. For a moment there wasn't a sound. Then, the peeper frogs began their chirping. They had surfaced from deep mud, having over-wintered in a small swale next to the river.

Ellen grabbed my arm. "What's that sound?"

"Peepers. Didn't you hear them on our tour?"

"No." She asked, "Do they chirp every night?"

"No, only in spring. It's a mating call, coming from the male."

"Oh." She commented, "I guess every creature goes about *it* some way or another."

"*It?*" I was relaxing with Ellen at my side. Sort of teasing, I wanted to hear her explanation of *it*.

"Well...you...you're joking." She playfully poked me. "You're the naturalist. Tell me about the sex life of peepers."

"All I know is what I've read. The female frog looks over the possibilities and selects the male frog with the best peep."

"Really! Then what?"

"I don't know exactly. She probably winks at him." I laughed. "He probably gets all excited and climbs aboard. In a while frog's eggs are born." I shrugged. "I'm making up most of the process. I do know frogs give off fertilized eggs, the source of pollywogs that turn into baby frogs.

"Sounds simple. That's all *it* takes?"

I chuckled. "*It's* just that simple with us, but as you know, what follows can be the hard part."

"Yeah, I agree."

I put my arm around her and kissed her neck. She returned a kiss. Sliding away from under the wheel, I pulled her willowy body into me.

She twisted around to sit in my lap with her feet and legs pressed against the door. Her hand was under my t-shirt exploring my bare back.

I did the same with my hand, pulling her even closer, cuddling tightly. This new experience made me light-headed.

Her mouth opened. She ran her tongue over my lips. I pressed my mouth for a wet kiss.

As the saying goes, she came up for air, "Wow!"

"Yeah... wow!" I gave her a kiss. Nearly speechless, I shuddered, Le...let's get out." I moved away from her toward the door.

She exhaled a deep breath. "Good idea."

Outside in the moonlit night, I picked Ellen up by the waist and sat her on the fender. I leaned beside the truck with my elbow resting on the hood and my arm around her. She bent toward me and whispered, "I've dreamed of this for a long time."

"Well, I'm lucky you gave me the wink."

She laughed. "Yeah, the wink without the consequences."

We stayed in the same position for a while, exchanging an occasional kiss and basking in the balmy air while quietly listening to the peepers. The time passed quickly.

After a half hour or so, I said, "I think it's time we left." I stepped back. "It's been a beautiful night."

She slid off the fender. "It has been." She put her arm around my waist, then we got in the truck.

The frogs stopped their singing when they heard the door open and our louder voices. Before leaving, I rolled down the window, and we sat in silence.

In a minute a chorus of *peeps* began.

I chuckled. "Poor guys, they're waiting for a gal to wink at them."

Ellen laughed.

eight

Ruth

On Sunday, after doing some computer entry, I decided that since Chris had been invited to dinner, I should attend Sunday service. I drove into town to the Huntersville Community Church—a church the Murrays had belonged to for generations. Mom and Dad were lukewarm church-goers, but they felt it their parental duty that Jason and I at least learn the Ten Commandments and the Lord's Prayer. Especially in recent years, my folks' support had waned ever since Reverend Bombbecker was minister. His pastorate hadn't gone well. He delivered lengthy and boring sermons, and consequently Sunday attendance had fallen.

However, I remember the last straw that caused Bombbecker to leave. He'd become too chummy with Missy Butson, a seventeen-year-old high school girl. Her parents, Mildred and Junior Butson, were concerned, knowing Missy often visited Bombbecker after school. Mildred decided to check to see what was going on.

Mildred told Mom that she entered the church by the hallway on the soft carpeted flooring that led to the office. Quietly reaching the door, she listened with her ear pressed against the wooden panel—no sound. Then a squeak of a chair, and low murmurs were followed by the rustle of clothing…next, louder whispers that Mildred couldn't discern. With her ear continuing to press the door, she knocked. A shaky "Yes," followed by a thump of feet landing on the floor.

"Missy, are you there?"

"Yes," Missy answered in a trembling voice.

Mildred opened the door and was shocked. Missy was pulling her sweater down. Her hair was a mess. Her wide eyes blinked from fright. "With a flushed face," Mildred told, "Missy gawked at me in amazement."

Bombbecker had his back turned, pulling himself together. Mildred, chair of the church's Executive Committee, fired Bombbecker on the spot as she dragged Missy from his office. It happened on Good Friday. Word of the incident traveled fast. Mom told me that by Easter Sunday Bombbecker had packed his bags and left town. The Easter service amounted to the singing of a few hymns, including *Christ The Lord Has Risen Today.* Some church members were devastated, while others remarked, "Hallelujah, the bomb has left town."

The scandal rocked the church. Members, including Mom and Dad, stopped going. But Bertha Bean and a few others hung on. Bertha eventually passed off the scandal. "None of us are perfect. We all have a few bats flyin' around in our belfries. Reverend Bombecker just let one loose."

Since Chris's arrival in town, forty-plus regularly attended Sunday service. When entering the church, I hesitated, since I hadn't been there in years. Bertha Bean winked when she saw me. She whispered in a loud voice, "We've got a good one this time."

Returning a nod, I took my favorite pew next to an ancestral stained-glass window named *The Good Shepherd.* It was dedicated to Captain Ezekiel Murray, July 3, 1863.

I felt I belonged here, sort of an inherited right. Ezekiel Murray was a brother of Marcus Murray, my great-great grandfather. Ezekiel was killed in the Civil War at the Battle of Gettysburg.

As a kid, I often sat admiring the window's beauty—the fatherly shepherd holding a staff and baby lamb. The variegated colors of red, blue, and green sparkled on sunny mornings, creating the likeness of a living shepherd in color.

Lately, there'd been considerable concern expressed over the safety of the historical treasure. There was no outside protection, such as an outer Plexiglass window, and some of the lead settings had deteriorated. The Booster Club had recently come to the rescue of the window and had hired a company out of Boston to repair it.

I relaxed in the warmth of the moment, watching and listening to Chris preach. He moved from side to side behind the central pulpit, preaching without any notes. I admired him and his Sunday morning message, centering on the biblical passage of love: 1st Corinthians 13:4-5. He read with clarity and expression: *Love is patient and kind; love is not jealous or boastful. It is not arrogant or rude. Love does not insist on its own way; it is not irritable or resentful.*

I found myself hanging on his every word. *"Love forgives all…"*

Even though a rather plain man at first glance, Chris held the congregation spellbound. He preached as if he was directly talking to each one of us, showing a ministerial demeanor far exceeding that of anyone I'd known.

"Christ came to show us the way, the truth and the life…"

At the end of the service, I stayed seated, basking in the warmth of his message and the flooding light streaming through the stained-glass window. I felt renewed, wanting to pause in my comfortable seat before returning to a secular world that didn't always practice the morning's message.

I was the last to leave. Chris stood at the back of the church. "Wonderful sermon." I shook his hand.

"Thanks." He smiled.

I could feel the warmth of the sun as I stood at the church door. "Ready for dinner?"

"Yeah, I'll be out soon."

"Why don't we ride to the farm in Jason's truck?"

"No." He pushed his horn-rimmed glasses back in place. "It's really best if I drive myself."

I went to Jason's truck, puzzled by his reaction. As I headed home, I passed Murray's Meadow where Jason was mowing. He'd nearly finished the fifteen acres of alfalfa with only a few passes left.

As I walked toward the house, Cooner was sitting on his bench. "How was church?"

"Chris is a good preacher." I sat next to him. "I'm puzzled, though. He turned down an offer to ride with me."

"'Course." Cooner chuckled. "Be seen with the best-lookin' woman in town."

"Oh, Cooner! That's no reason!"

"It tis." He pulled his Beechnut from his shirt pocket. "Bertha said the church don't want another Bombbecker."

"Ridiculous!"

"You try and get chummy with him." He popped a pinch in his mouth. "You'll see."

We all enjoyed Chris's company at dinner. During our conversation, he admitted he was a greenhorn when it came to the farm. I saw right away that he was a listener and asked good questions.

Jason answered most of them. "Why don't you come out Wednesday around noon?" He looked toward Chris. "You can help us, and learn how the haying process works."

"I'd like that."

By Wednesday morning the hay was almost raked and ready to bale. I'd finished my office work on the computer and headed for the door. Cooner sat on his bench. "Morning, Cooner, slide over and give me a seat." I patted him on the shoulder. "How are you doing?"

"Well, pretty good shape for the shape I'm in." He looked out across the meadow. "Yup, see that boy, rakin' like thunder?" He spat. "Soon's he's finished, I'll wait a couple of hours, then I'll go ta balin'." Cooner tapped the end of his cane on the earthen path. "Your great-grandfather would wait to mow the first cut way toward the first of July."

"How come so late?" I inwardly sighed, knowing the answer to my question, having heard the old man reminisce as he often did. My mind wandered, thinking about the Piedmont Center and how much I missed Anadeepa, about Chris, his sermon, his wild hair. I collected my own hair and tied my ponytail.

Cooner rattled on, "... back in the thirties there wan't no equipment like today. Hay had to be ripe before it was cut—half dried on the stem."

Knowing Chris would come soon, I ran my hand over my face, wondering how I looked.

Cooner was on a roll, talking non-stop. "...'course there wan't no barn dryers, like today. Heck, by chore time Jason will have that alfalfa in the barn all stacked. Good thing we have the dryer. That alfalfa's hard to dry."

He looked up at the clear sky. "Yup, the weather's 'posed to hold. 'Bout noon, I'll start balin'."

"We'll need more help." I slipped on a light, long-sleeved shirt over my t-shirt and buttoned it.

"Yup. Jason called Scoop."

"Chris will be here, too."

Cooner spat again. "I don't know's a preacher can handle hay."

"He can learn," I said defensively.

He looked at me and grinned. "Bertha was just sayin' she was wonderin' when a young gal might appear on the scene."

"Cooner! Really!"

"Who said, 'I think ye protest too much'?" He wiped the tobacco juice at the edge of his mouth.

I laughed. "I don't know, but it sounds too learned for you, Cooner." He chuckled, "I agree."

Cooner was right—by noon, Jason had him on the tractor, running the baler, pumping out bales that were being kicked into a wagon pulled behind the baler. Because the land lay flat, the windrows straight and long, the old man could handle the job. Ever since the Murrays had been baling hay, Cooner was the self-proclaimed baler operator.

I sat on the bench, bobby pins in my mouth, covering my hair with my bandana, waiting for the first load of hay.

Scoop's old van pulled in the yard. Tools rattled against the tin sides when the brakes squealed, bringing the truck to a stop. He jumped out, wearing a leather welder's cap, blue work shirt, jeans, and cowboy boots. His dark eyes gleamed as he said with a smile, "Well, well, the beauty of Huntersville." He put on a foxy grin. "All dressed up, ready for the haymow."

"Right." I pulled at my shirt, feeling the cool air pass over my front. "Alfalfa's scratchy."

"So...we're goin' to be in the haymow together?" He winked with a teasing smile.

"No." His remark gave me a jolt. "Chris Ball will be helping me in the mow."

"Chris Ball? Chris Ball?" He stroked his beard. "Oh, the preacher? He ain't like no priest, is he?"

"No." I laughed. "He's Protestant."

"I know." Scoop smirked. "I won't have to be sayin' my Hail Mary's while I handle hay." Walking toward the barn, he continued, "I'll have to watch my mouth, though. You know, bleep, bleep, instead of trash talk."

I chuckled. "He won't care."

We stood at the hay elevator outside the barn. It was placed to reach the second-floor haymow.

"Here comes Chris now." I left Scoop to meet him. I felt a flash of excitement, watching his tall, slender frame with long arms swinging as he came toward me. "Hi, Chris." His wild hair glistened in the sunlight. He had on worn jeans and a shirt split out at the elbows.

Chris smiled. "Hi." He was buttoning his shirt. "I hope I'm dressed okay to handle hay."

"Work pants and a long-sleeved shirt—perfect."

He met Scoop as he leaned on the end of the elevator. "I'm Chris Ball. Ruth says you're going to help."

"Right, Theodore LaQuine here. But everyone calls me Scoop." They shook hands. "So, you're the new preacher in town."

Chris shrugged. "Well, sort of. I've been in Huntersville several months now."

"I wouldn't know. You see church and I got off on the wrong foot when I was an altar boy. My old lady's idea."

Chris listened intently. "What happened?"

Having an audience, Scoop licked the mustache hair that was at the corner of his mouth. As Cooner would say, 'Scoop can talk the leather sole off a pair of shoes'."

I wasn't interested in hearing any more, but had no choice.

Scoop cleared his throat. "You see the first Mass I was to help at, I found the wine before the priest came. I chugged down what was left in the bottle."

"Really!" Chris was wide-eyed.

"The high-brow altar boy I was with looked like he could piss his pants. He said in a panic, 'That was supposed to be the blood of Christ!'"

"Right off, I felt silky warm. I said, 'Well, it's the right stuff because my blood sure as hell feels Christly hot'." Scoop roared. "The priest came, findin' out what I'd done, and dragged me to the side door, sayin', 'I need to see you at confession'."

Chris leaned forward. "Did you go?"

Scoop, not accustomed to another's attention, raised his voice, adding plenty of fiction with his facts. "Hell, no! That's the last time I darkened the door of the church. I never drew a sober breath for ten years. My old man and I drank steady."

"You're sober now?"

"Yup, two months, fifteen days, and"—Scoop looked at his watch — "ten and a half hours."

Chris patted him on the back. "Good for you."

Hearing a tractor, Scoop turned. "Well, nice meetin' you. We've got to get to work."

Inside the barn, I found a John Deere cap hanging on a nail. "Here, Chris, put this on. It'll keep the chaff out of your wooly hair." I reached and flipped it on his head. Tufts of hair squeezed out around the edges. I chuckled.

He took off the cap and looked inside. "What's so funny?"

"Nothing. I just noticed your hair."

He blushed slightly. "Thanks—I guess."

I climbed the wooden rung ladder to the haymow. Chris followed. The mow air was stuffy. Sunshine struggled through a small dusty window at the end of the barn. A few lights high in the rafters somewhat lit the dim cavern. Nesting birds screeched as they swooped with their long pointed wings. They echoed a sharp warning cry and dove at us within reach. Chris ducked. "What's with these birds?"

"They're harmless—barn swallows." I laughed, watching Chris.

He looked wall-eyed over his head. "Okay, if you say so. I've never experienced this."

"Relax. They'll probably take off when they hear the clank of the elevator." I led the way over the slatted flooring toward the end of the elevator. "Bales will be coming up there." I glanced ten feet above my head. "When they drop, we need to stack them on the slatted flooring."

Chris craned his neck, looking twenty feet toward the peak. "You're going to fill all this space with hay?"

"Yeah. Some years we run out of room and store bales in the shed outside."

His eyes scanned over the hayloft from end to end. "Gosh, such a huge space."

I pointed toward the end of the barn. "That section of the mow was built by my great-great-grandfather, Marcus. Notice the hand-hewed beams?"

"Yeah." Chris followed my direction toward the rafters.

"A hundred years ago or so it was a small hay barn used only for storage. Then my great-grandfather moved here in the thirties and built on the second section with rough-sawed lumber."

"I see." He continued studying the rafters.

I was pleased at his interest. "Before my folks were married, my dad and Cooner built this last section, using planed lumber."

He motioned. "What's that long rectangular thing, going the whole length of the barn?"

"The hay dryer duct. Jason and I helped Dad and Cooner build it."

"Interesting. This barn reminds me of a one-sided family tree."

"Sort of. It's been built by four generations of Murrays, Jason and I being the fourth."

"I never knew anyone that could stand in a building and account for their family roots."

I touched the sleeve of his shirt. "I think it's great you're so interested in hearing about this old barn."

He smiled. "You don't realize how unusual you are."

I was happy for the dimness of the light because he couldn't notice the blush I was feeling.

The clank of the elevator started. We watched the bales climb on the tubular frame and drop off the end onto the slatted floor. The mostly dried hay had a sweet smell with alfalfa leaves flying in a puff when the bales landed. I grabbed the bale's two strings and carried it to the furthest corner to begin the stacking process on the slatted lateral. The bales came at a steady pace while Jason and Scoop unloaded.

After the hundred or so bales climbed the elevator, it stopped. The first lateral has been covered by one layer of bales and a second layer started.

I sat on a bale. "Whew, time for a break." My clothes were covered with chaff. I brushed my shirt with my hand and pulled a cloth from my back pocket and wiped my face.

Chris sat a few feet from me. "This was a workout! My soft hands aren't used to this."

"Ooh, they *do* look sore."

He flexed his fingers. "I need some gloves."

"Let's go down to the milk house, get a drink, and I'll find some."

"Good idea."

In the milk room I handed him the hose with running cold water. He bent and slurped from the shooting stream.

I followed and wet a cloth. "Here, wipe your face." I chuckled, seeing the alfalfa leaves stuck on his sweaty face and glasses. "You're beginning to look like the 'Jolly Green Giant'."

"I do!" He held his glasses and covered his face with the cool cloth. "Feels good." He wiped it across his forehead, cheeks, and chin, and handed the cloth back to me.

"Here, you've missed some." I reached and wiped green specks off the bridge of his nose, then backed away, having felt a thrill scamper through me.

He smiled. "Thanks." He cleaned the lenses and put his glasses back on.

I looked out the milk room window. "Here's the second load and here's some gloves."

We hurried up the ladder and continued our work. By late afternoon the baling was finished. Chris and I had stacked more than a thousand bales six layers high on the dryer laterals.

In the yard, as he was about to leave, I took his hand. "Thanks a lot for your help."

He reached and firmly put his hand on mine. "It was fun. You know, helping one of my parishioners."

We both laughed. He got in his car and left.

nine

Jason

Having unloaded the last of the hay, I went to the electrical box to start the dryer. The switch was located at the end of the barn where the cows passed through a lean-to shed before entering the stable. The switch handle was at ground level several feet below the ten-horse-power motor that powered the dryer fan—a fan equal in size to the propellers of a small airplane.

I pushed the lever to the *on* position. The motor growled for a second and stopped. I tried a second time—nothing. I ran out the barn door and motioned to Scoop. "We've got a problem!"

He came and pulled the switch. "Probably a blown fuse." He opened the electrical box. "Cartridge fuses. I might have a couple on the truck." He left the shed.

Ruth stood with me, looking at the finger-long fuses, puzzled that the motor wouldn't start.

I yanked on the bill of my cap. "We've got to get this dryer going or we'll have a pile of spoiled hay." I shifted from one foot to another—waiting. "Where's that Scoop, anyway?"

Ruth went to the door. "Oh, no, Steven Iverson's here. They're visiting."

"What's Iverson doing here?" I whirled around, motioning to Scoop, and yelled, "Come on!"

Ruth went back to study the switch. "Maybe Dad told Iverson we'd meet today."

I snapped, "We can't meet with him now!"

Iverson and Scoop came to the shed. The older man looked at the box. "What's the problem?"

I scowled. "Blown fuses."

All of us crowded around the gray box that showed wires entering, and fuses between the wires leaving to power the dryer motor.

After putting in new fuses, Scoop threw the switch handle. The big motor groaned for a moment and stopped. He slammed the cover shut. "The starter motor's shot, drawin' power like a bastard. Too much for the fuses."

Ruth backed away and pulled on Scoop's arm. "Have you got heavier fuses?"

"No. There ain't none bigger that fit that box." He stroked his beard. "My old man and I will have to come back tomorrow." Scoop looked up at the screened dryer housing. "We'll heft that motor down and get it rebuilt."

"No way!" I demanded. "We've got to get this dryer running…now!" I pushed my cap back. "That hay in the mow will be steaming hot by morning."

Iverson opened the cover of the box. "Bypass the fuses." He studied the wiring closely. "When you throw the switch, manually spin the blades of the fan. It might start."

"Bypass the fuses?" Scoop whipped around. "That's crazy! Those wires will get hot as hell!"

"Yeah," Iverson nodded. "Use the heaviest copper wire you have."

Ruth looked toward Scoop. "It might work."

Scoop shook his head. "I ain't havin' nothin' to do with this!" His arms flew. "Bypass the fuses. Son of a bitch! If word gets out I did that, I'd never get my electrician's license!"

Ruth pulled his arm. "Let's go to your truck and give me the wire and I'll do it myself."

Scoop glared at Ruth. "You?"

"Yes, me!" She continued pulling. "Let's go. I did wiring at the Center. I can do this."

Going toward the truck Scoop warned, "Kill the power at the main entrance or you'll be knocked on your ass."

"Right."

On Ruth's return, I was in the process of removing the screen to get to the propellers.

She pushed the switch at the main entrance marked *Hay Dryer* to *off*, then began looping the heavy copper wire over the fuses. She attached the wire before the fuses and to the lug screw after the fuses. She went back to the main switch box. "Ready?"

I yelled, "Turn it on." I was outside the fan housing several feet above those watching me, manually turning the fan. It spun easily.

Scoop and Iverson stood back expecting to see electrical fireworks.

The motor continually groaned. The wires that bypassed the fuses started to get hot, sending off a burning smell. I increased the speed of the fan, and finally felt the motor start. I yanked my hand as it roared, backing away, within inches of being sucked in. I realized that the whirling propellers could cut me to shreds.

Over the roaring sound, Scoop explained as if he had been giving an electrician's lecture. "Soon as the ten-horse motor starts, it ain't drawin' as much power. Those bypass wires will cool down. But just the same, keep checkin' it."

I examined the open box closely. "Don't worry." I frowned. "This works, but it's far from safe."

Scoop reminded everyone as he left, "Just remember, this ain't none of my doin'!" He turned. "Drive a nail and wire that cover open. If the cover shuts by accident, the bare wires will arc like a bastard."

Over the noise, I turned to Scoop with a plan. "We'll keep it running until we get a rainy spell. Then we'll rebuild the motor."

"You might be runnin' that thing for most of the summer." Scoop jumped in his truck.

"With the fan going, haying won't take very long. We don't have to worry how dry it is when it's baled."

Stepping outside the shed, Iverson spoke in an almost begging tone. "I stopped by to see if I could sit down with you and Ruth."

For several days, I'd given continual thought toward the Iverson proposal. In a conciliatory tone, I offered, "How about tomorrow at two?"

"Sounds good." He went to his car. "I'll see you then."

After night chores and scrubbing my hands, leaving no trace of black grease or dirt, I went straight to Gilda's to pick up Ellen.

The daylight hours were longer now, giving us a chance to take a walk in our woods before dark. Besides, this gave me a chance to use my camera. I was anxious to finish the roll of film to see the pictures I'd taken. Ellen had planned a picnic supper that we were to share on our walk.

Nearing Gilda's, I saw Ellen in the parking lot. My throat turned dry. I gulped. I was learning that she had that effect on me. I'd never known what lovesick meant, but at that moment I felt this new sensation, like eating too much cotton candy. It was a thrill. You might say a thrilling sickness, if that's possible. But make no mistake, as she stood waiting, leaning on Gilda's car, I swallowed three or four times to try and settle myself.

Seeing me come, Ellen wildly waved, while running toward the truck. Her bright yellow summer jacket flapped and billowed in the breeze. She had on white sneakers, white pants, and a new t-shirt. She jumped in the truck. "Hi, Jason." She faced me and threw back her shoulders. "How do you like my yellow butterfly?"

"I like it. The yellow matches your hair." I couldn't help noticing the outline of her small breasts. She settled back in her seat, placing the picnic basket between us.

In the time it took to leave Gilda's yard, I realized Ellen felt good about herself. She was somewhat shy, but getting to know her, she seemed satisfied and thrilled with life. Best of all, she acted thrilled with me. I had a hard time not to stop and take her in my arms. In her innocence, she came across to me as luscious as a juicy peach waiting to be devoured.

On the road traveling toward the farm, her mood changed. "Something's bothering Gilda." She bent forward with a hand on each knee.

"How do you know?" We had reached the farmyard.

"She stayed in the apartment all afternoon."

"She didn't say?" I looked at Ellen. "Talk to her about it."

"I will tonight." She drew a deep breath. "Sorry to mention that." She jumped out of the truck. "Let's enjoy our picnic."

It was a typical spring night, cool, but not cold. I pulled on a gray sweatshirt over my t-shirt. We entered the bridge and saw, as we did recently, that the water level had dropped even more since our last date by the river. It was traveling under the bridge at a much slower rate, compared to the previous few days. Ellen stopped to look over the edge. I stepped back to take her picture. She gave me a smile while I clicked the shutter.

I carried the basket, telling her that a long walk was in store for us if she'd like to see a place we hadn't visited on the tour. When we passed the wrecked Hideaway, a feeling of regret struck me. I wouldn't be visiting it anymore or until I had time to put it back together.

Ellen looked up at it. "Some of Gilda's pans are still there. They aren't very valuable. Forget I mentioned it."

As I surveyed the damage, I couldn't see a way to get to the pans without a ladder. "Maybe late this summer I'll have some time to fix it up and recover the pans."

We continued on. When the heifers saw us nearing the fence, expecting salt, they came running.

I told Ellen about each heifer's pedigree. How I'd bred them to special bulls. She hardly listened. Never having been around cattle, she was darting glances, worried they might break out. So we followed the fence line outside the pasture. The lead heifer kicked her hind feet and snorted. Ellen grabbed my arm. "Yikes, are we okay?"

I laughed. "They'd never hurt you."

"They're so big!" She walked, firmly holding my hand, making sure I was next to the fence,

We left the heifers and followed an abandoned wagon trail. In a dip in the trail, we saw an old stone bridge, some of which had sunken into the ground. Headers about ten feet long lay either side of the road. The drill marks were visible where ages ago workers had cut and formed the granite bars. "Cooner thinks stone was taken out of here to build the road on Murray's Flats."

After walking a short distance, we came to a flat open area, showing where stone had once been quarried. White cedar trees about thirty feet high grew around the space, the size of a large room. The trees' limbs hung over the side of the walls, creating damp shade in the open area, perfect for growing moss.

"Let's stop here." I pressed my hand on the green velvety softness. "Like a carpeted bedroom."

"How about a living room?" She chuckled and turned to look around the edges. "These white pants easily show dirt." She spread a placemat on a discarded granite bar. "I have another for you."

"No, don't bother."

She opened and spread a flannel sheet on the ground next to us. "Ants and bugs." She scowled. "I don't want them near our food."

"Oh." I watched her run her hands over the material to pull and flatten the creases.

We sat side by side on the moss-covered stone and ate our chicken sandwiches. Ellen excitedly talked about the classes she was taking. Close by, chickadees chirped and flitted from cedar branch to cedar branch, making for friendly background music. I could hear, in the distance, the evening call of the white-throated sparrow. "Isn't that bird's song beautiful?"

"Which one?" Ellen turned to me with a blank expression.

"Listen. It's a ways away."

"Yeah, it's sort of haunting." She picked a crumb off her white pant leg and continued to look for more.

"That sparrow only stays here until late summer." I stood to take another picture. She zipped her jacket, sweetly smiling for the camera.

"I miss the song birds when they leave, especially the white-throated sparrow." I sat next to her, eating a piece of apple pie.

"I must confess." She sighed. "I don't know one bird from another."

I turned to her, asking in a hopeful tone, "Would you like to learn?"

"Maybe." Her answer wasn't convincing. "Becoming an RN is all I can handle right now."

"Of course."

Ellen nibbled at her small wedge of pie. Not finishing it, she placed the remainder into a Ziplock and gathered the used ones, folded them neatly, placing them in a brown paper bag. She folded the bag into a perfect rectangle, continuing to press and square it on her knee, placing it in the basket.

Watching her pack things with such care, I smiled, thinking she'd make a great nurse, neat and orderly.

There was a pause. Still seated, I turned and looked at her. My heart thumped in my ear. Her lips curled into a slight smile. Our eyes met, telling of eager anticipation. We threw our arms around each other. She buried herself in me and arched her head back as we kissed.

We gently rolled onto the flannel blanket, lying on our sides. I pulled her into me, pressing the yellow butterfly close to my heart. The feeling of closeness was familiar, since our previous date by the river. I was more sure of myself with her, letting my hands travel to new places. Ellen seemed eager for the journey.

She murmured, "Oh Jason, I love you."

Her admission of love was new, but it was exactly how I felt. "I love you, too."

She whispered, "This…this is wonderful."

"For me, too."

I began exploring beneath her t-shirt, cupping her breasts. Ellen didn't resist. Her hot breath made my neck feel on fire. I'd lost all common sense. My excitement was about to explode. This couldn't be happening but it was. A thought of a pregnancy swirled beneath the moment. Protection…I should ask.

Her pants slid easily over her slim hips. She rolled onto her back. I followed, taking off my pants, dizzy with anticipation…but protection…

Before I could say anything, she screamed, "Stop!" She squirmed out from under me. "God, Jason, we aren't peeper frogs. How about a condom?"

"Condom? I…I don't have one."

She wildly pushed on my chest. Her delicate hands felt like swords.

Immediately, the purr of sweetness had turned to bitterness. "What were you thinking?" She hysterically cried. "Sex without a condom!"

"I don't know. I thought you…you."

"Me! How about you!" She screamed. "I could've gotten pregnant."

"I…I know. I was about to ask." I rested my hand on her. "Believe me. I wouldn't have gone any further without…"

"Oh no?" She shook with anger. "It sure seemed like the real thing!"

"I intended to stop!"

"Stop?" She whimpered. "I doubt it!"

"I'm sorry, really sorry." I tried to hold her but she yanked away. "Besides, I thought you were probably on the pill."

"The pill! Why? I...I never..." She drew a breath from crying. "What a fool I was! Jason Murray, the big catch around town. He's such a great guy." She sneered. "What a joke!"

"Please know that I'm sorry." I felt helpless; what could I do or say? "Nothing happened! Aren't you being a little too emotional?"

"Emotional!" She continued to cry.

I sat rubbing her back. "This is all new..."

"To me too...being pregnant sure isn't in my plan."

"It...it won't happen again."

She started to calm down. "Jason, don't you understand my fear?"

"Sure, I do!"

She questioned me, slowly shaking her head while putting on a scowl. "Really?"

"Yes, really."

I withdrew my hand from her back. We sat side by side sort of in shock at the complete change in the atmosphere.

A feeling of gloom passed over me, having been accused of being thoughtless. I regretted not being more considerate. Of course, I didn't want to get Ellen pregnant. Fully as important, I wanted her to think of me as highly as she had before this botched incident.

In the far distance the evening whistle of the white-throated sparrow filtered through the silence, like a heavenly sound nestled in the clouds. For me, the song cut the tension and lifted my sadness. Ellen didn't talk for a while, but that was okay. We just sat and listened. I put my arm around her and she hesitantly leaned toward me. The crickets seemed louder as darker dusk filled the air while the sparrow sang through the mist of twilight.

After a while we left in silence. We hurried along. Daylight was quickly leaving the shaded road ahead.

ten

Ruth

The next morning it was sunny after our big hay day. I left the house to pick up the mail in the box at the side of the road. On my way, the dryer fan roared in the background. It sounded like a small plane ready for take-off. I hoped we could finish first cutting soon so we could shut it off. Jason had been mowing all morning so we'd have a big jag to bale. It was still the first part of June—early for first-cut hay. Although it was a beautiful day, I would be spending most of the morning in the farmhouse office.

Among the junk mail of ads and promotional flyers, there was a handful of bills, the milk check, and checks addressed to the florist shop for payment of spring deliveries. Continuing to thumb through the mail, I walked toward the house. One particular letter caught my attention:

> *The Elias M. Cole Foundation*
> *North Tower, World Trade Center*
> *39th floor, Suite 29.*
> *1 Trade Center, New York, N.Y. 10048*

I tore open the envelope addressed to Ms. Ruth Murray.

Dear Ms. Murray,
 The Elias M. Cole Foundation's Board of Directors regretfully informs you that the monthly funding of the Piedmont Community Center, Piedmont, Ga., will

be substantially curtailed at the end of our budget year, Dec. 31, 1995. Due to reversals in our portfolio, we've concluded that this will be necessary. A six-month lead time will give you an opportunity to find alternative funding.

However, at our July 14th meeting, we will be interviewing all the recipients of our funds. You are certainly welcome to appear before the Board on this date for a five-minute presentation concerning the worthiness of our $40,000 annual support of the Piedmont Community Center.

Please let me know of your intentions by returning the enclosed card.

Respectfully,

Charles M. Cobb, Director

cc: The Piedmont Community Center, Piedmont Georgia.

As I read the letter, my knees went weak. Finding a replacement for that amount of money was not going to be easy. Continuing toward the house, I was sure that if Elias M. Cole was living today he'd support the Piedmont Center. That was the one fact I hung onto. If only I could convey that to the Board.

When reading the biography of Elias M. Cole, I'd learned he'd been a slave owner before The Emancipation Proclamation was signed into law by President Lincoln. Cole had profited handsomely, having owned a large number of slaves. He worked them hard for long hours in the Cotton Exchange out of the port in Savannah, Georgia.

He was a respected community leader, but he knowingly short-changed the slaves' welfare. A religious man, Elias fervently believed in the concept of Heaven and Hell. In his failing years and eventually at death, he envisioned himself having to stoke the fires in Hell for the sins he'd committed during his earthly days.

I had read that as an old man, Elias came to realize to whom he owed a debt of gratitude. With no family or close relatives, he established the Elias M. Cole Foundation. Its mission statement read: *Revenue from the investment of these funds to be used for the education of the Negro.*

When I first located the Foundation, I realized it was a perfect fit for our purposes of tutoring children at the Piedmont Center. However, my request was a late-comer to an already long list of projects. The Piedmont Center's funding was granted due to an excess of revenue at the end of the 1994 fiscal year. I fearfully concluded that the board's assumption would be that the last project funded would be the first to be cut. Therefore, I definitely had to attend the board meeting in July to plead my case and remind the board that the Piedmont project very closely followed the objective of the Cole Foundation.

I entered the house, feeling devastated. There was a lot of work ahead if I was to ever replace the foundation grant. I went immediately to the office and wrote a letter:

Hi Frieda and Sara: *June 3, 1995*
Bad news from the Cole Foundation today. You undoubtedly have seen the notification regarding funding in a copy of the letter sent to me. Sara, regardless of the situation, I will find a funding source so your work can continue. I'll keep you informed.
Sincerely, Ruth.

I decided not to tell my family about the threatened funding as Iverson was due after lunch. This was serious enough to wait for a moment of calm. Anyway, I didn't expect Mom or Dad to be especially sympathetic to the cause. But I guessed Chris would be. If the weather held, he and I would be in the mow stacking hay for the next day or two. This would give us plenty of time to talk between loads.

As expected, Dad came to lunch all fired up. He was running his spread fingers through his short hair. "Gosh, I hope we can work something out with Iverson."

I warned, "You're forgetting Jason. He might be a drag on closing a deal."

eleven

Jason

On my way to the house after morning chores, the crisp air and bright sun told me we were in for a stretch of good weather. I planned to cut two fields of hay west of town. We were using the land rent-free in exchange for keeping them mowed. Dad feared that any day they'd be sold for housing. And as usual, the new owners would plunk a house right in the middle of the acreage, causing the land to be useless for agriculture. That fact, and comments from Ellen about not wanting to marry a poor man, made me willing to at least listen to Iverson's proposal. To support a family and especially live the life of Ellen's dreams, there was a good chance I would need more land to milk more cows.

However, our last date brought up questions as to how our relationship might continue. The whole subject of birth control was new to me. I didn't feel free to discuss the matter with her. Bringing up the subject might suggest that sex was the main reason I liked her, which was far from the truth. I would never outright ask her to start taking birth control pills. I decided to leave the subject alone until she brought it up herself.

In regards to using condoms, it was out of the question until I had a chance to go to Rutland. The only place that sold them in Huntersville was Chub's Variety. I drove up the road to Chub's with the tractor and mower, on my way to the fields that morning. I'd a plan to buy some— that is, if someone I didn't know well was behind the counter. After all,

I felt sex was a private matter. I was highly embarrassed even thinking about openly buying condoms. I decided I'd slap some on the counter with a bottle of Coke.

Entering the store, I tried to act relaxed and casual, but inside I was a mess, being on a mission to buy a very personal item. But I felt lucky, being the only customer. The condom rack was within easy reach for anyone buying merchandise. I checked out Chub's inventory—glancing out of the corner of my eye as I slid my Coke onto the counter.

Guaranteed Not To Break was the advertising claim printed at the top of the display. I shivered at the thought, realizing that nothing was a hundred percent. I went for the no-frills brand, starting to hesitantly reach for a few.

Suddenly, I heard a piercing voice coming from somewhere behind the counter. "Hi."

"Oh…hi." I quickly yanked my hand away from the rack.

It was my dumb luck that Herb Chub's daughter, Bubbles, was working today. She must have been reaching low for something. I hadn't noticed her. Bubbles and I had gone to high school together. I remember she'd kept a close eye on the condom inventory, telling all at school who was buying what and when.

Bubbles got her nickname from her wild head of tight curly black hair dyed in streaks of pea-green, plus she had a bouncy personality. She continuously talked. Her big mouth motored a mile a minute, usually telling more than anyone cared to know.

Stepping from behind the cigarette case, she smiled and purred, "Jason!"

"Oh, hi, Bubbles."

She had added a huge tattoo since the last time I saw her. The limbs of an apple tree were coming from her cleavage. Small branches with leaves reached her collar bone and shoulders. Bright red apples were nestled in the foliage. They were obvious since she wore a low-cut jersey, and the deep green leaves were vivid set against her milky coloring. I was mad at myself for gawking. But that was just what she wanted.

She continued in her loud voice, "I notice you were checking my apples."

"Well, they're sort of obvious." I arched my brow.

"I have more if you'd like to see?" She gave me a come-on smile. "I'd show my whole Tree of Life to a nice guy like you."

"No!" I realized I sounded blunt and rude. I managed a slight smile. "Maybe some other day." I shoved the Coke closer. "I just stopped for a drink."

"I hear you and Ellen Pierce are an item."

"An item? I wouldn't go that far." I placed a dollar on the counter.

"Oh, really?" She giggled. "I noticed you were checking out our condoms."

"I...I just stopped to buy this Coke."

Bubbles winked. "I see." She gave me an all-knowing smile and giggle. "Our supplier sends us all these weird varieties." She looked toward the rack and pointed: "Hyper Thrill, Bound to Please, Sugar Plumb—stuff like that. They don't sell unless you...you want something more than the regular." She smirked, loving to see me squirm.

"No...I...I just. I just want this Coke."

"You know what Scoop told me?"

I winced inside, knowing it would be some wild comment. "I can't imagine."

"Scoop said he just used a Hyper Thrill on Missy Butson. She screamed so loud, he called 911." Bubbles roared.

"That sounds like Scoop." I edged the money closer to the register. "Actually, Missy moved to North Carolina quite a while ago."

"Oh."

"You knew that!" Anger stirred in me that an innocent girl's name was being used so glibly.

Disappointed that I'd ruined her story, her shoulders slumped as she mumbled, "I guess you want to go?" She handed me the change.

"I've got hay to mow." On leaving, I vowed I'd never stop at Chub's again for condoms or at least not while Bubbles worked there. I headed for the field, thinking that birth control was way out of my league.

I had all morning to mull over my situation, a situation so distracting that I ran the mower into a ledge, smashing the machine. I was disgusted with myself because I'd been over the land many times, learning where the unforgiving ledges lay. My lack of concentration caused me to spend the better part of an hour replacing the knives and guards on the cutter bar.

While fixing the mower, I continued to think of Ellen. I wondered if I wanted to devote my whole life to managing a big herd of cows. Although I was sweet on her, I wasn't sure I wanted to change my life's plan just to make more money. Maybe we weren't even compatible. Just because she was beautiful didn't mean we were made for each other. Anyway, if I found I needed more income, I could always add a few more cows. This way, I could stay at the farm and continue gaining knowledge as a naturalist.

By noon, I'd finished and drove home. After lunch, Cooner got up from the table. "I'm leavin' to let you folks handle Iverson as you might."

Dad was so excited that I'm sure, in his mind, he had Iverson's fifty acres limed, fertilized, and planted before Iverson came through the door.

His old rusty Ford pulled into the yard. The car's muffler was blown, so it was no secret he'd arrived.

I answered the knock at the door. As hard as he tried to be light-hearted, Iverson's eyes and jowls drooped. It was easy to see the man had continued to slip. His clothes were grubby, even more so than usual. He didn't bother to tuck in his shirt. The tails hung over his gut. A gut so big he couldn't fully zip his pants.

He had an array of dog-eared papers stuffed in a manila folder. "Afternoon, Jason." He glanced past me. "Glad you're all here so we can talk business."

"Come in and have a seat at the table." I pulled out a chair. "Mom's got coffee on."

"Thanks." Seated, Iverson poured from the Forget Me Not creamer, draining it into his cup. He took a sip and placed the drink on the table. He knitted his fingers, resting his hands on his gut. "As you all know, I've been trying to interest you young people in joining my farm." He pulled his hands apart and opened his folder, pulling out a blueprint of a detailed drawing of his four-hundred-cow facility. Spread out, it included a double-ten milking parlor. "Two milkers can put through twenty cows in a matter of minutes." He looked to see if we were impressed. "In four hours you can easily milk four hundred cows.

"This is a great opportunity for folks that know dairy farming. I can't think of anyone more capable than Jason and Ruth Murray to make this work." He spoke with an encouraging tone. "I'll rent the whole place, cows, equipment, house and barn for ten thousand a month. With milk prices the way they are and four hundred cows, you can easily gross a million and a half a year."

"Why are you giving it up?" I asked the obvious, especially if he thought it such a good deal.

"My interests are in politics. It's taken me away from the farm too much." He looked at all of us. "Recently, I've experienced a situation that needs immediate attention." He cleared his throat and drew a deep breath. "Like forty thousand dollars."

Dad sobered. "Forty thousand? What do we get for forty thousand?"

"A security deposit and two months' rent."

Mom started winding her hair while staring at Iverson, letting Dad do all the talking.

Dad frowned. "I've been checking on land appraisals and other public records such as liens and mortgages, and it looks to me as though your back's against the wall."

Iverson's eyes widened. "So you've been sneaking around, checking up on me." He reached for the creamer and rolled it in his hands.

"I wouldn't say that. It's all public information." Dad raised his voice. "What do you want for the meadow?"

"The meadow is part of my farm." Iverson returned a sarcastic grin. "I'd take half a million."

"It isn't worth that! At the town office, I found out that it's zoned agricultural."

"Yeah, well, I'm not selling." Iverson gathered his papers. "I'm talking about renting."

Dad sat mum, his head down, with his hand on his cup. The gleam on his face had left. "You aren't mentioning that we'd have to buy a bunch of cows to make this deal work."

Iverson puffed. "Of course, you'd have to buy cattle. That shouldn't stop a Murray."

I spoke bluntly. "I have a feeling that as it is now, you aren't making it."

"I'm only milking a hundred and fifty cows." The creamer rolled to the other hand.

"How come?" I had to ask, but knew he had probably sold cows to raise money. "You don't even have close to four hundred milkers."

"Well, I've had to cull some." He cleared his throat again as his knuckles turned white while squeezing the creamer. He raised his voice, and with his free hand he pointed at me. "But you can buy cows and bring the place up to speed!" He placed the creamer on the table and started folding the blueprint. "You see, I'm on a couple of committees in Montpelier, Banking and Insurance, and Agriculture. My responsibilities have taken me away from the farm too much." He completed folding the blueprint. "I've enjoyed being the representative from Huntersville, but it's taken its toll." He closed the folder. "Yeah, taken its toll."

Mom fingered a strand of hair for a second hair wind. A ringlet hung by the side of her face.

Ruth looked up. "I'm not ready to commit to a big farm. Not at this time, anyway."

I nodded. "Me neither." I again mulled over Ellen's requirement for her man to make a lot of money. Coming face to face with the thought of managing a bunch of cows caused me to again question rearranging my life for the sake of Ellen.

Iverson's face turned red. "Marcus, talk some sense into your kids! What's wrong with you people?" He puffed. "Goddammit, these kids' heads are off in la-la land. I'd offer this deal to someone else, but you folks fit the situation better than anyone I know.

Dad sat stone silent, gazing at the table.

I got up and looked out the window over the kitchen sink, running cold water for a drink. The meeting was over as far as I was concerned. I changed the subject. "There's bobcats that roam Hardhack Mountain. I've heard their mating screams—sounding like kids in terrible pain."

Ruth carried cups to the sink. "Jason loves his cows and his hobby. Let's leave it at that."

Those at the table turned in my direction. Iverson glared at me. "I thought you were a smart kid."

"Yeah, smart enough to turn down your offer." I glanced out the window again. "I want to track those cats to see if I can get a good picture." I drained my glass and set it on the counter. "Seeing a bobcat means more to me than milking four hundred cows."

Dad groaned.

"Grow up! Jason, grow up!" Iverson roared. "I'd like to be governor someday, but it will never happen." He left and slammed the door.

Ruth gave me a sympathetic glance. "Jason loves the untamed wild. We all know that. I think he should do what he loves."

Dad raised his voice. "If you're turning down this offer, Jason, you're on your own. I wish you could see the chance you're missing." Dad turned red. His eyes narrowed to a squint—on fire with anger. "Well, you've just blown off a chance of a lifetime!" He glared at me. "There's no way Iverson can keep that farm! He's way in over his head!"

"Sorry. I'm just not interested!" I shot back. "Take it on yourself."

"I'm not into cows anymore or I would." Dad looked at me. "I'll bet in two or three years you could end up owning the whole place."

"Forget it! I'd be drowning in debt buying over two hundred cows. Then I'd have to buy feed." I backed away from the table. "I've got equipment to work on before we hay tomorrow."

twelve

Ruth

I hung up the phone after talking to Sara at the Piedmont Center. I worried that a well-qualified teacher like her might start looking for another position. Even though I'd sent a letter, I wanted to assure her personally that her salary plus money for running expenses would continue. I had no idea where the funds would come from, but in the worst case, I'd draw from my own small trust fund. But that could only be temporary as Mom and Dad had put restrictions on its use. During the call, Anadeepa asked to talk to me. She had learned to read a chapter book and wanted to show me over the phone. I held the receiver, hearing her soft voice, thinking how sweet she was. Tears filled my eyes.

After the call, I spent the remainder of the morning searching on the Internet for foundations that might be sympathetic to the Piedmont cause, writing several letters of inquiry. I left the house just before noon in order to catch the mailman. I was surprised to see Cooner on his bench. "What's up? I thought you'd be at Butson's."

"Well, where've you been? We're havin' one of the biggest hay days this farm's ever seen."

"I've been busy in the office."

"The roar of that dryer's drivin' your dad nuts."

"Me, too. I dread seeing next month's power bill." I stood next to him holding my letters. "I'll be right back after mailing these."

As I walked back from the mailbox by the road, I saw two tractors pulling haying equipment coming toward the farm. Reaching Cooner, I commented, "I see Dad's helping Jason?"

"Yup, with this dry spell, he wants to finish hayin'." He tapped his cane. "Get that confounded dryer shut off."

I laughed. "Also making a little peace with his son."

"That, too." Cooner spat. "I'm pullin' hay wagons with Jason's truck. It's at least three miles to the furthest field." He chuckled. "Got to keep the wagons comin'." He winked. "Can't have you and the Reverend sittin' in the haymow waitin' on loads."

I smiled. "Don't drive too fast."

"I won't." He spat again. "I told Jason I wan't balin' on those rough pieces, so your dad's doin' it instead." He glanced my way. "You've already lined up the preacher for the mow this afternoon?"

"No. I'd better call him to see if he can come earlier today, and I don't know about tomorrow." I watched Dad and Jason park the tractors at the shed. "I can't expect him to help every hay day."

"For sure." Cooner nodded. "The shepherd spendin' too much time with one lamb spooks the whole flock." He had a twinkle in his eye.

"I hear you." But I didn't laugh. I left to call Chris, who said he'd come right along. I returned and sat thinking about the Cole Foundation while I fixed my hair.

Cooner squinted. The edges of his eyes were deeply wrinkled. "What's wrong with you?" He rubbed the knob of his cane. "Some problem's whirlin' around in that head of yours."

"I'll tell you later. I have to get my bandana and cover my hair for the mow." I got up to leave.

"You'd better." Cooner turned to me. "They're hookin' up the baler right now."

Jason yelled to me as I was going in the house. "Scoop can help you in the mow if Chris can't come."

"Oh, God!" I yelled back. "Chris is coming!"

When I returned, Cooner was still there. I quickly filled him in on my problem with the Cole Foundation.

He rattled his cane. "Tell me a problem in life that ain't got money tied to it."

"You're so right." I looked toward Jason's truck. "You'd better get going or they'll be waiting for you in the field."

Chris came right after I called. He drove in the yard before the first load had to be unloaded. We went to the mow. It was actually a nice place to visit since the dryer blew cool air up through the bales. The swallows screamed their alarm and fluttered in the peak of the barn, but we ignored them. I was eager to tell him my concern.

Chris listened intently as we sat side by side on a bale. He commented, "It will be difficult to find another fund to cover that amount."

"You're right. I haven't found a promising source yet."

"This probably won't help a lot, but you could speak at a Sunday service about your work at the center."

"I can do that, but I agree, it won't solve my problem." I dropped my head and rested my hands on my knees.

His arm reached across my shoulder. "You'll find a way."

His touch was comforting. This I knew about Chris: he found it natural to show compassion. I told him about the meeting on July 14, and that I was nervous to make the trip.

"I understand. I've been before boards before." He withdrew his arm. "Your meeting's a ways away."

"I know. I guess I'm jumping ahead too quickly."

Within minutes a load of hay arrived, and the elevator started. We began stacking bales onto the next available lateral.

In between loads we got a drink and sat waiting for the next load to come. The mow was filling as bales were near the peak. Jason wanted to save a lateral for second cutting. At the end of the mow, we stood on several layers of bales looking at the empty space below.

Waiting for loads gave us plenty of time to visit as we sat feeling the pleasant breeze of the dryer fan. Chris asked several questions about the Center. He again suggested that I should explain to his church congregation the need for tutoring the children. He promised to set aside a block of time to give me a chance to speak.

During the few hours we were together, I felt he was interested in my dilemma, but I wasn't sure how he felt about me. He kept saying as he handled the bales, "This is good exercise." In a few minutes he repeated, "I need to do this. I can't sit in my office all the time."

I smiled at his rationale for handling hay in our barn. Even with the breeze, my shirt dampened with sweat, doing the hard work of lifting and stacking bales. I noticed he glanced at me with the shirt sticking like wallpaper to the cups of my bra. I pulled on the bottom edge, feeling a gush of air up my front. But in handling the next few bales, it clung to me again.

During short interruptions of taking bales from the elevator, I continually pulled my shirt. I noticed he watched, but he turned quickly when I caught his eye. He repeated his line, "I like this exercise."

I realized he was trying hard not to show any attraction toward me.

We sat quietly for a while. I purposely sat close to him, hoping he'd loosen up. I wanted our friendship to naturally blossom, but he shut me out, sitting with arms extended, hands clamped to each knee, looking straight ahead.

I turned his way. "A penny for your thoughts?"

He started cleaning his glasses with his shirt tail—blowing on the glass—holding them up to the dim light. "I've got so many things to do and parishioners to see." He slipped his glasses on. "I hope I'm not spending too much time here."

"Why?" I placed my hand on his arm, slightly pulling to get his attention. "You've said you need the exercise." I tried to lighten his mood. "You think spending hours in the haymow with Ruth Murray sounds scandalous?" I teasingly laughed.

"Ruth!" His voice rose in alarm. "You know with Scoop down there everyone in town will know I'm helping at your farm."

"Sorry!" I was taken aback by his abruptness. Maybe he didn't care about me. But I'd been around guys enough to feel when there was an attraction. Then again, maybe I was wrong.

When he saw the effect his strong reaction had on me, he put his arm around me. "I love being with you even if it's slinging bales. I look forward to our time together." His arm tightened. "But I'm tormented, not wanting to break an agreement." He let go. "When I was called to the Huntersville church, Mildred Butson, who was chair of the Search Committee, required that I sign a statement agreeing I wouldn't get romantically involved with a parishioner."

I nodded. "Oh, that's left over from the Bombbecker scandal."

"It sounds as though you're making light of it?"

"Absolutely!" I firmly said, "It's ridiculous!"

After the last load, we left the mow in a stand-off mood at odds with each other. Even if he wanted, Chris obviously wasn't about to break a promise in his contract and encourage a closer relationship.

The next day and the last of first cutting, the phone rang at breakfast. It was Chris. He told Mom he was sorry, but due to matters at church, he couldn't help. Only I knew the real reason he called.

I drove the tractor and ran the baler. Jason and Dad worked the mow. Mom and Scoop unloaded wagons. Bertha was called in to keep the florist shop open for a few hours while Mom and Dad helped on the farm. At the end of the day the first cutting was finished. In a couple of days, Jason pulled the switch on the dryer, disconnecting the bypass wires, shutting the cover of the fuse box.

I sat with Cooner on his bench. He spat. "Thank the Lord, the roar of the dryer has been laid ta rest."

thirteen

Jason

Moving into the third week in June, we had yet to have much rain. We needed some soon for the corn, pastures, and a second cut of alfalfa. Outside the barn after morning chores, it was a hot sultry day. The flies and bugs were out in force.

Late that afternoon, I walked to the ridge to salt the heifers and spray them for relief from the deerflies and horseflies. The birds were quiet. In fact all the wildlife was in hiding, waiting for the sun to set and for the woods to take on a night life of its own.

I took my camera out of the case, ready to take a picture at a second's notice. Nothing happened. If I was ever to see a bobcat, it was going to take patience. I needed to become familiar with their behavior and that would take a lot of time. A bobcat wasn't going to pop out of the woods and stand for a perfect pose. I grinned at the ridiculous thought.

After I got back from the ridge, I tried to locate Scoop to come and fix the hay dryer motor. No luck.

As I left the house, I glanced beyond our fields and saw Iverson's fifty acres. It was a field of weeds—unbelievable, just weeds. At least in years past he'd tried to grow a crop of corn, but this year—nothing. The rest of the day I checked through breeding dates and due dates to make sure the heifers that were close to calving were with the herd and not pastured on the ridge. I'd recently stopped milking Precious, drying her off for a rest period until her next calving. I could see her every day because she was too valuable to be put in a pasture away from the herd. Other dry cows were pastured with the milkers, but they quickly learned to stay away from the barn during chore time.

That night I headed to Gilda's. I hadn't seen Ellen since our disastrous date. I missed her. Before leaving the house, I made sure I had clean hands, trimmed nails, all things she'd notice.

Gilda's mom, Agnes, met me at the restaurant door. "Well, Jason. It's been a while since we've seen you."

"Yeah, I've been busy haying." Although friendly, Agnes was showing her age: gray hair, thin as a rail, her face puckered with wrinkles, her eyes anxious with worry.

Country music gave a soft, relaxing background, but I felt there was tension in the air. I glanced toward the furthest booth. Gilda and Iverson were locked in a heated discussion. Sheriff Krads sat at the counter drinking coffee. He was watching them and wasn't about to leave.

Agnes directed me to a booth away from the loud voices. I ordered a hamburger, fries and coffee. "Ellen around?"

Agnes motioned. "She's up in the apartment studying. I'm sure she'd love to see you."

"Okay, after I eat." At the moment Gilda and Iverson held my attention. One thing I knew about Gilda, she wanted her restaurant to be calm and peaceful. She wasn't going to carry on with Iverson much longer. As soon as I thought that, she stood and motioned for Jasper Krads. Iverson got up to leave when Krads stood by his table. As they passed my booth, I could see Iverson had been drinking. He smelled like a brewery. His face was red and his eyes were puffy and watery. "That bitch hasn't heard the last of me." He looked at Gilda. "I'll be back!"

Gilda said nothing, but her eyes were narrowed and her face looked drawn and ashen.

I'd finished my burger. Gilda stopped by my table. "Why don't you go up and visit Ellen?" She forced a smile. "I'll call the apartment and let her know you're on the way."

For some reason, I had a feeling this woman would just as soon I leave, especially since her heated discussion with Iverson had not ended. Why didn't she want me around? Maybe it had something to do with the meadow, the farm, the Murrays. I wasn't sure. Gilda even spoke to Bertha, who promptly went to the kitchen to begin her cleaning detail.

There was only an elderly couple in a booth, and they'd almost finished their meal. I gulped my coffee and left.

Before knocking on the apartment door, I quickly checked myself for anything out of place, like a stray thread.

Ellen met me. "Hi, Jason!" She motioned. "Come in!"

She looked like she'd just walked off the pages of a fashion magazine—not a wrinkle in sight. She was stunning in a navy jumper and light blue blouse, both matching her eyes. Every hair of her shingle cut was in place.

I caught my breath and swallowed hard. A flutter flashed through me. "Hi." My face reddened. "I...I've missed..."

She threw her arms around me. Her feather-weight body filled my arms as we kissed. She whispered, "I've missed you lots."

"Same here." I didn't want to gush over her too much for fear she might pull away. I struggled to find the right words. "I...I miss you... every day...you're with me all the time."

Ellen reached for my hand. "I've often dreamed of being here with you, snuggled in your arms, planning our future."

"Do you ever think...about...about..."

"Marriage?" She brightened with a broad smile.

"Yeah...yeah...that's what I was wanting to say." I hugged her for the longest time. "Would you...wear...wear a ring?"

"Engagement ring?" She squirmed tightly, reaching to kiss me on the neck. "Whew...really...you're asking me to marry you?"

"Well...well...not right away." I didn't want her to say no. "Maybe in a year or so. Or after you graduate and get a job."

"I'd be so proud to wear a ring." She jumped up from the couch and sat to curl in my lap. "But I want it special, reminding me that it's from a special guy."

I was delirious with excitement.

Gilda's apartment was beautifully decorated in a soft blue with over-stuffed furniture that looked and smelled new. The setting was definitely romantic.

Although the moment was made for lovers, I felt reserved. I didn't want a repeat of our last date. She didn't mention the pill, and I didn't mention my stop at Chub's Variety. We stayed on the couch in each other's arms, but neither said anything about our last date. Ellen excitedly broke the silence. "I really like the course I'm taking, Epidemiology 101." She sat up. "Wow, the professor, Dr. Reed, is he ever handsome!"

A bolt of jealousy blew through me. "Is it Dr. Reed or the course?"

Ellen giggled. "The course, silly." She smiled. "Epidemiology."

"Epidem... what?"

"Epidemiology." She reached for the text book. "An epidemiologist is one who investigates the cause of an epidemic."

She burst with information. "Anthropologists believe that epidemics are as old as mankind." She read from her textbook. "Over three thousand years ago, the Anasazi Indian tribe in the southwestern United States became extinct caused by what some believe to be an epidemic."

"Really. How would they know?"

"Well, they don't really. It's only speculation. But through hieroglyphics seen in caves, it's known that a man called the Kokopelli was a flute player who travelled long distances from tribe to tribe, bringing joy and celebration. On his back he carried seeds, mostly corn, precious stones and beads that he used for barter. In the cave drawings, he's always shown with a humped back, carrying his goods while playing a flute."

"I get it. He also spread disease from tribe to tribe."

"Yeah, that's the idea." She continued, "A modern example of an epidemic is the spread of AIDS or Acquired Immune Deficiency Syndrome."

"I don't know much about AIDS. All I know is that it scares me."

Ellen nodded. "We didn't always have the disease in this country. Several years before AIDS was identified, people in West Africa became sick with no known cause. No one had heard of HIV or Human Immune Deficiency. But this strange virus was occurring. It's theorized that some West African cultures ate monkey. The virus found in monkeys mutated and infected humans. Eventually in the 1980s, AIDS had spread to the US. It was discovered that it passed by blood through the use of dirty hypodermic needles and the practice of unprotected sex."

"Through sex?" Scoop might be right when he said, "Ellen Pierce is so fussy about bein' clean, she'd probably make a guy wash his dick in alcohol before crawlin' in bed with her." His comment was buzzing through my mind as she continued on.

"…usually in the sex act tiny blood vessels are broken and partners' blood is exchanged. That's why condom use is important."

I was beginning to feel defensive as if she were suggesting that I could be a potential carrier of AIDS. "Hey, I've never been to Africa."

She turned to me. "You never know who your partner's been exposed to."

I raised an eyebrow. "Don't look at me!"

She laughed. "I was just talking in general terms." She looked at her text book again. "Disease can also spread from isolated group to isolated group of farm animals when selected individuals join a new environment."

I immediately thought of the Iverson herd. Since for generations, we hadn't added purchased cows, I wouldn't know how my cows might be affected if I accepted his offer and joined herds.

We resumed cuddling on the couch. The frank discussion of AIDS and the need for condoms had killed any thought that our romantic night could go any further.

It was pouring rain when I left the apartment. In spite of getting wet, I felt like cheering—it had been so dry. I ran for my truck parked at Gilda's. Krad's police cruiser, Gilda's dad's old Plymouth, and Iverson's white junker were the only vehicles left in the lot. A sign was hanging in the door, "Restaurant Closed".

I went home wondering what was going on.

fourteen

Ruth

I had just gotten off the phone with Chris. He came across as stilted but nonetheless pleasant. I was hoping for some enthusiasm from him on hearing my voice—like I was feeling when hearing his. He seemed indifferent, like I was an ordinary parishioner—asking me to donate a dozen cookies for a church bake sale. However, he was planning the Sunday service, and asked if I would give a short talk about my Georgia experience. My reply must have sounded rather flat because that was the way I was feeling. "Sure, I'd be glad to." I know I sounded disappointed. Little did he know how I dreamed of him, hoping that someday he'd be my man. But that morning from the sound of his voice, I could tell that a love affair wasn't going to blossom anytime soon.

"Good. I'll see you Sunday." Chris hung up and that was it.

I stood numb. He wasn't about to break the terms of his contract. He was just a preacher taking care of business. I could have cried over our flat conversation, but I sucked in a deep breath and went to the kitchen for breakfast.

It had rained hard all night with a slight let-up at dawn. Everyone around the breakfast table was in good spirits. The badly needed rain would give the crops a big boost.

Jason left after breakfast for a dental appointment in Rutland. He was also anxious to pick up his developed pictures.

Mom and I cleared the breakfast table. She was carrying dishes to the sink. "Emily Ann stopped by the shop yesterday." She glanced at me.

"She wants one of us, your dad, you, or me, for a nine o'clock meeting at the bank."

I stopped rinsing the dishes. "What's that all about?"

"I don't know. She seemed uptight, said it was in regards to finances." Mom started getting ready for work, combing her hair, using the kitchen mirror. "I told her that you were in charge of our accounts, and that you would be the one to go."

"Okay." I looked at her puzzled. "Kind of odd, don't you think?"

"I agree." Mom clipped her hair back. "You know Emily Ann better than I, but she always seems to me to be stiff and closed-mouthed, especially yesterday."

"She has to be, dealing with other people's money."

"Yeah, but she could at least tell me the purpose of her request." Mom slipped on her jacket and left.

In regards to the meeting, I also wondered what the problem was. Just yesterday morning I balanced the checkbooks and reviewed the financial reports. Everything was in order. The Murray investments were conservative and sound—so, why the meeting?

Leaving the house, I noticed that everything was lush and green. The alfalfa on the meadow especially looked like it had taken on a new life. The hydrangea bush by the back door was starting to develop its white snowballs. The sun was high above Hardhack Mountain, bringing the world alive. I looked for the headwaters of the Blue, an open spot on the mountain, but the leaves were hiding it.

On my way for the meeting, I recalled interning at the bank. Emily Ann Gray, president of the Huntersville National Bank, a spinster in her late fifties, handled her position with integrity, albeit with a strong dose of aloofness. She had few, if any, friends. When I was at the bank, I felt she clung to me, wanting companionship. At the time, we didn't have much in common, except bank business.

I often wondered about her. I was told she had been adopted from a Huntersville family—the result of a teen pregnancy. Her adoptive parents lived in the Boston area. A few years after leaving Huntersville, Emily Ann's adoptive mother died of cancer. She returned to town in 1948 when she was nine and lived with Joe and Shirley Iverson.

Shirley, on the Harold Tully farm, had needed someone to care for her infant son, Steven. Emily Ann moved to the farm and took on child-care responsibilities: bathing him, changing diapers, feeding him, and going for walks. Throughout the years she watched Steven grow into manhood.

Hiram Silver was Emily Ann's grandfather. A majority stockholder in the Huntersville National Bank, he took a special interest in his grand-daughter. In high school she became a part-time teller—soon a loan officer, next a trust officer and eventually was made president of the bank at twenty-eight.

Hiram's youngest son, Buddy, worked at the bank. He was bypassed in favor of Emily Ann. She had told me immediate friction set in between the two. However, from what I understood, she performed her duties admirably. A conservative lender, she tallied handsome profits for the bank. Her delinquency rate was rock bottom compared to that of other lending institutions, with one exception—Steven Iverson.

Emily Ann broke the rules when lending to Steven. He carried a staggering debt, frequently not meeting the payments on his loans. Emily Ann confided in me that she often used her own money to make his payments. She sometimes called Shirley Iverson, asking her to make certain payments, especially if she feared the bank examiners were due.

I learned that her reckless lending to Steven didn't go unnoticed by Buddy Silver. She feared that Buddy might report her to the Board of Directors if Steven's loans weren't kept current. Their relationship became even more contentious when Buddy was named Chair of the Board of Directors.

Now he lives out of town, spending most of his days in a fitness club and on the golf course. Living the life of leisure, he's not very often in his office.

I parked in front of a square brick building located on the corner of Main and Silver. I entered the bank, passing two teller windows and a cubicle with two middle-aged folks speaking French to Eve Hebert, the loan officer. I passed Buddy's plate-glass office. He happened to be in, humped over a golf club, practicing putting on the carpeted floor.

At the end of the hallway, I stopped in front of Emily Ann's office and knocked. She came out, pulling the door closed behind her. Her hand slightly shook as she slipped it from the door knob. Behind steel-rimmed glasses, her brown eyes darted anxiously. Her thin colorless face had hardly a smile as she welcomed me in an edgy voice. "It's good to see you! Thanks for coming."

"Sure."

"We're meeting with Steven and Gilda Pierce." Emily Ann rolled a ruby ring on her finger. "Somehow, I need to lend forty thousand to Steven."

"Why the loan?"

"Well…" Emily Ann's face flushed. "Gilda's demanding payment from Steven on a long-standing debt."

I reacted matter-of-factly. "So?"

"Gilda's threatening to file for Steven's seat in the legislature if she isn't paid."

I started to go. "So why am I here?"

"Please bear with me." Emily Ann held my arm. "Steven lacks equity in his farm."

"That's not your problem," I said in a disgusted tone. "He's no longer a kid."

"I know." Emily Ann darted a glance toward Buddy's office.

I bluntly asked, "When do you give up on the guy?"

"He's like a son I never had." She clenched her hands. "My very own."

Her frown and desperate tone made me realize how much she wanted me in on the meeting. "How can I help?"

"I'm not sure." She shrugged. "Steven might have a workable plan."

"Well, let's see."

Emily Ann opened the door, gesturing for me to enter. I quickly scanned the office. It hadn't changed since high school. Norman Rockwell paintings decorated the walls. I was looking straight ahead at a Boy Scout saving a little blond girl, dripping wet, wrapped in a blanket. At the back wall, a five-foot-high rack stood, partly filled with Emily Ann's coats. Beside it, a pottery crock held several of Hiram Silver's ornate wooden canes.

I turned my attention to Gilda, seated at the far edge of Emily Ann's desk. She didn't smile on seeing me. She'd lost the spring in her ringlets—straight hair was held in place by the same sequined barrettes she regularly wore. Presently, her charm was hidden under a layer of frosty emotion. She sat stiffly, with lips pale and drawn. Her steely glare toward Iverson could wither the boldest of men. At the restaurant, days ago, they had acted intimate. But at the moment, Iverson seemed to be Gilda's arch enemy.

I nodded toward him. He sat, looking sour and glum, at the opposite end of the desk from Gilda. He wore the same grubby clothes. He clenched his fists with thumbs nervously in motion.

I chose a chair away from the desk and glanced at Gilda to my left and Steven to my right. I was wondering how I fit into the situation. Emily Ann drew her seat into position as she leaned forward onto her desk. A computer screen was at her right elbow.

Catching my attention, Emily Ann announced, "We're meeting today to try and resolve a difficult situation."

Gilda became teary. "Dad has terminal cancer." She sighed. "I want to pay off the mortgage on my folks' house to help my mom."

Emily Ann continued, "Gilda wants Steven to pay back a long-standing debt of forty thousand dollars." She glanced at me. "We want to keep this from becoming scandalous."

"Scandalous!" Gilda reacted in an angry voice. "I guess. A lawsuit would surely make the papers."

"Well," Steven reasoned, "give me some time!"

"Time!" Gilda waved her finger. "I loaned you that money years ago with the promise you'd pay within months."

Steven blushed and mumbled, "I don't have it."

Gilda slumped. "You're pathetic!"

"Steven." Emily Ann leaned forward. "Let's stop acting so hopeless. Decide how you can pay your debt."

"Right!" Gilda fumed. "And the check gets made out to me before I leave!"

Iverson snarled, "What check?"

Gilda snapped. "A check for forty thousand dollars!"

"And just where do I come up with that amount?" He paused, turning to me. "I did mention to Emily Ann that Jason might be willing to merge our farms for a price."

"No! You know Jason's against the idea," I said emphatically. "A merger will never happen."

"We can't loan Steven anymore." Emily Ann flatly stated. "His loans already are more than the farm's worth."

I turned to Iverson. "Sell us the meadow."

"That's my best land!" He grabbed the arms of his chair. "I'm *not* selling the meadow!"

Gilda plunged toward Iverson. "And I'm *not* leaving here empty-handed."

"Go ahead—sue!" Steven settled back in his chair. "This well is bone dry."

"Okay." Gilda threatened. "I'll file for your seat in the upcoming election."

Steven laughed. "What a threat!"

"Oh, yeah? Try me!" Gilda darted her big brown eyes at him.

Emily Ann turned to Steven. "If you settle this peacefully, you have no choice but to sell property. Murray's Meadow is the only land you own that's not adjoining your farm. That being the case, you can pass the title to the Murrays once the encumbrances are paid." She looked toward the door. "Buddy, the directors, and I will also require that all your other notes be current."

Iverson jumped up, his loose tie flapping. "Son of a bitch! You're all a bunch of thieves!" He settled back in his chair. "You're vultures picking on a down-and-out guy who's run onto some bad luck." He waved his arms. "Yeah, a bunch of turkey vultures!"

Gilda retorted, "I'm only here to get what's due me!"

"Yeah, well, I'll tell you if the Murrays buy the meadow," he wagged his finger at me, "you're paying through the nose."

His bluster didn't faze me. "Not for any half million."

"You bastardly Murrays could buy the whole town if you had a mind to!"

"So?" I snapped back. "Dad's not a fool."

Emily Ann sent a message on her computer. "I'm having Eve Hebert go to the town clerk's office next door to tally the attachments on the meadow." She glanced from her computer to Iverson. "Think in terms of a reasonable price for the land."

"Reasonable, huh! Reasonable means I won't end up with a god-damned thing." He sneered. "The bank and all those greedy suppliers will come in for the kill." He slumped. "I'll have nothing." He put on a poor-me look with arms hanging by the side of his chair. "A river rat can live better than I can."

"I don't feel sorry for you," Gilda sneered. "I can't believe I loaned you my total savings."

Iverson shrugged. "You agreed."

A half hour passed while we waited for Eve. I got up and circled the room, looking at the Rockwell paintings.

Iverson paced the floor, swearing a constant string of four-letter words. "Letting that meadow go will do me in!"

Gilda watched him as he paced. "You might as well sell. All you've grown for the last few years is a crop of weeds."

He glared at Gilda while taking his chair, mumbling, "I know Jason could get me up and running—plant that field and get a good crop." He glanced toward me and yelled, "But no! The son-of-a-bitch would rather watch the birds!"

Seeing he was about to flair into an uncontrollable rage, I held my breath and said nothing.

Thankfully in the next moment, Emily Ann announced, "Eve has a closing figure." She turned to Iverson. "The amount owed the bank and attachments on the meadow come to eighty thousand."

"I'm not selling for no eighty thousand!" Iverson barked.

Emily Ann took a deep breath. "Right, but start at eighty."

"I'll put it on the market for half a million." Iverson pulled on the lapels of his coat and settled back in his chair.

Gilda fired back, "If that's the case, as soon as I leave the bank, I'm starting a petition for your seat in the legislature."

"You wouldn't." Iverson jumped up.

"Try me." Gilda glared. "Just try me!"

Emily Ann offered, "If you sold for two hundred thousand, you'd have enough to pay the bank, the attachments, the taxes, and have a little left over." She paused. "Considering the losses on your farm, you might not have any tax to pay."

Iverson slumped in his chair. "I'm sure as hell not letting Gilda run against me." He said, resigned, "I'll sell for three hundred thousand."

"Not to Marcus and Maggie Murray!" I said with determination. "Two hundred is more than fair." I knew from previous discussions the amount Dad would be willing to pay for the meadow.

He countered. "Two seventy-five!"

"No, two hundred."

Iverson grumbled, "My place will never attract a farmer without the meadow!" He sagged in his chair. "I was planning on farm rent for part of my income." He jumped up red-faced. "I'm screwed!"

The room was silent. I could feel tension gripping us all.

Suddenly, Iverson's fist flew, punching air. "I hate the Murrays. They're the son of a bitchin' richest people in town and Ruth, you're stealing my land!" He paced the floor. His red puffy cheeks, wild eyes, and spitting profanity made him look and sound like a mad bull. He grabbed his captain's chair and charged at me, holding it over his head, yelling, "Okay, you queen of finance, I'll sell for a measly two hundred thousand!"

Emily Ann and Gilda jumped to grab his arms. He spun, shaking them free. They stumbled backward, nearly losing their footing. They both screamed, "STEVEN!"

I sprang up, backing against the wall.

He continued toward me. In a fraction of a second, he flung the chair. I ducked. It hit the Rockwell picture of the Boy Scout holding the little girl. *Crash!*

Glass sprayed in all directions. Gilda and Emily Ann tried to stop him. I was cornered by the desk on my left, plus a chair and broken glass on my right. Iverson was close enough for me to smell his sour sweat. He was within inches of grabbing my throat. My hands, holding him back, were sunken into his flabby neck. I was speechless with fright.

Suddenly, Buddy Silver came barging through the door. "Hey!"

Iverson turned.

Buddy grabbed the portly man, shoving him into the coat rack. Iverson's red cheeks turned pale. Lying in a heap under the hanging coats, he looked as helpless as a bag of trash. Buddy lunged for one of Hiram Silver's canes. "You make one move and I'll split your head like a block of wood."

Iverson mumbled, "Show me where to sign."

I ran out of the room shaken to the core. With a quivering voice, I called Dad. "Iverson will sell the meadow for two hundred thousand." I gasped. "He tried to attack me."

"What... you still at the bank?"

"Yeah, he's lost it!" I could feel the tears edging down my face.

"Do you want me to come right down?"

"Yeah, you and Mom need to sign for the title." I sniffed. "Buddy has Iverson under control."

"We'll be right over."

"Thanks, Dad." I sat for a while to get settled, and then I went back to the office. Buddy was standing guard. Iverson's watery eyes followed me when I entered. I could feel his hatred.

Late in the morning after everyone had signed papers, Gilda sighed, "I'm just happy for my poor dad and mom that they don't have a mortgage hanging over their heads."

I didn't comment, not wanting to gloat. My folks were the winners. No one wanted the fifty acres more than Dad. I started to leave the bank, passing Buddy's office. He was in the same position hunched over his putter like nothing had happened. I stopped briefly at Eve's office to say, "Hi."

She came from behind her desk. "Isn't that Gilda something else? She sure put Steven in his place."

I kept my thoughts to myself. Eve would talk plenty. I didn't want her to relay any hint of a Murray victory. It was already troubling to know that Iverson's feelings ran deep against the Murrays. Many Huntersville folks would side with their state representative, the underdog.

Eve was an Iverson supporter. "I feel sort of sorry for Steven. He's been good to me."

What could I say? I just turned and left. Dad and Mom were still in Emily Ann's office.

That night around the supper table, Dad acted as if he'd taken on a new life. "I'll have Scoop plow that fifty acres. We'll lime and fertilize it and plant rye. It's too late to get a crop this year." He paused. "I've got a lot more to learn before I start growing turf."

Coffee was running down the edge of Cooner's mouth. He grabbed a napkin. "You folks buyin' that meadow caused quite the stir around town." He held the napkin. "Word has it that Iverson ain't seen the end of his money problems."

I was about to leave the table. "Who says?"

"Bertha told me."

"She's probably right." I headed toward the office.

fifteen

Jason

I pulled into the farmyard after my trip to Rutland. Aside from the few photos that Iverson had taken in his messy kitchen, the pictures from the first roll of film looked great, especially of the white-throated sparrow. After several attempts, I had a perfect one of the bird: reddish brown, white at the wing tips, a white throat, clean gray vest, with a dash of yellow between his eye and beak. In the best photo, his beak was opened wide. As I studied the bird, I could almost hear him whistling his soprano song.

The ones of Ellen were especially nice. In fact she was beautiful. After looking several times at the pictures, I planned to get my favorite enlarged, her wearing the butterfly t-shirt, standing by the bridge.

A gush of pride flashed through me. Did I love her because she was star-struck beautiful, and I was proud to be with her? Or did I love her because she was fun company? Still sitting in my truck, after looking at my pictures—especially of Ellen, I put them in the glove compartment along with a paper bag of condoms that I'd bought while in Rutland. I opened the bag and looked inside. Just seeing the box sent my heart racing.

Minutes earlier, as I drove through town on my way home, I saw Scoop by his van outside of Chub's Variety. I rolled down my window. "I've just been in Rutland. Can you come to the farm and we'll start the process of fixing that dryer motor?"

"I've got to see Bubbles, then I'll be right along." Scoop left for the store.

It was obvious that I was going to have to take the lead if the motor was going to be fixed before second cutting.

After a while, Scoop's van rattled into the farmyard. He got out and met me. "My old man says we can fix that motor without hefting it to the ground."

"Well, geez, Scoop, let's get moving on it." We walked toward the barn. "Second cutting will be here in a matter of weeks."

We headed for the shed to check out the motor.

Scoop stood, stroking his beard. "Let's get up there and take down some serial numbers."

"Good." I led the way on ladder rungs nailed to the barn. We hovered over the motor. I rubbed away some grease and dust with a rag. "Here's the plate with all the information."

He bent over, reading the numbers. "This motor's an old bastard." Scoop wrote in his small Butson's Feed booklet. "I'll check on this today."

"Good. Let's get cracking." We climbed down.

Scoop tucked the booklet in his vest pocket. "You know I've been busy as hell with AA, electrical classes, and seeing the probation officer. All stuff I have to do or I'd been here sooner."

"Yeah, and hanging out at Chub's." That place attracted the young crowd. Scoop loved their company.

He smiled. "You know that Bubbles is something else." He broke out laughing. "She showed me some of her tattoos. Son-of-a-bitch, she's covered. The Tree of Life, she calls it, grows from her belly button up between her boobs and branches out across her shoulders." He continued to smile. "A copperhead snake is wrapped around the tree trunk. Bright red apples hang from the branches." He shook his head. "She's a real live Garden of Eden."

"Bubbles' tattoos are unbelievable." I said in a tone of amazement. "Seeing the tree branches on her shoulders is enough for me." I started walking away.

Scoop turned toward me with a smirk. "Bubbles told me about you stoppin' in the other day."

He caught my attention. "Yeah."

"She says in nine or ten months there's goin' to be a population explosion in Rutland."

"Why?" I stood by my truck.

"Didn't you hear?" Scoop continued smirking.

"No."

"Well, the rubbers sold in Rutland leak like a watering can." He nodded, affirming his statement while jumping in his truck. "Ellen will have one in the oven by fall!"

My face turned red. A bolt of fear struck me like a rock. I yanked open the passenger-side door of my truck and fumbled for the glove compartment, opening the bag to examine the condoms. I looked up and Scoop was laughing so hard I didn't know if he was fit for the road.

I shoved the bag back, slamming the truck door when I realized I'd been had.

While doing chores Sunday morning, Ruth asked me if I'd go to church with her. She was giving a talk on the Piedmont Center and would like me along. I hadn't been to church in years, but I agreed to support her. She also invited Eve.

We picked up Eve at her apartment above the bank. She was waiting by the door, dressed to kill: long brunette hair lay over the shoulders of a light brown blouse, worn daringly. Her outfit was coordinated with a dark brown skirt. Coming toward the truck, I could see she had used plenty of makeup: beige facial cream, dark brown on her eyebrows, and brown pencil outlining her eyes. She was quite the contrast to Ruth who never used makeup and who wore a white blouse and navy slacks.

Ruth opened the truck door, then slid over next to me. She glanced toward Eve. "Good morning, thanks for coming."

Eve mumbled, "Morning."

She either had a wicked hangover or was depressed. She was close to tears. "I've got to see you guys, especially you, Jason."

I left the curb and shifted into second gear. "Sure, maybe this afternoon."

"Well, I'm at my folks all afternoon." She sniffed. "Let's go to Gilda's tonight after your chores, and we can talk."

"Around seven." I glanced toward Eve. "What's this all about?"

"It can wait." The truck came to a stop in front of the church. "This is not the time or place right now."

I couldn't imagine what her problem was as we entered church and took our seats. Eve, Ruth, and I sat in the pew next to a window opening covered by a temporary sheet of plastic. The stained-glass window, *The Good Shepherd,* was being repaired. A dedication of the newly refurbished window was set for July 16.

Ruth seemed relaxed in the warmth of the moment. Chris's sermon was on *Compassion.* It was short and to the point: "All of us are warm, have plenty of food, drive decent vehicles, and most of us have been given an education."

He spoke with clarity, scanning the congregation for eye contact.

"Many of the world's population are underfed, have no source of income, no education, and no way to improve their station in life. Our faith tells us to be caring, requiring of us to be compassionate, reaching out and helping the less fortunate."

He paused to draw our attention and continued: "We're not called to lay down our lives for others but to do daily acts of kindness for one another." He paused again. "This morning we'll hear from Ruth Murray who has done more than most of us, more than small acts of kindness."

Ruth left her seat and walked up front toward the podium. On her way, she looked straight ahead, moving with a confident stride.

Chris continued from the pulpit. "After college, Ruth joined Volunteers in Service to America to improve the lives of others in Piedmont, Georgia. As most of us know, she has recently returned home. This morning she'll tell us about her work."

Ruth walked up to the pulpit and grasped the edges of the lectern. Her alert blue eyes, welcoming smile, and steady pleasant voice greeted us.

I was amazed at how she delivered her message without stumbling or hesitation. She held the attention of the congregation, and I noticed that Chris seemed fixated by her.

I felt proud to be her brother. I also realized that emotionally she was still in Piedmont, Georgia.

"At the Center, I came to know a little nine-year-old, Anadeepa." Her voice broke, but she quickly recovered.

"Anadeepa had no parents. Her mother, at thirteen, was a prostitute in Atlanta. After Anadeepa was born, her mother, deathly ill, returned to live with a relative and died soon after. A distant aunt, who looked after her daughter's four preschool children, took Anadeepa as an infant. An eighty-year-old grandmother watched the children while the aunt worked as a cleaning woman in a nursing home. There were no regular meals. The children learned to fend for themselves through Food Stamps plus what clothes the aunt could provide."

Ruth paused for a drink of water.

"The Piedmont Center, where I was placed by VISTA, is under the direction of Frieda Angrish. She took in Anadeepa along with the other four children. Others at the Center were from similar situations. The place has a capacity of forty children. Only the neediest are given residence, while a number of kids come to the center for an after-school program.

"Local black churches help to support the place, but it struggles to keep the doors open. When VISTA placed me there, the Center had a hard time to provide the basic needs such as food and clothing. In addition, many students were behind in their reading, writing, and math.

"Many of us in the north don't understand some places in the deep south and its society. For the most part, in Piedmont the white kids go to superior Christian or private schools, and the black kids attend public school. Segregation continues with the black children receiving inferior schooling.

"Frieda's often-repeated line was, 'I want these kids to make it to the top. I want them to have a chance in life. We need money for food and clothing, and a full-time tutor.'

"Right away, I could see the need, but finding and paying a full-time tutor was a tall order. After many letters and contacts with non-profits and foundations, I located the Elias M. Cole Foundation. The Foundation funded essentials for the kids, as well as a tutor, Sara Patch, a young, highly trained black woman. She's an excellent role model, and she's making progress with the kids.

"Just days ago, I got word that some of the Foundation's investments have gone sour. Through a letter, I've been informed that on July 14 the

Board of Directors will decide the funding for the Piedmont project. I've been advised that support for the Center won't be adequate."

I watched Ruth's eyes widen and her brow furrow. She leaned over the podium. "I intend with every fiber of my body to give these kids the chance they deserve. I'm going to New York on the 14th to plead for them—especially for Anadeepa."

Ruth paused. "If any of you would be willing to support this cause, I'd be grateful to receive your contributions."

As Ruth left the podium, I believed that somehow, some way, she would see to it that the $40,000 a year cost would be covered in spite of the pullback by the Elias M. Cole Foundation.

After church, members gave her generous donations. Ruth looked particularly surprised when Bertha Bean handed her a fifty-dollar check. Bertha's carrot-red hair showed at the edges of a pink hat. "You gave a good talk."

Ruth smiled. "Thanks, Bertha."

While I was standing with Ruth, Chris came up and shook our hands. "Ruth, that was outstanding."

"Thanks, Chris."

He offered, "If you need any help with your project, let me know."

"Thanks, again. I just might call on you."

I could see Ruth's mood change to a cheerful smile on hearing the offer from Chris.

That night after chores Ruth was deep into office work and writing letters. She didn't care to go to Gilda's.

Since it was Sunday night, I intended to see Ellen, who was home from school. I planned to pick up Eve, have dinner, then take her home. Afterward, I was excited and ready for a romantic night with Ellen.

At seven I pulled up to Eve's apartment in my red truck. She came out wearing a light summer knee-length coat, slacks, and sneakers. She opened the truck door and fell onto the seat.

"Hi, Jason. Sorry. I tripped."

"Hi." The strong smell of liquor filled the cab. Her hand groped for the door handle.

"Eve. You've been drinking?"

"Yeah, I need some comfort." She slammed the door.

I headed toward Gilda's. On the way she reached for a bottle in her coat pocket.

I pulled into the yard and parked. "Here, give me that stuff!" I slid to the center of the seat, took the liquor from her and placed it on the dashboard. "Seeing the shape you're in, Gilda won't let you through the door!"

Eve, sobbing, threw her arms around me. Her long hair flew in my face. I wiped strands away from my mouth and nose. "What's your problem?" Her large breasts pressed into my chest, feeling like soft pillows. Her head lay on my shoulder. She turned, resting in my lap with her feet and legs folded under her.

I held her like a big baby. To support her, my legs were jacked high with my feet placed on the hump in the floorboard. I thought of Chris's sermon that morning: *small acts of kindness.*

"I...I don't know where to begin." Eve caught her breath in a sob. "Charlie's gone." She inhaled a shudder. "He was mean...didn't love me."

"Gee, you two have lived together since high school." I readjusted her bulk. Her head slid to rest in the cradle of my arm.

"Yeah, he'd come at me as if I was a slab of meat." She reached in her pocket for a hankie and blew her nose. "He was a mean drinker, slapping and shoving me around."

"Really? How long did that go on?"

"Too long. I...I gave him a place to live, and food. He treated me like an animal."

"That's awful!" My expressed sympathy brought on more drunken crying.

"Just lately Steven Iverson got friendly. He kicked Charlie out. Steven stayed a couple of nights."

"Oh no!" I couldn't imagine it.

"Steven slept on the couch. He snored like a hog."

"Eve, you can do better than Steven Iverson."

"He...he's a good friend!" She sniffed. "At least he treated me decent and got rid of Charlie."

"I guess, sort of a mixed blessing."

"That's—that's the point." She whimpered. "I…I feel like I'm stabbin' him in the back."

"Why?" I shifted my arms. She was getting heavy.

"Buddy Silver came to me Friday and told me to get the legal work in…in motion to…to foreclose on Steven." She started crying, burying her face in my shirt.

"This isn't your fault!" I could feel her hot breath and warm tears dampen my chest.

"He…he set the foreclosing date for November 1." She wiped her tears. "This will ruin him."

"He's already ruined."

"Don't you see!" She sat up and slid her arm around my neck, leaning into me. "If you took over his farm, it would save him."

"Gosh, is that why you wanted to talk to me?"

"Yeah, you can help Steven, me, and the bank."

"Eve, you're asking a lot—to change the whole course of my life."

"I haven't told you all." She reached for the bottle, but I held her arm from getting it. "Buddy has threatened to fire me for drinking too much." She looked at me. "If I can save the farm, Buddy and the bank will think more highly of me." She burst into a steady cry.

"Eve, this is ridiculous! I'm not making what amounts to a career change to help you, Steven, or the bank." I put the bottle under my seat. "Your drinking is a separate issue."

She moved toward me, kissing me on the cheek. "Please!" She kissed me again. "You're the…the key."

I pulled my arm from beneath her and rested it on the back of the seat. Eve took the opportunity to slide even closer with her right leg sliding over my lap. I wanted to shove her away, but I felt sorry for her. She'd certainly been a successful young woman, but alcohol and the wrong man had derailed her. I could listen to her woes, but I certainly wasn't the one to get her back on track. "You need to stop your drinking." I held her head for eye contact.

"So you're going to lecture me." She sobbed and again buried her face in my shirt.

"Right." I pushed her so she'd look at me. "Join AA and get a hold of yourself."

She flopped back, resting her head on my shoulder.

Suddenly, the driver's-side door flew open. Ellen stood with her hand over her mouth.

Eve didn't move. Seeing Ellen, I jerked forward in alarm. I was speechless.

The door slammed before I could explain. Anyway, what could I say? Our closeness spoke volumes.

I turned and watched Ellen run toward Gilda's. I gulped. I convinced Eve we should go to her apartment. We could cook something to eat at her place. Even if Gilda allowed her in the front door, I didn't want folks to see Eve drunk—further damaging her reputation.

Back at her apartment, she was so unsteady, I held her by the arm as we climbed the stairs. Opening the door, I saw that her place was neat and orderly. However, she was in no shape to prepare a meal. She sat at the breakfast bar, watching me fry hamburgers and heat some corn from a can.

Her tears flowed freely. She dabbed her face with Kleenex. "I'm so depressed." She whimpered, "I need a drink."

"Eve, eat something!" I shoved the hamburger and warmed corn in front of her.

"Jason, I want a man like you."

"We've been friends forever. Let's keep it that way." I sat across from her. "Will you promise me you'll go to AA? Forget about Charlie. Forget about Iverson." I reached and held her arm, slightly shaking it. "Don't blow off your bank job."

She sniffed. "I'll try not to."

I wasn't convinced of her promise, but in her condition, I couldn't expect anything more. I made her a cup of coffee, turned on the TV, and got her settled on her couch. I'd helped her all I could, or all I wanted to help. Eve cried mournfully, seeing me leave.

Ellen was on my mind. I heard Eve all the way down the stairs. I raced across town back to Gilda's. I had no idea of what I could say to Ellen. I was uptight as I left the truck. Gilda met me at the door. "Hi, Jason." The tone of her voice was cool. "You here to eat...or...?"

"For Ellen." I looked around, seeing those I recognized but not her.

Gilda motioned with a glance. "In the back room."

I brushed past her and the folks seated at the counter. Iverson sat slouched, drinking beer. He gave me an ugly look. I said nothing as I went toward the back room. I could feel his stare following me until I turned the corner.

There were all sorts of things in the merchandise room: children's furniture, tools of all descriptions, and a case of guns. Ellen was at the far end, sorting clothing. She held up a large long-sleeved shirt, inspecting it. She didn't notice me.

"Ellen." I spoke softly.

She dropped the shirt. "What are you doing here?" she demanded in a stern voice.

"I want to talk to you."

"You and Eve Hebert! My God!"

"She needed a friend." I stepped closer. "She's troubled."

"Yeah, troubled right into your arms." She motioned. "Get away from me!"

"You've got the wrong idea." I reached out. "She was drunk."

"Eve Hebert... drunk." She held up the shirt as a shield between us. "Huh!" In a second she dropped it back onto the pile. "What else is new?"

"Could we talk over a cup of coffee?"

She shook her head in an angry squinty-eyed look. Then all of a sudden...silence. She turned white, covered her mouth, and a muffled scream blew through her fingers.

I turned. Iverson had a rifle pressed to his shoulder. He was looking down the sights, aiming at me. The barrel was weaving as he yelled, "I had a great plan!" He cocked the hammer. "You could've done a hell of a job at my place. But, no! You Murrays are too good for me!"

My throat tightened. Was this a joke? Was the gun loaded? I watched his finger slide onto the trigger. He was within a few feet of me. There wasn't time to move. "You're crazy!"

"You're the crazy one...not seeing a good deal!" He had a sneering smile. He pulled the trigger.

The click against the firing pin magnified to a loud *snap*. It wasn't loaded. Iverson bent over in uncontrolled laughter.

I grabbed the barrel, yanking the gun from his hands. "I should report you!"

He stumbled backward. "Go ahead." He crashed against a baby's crib, yelling, "Goddamn!" His deep voice boomed in the restaurant. "You've ruined me!"

The loud noise brought Gilda running, with Sheriff Krads right behind. Gilda put the gun back in its case. "Pointing a gun is serious stuff."

"Oh, hell, Gilda." Iverson straightened his suit coat. "You know I was only joking." Gilda motioned toward the door. She demanded, "Leave!"

I was shaking. Ellen was crying. I hurried to her...threw my arms around her. She didn't pull away.

sixteen

Ruth

July 1st, Jason ate breakfast and left early. He headed with his camera for the ridge to check the heifer, Penny, who was hopefully carrying a red and white calf. Due to the dry weather, he also worried that they might have run out of pasture.

After eating, I went to the barn before Judge Crabtree, the insurance agent, came to okay the coverage increase.

Leaving the barn near noon, I stopped for Cooner who was on his bench in deep thought. I patted him on the shoulder and sat down. "What's on your mind, old man? You haven't gone to Butson's?"

"Well, I was thinkin' about the sunrise earlier this mornin'. What a sight. The shades of red across Hardhack Mountain were…well nothin' I remember seein' before. 'Course Wunderland and the Blue are hidden by the leaves on the trees. When ya get to be my age ya see more with a poorer set of eyes." He turned to me in my spattered t-shirt and jeans. "I was thinkin'. The older I get, the younger-lookin' ya get."

"Thanks, but gosh I feel older than my age right now." I tucked hair behind my ear.

He chuckled. "A little cow manure don't age ya none."

"It's problems." I sighed. "Yeah, problems age folks."

"What's on your mind?" He packed in a pinch of Beechnut.

"I'd like to say 'nothing,' but that's not so." I rested my forehead in my hand.

"What is it?"

"Like I told you before, the Cole Foundation is cutting their funding to the Piedmont Center."

"What does that mean?" Cooner spat.

"A cut of up to forty thousand a year." I paused. "I'll find out at their board meeting in New York."

"Golly, yer talkin' real money." He turned to me. "Sure wish I could help."

"Thanks, Cooner, but I need to find money somewhere."

"Well, ya handle the Murray money." He spat. "Write a check."

"Cooner, that's called embezzling."

"I know. I hope ya ain't that desperate."

"I'm desperate but I'm not a thief." I turned to him. "I was thinking of asking Mom and Dad."

"For money?" He scowled.

"Yeah."

"Oh gosh, Ruth." He spat again. "Your folks have been good to me, but I'll tell ya they're tighter than new skin on a snake."

"I know. They're Murrays." I gazed off, glum.

"That's a lot to expect, havin' them shell out for a place they ain't never seen and for kids they ain't knowin'."

"Yeah." I felt defeated. "You're right."

"Anyway, yer puttin' the cart before the horse." He tapped his cane. "You ain't sure how much ya'll be needin'."

"I know. I guess I worry too much." I felt teary. My voice broke. "I'm all alone in this. Pleading my case before people I don't even know. It scares me." I sniffed and wiped my nose.

Cooner reached and put his hand on my shoulder. "I know if I got plunked in the middle of New York City, my timbers would shiver."

"Well, New York doesn't scare me. It's the thought of going alone." I sat for a moment. "Maybe I should take Chris up on his offer to help."

"Why not?" He tapped his cane. "This should be right up his alley."

"You're right." I thought a minute. "I just wish he wasn't so uptight, worrying over a close relationship. It takes all the fun out of being around him."

"It's Mildred Butson. She has him hog-tied, causin' him to be afraid he'll lose his job."

"That's ridiculous. Folks love him."

Cooner looked at me. "Ask him for help. You might be surprised." He lurched ahead as I helped him stand. "Let's get somethin' ta eat."

Around the dinner table, Dad was full of talk about turf farming. With pamphlets in hand, he was like a kid with a new toy. He mentioned the start-up costs were around a million and a half.

Mom's brow furrowed and her smile vanished. "Marcus, the cost!"

He kept on reading as if he didn't hear her.

I gulped. Forty thousand a year seemed like chump-change in comparison. It became clear to me that I was a family oddball. My real interest lay in helping the less fortunate. Making money at turf farming didn't interest me one bit. Consequently, I finished eating and went back to the barn.

All the cattle were out to pasture except for a few calves. The place was cool and quiet. A few birds had flown through the open windows to feed on bits of grain in the mangers.

I cleaned and bedded the pens, feeling it a welcome change from the table discussion.

I had just started sweeping the aisle when I heard Scoop pull in the yard. Although he was a flirt, I'd come to realize, even considering his prison time, that he was harmless.

He sauntered into the barn. His leather heels clicked on the walk. "Howdy, gorgeous."

"Hi, Scoop." With my back turned, I pulled on my shirt, shifting my shoulders.

He leaned against the barn wall and rolled up his sleeves to his elbows, acting as if he didn't have a thing to do except to try and impress me. "Well, all the primpin' gals do don't matter. I like the plain down-home type."

I laughed. "Scoop, what's on your mind?"

"Well, I've got myself a girl."

"Oh, who?" I leaned on the broom handle.

"Herb Chub's daughter, Bubbles." He smacked his lips. "Well, sorta. She showed me more of her Garden of Eden."

"You mean her tattoos?" I continued sweeping.

"Yup, but I got to get tested." He followed me and the broom. "Bein' a jail bird and all, there's a lot of weird shit that goes on." He tapped me on the shoulder.

I stopped and turned.

"You know what she said?"

"What?"

"She told me I ain't to taste the apples until I pass the test."

"You mean her apple tattoos?" I continued sweeping.

"Yup, she's waitin' on me before gettin' too serious."

"Good for her!" I stopped. "When are you going to fix that dryer motor?"

"The parts are back-ordered. I've come to check the shaft size."

"Well, something should happen soon. You've sure dragged your feet."

"I've been, well…swamped with work." He followed me as I swept. "Besides, your dad asked me to plow the Iverson land."

I said emphatically, "The motor is top priority!" I looked out the barn window at the field of alfalfa. "It's just a matter of days until Jason will want to do second cutting."

"Okay. But there're problems. I told Jason when we read the serial numbers that the thing is old—outdated."

"Buy a new one!" I was getting frustrated that we hadn't been more aggressive in taking care of the situation.

"It ain't that easy." His fingers raked his beard. "Most motors that size are three-phase. Power leadin' to this place ain't three-phase. Besides the shaft size on new ten-horse motors is usually bigger than this one."

I raised my voice. "Well, let's get tending to business and do something!" I motioned with the broom.

"Okay, okay, I'll measure the shaft." He headed toward the mow. "I'll check with Electrical Supply this afternoon."

"Maybe if you weren't hanging out at Chub's so much, you could get more accomplished." I stopped and watched him leave. He acted as if he didn't hear.

A few days later when we were coming home from church, Jason glanced at the alfalfa on the meadow. "Even with the dry weather, the crop looks to be heavy and lush."

I nodded.

"After dinner, I'm mowing, since the forecast looks good." He pulled in the yard. "With no rain, by Tuesday, late morning, Cooner will be baling."

"How about the motor?"

"There's no choice but to by-pass the fuses again." Jason pushed his cap back. "I should've been onto Scoop a lot sooner. For sure we'll take care of it before another cutting."

My brow arched. "Gosh. I hope so!"

Tuesday morning, Jason asked me, "Will you call Chris and see if he's free for a couple of hours? He's good help stacking hay."

"Okay, I hope he's around."

When I called, he agreed to help. I also mentioned that I would take him up on his offer to help me with the Center project.

Tuesday afternoon, before baling, Cooner watched me by-passing the fuses to start and run the hay dryer. Before the motor kicked into full speed, the area around the dryer fan filled with electrical smoke from hot wires. Scoop stood back, declaring his innocence of the make-shift arrangement. Cooner leaned on his cane, chewing a mouthful of Beechnut. He spat and pulled his handkerchief, wiping his mouth. "This boondoggle thing I'm watchin' worries me."

Scoop nervously bit his lip. "I know. What I'm seein' ain't right."

I stood at the switch.

Jason was spinning the blades of the fan as fast as he could.

Cooner cleared his throat. "There's a time *to* do and a time *not* to do. Someone ain't done the *do* as they should."

Scoop turned to Cooner. "You talkin' about me, old man?"

"Well, as Bertha says, 'If the pants fit, put them on'."

Suddenly, the dryer motor began to roar. If Scoop had a comment, Cooner in no way could hear it. He gimped away to start baling.

Chris drove in the yard. As he came toward me, his warm smile thrilled me. "Hi, Ruth. How are you?" I was excited to see him. From the tone of his voice, I felt he'd mellowed toward me, and that we connected in a warm sort of way.

I caught myself from gushing over him too much. "I'm great, especially happy you're here to help."

He continued toward me with a broad grin. "I'm ready for a break, to do some physical work."

"Let's go then."

The swallows screeched as usual. Most of the mow was stacked into the rafters with hay. Space on the dryer lateral had been saved for second cutting. Chris and I sat closely, waiting for the bales. A gentle breeze crept up our pant legs from the dryer fan.

Chris turned to me. "I've missed seeing you."

I smiled. "I feel the same."

He asked, "What are your plans for New York?"

"I've got to give a five-minute talk. Just thinking about it fires my nerves."

"You did well in church." He cleared his throat. "Pictures would help."

I nodded. "That's a good idea."

"Come to my office." He reached for my arm. "We'll work on your talk."

"Gee, thanks." I smiled. "That would be a big help."

The elevator started clanking. We jumped up as the bales came within reach.

seventeen

Jason

Lately in the heavy air of the mornings, I could smell the pollen from the tasseling corn. Although it had been dry, there was enough rain from the last shower to jump-start the crop.

However, the pasture on the ridge was a different matter. The heifers had grazed every available blade of grass. The pasture had a brown shriveled-up appearance. I had to begin taking hay and grain to them every day in hopes that a pattern of wet weather would revive the pastures.

On my way to the ridge, I had to pass the former Hideaway. It gave me a pang of regret to see it torn from the tree, pulled at the seams, resting on a large limb. It looked like it had been hit by a wrecking ball. I no longer had a retreat to write in my log book and no chance to recognize familiar songbirds at the bird feeder.

The next morning after checking the second-cut hay in the mow, I pulled the lever on the dryer and disconnected the wires that bypassed the fuses. I laid the short copper wires in the bottom of the box and shut the cover. Before another season, I was sure we would repair the motor or, better yet, buy a new one. I certainly didn't want to again use this makeshift arrangement to dry hay.

Before going to give my daily feeding of the heifers, I looked out the barn window and watched Scoop driving our tractor, pulling a drag. He was covering the rye seed just sown on the fifty-acre former Iverson land. It occurred to me that he could help me repair the Hideaway.

After parking the tractor, Scoop came to the barn. "Well, I've finished. It came out lookin' smoother than a cow's hide."

"Good job." I pushed my cap back. "How about helping me this afternoon? We'll start fixing the Hideaway."

"No kiddin'?" His eyes widened. "You're puttin' that thing back together?" He thoughtfully stroked his beard. "You know, climbin' ain't my bag."

"Scoop, after I feed the heifers, we can do it with ladders and a come-along."

"Yup, with me hangin' in mid-air."

I laughed. "Don't worry."

When I headed to the house for lunch, Cooner was talking to Mildred Butson. He acted as a verbal historian in regards to the Murray family. He was telling Mildred what he remembered hearing about Capt. Ezekiel Murray, who was killed at the battle of Gettysburg. Mildred, president of the Booster Club, was planning to rededicate the newly refurbished Capt. Murray stained-glass window in church on July 16.

Besides her prepared dedication, Mildred wanted to recognize Capt. Murray's descendants. My folks groaned at the idea, but agreed to attend church. Ruth, of course, would be there and I was willing. I hesitated calling Ellen at school to invite her, since I wasn't sure she'd forgiven me yet for the incident with Eve. But I held my breath and called anyway.

"To church?" came her unenthusiastic reply.

"Mom is planning a big dinner afterward. I'd like it if you'd come."

"Oh...Okay." She continued to sound cool.

"I'll pick you up." I injected some life into my offer. "A few minutes before church at eleven."

"O...kay." Came her monotone answer.

I hung up, feeling deflated. Obviously, she was still put out with me.

Of all of us invited to church for the ceremony, Cooner acted the most excited. He'd never been to church except for weddings and funerals. This was a big deal for him.

In the afternoon, Ruth went to get help from Chris for her speech to be given in New York. On returning for night chores, she was encouraged. "Chris has offered to go with me. We're leaving Friday on the five a.m. bus."

"I'm surprised he's willing to take the time."

"I'm not." Ruth passed me with calf pails full of milk as I put a machine on a cow. "He's really into my project." She sounded light-hearted.

"Good." I stepped to the aisle. "I'm glad you have his help."

Ruth set the pails on the floor "Oh, by the way, thank goodness you shut off the hay dryer. We won't have to hear that thing anymore."

"Yeah, and I disconnected the jumper wires you used."

"Good; did you throw them away?"

"No, they're in the bottom of the box. Just in case we need to start it again."

"Well, I hope we don't."

eighteen

Ruth

While I'd shared my problems of funding for the center with Cooner, I felt I had to bring my folks up-to-date with what was going on—why I was leaving the next morning for New York. I dreaded discussing the trip. Cooner had told me what I already knew. My folks weren't interested in a project unless it made money.

Cooner, Mom, Dad, and I were seated around the dinner table. Jason stood at the kitchen sink, looking out the window, probably dreaming of Ellen or the bobcat picture he hoped to take someday. Dad, studying his leaflets, continued to try and make sense of the turf business. Mom sat with her hand on her coffee cup. Cooner left for the living room to watch TV.

This was my chance. I was nervous, because I knew I was facing disapproval. I launched into the subject with the grace of a pitchfork rather than a smooth entry such as "By the way."

"I...I'm leaving in the morning for New York." My words sort of hung in suspension...silence. I shifted my feet under the table.

Dad looked up. "New York?"

"Yeah, Chris and I."

Mom brightened. "To see a show and the sights of the Big Apple?"

"Well... not really." I glanced at my plate. I didn't want to revisit the sharp contrast in our values and witness their disappointment in my humanitarian efforts. However, they deserved to know the purpose of my trip. "I'm meeting with the Board that funds the Center."

"Why?" Dad asked, sounding uninterested.

Mom rolled her eyes. "Haven't you already served your time?"

"Certainly not!" I was annoyed. "Look. This is something that's very dear to me. I want my efforts at the Center to continue!" I drew a deep breath. "Plus, there's a little girl there that I love as if she were my own."

Dad scowled, saying nothing. He put aside his turf information and left the house.

Mom knew I was angry, so turned her back and started cleaning up the kitchen.

I went to my room with a hollow feeling—a feeling that I didn't belong. But I vowed that my folks' values wouldn't stop me from my desire to help these kids.

Friday morning, Cooner brought me to meet the five a.m. bus. We were in his truck, waiting in front of the Huntersville Town Hall. My stomach felt knotted as I bit my bottom lip. "I hope this trip amounts to something."

Cooner turned to me. "Ya can't say ya ain't tried." He patted my arm. "They'll like what ya say."

"I love you, Cooner." I nervously chuckled. "I hope the folks in New York doling out the money will think the same."

He took some Beechnut from his shirt pocket. "I wish I was goin'." He put a pinch in his mouth. "I'd tell 'em, ya betcha, I'd tell 'em!" He spat. "About the girl I raised."

"I'm sure you would."

We sat in silence. I rolled down my window. The village was quiet with no traffic. All I could hear, some distance away, was a barking dog. The early light cast shadows over the brick buildings along Main Street. The outline of a dark figure walked toward the truck. "Here comes Chris." I grinned. "He's sneaking out of town."

"Well, I ain't tellin' nobody." Cooner spat out his window. "There's a lot more worse things goin' on."

"Thanks for your unbiased opinion." I chuckled and listened intently. "The bus is coming." I jumped out of the truck with my overnight bag in hand. "I'll see you tomorrow night."

Cooner yelled from his window, "Stand right up to those city folks, now." He chugged away in his old Chevy.

Chris came from across the street. "Good morning."

"'Morning, Chris." I looked up at him. "You've gotten a haircut."

"Yeah, primping for the big city." He smiled.

The Vermont Transit bus came to a stop. The air brakes blasted a loud *hiss* as the door flew open. Chris pushed his glasses in place and looked up and down the street—no one. I heard his "phew" as I stepped onto the bus. He followed me. There were just a few passengers. We put our bags overhead and got settled.

Chris was good company. We talked about places we'd been, my mission to help the Piedmont kids, and some about past friends. Talking with him eased my mind as to what lay ahead. By mid-afternoon we were in Manhattan, passing the Theodore Roosevelt Park on 77th Street. The bus continued on to the New York Port Authority, traveling to the lower level into relative darkness as it passed a long line of parked buses at specified gates called the North Terminal. Our bus parked at a Vermont Transit gate.

My expectations were restrained. My nervousness intensified as I took a deep breath, wondering if I could say anything convincing enough to move the Board.

We flagged a taxi and hurried to the World Trade Center. I checked the directions—the 39th floor of the North Tower. We had a four-thirty appointment at the office of the All World Bank, the financial institution that administered the Elias M. Cole Foundation. We easily located the place. Large gold lettering on glass, *All World Bank*, faced us as Chris swung the glass door open. I felt my feet sink as we stepped onto the thick carpeting. We passed between two Greek-style columns of gray granite at the entrance. A gold-plated map of the world spread across the fabric walls on both sides of a receptionist. She was seated in a black leather chair behind a marble-top desk. She greeted us pleasantly and led us to the vestibule of the board room where we were to meet Mr. Cobb, the Cole Foundation director.

The image of the village of Piedmont flashed before me with its red dusty roads and junk cars as we passed through the richly furnished offices. The place was filled with busy cosmopolitan-type professionals. I was reminded of old black men, shriveled from age and the sun, seated on empty five-gallon oil cans, drinking sweet tea in the town square under the shade of a chinaberry tree. Young kids, in shorts and barefoot, excitedly screamed while shooting baskets with a ball of crumpled paper wrapped with duct tape. Young girls watched as stray dogs snuck behind makeshift sheds looking for something to eat. I blinked to bring myself back to my elaborate surroundings, turning to glance at Chris who followed me.

We met Mr. Cobb coming from the board room. He introduced himself—a dark, handsome guy in his thirties, a preppy sort—three-piece suit, highly polished tasseled shoes, and neatly trimmed hair. He showed no particular interest when meeting Chris and me. He waved the flat of his hand at chairs. "Have a seat, and you'll be called in due time." Far from engaging, he said in an aloof tone, "Remember, make it short and to the point."

As he walked away, Cobb's tasseled shoes caught my eye. I was reminded of some old men in Piedmont, wearing rubber clogs cut from discarded tire treads. They were held in place with rawhide.

I wore a business suit and hadn't yet allowed myself to be intimidated by the posh atmosphere. However, I felt tension building—a familiar tightness in my stomach. I swallowed to clear a dry mouth. There were others also making their requests. I noticed all sorts of visual aids such as charts and graphs that people had brought to plead their cases. I reread the presentation that Chris had helped me prepare.

He leaned over and said quietly, "Show just the one group picture of the kids. That should be enough." Even he was getting tense.

I jokingly whispered, "I should have worn my bandana and jeans; that would really impress."

Chris smiled and silently sat.

Names were called and presenters left for the board room. They filed in and out in a rather rapid fashion. Even though I'd checked my appearance in the women's room, I reexamined the front of my jacket.

The receptionist called out, "Ruth Murray," and we entered the room.

Chris sat in a corner in back.

I was seated at the head of a mahogany conference table. I smiled, while facing three men and four women. Probably most were in their sixties. They had pads of paper, pens, and spreadsheets resting on the shiny surface. All were wearing dress suits. I surmised they were middle to high-end bank executives. I wondered if any were hard-driven activists for the underprivileged, or could they remotely understand deprivation in a far-off place in our country? The thought occurred to me that some had tried to put the brakes on the aging process, considering their hair coloring. I inwardly sighed; these folks might be a hard sell. I was caught off-guard by a balding, portly guy seated at the far end of the table. He was giving me the once-over with searching eyes. I figured he was more interested in me than in what I might have to say.

Mr. Cobb, in a tired voice, introduced me, "Ruth Murray represents the Piedmont Community Center in Piedmont, Georgia. The religious community has been helping to support the Center. We fund a staff person for the purpose of teaching and tutoring forty children, plus help with the running expenses."

Rapidly, he read from a prepared script of the Foundation's benefactors.

"Last year at this time, we committed forty thousand to the Piedmont Center. We agreed to support it due to a surplus of revenue. The project fit the goals of our Foundation: the education of disadvantaged African-Americans."

His voice rose on "disadvantaged," probably to impress me or the board. I wasn't sure.

Mr. Cobb continued, "Since our support of the Piedmont Center is relatively recent, and since there have been reversals in the Cole portfolio, I'm suggesting that Board members keep that in mind while considering Ms. Murray's request."

My aggressive juices kicked in, having heard Cobb's veiled hint to drop funding altogether. I knew I had to use plenty of passion to move the group. I glanced at the portly detractor at the end of the table. He was doodling on his pad of paper, seeming to be totally bored. Cobb fidgeted, his legs nervously jouncing. He seemed eager to end the meeting—no doubt thinking about his Happy Hour.

I cleared my throat. "Thank you for inviting me here today. And thank you for funding the Piedmont Center this past year. I became involved in working at the Center through VISTA."

The big guy's eyes honed in on the front of my tailored suit jacket. I felt fired up and stood up, in spite of being thoroughly examined. "I'm here today as a daughter from middle-class America—a well-dressed, well-educated woman of comfortable means. I ate decent meals today—a fact that no doubt matches most of you seated at this table."

My riveting eyes and clear voice appeared to capture the attention of most of those seated. I continued, while scanning the group for direct eye contact, noticing a diamond brooch on the lapel of one woman, a guy with a gold watch, and the blazing blue tie of another. I used my hands to help encourage the Board to envision each point. However, I didn't have the attention of Cobb or the big guy.

"Imagine for a moment that your mother is thirteen years old—a homeless street girl in Atlanta—a prostitute. She has no home, no parents, no way to earn money except to sell herself. She becomes pregnant. After months of roaming the streets, labor pains begin. She finds refuge under the cover of a cardboard refrigerator box."

My dramatic description stirred several as they winced and "ooed" in disbelief. I paused, glancing at faces, the watch, the brooch, the tie. These folks were with me. Cobb and the big guy still weren't.

"This wretched girl, who soon would be your mother, can only do what others have done: leave you on the steps of a church or at the entrance of a police station. The only gift given you is a name on a scrap of paper, *Anadeepa*, pinned to your blanket."

I raised my voice, hoping to further stir the Board, especially my two detractors. Mr. Cobb looked at his watch.

"A year ago, Anadeepa was taken into foster care along with four other preschool children. The caretaker was a cleaning woman at a local nursing home. An old woman, suffering from dementia, babysat the children during the day. The Piedmont Center knew of the situation and took those children, and others in similar situations."

I stopped to allow the visualization of the last few words. I breathed deeply and continued.

Cobb stared off. The big guy continued doodling on his print-out. Despite their disinterest, I felt most of the board's full sympathy for the cause. The brooch lady seemed especially interested.

"The Elias M. Cole Foundation provides a home and education for these children, through the employment of a highly qualified black teacher. Because of the funding, you give these youngsters a jump-start in public schools."

I took a drink from the glass resting in front of me.

"In Piedmont, the public schools are overcrowded and underfunded. The white children, for the most part, go to private or religious schools. Most of the children at the Piedmont Center were performing well below their grade level before Sara, the teacher you're supporting, came to the Center. I'm happy to report that since her arrival there has been a noticeable improvement in test scores."

I hesitated for a moment.

"If…if it were not for the Center and your Foundation, many of these children would drop through the cracks, ending up in the streets, turning to drugs and the sex market."

I glanced at my watch. "Right now, Sara is working with the children in an after-school program." I held up an enlarged group picture of the kids. "These are the children you're supporting."

I sensed my message had moved most because they sat quietly, watching me as if I might have more to say. I glanced from face to face. "Are there any questions?"

The brooch lady commented, "This is a worthy project we should fund." Several nodded in agreement.

The big guy off-handedly grumbled, "So are all of the causes we support."

Cobb added, "We just simply don't have the resources to cover all the needs."

I nodded. "I've appreciated my chance to be here." I turned to leave. "Please keep the children of the Piedmont Center in mind when considering your funding. Thank you again for your undivided attention."

Mr. Cobb led us from the board room. "I'll notify you by September 15 as to the adjusted amount of our support."

I nodded.

He spoke in a matter-of-fact tone. "You'll need an additional major sponsor if you continue the work at the center."

"I understand." I turned to leave. "Please do what you can."

On our way to the elevator Chris caught my arm. "You sure captivated those folks."

"Thanks...maybe so." We stepped into the elevator. "Regardless, I've got to search for more funding."

Riding down from the 39th floor, I watched as the numbers zipped by. Suddenly, I felt a flash of fear, awakening to the fact that little to no funding would mean some of the children I'd grown to love would languish at the Center. Earlier, I'd thought as much, but now reality had set in—seeing homeless children, mostly girls, roaming the big city streets after they are too old to stay at the Center and too behind in school to warrant more education. The thought froze me in place. I imagined being lifted from the elevator and placed at the door of the Piedmont Center, pushing children like Anadeepa out on the street. "Go, you're on your own. Public school has given up on you."

I was gripped by the reality that I just had to find more funding. Even in the face of Cooner's doubts—maybe I needed to ask my folks. They'd never supported a non-profit or given much to the church.

Beneath my feet, the elevator settled to a stop. I stood in another world stunned, thinking of Georgia, yet vaguely aware of my surroundings: the antiseptic smells, the rush of air against my face as the elevator door swished open, the feel of Chris's hand as he pulled me forward, the sound of voices, and the sight of busy traffic. My thoughts continued to be in rural Georgia, red dust wafting toward me, dogs barking, roosters crowing, the thermometer hovering in the hundred-degree range, the baked roads burning my feet. I was soul-bound to each child, fearing that no support would surely mean wandering in a dangerous world—homeless.

"Ruth!" Chris shook me.

"Oh...what?"

"Are you okay?" He held me by the arm. We weaved around and between busy pedestrians, scurrying somewhere at the close of the workday.

I sighed in deep thought, while looking down at the sidewalk. "I'm so worried for those kids."

"You can't deal with the problem now." He put his arm around me as we walked.

"That sounds logical, but something needs to be done about it real soon!" I pulled away from him. "I know acquiring funding takes time. Solicitations have to go before boards. Even if the request is honored, months can pass before any money comes."

"Well, let it go for tonight!" he urged.

I turned to Chris. "After dinner, I'm going to spend some time on the Internet."

"Okay, but right now I'm hungry." Near Times Square Chris found a restaurant. He led me through the door.

I was totally distracted. A host dressed in black greeted us. "Dinner for two?"

"Yes." Chris held my hand, dragging me along. A waitress seated us and left two menu folders. At the table, I gazed onto the street, watching the hurried cosmopolitan crowd pass by—men in suits, women in business attire. Several poodles on leashes trotted by, immaculately groomed, sporting pom-pom hair balls —their handlers dressed to the nines. The display of opulence began to depress me. I felt uneasy. This wasn't where I wanted to be. These weren't my people. People in this world had so much.

A waiter came to our table and flicked his lighter, reaching for the wick in the wax-filled goblet. He filled our water glasses that rested on white linen—clutching the glass pitcher to his chest as if it were valuable crystal. He asked in a high nasal voice, "What's your pleasure for a drink?"

Chris reached for my hand and jarred me to attention. "What would you like?"

"Just water." I returned to my shell.

He glared at me, pushing his glasses in place. He blurted, "A dry martini. Very dry!"

The waiter left. I glanced at the menu—thirty and forty-dollar entrées. I winced and closed the folder. I glanced toward the window again, not focusing but in a daze. Finally, I turned back, looking at those seated. Waiters carried dinner plates on huge circular trays above their heads, swirling them like flying saucers to land on tray stands. The heaping portions, beautifully garnished, filled white porcelain plates. The sight sent me into yet a darker mood—hating where I was. I surmised that the total take for one week in this place would more than cover the expenses of the Piedmont Center for several months.

Chris studied the wine list, turning it toward me, pointing in jest. "Let's splurge and order this bottle of chardonnay, a 1934 vintage." He chuckled. "It's only eighty-five dollars."

"Unreal!" I was about to explode in a mixture of depression and anger. I felt my heart beat in my throat. My head began to pound. My sight was blurry. "I've got to leave," I blurted. "Blowing money on an expensive dinner just doesn't seem right!"

Chris nervously laughed, "Gosh, Ruth, let's not take on the world's problems tonight."

"I...I can't take this!" I began to cry. "Dammit, Chris!" I madly waved my arms. My voice trembled. "Doesn't this bother you?" I lurched toward him, wildly yelling, "I can't stand being here!"

The waiters and the dinner crowd stared as if I were at center stage. Seeing the host rushing toward me, I jumped up and ran for the door.

As I rushed by, a dinner guest in a deep voice loudly grumbled, "She's drunk as hell."

The comment infuriated me. I turned and yelled before I shoved the door open. "No, I'm not!" I left crying.

Chris, dumbfounded, was right behind. "Let's go to the hotel before you end up in jail."

Out on the street, the fresh night air felt good. I settled down and said, chagrined, "I'm sorry, Chris. I lost it."

"Oh, no kidding!" He looked on both sides of the street. "Let's find a deli."

I grabbed his hand. "Are you mad at me?"

"No." He chuckled. "But I didn't think dinner would be such an adventure."

"Sorry."

"It's okay." He looked from side to side. "I just need something to eat."

"After dinner, using the hotel computer, I do want to continue to explore possible organizations that might support the Center."

"Go ahead." Chris was searching. "There's a place down the street... a deli."

Finally, with a bag of food, we headed for the hotel. Seated at a small table in our room, I commented, "This is a little more my style."

He hungrily munched a quantity of egg salad from a Styrofoam dish—then took a sip from a Coke can. "I agree." He chuckled. "At least we won't be shoved out the door." He smiled. "With you, I'm never quite sure."

"I'll try and control myself." I ate some cold chicken. "I'm sorry this trip hasn't been much fun for you"

"That's okay." He reached for my hand. "The effort was for a good cause."

"Thanks for your support." I squeezed his hand. "It means a lot." I got up to leave. "If I can get the use of a computer, I might be gone for a while."

He flopped on his bed. "I'm tired. I'll be dead to the world when you get back."

I spent an hour or so in the hotel office on the Internet. While searching, I located The Child Welfare Information Network (CWIN). This organization showed promise. It more closely matched the Center's needs. I composed a letter, hoping to contact a Network representative.

I returned to our room, changed into my pj's, and crawled into bed. Chris slept soundly several feet away. I smiled, thinking of the people back home and what they might be saying: "Reverend Ball left town with Ruth Murray and they shacked up in a New York hotel." I chuckled. Guess what, folks? It wasn't romantic.

Early the next morning at the Port Authority, we boarded a bus back to Vermont. I took the window seat, and Chris flopped into the aisle seat. He acted like a zombie.

An hour later, he woke. "I didn't realize how tired I was."

"Well, you were sound asleep."

He reached for my hand. "I'm hoping your effort might yield some results."

I lurched forward and covered my face, holding back tears. "I'm doubting it will."

"I understand." His arm slid around me.

"No, you don't understand!" I shook off his arm.

"What are you saying?" He turned to me puzzled.

"I feel very alone in this cause."

"Alone!" He raised his voice. "I helped you!"

"But my talk didn't work and the Center is short of funds." I spoke in a defeated tone.

"Well, you tried." He sat forward for eye contact.

"Where do I go from here? I'm on my own." I grabbed his arm. "Right?"

"As much as I'd like to, I can't continue to spend a lot of time with you." He paused. "My job and the agreement."

"Yeah, the agreement!" I sighed. "Chris, I'm not going to…" I paused. "Expect anything more from you." I turned my head toward the window. The bus whizzed past a grove of white birches. "We'll be home soon. Let's be honest with our feelings." I looked at him. "Let's decide right here and now. Where do we go from here?"

"Nothing has changed." Chris pushed his glasses.

"Okay." I turned back toward the window. "In other words, spending more time with me is out of the question."

"It is, unless I can get the Board to agree to a change." He rested his hand on my shoulder. "I'll ask at our next meeting."

"Gosh, so damn formal!" I watched for his reaction.

He nodded.

"Look, I like being with you. We have similar interests. I suppose the clergy aren't supposed to have sexual desires?"

"Hey, I'm a normal guy. Falling in love…would…would be easy."

I looked straight into his eyes. "Thank you. I wonder at times."

We said nothing for a while. The hum of the bus and singing tires filled the void of quietness.

"You don't have to wonder about me." He slid his arm over my shoulder

"Chris…I…I already love you." Our eyes met. I hesitated and held his hand. "Love…isn't something…you can turn on and off."

The bus purred along. There were few passengers. No one could see us.

Our heads rested on the seat back, nearly touching. I reached for his upper arm and pulled him closer. Our lips were warm as we kissed. We held each other in a hug for long moments.

"I love you, too, Ruth."

We hugged and kissed again.

It was late Saturday afternoon when the bus pulled to a stop in front of the Huntersville Town Hall. We said our goodbyes. Walking down the aisle of the bus, I turned to him. "Oh, by the way, you'll be at the house tomorrow after church?"

"Sure." He stepped onto the street.

"Good. Mom's planning a big dinner."

He didn't look left or right but headed down the street toward the church.

I went to Cooner's truck parked in the shade of a maple. He was sleeping with his head resting on the closed window. I smiled and knocked before opening the door.

He jerked awake. "Well, well, my girl's home." He sat forward. "How did it go?"

"It doesn't look good. I'm worried sick about the Center." I jumped into the truck.

"Don't worry, ya'll find a way."

"We'll see." I reset my ponytail. "I'm not giving up."

His face brightened as he smiled. "Ya'll never guess what happened while you were gone."

"I wouldn't know...you and Bertha got engaged?" That was the first thing that came to mind, wanting to lift my glum spirits.

He laughed. "Heck, no. My clock's windin' down and old father time ain't about ta rewind it." He sniffed. "Bertha *was* some curious, though, as ta where her young minister disappeared to. She cleaned the church and he wan't nowhere ta be found."

I quickly looked his way. "What'd you tell her?"

"Nothin'. I ain't about ta go back on my promise ta ya."

"Well, tell me then. What *did* happen?"

"The stained-glass window came to town." He reached for the key. "The dedication is happenin'."

"Good! You got your church clothes all laid out?"

"Well, not exactly. I ain't gettin' too fancy for church. The timbers might bust when I walk through the door."

I laughed.

He started the truck. "When I told about the window at Butson's, Clyde Shanks said kinda sneerin', 'Don't the Murrays get all the glory in town? If a Murray steps in gutter slop, their foot turns ta gold'."

I glared toward Cooner, raising my voice. "Yeah, well, Clyde's jealous. He can't claim any of his forefathers served in the Civil War!"

Cooner glanced my way. "What's ailin' ya? You act as high-strung as an old hen."

I sighed. "I wonder what will happen if I can't find support."

He reached with one hand off the wheel and patted my forearm. "Keep tryin'." He spat out his window. "Somethin' will come up."

nineteen

Jason

The day Ruth was in New York the temperature at the farm rose to 90 degrees. In fact, all month the July heat bore down on us. The grasses turned brittle and appeared dead. The corn was beginning to curl. The weather forecast showed there was no rain in sight. Due to the intense heat and no grass for the animals to graze, I started barn-feeding the milking herd. I used portable fans to try and keep the cows cool.

Daily I checked the Blue River. In twenty-four hours it had slowed to a trickle. I walked along the riverbed to where the heifers drank from a water hole. They pushed and shoved to get at a small riled pool among the boulders. Alarmed at the lack of water, I decided the heifers had to come home.

I also worried that one was missing—Penny, one of the three black daughters of Precious. She was carrying a calf that could be the red and white bull.

I charged up the steep cow path, the path the heifers used to come for water. Animals seldom leave the herd unless they're in trouble. Most of the heifers were due to calve in August and early September. Perhaps an early calving was the case with Penny. As I hurried over the land, the dry ground crunched underfoot. The landscape ahead was tinder dry. Even the thistles and goldenrod were curling to a crispy brown.

I was anxious, thinking of a bull contract for five thousand dollars. I checked on Penny only yesterday. Although she was developing an udder, I never suspected she was close to calving. "I hope she's okay." I stopped on high ground and closely searched the open pasture. The only place she could be hidden was along the hedgerow in the tall weeds next to the pines.

Although hot and short of breath, I continued to run the quarter mile to the pines. I spotted her along the fence. She was flat out on her side, her legs periodically kicking, the tell-tale sign she was trying to calve.

When I reached her, I could see that her water bag had broken, and showing from her vulva, two dry hooves faced skyward. The calf was coming breech. The dryness told me she'd been trying for a while. She couldn't calve without my help. By nightfall coyotes would have picked up the birthing scent and killed her in minutes.

I didn't dare take the time to go back to the barn to get the calving chains and puller. For all I knew, coyotes could already be lurking in the cover of the pine grove.

Thankfully, I wore a wide leather belt. The width would allow for the hard pull I needed. I slipped the length of the belt through the buckle, forming a loop I put around the hooves. I had length enough to put the remainder of the strap partly around my middle. Since she was early, the calf's feet and legs were small.

I sat on the ground with my knees bent and feet pressed against the heifer's rump. With each contraction, I held tightly to the end of the belt, pulling with my arms and pushing with my legs. Breech births are not always successful. When the umbilical cord breaks, the calf has to come quickly, which is not always possible. I'd experienced stillbirths before, when the calf came through a tight birthing canal too slowly and was born DOA.

This calf's legs came easily. But Penny's cervix had not yet stretched enough for the hips to pass through the canal. I doubled down on my effort. The torque of the belt squeezed my fingers and knuckles. The calf inched out ever so slowly. Suddenly, there was a release. The hips had passed the cervix. The cord had broken.

Now a couple of feet from Penny's rump, I dug my heels into the ground. The calf had to come fast or it would take on fluid and drown. I didn't wait for a contraction. My hands hurt and the belt cut into my back, but that wasn't a concern. I saw the calf was red and white. I was excited, seeing color, and all the more determined to deliver a live calf. One more gigantic pull—the calf slipped out. I quickly put its hind legs over my shoulders and stood. Its head hung near the ground. A string of thick fluid flowed from its mouth. Its muzzle twisted in a sniff to draw a breath. The calf had survived the journey. I quickly looked for the sex. There it was—a white scrotum the size and shape of a change purse. I could have danced a jig—a potential sale to Canada.

Penny lifted her head and let out a motherly *moo*. I carried the calf within her reach. She stood and started drying him with her rough tongue. Now, she would be able to fend off any predator.

I ran toward home. I needed water for Penny, and I had to be sure the calf nursed his mother's first milk. I charged from the ridge, down the wood's road, my feet pounding over the bridge, reaching home. I jumped on the John Deere and hooked up the two-wheel trailer. In the milk house, I ran water in a bucket and brought along a nipple bottle just in case I couldn't get the calf to nurse right away.

Luckily, Cooner drove in the yard. I yelled, "I need your help! Ruth's working on accounts at the shop!" I loaded the water and jumped on the trailer. "Drive the tractor to the pines. We have a red and white bull calf!"

"Well, I'll be!" He gimped from his truck and climbed aboard the tractor. "What are you namin' him?"

"Rover Red."

Cooner drove in first gear. We soon reached Penny and the calf. After watering Penny and helping the calf nurse, I sat on the back edge of the trailer and held him in my arms. Penny followed. By this time the other seven heifers had joined us.

Arriving home, Cooner stopped the tractor at the back of the barn. I carried Rover Red. All the heifers crowded to enter the barn. Cooner was in back of them.

I jumped in surprise. "What the...a rat!" It scurried between the heifers' legs and climbed the electrical cable leading to the hay dryer motor. I shivered, seeing its long brown body, sharp claws, and grisly tail traverse the cable in a matter of seconds.

"Geez!" Cooner yelled. "Even the rats are lookin' for a home!"

"After we tie up these heifers, I'll set out some poison."

twenty

Ruth

Sunday morning Jason and I hurried through chores. All of us Murrays were due in church for the dedication of the stained-glass window. Jason left the barn early to get cleaned up, thinking of Ellen. I swept the hay into the mangers and washed down the floor in the milk room.

After finishing, I went to the house. Mom was busy making salads for Sunday dinner. Dad was in the house office, deep into the study of turf farming.

I showered and went to my room. Since I was going to be introduced to an expected big crowd, I put on a white blouse, my light powder blue jacket, and navy slacks. Cooner, never having worn dress clothes, wore a Carter work shirt and denim work pants. Dad and Mom dressed casually.

It was a beautiful day, except for an unusual easterly breeze sweeping the valley. The stiff air moved the pungent smell of the parched land. The leaves rattled in the maples.

The farmstead looked great. The late morning sun glistened off the red cow barn. Yesterday, Jason had mowed the lawn in front of the barn. Since we had a driven well that never went dry, we had a dependable source for the house and barn and extra water for the lawn. We left the farm in two vehicles for the eleven o'clock service. I rode in Jason's truck.

On the way to church he was in high spirits. He was telling me about the sales contract for Rover Red he'd received in Saturday's mail. "The contract has plenty of contingencies, but I hope we can make the grade on them." He turned to me. "The big question will be if Penny passes the buyer's inspection."

"Let's hope." I looked at his smooth-shaven face, square jaw, deeply set blue eyes, and neatly trimmed short hair, realizing, not for the first time, that I had a handsome brother. His casual dress, shirt opened at the neck, tucked into a neatly pressed pair of khakis, added to his good looks. But looks wasn't what I most admired about Jason. It was his assertiveness, strong-willed direction, and leadership that I was most proud of.

Jason pulled into Gilda's yard to pick up Ellen. I smiled, seeing slender Ellen in her bright yellow summer jacket, running toward the truck through the wind with her hand holding her hair in place. She carried a small white bag in her other hand. "She's beautiful, Jason."

Jason blushed. "Yeah."

"Hi, Ellen." I jumped out of the truck. "Quite the wind!"

"Whew, I guess." She slid in beside Jason. "Hi, there."

He glowed, I think because it was obvious Ellen had forgiven him for the Eve incident.

Going into the church, we all sat in two pews next to the stained-glass window. It had a drape covering it.

Following the church service, a short special program was held. Eve, vice president of the Booster Club, unveiled the work of art of the kindly shepherd holding his lost lamb. The church was filled with folks wanting to see the refurbished window.

Several came just for the dedication. Iverson, having brought Eve, was there, not wanting to miss a chance to hobnob with his constituents. He had even cleaned himself up for the occasion.

Mildred Butson did a good job of extolling the virtues of Capt. Ezekiel Murray. She told of his heroism, plus his gift to the Union of his Morgan stallion, Star.

At Gettysburg, Murray, on his rugged mount, charged the front line to hold back the Confederates. Star went down, having been struck by a rain of fire. On foot, Murray pushed forward in hand-to-hand combat. He was killed minutes later.

Cooner hadn't left anything out in giving Mildred information that lavished the long-departed Murray with praise as a successful breeder of highly valued Morgans. Introducing his descendants was painless since we all stood as a group. The service ended with Chris offering a short prayer.

At the farm, after church, the strong easterly breeze continued, pushing at our backs as we ran for the house. Mom started putting the meal on the table.

Jason and Ellen sat on a bench in the kitchen. I noticed she pulled a new Red Sox cap from her bag. It was blue with a white **B** on the front panel. "Here, Jason, try this." She reached and put it on him. "It's brand new." Her color slightly changed. "Doctor Reed gave it to me. He was at a game last week."

"Oh, Doctor…"

Ellen smiled. "He's just a friend."

Jason adjusted the cap. "Gee, thanks." He put his arm around her and gave her a hug.

I was anxious to see Chris. He must have been held up at church. I kept checking for him through the side window that faced the yard. Dust and small twigs scattered across the paved drive toward the house. Through the slightly raised window, the curtains fluttered.

When I checked again for Chris, the aluminum fan shroud on the side of the barn caught my attention. I was curious about the strange exhaust—unusual coming from the barn, similar to the morning mist rising from a plowed field.

The mist was smoke!

"Fire!"

Jason charged for the door. "Call the fire department!"

We ran, flinging the barn door open. Smoke was coming from the hay dryer. I could hear the crackling. "The cows!"

We hurriedly unhooked each cow. Fire and smoke shot from the exit door where the herd normally left. The cattle balked and turned in confusion and ran back to their stalls. We had no choice but to force them to leave by a narrow door they had never used before. We pushed Precious toward the opening. She reacted, hesitating and bracing her legs. We continued pushing on her butt, moving her foot by foot. Finally, she jumped to safety. The herd followed easier since they saw Precious outside, but it was taking too long to free the cows. The fire increased rapidly. The stable was packed with smoke. We pushed calves and skittish heifers out the door. Rover Red was the last to leave.

After emptying the stable, we hurried out, coughing. The stiff breeze buffeted the back of the barn. The fire roared like a blast furnace through the overhead hay dryer duct that ran the length of the barn.

Ellen and Cooner helplessly watched as they stood in the yard.

Jason and I ran to where the hay dryer was located. We were stunned seeing the flames lap up the back of the barn. Jason yelled, "Round up the cattle!"

We ran to control the herd. The heat was too intense to be near the barn. We were trying to direct the cows from the yard toward the meadow. A bellowing Precious stood by the farm sign. Just as she was about to head in the right direction, screaming sirens entered the yard. Firefighters in yellow suits poured out of the trucks. An ambulance pulled onto the lawn next to the road.

The noise scattered the herd in several directions; they ran for the meadow, the yard, the road. The red bull calf raced past me back into the barn. I yelled, "Rover Red!" and lunged to catch him. The calf charged into the dense smoke. I followed.

I could hear Jason yell, "It's too late!"

Past the door the smoke overcame the calf. He fell to his knees and collapsed. I instantly lost my strength and fell onto Rover Red. My face rested between his out-stretched front legs. I gasped for a breath. On the floor there was less smoke. I gagged and drew another breath. The heat overpowered me. I lost all consciousness. Dizzy…that's all I remember.

twenty-one

Jason

"Ruth ! Oh my God!" My mind frozen in fear, beyond all reason, I dove through the smoke to catch her—but it was too late. My chest felt like it could explode. I bent over, gasping for air, and backed out of the barn. The heat felt like I could turn to flames in seconds.

"Ruth!" Mom and Dad screamed. "She's in the barn!"

Two firemen wearing breathing apparatuses and protective clothing ran in after her. The seconds ticked by.

Flames curled out the barn door and shot up the outside of the barn. I heard something collapse onto the stable floor. Fiery particles landed on me. They were burning through my shirt like a branding iron. An ember landed on my new cap**,** scorching a hole, singeing my hair. I brushed them off. Later, I realized the heat had scorched my face. At the moment, I was paralyzed in fear for Ruth. I stood in place waiting, willing the firemen to come from the smoke bringing Ruth.

"They've got to save her!" I pressed my clenched fists against my head.

Within seconds a fireman hurried from the barn with a limp Ruth in his arms. Her head hung lifeless. Her ponytail was gone, arms dangled, with hands cranberry red. The sleeves of her powder blue jacket were scorched to a brown. The fireman rushed her toward the ambulance and laid her on a waiting stretcher. Dad, Mom, and I rushed to follow. The stretcher slid instantly into the ambulance. The doors slammed shut.

Taking off his breathing apparatus, the fireman said, "Luckily, she wasn't far inside."

I looked toward the barn; the second fireman came out carrying Rover Red. The bull's mouth hung wide open, showing his tongue. He was coughing, gasping for air.

Chris had just arrived at the farm. Dad and Mom and he followed the screaming ambulance in their cars. Ellen and Cooner were in his truck. His head lay on the steering wheel. Ellen, trying to console him, rested her arm on his shoulder.

The firemen were desperately trying to stop the fire from spreading to the house. The house was being soaked with torrents of water coming from two hoses.

Stepping back from the fire, I could see the end of the barn where it had started. The trusses, boarding, and roofing caved and fell like matchsticks. Suddenly, there was an explosion. The barn roof heaved off its bearings and settled back. Fire poured out the mow windows.

Stunned in my tracks, I felt my face, stiff, hot, and burned. I repeatedly ran my tongue across my burned lips. My eyebrows were prickly stubble. My dress shirt and khakis were peppered with black marks. I took off my cap. It too was covered with burn holes.

I tried to gather my thoughts while feeling my scorched forehead. The sight of Ruth flashed before me. I wanted to run to my truck, tear off after the ambulance, but I couldn't—the cattle. They had charged toward the meadow. They scattered like ants on the run. I stood in shock, trying to get my bearings. I looked over the disorder. Neighbors and friends had gathered. Cars and trucks had pulled to the side of the road.

With the barn fully involved, the intensely hot clapboards crumbled. The roofing caved as if it was paper. Burning roof trusses continued to topple. The crispy-dry hay sent smoke and burning particles hundreds of feet high. The easterly breeze pushed the smoke and flames toward the shed and house.

Friends and neighbors had quickly emptied what they could from the barn: bulk milk tank, vacuum pump, hot water heater, desk with important papers, forks, shovels and small tools were brought to the lawn, a safe distance from the fire. The medicine cabinet and contents were rescued. People were rushing into the house to save the furnishings. I saw that the computer with the financial information, the cattle breeding records, and important letters were taken to my truck and placed on the seat.

The fire jumped from the barn to the shed. It was inevitable; the house was next. Steam rolled off the house clapboards, soaked to stop the flames, but the relentless breeze was unforgiving. The firefighters had run out of water. A hose leading to the Blue River lay flat. Water tankers from area towns were empty. There was no way to hold back the destruction. Electrical lines had fallen, cutting power to the driven well. More water was coming, but it would be too late to save the house.

I willed myself to hold back from totally collapsing. Before dealing with the immediate problems, I ran to a fire truck and asked the chief, "Any word on Ruth?"

The chief called the ambulance. "Jason Murray wants to know about his sister."

"Patient is breathing normally."

I ran to Cooner's truck.

Ellen rolled down her window and gasped, "Jason, you look awful!"

Cooner cried, "Ruth!"

"She's stable." I tried not to stir too much emotion. I took a deep breath. "That much we know."

Cooner pushed back in his seat and lowered his hands. His jowls were streaked with tears. He moaned, "But her hands...her hair." His deep wrinkles pulled taut with grief.

I'd never seen Cooner so distraught—gut-torn and limp as a dead man.

I licked my burned lips, forcing myself to push forward. I was aware of the milling cattle. I stood considering, sighing deeply, feeling turmoil. What to do? Standing next to Cooner's truck, I looked down at the ground in deep thought. Something had to be done immediately, no time to consider ramifications or to make financial decisions. Where was I going to bring these cows? Where? Where? They had to be fed and milked in a few hours. The Iverson place was my only choice. There was no other farm close by or empty barns that could stable our cows.

Through the open truck window, I spoke solemnly to Ellen and Cooner. "We're driving the herd to the Iverson place."

Cooner rallied. "Iverson's?"

I grimaced. "We have to."

Resigned, Cooner mumbled, "Yup. You're right."

I reached and held Ellen's forearm. "You drive Cooner to Butson's."

He sat up, pulled his red-checkered handkerchief from his back pocket and wiped his face.

"Cooner, have Butson's men bed a place for our herd at Iverson's." I visualized the conditions even though I had never been near his barns. "Our cattle are to be kept separate from the Iverson herd."

"I'll drive my own truck." Cooner began to cry. "Oh, Ruth...why did she?" He slouched, shaking in grief.

I said sternly, "Ellen, you drive."

I ran to my truck and jumped in the back. A crowd gathered. I looked into the faces of helpers. I couldn't believe what I was being forced to say. Over the sound of the raging inferno, I yelled, "We've got to round up the cattle. We're driving them to the Iverson place."

A young fellow asked, "Right through town?"

"Yup." I shouted, "Several of you go on ahead and clear the traffic."

Helpers and kids ran through the meadow to round up the cattle. After some doing, a human corral bunched the eighty head of cows and young stock. Counting heads, I yelled, "They're all here."

With urging and arm waving, Precious headed onto Murray's Flats. She was making up an udder, showing she was soon to calve. I hoped she could stand the trip okay. One by one, the herd followed, going east toward town. My pick-up truck, driven by a neighbor, had sideboards holding the baby calves and Rover Red. It slowly followed the line of cattle. A teenager stood on the bumper, keeping the unsettled calves from jumping out over the tailgate. I walked behind my truck.

I turned, watching the fire. It fully engulfed the house. From a distance, the lawn looked like a giant yard sale. A patch of darkness overhead caught my eye. A vulture soared, reminding me of the shadow of death—death of the Murray farm. I quickly turned, walking behind the procession.

We were passing the corn. The broad leaves on the densely growing stalks rubbed from the stiff breeze, sounding like clashing swords.

We were traveling a stretch of road that pulled me away from a place I'd always known as home. Off to my right, beyond the huge column of smoke, I could barely see the Hideaway. A pang of separation hit me. I was filled with anxiety, realizing I wouldn't be visiting my favorite place for some time to come. Further east on the ridge, I noticed the deep green pine grove, standing as a marker for generations of Murrays that had farmed in this place. But in a flash, there was no choice but to move on—to be transplanted to another part of town. I felt like a tree, being yanked up by its roots.

The herd had settled. They were walking nearly single file at a slow, dogged pace. The line stretched for over three hundred feet. Their sleek, finished coats shone in the afternoon sun. The drum of their hooves on the pavement sounded similar to hail on a tin roof, but it was a softer, more rhythmic sort of cadence. Except for the sound of hooves, they were quiet, no bawling or bellowing as they moved along. They were satisfied, instinctively realizing their herdsman knew what he was doing.

I hoped the cows could make the three-mile trip without faltering. They, of course, had never been put to such a test of their endurance. I turned, walking backward for a few steps. The cement silo would be the only thing left of the Murray place.

Helpers were keeping the line moving in the road. The wind had settled to a soft breeze. When I went under the shade of old roadside maples, the cool air felt good on my burned face, giving me a shiver. Plodding along, I wondered what had caused the fire. I'd disconnected the jumper wires in the fuse box—maybe rats chewing on a hot electrical wire.

The herd was passing houses with neatly trimmed hedges and manicured lawns. I yelled to the crew, "Keep the cattle in the road. They'd love to walk on soft grass."

We approached Chub's Variety. Bubbles ran out to meet me. "You look terrible. This is awful!" She passed me a Coke. "You must need a drink."

"Thanks, Bubbles." In spite of the situation, the tattooed red apples nestled in greenery across her bare shoulders brought me up short. I drained the can and passed it back. "I didn't realize how thirsty I was."

"You poor guy." She grabbed my arm to stop me. "You look like a barbecued hot dog."

"I feel like one." I pulled away. "It's best I don't think about it."

But I did think about it, after leaving Bubbles. I felt under my cap. My hair was singed under burn holes in my cap. My hands were covered with burn marks. After rubbing my neck, I realized I resembled a burned coal miner. I could smell the smoke on myself. Although I was at least a mile or so away from the fire, each breath brought the lingering odor.

The herd was tiring, carrying their heads lower, but they kept plodding. Up ahead, Dunkin' Donuts was on the left and McDonald's across the street—next came the Huntersville Motel, where the sign read "*Low Rates and A Great Breakfast*," then Flood's Quick Stop and The Tire Store.

In the older section of town, folks lined the street. Traffic stopped, cars pulled to the side, giving the cows the right-of-way. The atmosphere was solemn. The shopkeepers had left their stores and stood watching cow after cow plod along. Even the children sensed the tragedy and quietly stood.

"Where are you headed?" a guy asked.

"The Iverson place."

He shook his head. "Oh my God, good luck!"

"I have no choice." I sensed he knew more than I did.

Eve ran from the Huntersville Bank. "So sad, Jason!" She slid her arm in mine and we walked a few steps. "After work, I'll help Gilda with the food."

"Thanks." I doggedly continued on.

"Sorry, Jason!" A former classmate rested his hand on my back. "I don't know a thing about cows, but call me if you need any help."

"Thanks." I was dazed, forcing myself to move beyond the events of the last hour.

Precious continued to lead the string of tired cattle. Some cows were slowing their pace, leaving gaps from cow to cow. The plodding line had grown to at least four hundred feet long.

We were passing Gilda's. She was there to meet me. "I'm cooking a big dinner for all the helpers."

"Thanks. We'll need some of your good food."

"I've talked to Steven. He'll be at the farm later today. He wants you to settle in wherever." Gilda left, going back to her diner.

I turned and raised my voice. "Call the hospital, will you? Check on Ruth!"

Gilda waved. "I'll send word with Ellen. She's come back and is changing at the apartment."

I was most worried for Ruth, seeing her lying burned and unconscious. I could feel my throat tighten, thinking of all the help and outpouring of sympathy coming my way, but I couldn't dwell on the fact. Even though I felt wobbly, I couldn't drop in my tracks.

The Iverson place was diagonally across the road from Gilda's. Precious was about to enter the driveway. My worries about her making the trip were for naught. She started climbing the drive, still in the lead. Seeing the place, I felt like gagging.

twenty-two

Ruth

"Oh my God! Where am I…my hands! Dad…Mom, is that you?"

Mom stepped close. "You're a lucky girl to have escaped. But hot… like an oven."

Dad stood at the other side of the bed. "The doctor says you have second-degree and some third-degree burns on your hands, and first-degree burns on your face."

"Whatever that means." I tried to focus. "Chris, is that you?"

"Yeah, you can see?" He stood at the foot of the bed.

"Barely." I must be wrapped like a mummy. "Whoa, this pain!"

A nurse checked the monitor and injected a pain killer into the saline line connected to a shunt between my neck and shoulder. "This will ease your pain and put you to sleep."

"What happened?…Jason."

I heard Mom's voice. "We'll tell you later."

twenty-three

Jason

I slowly climbed the grade into the yard of the Iverson place. The drive-way was lined with broken-down equipment: an old spreader half-full of manure with several seasons of dead weeds growing, a hay baler with rotten bales still in the chamber, wrecked hay wagons, an old gray ton-and-a-half truck with a missing door, and a set of broken harrows next to the truck. Several seasons of dead grass and weeds stood in and around these relics.

Taking a deep breath, I studied the buildings. The New England red-faded barn was where it had been for over a hundred years—a tall three-story structure. I noticed through the windows that the milk house and milking parlor were in the old barn at ground level. A modern, single-story, three-hundred-foot-long red barn was attached. It had narrow windows under the eaves, extending the full length.

The story-and-a-half farmhouse sat a hundred feet from the barn. The buildings were equidistant from the road. A modern addition on the backside of the house had been added. It was small. I surmised it was where Iverson lived.

Ellen ran from Gilda's to catch up to me. I waited for her. She gave me a broad smile and a kiss while she reached for my hand. "Ruth is at the Huntersville Hospital. Your mom reports that her condition is not serious enough to be transferred to a burn center."

"That's good news!" I stopped. "She's going to be okay, then?"

"Jason, I've told you all I know."

"I wish I could see her." I scuffed the gravel. "But I can't right now."

Ellen looked me up and down. "Let me get you some better clothes."

"There're more pressing things." I paused, thinking. "There's… there's all our stuff on the lawn. I hope it doesn't rain."

"Don't worry about it." She squeezed my hand. "We have plenty of help."

"Bring our things here and we'll decide what to do."

"Okay. I'll round up some trucks." Ellen left.

The cows were driven toward a vacant shed in back of the barn and house. It was a big enough area for the herd to bed down. Sonny Butson's men and helpers were spreading straw and hooking up a water tub for the herd. Helpers were in the process of separating the young stock, sending them to a pasture. As soon as most of the cows reached the straw bedding, they sniffed at it and flopped down, relieved to be off their feet. Some were thirsty and went for water. Butson's truck, loaded with hay, pulled in the yard.

Cooner sat on the tailgate of his truck, leaning on his cane.

I stopped by him and looked into the shed, watching the herd.

Cooner shook his head. "Any word on Ruth?" He tapped his cane.

"Ellen heard from the hospital. Ruth's going to be okay."

"That's good." He sighed. "Seein' her chase after that calf. I…I thought she was a goner."

"I agree. The heat drove me back. I can't believe she dove in the smoke and flames." I glanced around, sizing up the place. "Well, we've got to move on."

Cooner spat. "This ain't no place ta bring a herd of fancy cattle."

"I know, but it's the best we can do."

"Nothin's right." He tapped his cane again.

Emphatically I said, "We have no choice. We'll have to make it right!"

"Iverson ain't no housekeeper." Cooner glanced toward the barn. "That place ain't fit for cows." He wiped his mouth with his handkerchief. "Worst yet, the creamery shut him off."

"Shut off!" I stared at Cooner. "I'm not surprised."

"Iverson's dead in the water, belly-up." He spat again. "I went to the milk room. It stinks of sour milk and there's no hot water." He shifted and looked for my reaction. "I had to order propane under your name."

I scowled. "Way worse than I thought."

"Wait till ya see what he feeds his cattle." Cooner added, "It's crap!"

"I'll go to the barn and figure how we can get our cows milked."

I headed toward the barn, noticing broken, discarded parts, old electric motors, empty plastic pails, and a transmission from a truck that I recognized. When I opened the door to a hallway, a sour smell struck me. A Mexican couple met me. I assumed they were probably father and daughter.

"Hola." The older man raised his hand. "Mi José." He turned toward the girl. "Iz Rosita, mi hija."

"Your daughter?"

"Sí, sí, mi dautter."

They weren't much over five feet tall. Their jet black hair was mostly covered by their caps. José had a carefully trimmed mustache and carried himself confidently. Rosita's engaging smile caught my attention. They both wore green coveralls, and boots. She could have passed for a fine-featured young boy.

"Hi, I'm Jason, your new boss."

"Boss, sí." José nodded.

"You milk cows?" Their faces were blank. I motioned with clenched fists as if milking by hand.

"Sí, ordeño las vacas," José said.

I opened a door to the milk room. Light from an outside window revealed dirty walls. A seven- or eight-foot tall bulk milk tank faced me—oval in shape, stainless steel, with a ladder attached. I climbed and opened the cover. Immediately, a putrid smell rose from inside. I reached in and slid my finger down the flat inch-and-a-half-wide measuring stick. My whole upper torso hung in the tank. I pushed myself out to get a breath of air. "Geez, this is filthy!" I showed the jelly-like milk slime collected on my finger.

José pointed at the drain. "Leche."

"All the milk down the drain?"

"Sí, sí."

"Aqua está fría." José pointed to the portable tank washer. "Está braukan."

I pushed back my cap. "What isn't broken?"

There was a tank brush with a four-foot handle leaning in the corner of the room. The propane truck flashed by the window. Shortly, the deliveryman entered to light the flame in the water heater.

I figured with hot water and detergent either the father or daughter could get in the tank and at least start the cleaning process. I held the brush, wondering how to communicate what I wanted. Without a word, Rosita washed her boots. She climbed the ladder, swung her small frame on top of the tank and dropped through the circular opening, smaller than the cover of a municipal manhole. The water from a hose started running into the tank. Her delicate hand with child-like fingers waved out the hole. José handed her the brush.

It was obvious, she'd done this before. I noticed the drop-light and pushed the black switch. The light came on. "Hey, it works!"

I hooked it over the opening so Rosita could see. With the aid of hand directions from José, I figured out the automatic washer for the milk line, leading to the milking parlor, and then I added detergent.

Outside the milk room in the hallway, I cringed, glancing toward the milking facility. The stainless steel panels with ten milking machines attached were coated with dried milk and splattered manure. There was a narrow work alley with five milking units on each side.

Checking the rubber lining of several teat cups, I found them greasy, cracked, smelling sour. They needed changing before I could use them on my cows. And of course there were no replacements on hand. I went to the phone in the barn, surprised it hadn't been disconnected, and called the dairy supply dealer. It would be at least three hours before the changes in teat cup liners could be made. Milking probably couldn't begin before six o'clock. Besides, before the creamery would accept milk, an inspector had to give approval.

The tractor that cleaned the barn wouldn't start. I was told Butson's rig was on the way.

As I left the barn, Iverson pulled in the yard and parked his beat-up Chevy. He smiled sympathetically, gesturing as if visiting a family at a funeral parlor. "Sorry about the fire."

I looked at the gravel underfoot. "Thanks." I cleared my throat, fighting my emotions.

"How's Ruth?" Iverson leaned his butt against the car door.

I mumbled. "I'm told she'll be okay."

"What started the fire?"

"Rats, maybe… I don't know."

"Rats?" Iverson said in disbelief.

"Yeah, gnawing a hot wire." I wasn't interested in continuing to visit with him. I wanted to go to the shed where the herd was. I still thought of him as an enemy since the gun incident. But I was on his property; I had to at least be civil.

"What about wet hay?"

I sighed, "No," and mumbled, "I checked it before I shut off the dryer."

"Really?" Iverson shrugged. "I wanted you and Ruth to join me, but not under these circumstances."

"I must admit." I paused, not wanting to sound outright rude. "I'd give anything not to be here."

"Why?" Iverson adjusted his pants around his big gut.

"Well, your place…your place seems…seems like a huge undertaking." I moved small stones with the toe of my shoe.

"Let's go to the house and we'll talk about it."

"Ah…" I reacted tiredly, hoping I could skip further visiting. "Let's wait on that."

"We're both here." Iverson nervously cleared his throat. "It's only fair that I know what you're thinking."

"Well… okay." I hunched from exhaustion. "I'll take a few minutes. I've got a lot to do."

We headed toward his apartment. Iverson opened a wobbly aluminum storm door with no glass. It rubbed on the threshold. While passing through the entry, he flicked on the light in the two-room apartment. The entry was filled with an array of junk: pieces of roller chain, sprockets, a bottle jack, tire irons, and an empty tool box. The pathway from the door to the kitchen table was caked with dried mud and manure. The kitchen counter was piled with clothing, an opened loaf of bread, beans, catsup, Cheerios, and a jar of what looked like sugar. The sink was loaded with dirty dishes.

The table was covered with tools, junk, and clothing. "Take a seat." Iverson pushed aside an electric drill and a set of bits; three various-size drill buffers were opened, resting in a plastic case. A pack of wrenches lay opened beside the buffers. A pile of shirts, pants, and socks were at the end of the table.

He pulled out his chair and sat. I would have done the same opposite him, but there was a broken bearing lying on my seat. I picked it up and laid it on the table. It was covered with black grease. I scanned the table and pulled a dirty t-shirt from the pile, wiping my hand.

Iverson seemed unfazed by our surroundings. "How about a cup of coffee?"

"I…I don't…think so." I expected some excuse from him, regarding the mess, but it didn't come. Above the table, a circular fluorescent light hummed. I tried to collect my thoughts. A group of flies buzzed around the light. Stumped on what to say, I continued to watch them.

Iverson cleared his throat. "What do you think?"

Silence other than the endless buzz of the flies. I was speechless. I took off my scorched Red Sox cap and dropped it on the table, rubbing a burn hole above the B. I looked down at the black holes in the sleeves of my dress shirt. I wanted to flop on a bed and just cry, but I couldn't.

I noticed an open wrench set on the table by my left elbow. The plastic case had white lettering beneath each size. Most of the wrench pockets were empty but some odd sizes remained. The buffer set next to the wrenches was unusual. For some reason I studied them closely, probably to avoid facing him. The buffing material felt stiff and probably heat resistant. They also had threads of steel woven into them. I ran my finger over the three remaining tools in the opened package.

I wasn't surprised by his living conditions because of how he dressed in public. Also, the test pictures taken on his new camera his mother gave him for Christmas showed the same general messy disorder.

Suddenly, anger welled up in me. I shoved the wrenches and buffers aside, lifted my head and raised my voice. "Your farm's a goddamned disaster! Everything is either filthy or broken!" I glared at Iverson. "If I stay, I'm going to have full control of this place, and the milk check is going to be in my name."

Iverson's droopy eyes widened. His face tensed but he was controlled, reacting with a slight fake smile. "Okay, I'll rent."

I banged the table with my fist. "Damn, why haven't you gotten out of this god-awful mess."

Iverson lowered his voice. "It's not worth what I owe."

My elbows rested on the table with my hands covering my face. "Geez, the money it'll take just to get this place up and running."

He tried to lift my mood with enthusiasm. "I'll rent for three thousand a month, since your dad now owns the meadow."

"Let me think about it." I lifted my head and sighed, "I might just sell the herd."

"Rent would include the house." Iverson heightened his sales pitch. "Remember, all kinds of space. Room to store your stuff."

"And live with the Mexicans?"

"It's a big house." Iverson smirked. "Or Ellen lives just down the road."

I snapped, "No comment!"

Iverson nervously laughed. "You wouldn't mind living with the Mexicans?"

"More to the point, would the Mexicans mind living with me?"

He hesitantly answered, "I...I don't...don't think so."

"How long will they stay?" I looked at him. "They have any papers?"

"Do any these days?" He smoothed his slick hair. "They're all illegal."

"Undocumented?"

"Yeah." He shrugged. "Whatever."

"What're your plans for your cows?"

Iverson hesitated. "I'll find out what leased cows are worth."

"Okay." I looked down at my cap—feeling leery of any deal including cows. "I've got to check them out first."

"Well, you can buy my feed."

I inwardly groaned. "We'll see about that, too."

"Sure." Iverson nodded.

I shoved back from the table and walked toward the entry. "I'll let you know in a couple of days." I pushed to open the sticking storm door, kicking the bottom edge. It flew open, wobbling on its hinges.

After leaving Iverson's, I headed toward Ellen who was waiting in my loaded truck. She rolled down the driver's-side window. "I've got something for you."

I tensely asked, "Any word on Ruth?"

"Not yet. After we unload, I'll stop at the restaurant. Gilda will call your folks again." Ellen motioned. "Get in."

I opened the passenger-side door and slid in, resting my head on the back of the seat. "I swear Iverson's the biggest slob that ever hit Huntersville." I paused for a moment. "If I was smart, I'd call my cattle dealer and sell...be done with this place."

"You love your cows." She moved next to me, touching my face. "It must hurt?"

I pulled away. "It does."

"Don't move." She reached in a bag on the floor. "I'm going to help it with this cool wipe. It will feel good along with the special cream I have." She spread the wet cloth, completely covering my face.

"Ooh, that is nice." I squeezed her hand. "Thanks, Ellen."

She gently removed smudges. "I've got a hat my dad never wore and a t-shirt here in the bag." She continued applying the face cream. "Now, I hope this feels better."

"It does." I reached for the cap. "Thanks for this." I looked at it. "Neat, a chicken for a logo—*Lay or Bust*." I adjusted it to my head, and changed my shirt.

Ellen smiled. "Now you're in the chicken business."

I grinned at the comment. "We've got to figure where to put this furniture." I ran my hands down the new shirt. "Hey, thanks for this." I started to leave with my hand on the door. "We've got to get going."

"Just relax a minute." She held a brown paper bag. "I have a sandwich and a cup of coffee from the restaurant."

I settled back. "You thought of everything."

"I thought of you." She kissed me. "You can relax a while longer. A truck has already brought Ruth's and your folk's things to the homestead. Scoop and the guys are bringing the office equipment and your things here. They've stopped at Gilda's for a break."

I kissed her. "When I get settled by this weekend, we'll go to the Hideaway and stay overnight."

"Overnight?" She brightened. "Sounds great!" She hugged me. "I've got classes at the hospital all week. I'll be home Friday afternoon."

"Super, this will give me something to look forward to." I hugged her tightly, and then downed the sandwich and coffee. "Let me check on my cows, then we'll go to the house and find a place to store my stuff."

After finding that the herd had settled okay and was drinking water and eating some of Butson's alfalfa hay, we entered a neat kitchen that had a Mexican touch. A rectangular wooden table with four red ladder-back chairs were in the center of the room. A white oil cloth covered the table. In its center, a tall-stem vase held a single wild rose. The whole room had a bright look. There were curtains in two windows facing the barn. An eight-inch-high crucifix was placed above a door that led to a hallway. The likeness of the crucified Christ had dried palm fronds placed at the base. The fronds spread over the top board of the door casing.

I stepped lightly. "I feel weird being in someone else's space." I continued to check out the rooms. On either side of the darkened hall, there were several doors. I opened the first one. The room had a single bed, a bureau, and a pegboard to hang clothes. It was stark. I commented, "This must be José's room."

"You know his name?"

"Yeah, we met at the barn." I quietly closed the door.

I opened the next.

Ellen peered over my shoulder. "Obviously, a woman's bedroom."

"Rosita's."

"She must play the guitar and has a flair for brightly colored skirts and blouses." Ellen stepped around me and walked in, looking toward her bureau. "Interesting jewelry."

I motioned, feeling like an intruder. "Let's go."

Ellen backed from the room and closed the door. "Well, the next room can probably be yours."

The door being ajar, I pushed it open. In amazement, we both said, "Oh…what!"

A life-size crucifix stood against the back wall between two covered windows. The cross, constructed from weathered boards, reached the ceiling. The body of Christ, appropriately painted, was made from stuffed sheeting. The arms and hands were realistic with the black head of a nail in each palm. Christ's head, crowned with a wreath of thorns, hung forward. His features realistically expressed his pain and sorrow. His feet were nailed at the base. Two plank benches were placed in front of the altar. Three candles glowed in pint canning jars at the feet of Christ. An angel, painted on sheeting, hovered, loosely hung from the ceiling.

The flickering candles cast shadows off the darkened walls. But there was a pleasant smell coming from the room.

I took a deep breath. "What is it?"

"They burn incense." Ellen pointed. "See the bowl?"

I looked around the room. "This is something else!"

"Yeah, sort of . . . sort of different." She backed away.

"It's their chapel." I quietly closed the door.

Ellen went to the next door. "Well, this can be your room." She flicked the switch. "It works. We'll move your stuff in here. Your folks have taken their things to the Homestead.

"Thanks, I'll have a bed to fall into tonight." Other than a bunch of dead cluster flies on the floor by two windows and a stale smell, the room was nondescript. It probably hadn't been used in years.

I opened the doors at the far end of the hall. "Put the rest of the furniture and office equipment in these two rooms."

There was also an open door leading to a sitting room. It had a couch and two over-stuffed chairs, plus a TV.

Walking back down the hall toward the kitchen, I found the bathroom. We left the house.

I sighed. "Now, I've got to face the barn." My arm slid around Ellen's waist. "I love you." I tightly hugged her. "I can't wait to buy a ring for you."

"Ooh. . .you've just sent shivers through me." She clung to me in excitement. "Not an engagement ring?"

"Well, yeah." I looked at her surprised expression. "We could get married in a year or so."

Still pressed snugly, arching her back for eye contact. "Oh, I love you!" She looked away. "There's no need to hurry into marriage."

"But you'd wear my ring?"

"A sparkling diamond! How exciting!" She kissed me. "I'd be the envy of all my friends! A ring from Jason Murray!" Her fingers touched my burned face and lips. "Does it still hurt?"

"Not that much." I smiled. "You're good medicine."

She raised herself on tiptoes and murmured in my ear, "I can't wait for this weekend."

Tiredly, I smiled and kissed her again.

The sky was clear with just a few white clouds. In the distance, a pillar of smoke rose into the sky, reminding me of an exclamation mark against a background of blue.

I headed for the barn. Sonny Butson's men and helpers were still working. One was driving a tractor and loader, cleaning the barn. José and Rosita were raking out the manure-packed cow beds. A load of sawdust had arrived for the stalls.

I checked over Iverson's cows. They were thin with rough hair, caked manure on their flanks, and generally small udders. It was obvious they hadn't had much of a chance to be good producers.

Stanford Curry, the dairy fieldman for the creamery, had come earlier to inspect the facility. He entered the barn, walking with an all-business stride to meet me. "Sorry about your fire."

"Thanks."

"In spite of the circumstances," Curry looked at his clip board, "I'm personally happy to have you here. Steven Iverson has been on thin ice with us for years."

I pushed my cap back—a habit. But now it reminded me of my burns. "Well, I can change some of this mess, but it can't be immediate."

"Yes, I know. At least the equipment and barn are being cleaned." Curry glanced over the herd. "The udder health of these cows is poor." He showed me milk sample results. "Way too much mastitis—half or more of Iverson's cows should go."

I looked at the bacteria counts and raised my eyebrows. "Oh... terrible!"

"We'll pick up your milk in the morning." He handed me a list of improvements to be made immediately. "I'm going now, but I'll stop by tomorrow."

I nodded. "Tonight I'll start sorting Iverson's cows that show signs of mastitis."

I was standing in the yard, scanning the list of inspection requirements, when Cooner's truck came up the drive and stopped.

I leaned on his open window. "What's the latest from the hospital?"

"Maggie called and told us that Ruth will be okay, but she needs ta stay in the hospital for a while."

"That's good news!"

"Now, there's one plucky gal." Cooner shook his head. "Seein' how she looked comin' outta that fire." He spat. "I figured …" He sighed. "I figured the worst."

"I agree." I looked past Cooner to the barn. "I don't know about this place."

"I can't believe how bad it is." Cooner paused. "His cattle ain't nothin' but skin and bones. They might's well go."

"I agree. We sure walked into a mess, and the surprising thing is, Iverson doesn't seem to get it."

"That's Iverson. He's swamped with problems." Cooner slipped some chew in his mouth. "Oh, before I forget. Your folks said they'll be here soon ta talk over the situation."

"Good, I need that."

"I'll be here in the mornin' with Scoop." Cooner started to leave. "I'm headed ta the old homestead ta get settled in my new room."

"Thanks, Cooner." I stood back from the truck.

"Much obliged." He chugged away.

I was troubled, heading toward the milk house. Should I stay at this place or do the easiest thing and sell my cows? And I was concerned about my folks. Ruth and I had never been badly hurt, and I wondered how they would deal with Ruth's burns.

Up until now, Cooner had always been the substitute parent who was ready with the Band-Aids. When we were kids, I remembered him comforting Ruth and me when there were tears. It was Cooner who took us to the doctor's—held Ruth when she fell out of a tree and broke her arm. He also held her when the doctor put on the plaster cast.

I remembered eighth-grade football when I was flattened on the field, writhing in pain. It was Cooner who ran to be with me, worried over my condition. Mom and Dad were at the florist shop or occupied with farm business—not wanting to be bothered with football. They left the day-to-day, what they considered kids' stuff, to Cooner.

Although Ruth's condition didn't sound grave, it would take some time before she would be on her own. For a while, they would have to be responsible for her day-to-day needs.

As for my situation, Dad wanted to consider the Iverson proposal, but not under these circumstances. I knew once I told him the cost of continuing at this place, he'd have second thoughts about joining farms, especially since he owned the meadow. Now, I was at a crossroads. They would hopefully involve themselves in helping me decide my future.

Later, as promised, Dad and Mom drove into the yard from the hospital. Anxious, I went to their car.

They looked tired, with shadows beneath their eyes. Mom met me with a weary smile and a hug, shaking with emotion. "How are you, Jason?" Tears streamed down her face. "I can't believe what you've been through."

"I'm okay." I stepped back and looked at her. "How are you, and how about Ruth?"

"I'm all right, but when we left, your sister was in a lot of pain." Mom continued to wipe tears. "She's kept sedated most of the time."

"Her face?" I scowled. "And how about her hands?"

"We hope her face will heal quickly." Mom pulled a Kleenex from her pocket. "It's her hands. They'll be an issue for a while."

"I wish I could be with her." I paused, deep in thought. "What can I do?"

"At this point—nothing." Mom stared, hopeless. "In and out of sedation, she mumbles 'Anadeepa' a lot."

"The picture, Mom. You know, the picture of her kids." I brightened. "She'd love to see it."

"Good idea. I'll have to find it." Mom nodded. "She worries so about those children."

"They mean the world to her." I glanced at Dad and Mom for agreement.

"I know." Mom pondered in silence, looking down at her clenched hands. "Now, she's helpless to do anything for them."

Dad stood with Mom. "Jason, this has been terrible." He rested his hand on my shoulder. "How are you?"

"Okay." I breathed deeply, holding in my emotions. "But I think I want out."

Dad paused. "You mean sell the cows?"

"Yeah." I looked up for reactions. "That's right."

"Gee, are you sure?" Dad searched me for eye contact. "I've wanted to sell for some time, but the cows have meant a lot to you."

"Well, we'd have to buy a winter's supply of hay." I moved some gravel with my foot. "It's too much."

Dad stood looking around. By nature a neat-freak, he wore a dour expression. "This place looks to have its problems."

"I guess!" I glanced at him. "What are we going to do or what should I do?"

Mom reached for my arm. "Let's go to Gilda's and get something to eat. We'll talk about it."

"Okay, I've got an hour or so before we have to start milking."

We entered the restaurant and were met by several people extending their condolences. The most often-asked question was "What are you going to do?"

I just shrugged. I was mystified myself in regards to the right decision.

I pulled Gilda aside. "Mom, Dad and I have to talk business. Can you give us some privacy?"

"Sure, I'll set a place for you out back." Gilda turned. "Follow me."

We were led through a side door to a table in a nook which was used by the employees. We took our seats. Gilda brought us drinks and food she'd prepared for the helpers. "There's more chicken, salad, and rolls if you're really hungry."

Mom smiled. "Thanks, Gilda. This is plenty."

Dad leaned toward me from across the table. "What's the situation with Iverson's cows?"

I shook my head. "Skinny, underfed, and loaded with mastitis."

Mom suggested, "But this may be an opportunity for you."

My voice rose. "Opportunity!"

"Why not look past this winter? Act on the chance to eventually own a modern dairy facility."

"That's true." I pondered for a moment. "It would be foolish to build a barn and house when they're right here."

Dad glanced toward Mom. "We'll support whatever you decide."

"What about turf farming?" I buttered some bread. "What happened to that idea?"

"The start-up costs are too high, and besides..." Dad looked onto his plate. "Ruth..." His eyes blurred with tears as he sniffed.

Mom rested her hand on Dad's shoulder. He covered his face.

Silence.

He turned and dropped his hands and took a deep breath. He shut his eyes.

Mom darted a glance at him.

I looked down.

"Hum." Dad reached for a napkin and blew his nose. "We want what's best... for you and...Ruth." His face reddened. "The fire...well...it's caused me to...well, to see things...well, differently...to change."

"Change?" I wondered just how?

"Yes...change." Dad drank some tea. "We won't, or we *can't* decide your future."

"My future?" My fork moved some salad around my plate. "Gosh, I don't know what's best. There're so many possibilities."

"Give it time." Dad's eyes met mine. "What do *you* want?"

"I...I never thought I'd have all these options." I bit into a mouthful of bread. "It's always been the cows and nature."

He reached for my forearm. "It's different, now... you're at a crossroad."

"What should I do?" I felt challenged, having just been cut loose. There was no voice telling me what path to take.

Mom looked over her tea cup. "Go to college for another two years." She took a sip.

"College?" I swallowed hard. "Leave town?"

"Yeah." Mom looked at me for my reaction. "Why not?"

"I don't know." I felt myself blush. "Ellen ..."

Both Mom and Dad leaned toward me. "You're that serious?"

"Well, yeah...Ellen graduates next May." I looked down. "She plans to nurse here in Huntersville."

Mom's eyebrows arched. "Oh."

I took another bite of my bread. "Keeping the cows makes sense."

"Yeah, if that's what you want." Dad stirred his coffee. "You can build your future at Iverson's. The insurance money will be coming."

"What if the fire marshal finds a good reason not to settle?"

"They won't find anything." He glanced toward me for agreement.

"I'm not sure." I finished my bread. "A fire doesn't just start."

"Have you got any idea?"

"I haven't." I shrugged. "Maybe rats."

"Well." Dad held his cup. "We'll let the fire marshal figure it out."

"The Iverson place fits me and the herd about as closely as anyone could expect." I collected my thoughts. "I'm right back to realizing that I either have to make a deal with Iverson or I've got to sell."

"You're young." Dad drained his cup. "It looks like you want to settle down. You have the foundation to start building again."

"This would be my deal." I sipped some tea. "I can't plan on Ruth. Her heart's in Georgia."

Mom cried, "Jason, don't say that!"

"It's true."

Mom held her cup. "I hadn't thought ahead that much."

"I've got to start milking." I got up to leave. "Thanks for the talk."

"Now, consider all options." Dad stood. "Don't commit to anything for a while."

Mom nodded. "Especially marriage."

We left Gilda's.

After night chores, José, Rosita, and I walked toward the house. The moon in a cloudless sky lit our way. It was nearly ten o'clock, the workday had ended. When we entered the kitchen, there was a plate of fried chicken, a chocolate cake, and cookies with a note on the table:

Jason, have a good week. I'll be thinking of you.
I love you, Ellen

I took a kitchen chair and looked toward the bathroom for Rosita. "Shower?"

She waved her hand for me to go first.

"No, you." I sat, reaching for some chicken. Eating, I began to relax, wondering about my new home, living with two Mexicans and their culture. Something I'd never dreamed of hours earlier.

In just the short time I'd been with José and Rosita, I appreciated their quickness and ability to work. More importantly, they were good around the cows. My herd went through the milking parlor with unbelievable ease. Yes, the cows were hesitant, stiff-kneed, bracing themselves against taking their place to be milked. But Rosita spoke softly, gently urging the cows to move forward and, for the most part, they responded to her calm and patient touch.

After I showed José and Rosita that each Iverson cow had to be checked for clinical signs of mastitis, they understood and held the milk from being pumped to the tank. Each cow that showed the soft stringy white clots was banded on the leg with a red wrap.

Now, I sat at the kitchen table, taking time to reflect on my situation. Rosita came from her room wearing a red blouse, a brightly colored skirt with ruffles, and long dangling earrings. Her straight black hair flowed down her back, reaching her waist. A shiny red and yellow band kept her hair in place. I was surprised how in a matter of minutes, she'd been transformed from a common laborer to a beautiful girl.

She went to the kitchen cabinet and opened a five-pound bag of cornmeal, poured some in a bowl, added salt and water, and mixed the dough. Then she pulled a tortilla maker from the shelf. With rolled dough the size of a golf ball in her hand, she placed it in the center of the circular gadget—pulled the cover down and pressed. She lifted the cover and peeled a tortilla, the size and shape of a large pancake, from the surface, and transferred it to a heated pan, lightly frying both sides of the pastry. After making about a dozen, she placed them on a plate, ready to serve her father who had just come from the shower. I was amazed at how effortlessly she'd prepared their meal. Obviously a routine she'd done hundreds of times.

She held the plate for me. I took one and held it in my hand. Realizing I didn't know what to do with a tortilla, she placed another one flat on a plate, put strips of Ellen's chicken on the pastry and rolled it. "Es tortilla." She slid the plate toward José.

192 | John S. Hall

He munched and said with a mouthful, "Es buena, sí?"

I nodded. "Yes."

Although the tortilla had a rather bland taste, I overlooked the fact. After eating, I left for the shower. She smiled. "Buenas noches."

I raised my hand and managed a weary smile in return. "Good night."

After cleaning up, I went to my room, passing the chapel, and saw that the door was ajar. The candles at the altar cast a yellow light across the darkened hallway. In my room, I noticed that the windows had been opened, giving me some fresh air; however, the stale smell lingered. The faded wallpaper had jagged breaks running kitty-corner from ceiling to floor. No doubt the cracks were caused by the house shifting from season to season through the years. The scene on the wallpaper pictured a nineteenth-century lady wearing a bonnet and a man wearing a stovepipe hat, both in a carriage drawn by prancing horses.

My bed had been made up, and my bureau had been brought to the room along with clothes that Ellen had hung in a small closet. She'd laid a small braided rug beside my bed. A clock on a nightstand showed eleven.

I slid between the covers and shut my eyes. The picture in my mind of the raging fire and Ruth's burned hair and scorched face gripped my thoughts. The image was so real I felt like I was in the fire. Even with the shower, the smell of smoke lingered in my nose. Thinking of Ruth and my terrible loss, plus living in a strange home, overwhelmed me. I began sobbing; shaking in grief, I rolled over and buried my head, finally falling into a fitful sleep.

In a nightmare, I raced down a road, being chased by a rolling ball of fire. I was about to be sucked into the blazing mass. In the background, jumbled in my vivid dream, I could hear singing.

Suddenly, I was jarred from my sleep and sat up with my feet on the rug. It was eleven-thirty. The singing came from the next room, from the Mexicans' chapel. Fully awake, I blinked my eyes and realized it was Rosita. I was amazed by the flawless tone of her beautiful voice.

She repeated a chant, holding high notes for long periods. I had no understanding of the words but the sharp clarity, though different, mesmerized me the same way the white-throated sparrow did. I lay back and relaxed as Rosita's voice continued to float through my bedroom walls. At some point, I fell asleep.

The next morning, I woke, dressed, and went to the kitchen at four-thirty. José and Rosita were at the table drinking coffee and eating tortillas. Rosita's face glowed with a broad smile beneath her high cheekbones. Her deeply-set brown eyes and black eyebrows blended nicely with her bronze complexion. "Café, sí?"

I took a chair. "Sure." On seeing her in her overalls and bandana, I found it hard to believe the voice in the night came from her.

She passed me a cup and three tortillas on a plate. The coffee and tortillas, filled with jelly, were delicious. I caught her attention. "These are bueno."

She smiled and went to her room.

José ran a finger over his mustache. "Señor Iverson no paga, no dinero."

I translated the statement easily, realizing by now that Iverson hadn't paid anyone. "I'll pay you this afternoon."

José, who seemed never to smile, understood. "Sí."

After eating, José and I left the house. The light from the kitchen shone through a heavy fog. The broadleaf plantain beside the path leading from the house was dripping with dew.

Cooner's truck came in the yard, its lights stabbing through the dense fog. When it stopped, I saw that Cooner, Scoop, and Scoop's younger brother, Jared, were in the cab. Scoop rolled down his window. "We can give you a hand for a couple of hours."

"Thanks." I looked in the open window of the truck. "Gosh, Cooner got you guys up early."

"No problem." Scoop stroked his beard. "My brother and I used to work here."

Jared, about sixteen, said, "Yeah, until Iverson stopped payin' us."

"I'm hearing that a lot." I looked toward the barn. "I think we can get these cows sorted and the barns cleaned out in an hour or so. And then you guys can leave."

"Good." Cooner reached for his handkerchief. "Since my workin' days are over, I ain't use to gettin' up before the roosters."

Everyone laughed.

I looked at the old man. "Could you come by at about two and take José and Rosita shopping in town? They need some food."

"Sure. I ain't got nothin' planned."

The cows with leg bands were sorted into one group of about a hundred. The remaining hundred and fifty were divided into two groups, leaving a fourth section of the barn for my herd. The LaQuine boys cleaned the empty section. Hay and grain were brought in to feed the cows. At five-thirty my herd was driven from the open shed to their new home in the barn and on to the milking parlor. José and Rosita began washing udders and attaching the machines. Most of my herd entered the milking parlor quite easily, since they were being milked for the second time in their new surroundings. They had made the transition with no problem.

While feeding Iverson's cows, I thought of the costs to be borne if I stayed. I dreaded seeing the actual figure.

I estimated that at least half of the hundred Iverson cows would have to leave and be sold for beef—a fact that wouldn't go down well with him.

By mid-morning, I had fixed the bulk milk tank washer and showed José and Rosita how to use it. I was on my way to the house when a car with official Vermont plates pulled in the yard. A balding middle-aged man with a puffy face and squinty gray eyes left his car. He walked toward me with a brisk stride. "I'm Stanley Whitaker, Vermont State Fire Marshal. I'm here to ask a few questions."

I stopped. "Sure."

"I know this must be a difficult time." Whitaker said briskly. "I hear your sister was badly burned."

"Yeah, bad enough."

"Let's go to my car and talk." Whitaker slid in his seat and placed a clipboard on the steering wheel. "I'm going to ask a few routine questions." He slipped on reading glasses that rode low on his nose.

"Okay." I got in on the passenger side. It felt good to sit and relax while resting my head on the back of the seat.

Whitaker began. "What caused the fire?"

"I don't know. Rats might have chewed a hot wire."

The investigator jotted notes on his clipboard. "Were rats a problem?"

"Yeah, I set out poison last week."

"When did you first notice the fire?"

I looked at the gray visor above the windshield. "About twelve-thirty."

He turned toward me. His steely eyes looking through narrow lenses. "When were you last in the barn?"

The question startled me. Whitaker's visit was more than to fill out a report. I sat up, not so relaxed. "I left at about ten. Ruth followed."

"How long was she alone in the barn?"

"Oh, I don't know—fifteen minutes."

"Then what did she do?"

I raised my voice. "We went to church."

"Was anyone else at the farm?"

I answered emphatically, "No!"

Whitaker continued writing on the clipboard. "Do you go to church every Sunday?"

"No. This was the Sunday the stained-glass window was dedicated. We all went." I glared at the investigator. "Just what are you driving at?"

"All I want are a few answers." Whitaker studied my reaction. "Where did the fire start?"

I tensed, thinking of the illegal wiring, but since disconnecting them they were a dead issue. "The hay dryer."

"The hay dryer!" Whitaker sharpened. "Was it running?"

"No." I said assuredly. "I shut it off days ago."

Whitaker's eyes narrowed. "Are you sure?"

I raised my voice. "Very sure!"

Whitaker clipped his pen on the paper and leaned back, shrewdly looking at me. "Why did you recently raise your coverage issued by the Eagle Insurance Company?"

"Oh, for God sake!" I glared. "Because it needed to be. Judge Crabtree recommended it."

"Jason." Whitaker lowered his voice. "Calm down."

"Calm down!" I threw my hands. "You haven't just been wiped out with a huge loss!"

"Of course." Whitaker tapped me on the arm.

"Sorry. I'm shot." I ran my hand over my burned eyebrows. "Can't we do this another time?"

"It's my job to gather information." Whitaker took a deep breath. "Now, let's continue. Was anyone in the barn when you first noticed the smoke?"

I sighed. "Not that I know of."

Stanford Curry drove in the yard.

"The milk inspector just came." I held the door handle. "I've got to go."

"All right." Whitaker placed the clipboard on the seat. "I've asked enough questions for today. But I'm not done with this matter." He turned to me. "Our forensic investigator will be examining the site."

I said crisply, "Good! Have a great day!" Getting out of the car, I slammed the door.

twenty-four

Ruth

The third day after the fire, I lay in my hospital bed. I turned onto my side and looked at the picture Mom left of the Piedmont Center kids. I was really sad not being able to be with them. Here I was, helpless and feeling like crying. I should've been happy because I was being discharged and going home.

With help, I was eating and drinking normally. The shunt had been removed below my shoulder, and the plastic glucose bag that hung over my head was gone. The pain wasn't as bad, but at times I felt sharp twinges in my hands. When it became intense, I was given a pill. I was going to continue treatment as an out-patient. Concerning the back of my hands, the doctor was confident that the danger of infection could be averted. Although there were some small areas of third-degree burns, he didn't think skin grafting would be necessary.

During the fire, I was lucky to be within inches of the cement floor. I only had first-degree burns on my face, similar to a severe sun-burn. This morning the bandage had been removed from my face. The nurse removing the bandage told me that I was healing very nicely, as there was considerable lifting of dead skin. But I had yet to look in a mirror. The head nurse warned against hurrying to improve my awful appearance by peeling dead skin. But of course, I wanted to see how I looked.

My nurse came in and placed a compact mirror and a jar of white face cream on my bedside table. "You'd be much better off if you didn't look at yourself for a few more days."

"Pretty bad, huh?"

"Yes, but in time, your face will heal."

"Would you hold the mirror for me?" I saw it on the table but was helpless to do a single thing for myself.

"I wish you wouldn't." She hesitantly held the mirror.

I took a deep breath, squeezed my eyes shut—then opened them. "Oh, my gosh!" I looked like a character in a horror movie.

Bubbled skin covered both sides of my face. I ran my tongue over my lips. They were tender and felt like sandpaper. My eyebrows were stubble. My forehead showed transparent flakes furrowed in wrinkles. My nose was the most alarming. It too had bubbled skin, but near the tip it was deep red. My head was mostly bald, but the doctor said that my hair would grow back.

I never considered myself the vain movie star sort, but I looked awful. I tensed, as I knew that Chris would be the first to see me when he came to pick me up. He'd be shocked but probably wouldn't say any-thing—showing concern without acting alarmed. After all, I knew that the guy was full of compassion and kindness.

Just the same, before Chris came, I wanted to be hidden. The nurse stood by my bed with a sympathetic expression. "I'm sorry. Your healing, shall I say, is at an awkward stage."

I glanced at the jar. "Would you cover my face with that white cream?"

"That's really not necessary." She closely examined me. "Your nose and the edge of your ears could use some."

"Please. I want my whole face covered."

"Okay. If you say so."

The cool cream felt good as she gently applied it. "You're begin-ning to look like a ghost." She smiled. "Casper the friendly ghost." She finished.

"Let me see."

The nurse held the mirror.

I chuckled. "Yeah, I'm a dead-ringer for a ghost."

After having my face covered with the cream, and being helped to the bathroom, I'd had it. My hands started throbbing. "Damn, I need some pain meds."

"Well, you're due for a codeine pill." She gave it to me while holding a glass of water with a straw. "You'll be asleep in minutes." The nurse opened the privacy curtain that surrounded my bed.

A man with a briefcase stood at the door of my room. "I'm Stanley Whitaker, fire marshal. I'd like to ask a few questions?"

"Sure. If I can stay awake." I glanced at him. "I'm sorry for my weird appearance."

Whitaker was in a business suit, shirt and tie. He pulled up a chair and reached for his glasses. "Your looks don't bother me." He crossed his legs and placed a clipboard on his knee. "Just answer my questions. I assume you're Ruth Murray."

"Yes."

"The forensic investigator needs this preliminary information."

"Okay." I turned toward him. "I'll do the best I can."

"Do you have any idea how the fire started?"

"No." Already, I was feeling the effects of the pain pill.

He was writing. "I understand from your brother that you were the last to leave the barn on the morning before the fire."

"I'm feeling foggy." My head swayed. "Yes."

"Your brother has filled me in on most of what I need." He continued as if he were cross-examining me in a courtroom. "Was anyone with you?"

"No." I was fighting to stay awake.

He calmly asked, "Was it your idea to raise the Eagle Insurance Company's coverage?"

I was aware he watched for my reaction. "No. The insurance carrier suggested it."

"Your idea?" His eyes continued to be locked on me.

"I just told you. No!" Even in my groggy condition, he angered me. "Judge Crabtree, our insurance agent, showed me the letter."

"Was it required?"

"Well…what …would you…do?" My head dropped on the pillow. I didn't remember anymore of our conversation.

I woke early in the afternoon, free of pain. My lunch was in front of me, but I couldn't use my hands to eat. I could hear Chris at the nurses' station so I pressed the call button with my elbow. He came to my room with a nurse. He smiled. "You're awake."

The nurse held a thermometer. "Let me check you before you go." She read the results. "Normal." A moment passed. "Blood pressure—normal. The doctor's orders are for you to walk the halls for a while." The nurse looked at Chris and then me. "If you feel okay, you're good to go. After you eat, I can help you get dressed."

Chris helped me with a sandwich, and I drank a glass of milk using a straw. The nurse returned. Behind the pulled curtain, she slipped a shapeless dress on me. One Mom had left. I probably looked like a bag lady. The nurse tied a blue-and-white checkered bandana around my bald head.

I came from behind the curtain. My knees felt weak but I was ready for a walk.

Chris stood. "Do you feel okay?"

"Sure. Let's go."

Walking the halls felt good. I found that if I held my hands above my mid-section, it lessened the throbbing. "Well, here comes the ghost of Ruth Murray," I chuckled.

"You sure sound lighthearted for being in your condition." Chris was watchful, directing me around obstacles. "How are you feeling?"

"Frankly, I feel like crying. But what good would that do?"

"I understand. Who wouldn't?" We dodged around a food cart. "How are the hands?"

"Fine, I'm ready to go." What a lie! I was ready for another pain pill. I couldn't wait to get home—take a pill and crash on my bed.

"Your mom will meet us at the old homestead. She has your pain prescription." We stopped at the nurses' station. "We're leaving."

"Okay, sign this discharge paper and you're free to go. Here are the doctor's instructions, plus a bag with your personal items."

Chris signed for me. Walking to his car, aching really kicked in. I wasn't so sure about leaving the hospital. The pain was so bad, I wanted to scream. Nevertheless, I found it felt best with my hands raised above my head. I tried to force myself to think humorously—imagining that I was an Olympic swimmer about to take a high dive.

I sat in the car with the tips of my fingers touching the inside vinyl cover of the car roof. "Sorry, I must look like Casper the Friendly Ghost in a holdup."

"I feel badly for you." Chris checked on me. "Your humor can't cover the pain I know you're feeling."

"I'm trying." I was about to burst, holding a deep breath. Tears were trickling down my face. Within minutes, I saw the homestead up ahead. "Thank God!"

Mom must have heard Chris's car drive in the yard. She came running down the back steps. I broke down in a torrent of tears. "Mom, I...I need a pill."

twenty-five

Jason

I took a few minutes to see Ruth, knowing she'd just come home, but when I stopped at the homestead, she was sleeping. It was strange to see Mom in the house and not at work. She was doing the dishes when I entered the kitchen. "I'm going to be Ruth's nurse until she can use her hands. We've put her bed in the front living room."

This was a first for Mom, taking care of Ruth. "Who's at the florist shop?"

"Bertha's filling in as much as she can."

"How's Ruth doing?" I took a chair.

Mom sat down. "She's in a lot of pain."

"Gosh, I hope she improves quickly."

"Time." Mom looked toward the front of the house where Ruth was sleeping. "The doctor says it will just take time."

"Gee, all of this because of Rover Red."

Mom's eyes became teary. "That's your sister." She sniffed. "As you know, she has a kind heart for all living creatures, especially those that are threatened."

"I know." I got up. "Please tell her I stopped by."

It was too late to bother Mom for something to eat, so after night chores, I headed to Gilda's. The air felt cool in the clear dusk before sunset. Off in the distance a lone crow called through the closing shadows of the day. Mourning doves roosted in the shed, cooing to one another.

The alfalfa hay, delivered and unloaded just hours ago, filled the air with its sweet scent.

I sank my hands into the pockets my jacket and headed across the street. While walking to Gilda's, I thought of the decisions that had to be made. Dad and I had worked for years developing our well-bred Holstein herd. Now the fire had changed everything. Fifty cows couldn't support the running cost of the Iverson place. And more importantly, I didn't want my cows being infected with the mastitis bug that was running through the Iverson herd.

My best option was to get Iverson to sell his cows. I'd decided I wouldn't stay and risk infecting my herd unless he sold. As it was, I worried that an outbreak might happen anyway even though we milked my cows first, washing and sanitizing the equipment before and after milking. I also insisted that José and Rosita thoroughly wash their hands after milking the Iverson cows. I was very aware that a case of some forms of mastitis could destroy a cow like Precious and others of my herd. I shivered at the thought of feeling the swelling in an udder—seeing the clear fluid and long white strings of mastitis clots that could come from the teats of an infected cow. That being the case, perhaps I should sell my herd now while I had the chance and get out of the dairy business.

On the other hand, if the Iverson herd went, it would make sense to stay. I would have to thoroughly disinfect the barn and milking area with a pressure washer. I could then buy valuable selected cows. I didn't want commercial cows to fill the barn—cows that in no way would equal the breeding value of my present herd.

I had to agree that the large herd, commercial or registered, was the wave of the future. Profit margins were narrow, so volume was the logical way toward making a decent living. I didn't have a choice but to agree with Dad—the Iverson place was an opportunity not to be overlooked. However, I'd not closed my mind to other possibilities for my future. I didn't want to be pressured into making a quick decision. Even if Iverson did sell his cows, I could take some time to firm up my future.

I walked into Gilda's parking lot, thinking that our town representative needed me as much as I needed him. I surmised that he would be anxious to salvage something of value from his farm before the bank took control on November 1st.

I opened the restaurant door and Gilda greeted me with her usual welcoming smile. "Hi, Jason. How are you doing in and amongst the junk heap?" She cocked her head toward the Iverson place.

Not knowing quite what to say, I just smiled. It was unlike Gilda to talk disparagingly about anyone, but I realized Iverson was on her black list. "Oh, I'm managing." I felt my face redden. "Heard from Ellen?"

"No. Not since she left." Gilda smiled. "Counter?"

I frowned on seeing Bertha and the counter crowd. Upon hearing me enter, most turned on their stools. I was bombarded by questions and comments: "What's your plans? Don't stay in town. Sell real estate. Coach football. Log off the Murray pines. Build new."

I backed toward the door. I couldn't believe so many had given thought to my future.

Scoop puffed his chest. "That Iverson Place is a son-of-a- bitchin' hole." He stroked his beard. "I'd pull your cows outta that place."

Bertha broke in, "Lay off!" She slipped off her stool and motioned for people to stop. She laughed. "Jason, don't mind us. As you know, we're called Huntersville's counter-intelligence."

Judge Crabtree, who seldom talked, said with a smile, "Or counter-irritants."

I grinned and turned to Gilda. "Give me a place where I can eat in peace."

She led me toward the far end of the restaurant.

I mentioned in a low mumble, "Gosh, I'd like to talk to Ellen!" I slid into my seat.

Gilda sat on the opposite seat with her feet in the aisle. "Problem?"

"Yeah, I'm trying to come to the point of deciding what's best to do." I sighed. "I just want to talk it over with her."

"Call her!" She nudged my hand. "Whatever, don't get sucked in by Iverson. Believe me, I know." She got up. "I'll bring you something good to eat." She paused. "How about a big plate of fried clams, French fries, and a glass of iced coffee?"

I nodded. "Sounds good!"

While waiting for my dinner, I mulled over other possibilities. As Mom suggested, I could go away to college. It would be neat to major in ornithology and know more about the birds. But I suspected ornithologists travel a lot in search of rare birds and are away from home for long periods. I couldn't bear the thought of leaving Ellen. She'd been gone for a day and I already missed her.

I could work as a florist, learning the tricky business of timing the flowering of plants—managing full bloom by Mother's Day, Valentine's Day, Christmas, and Easter. I remembered seeing a whole greenhouse of beautifully grown geraniums. They were worthless because they didn't blossom in time for Memorial Day. The memory left me cold.

I could learn a trade, be a carpenter, a plumber, an electrician, start a business, stay in Huntersville, and hope to make a living—somehow. I sighed—learning a trade didn't appeal.

My thoughts came full circle to realize that it made sense to stay at the Iverson place, eventually buy it, fix up the house, marry Ellen, and raise a family.

I smiled in relief. I felt the fog was beginning to clear—showing a more sensible direction.

A waitress brought me my food.

While eating French fries, I looked up and groaned. Iverson had just come through the door. The Huntersville representative was way too happy and way too drunk. I slid my plate and glass toward the wall, hoping not to be noticed. While I needed to talk business with the man, I wanted a few minutes to eat and relax. I sank in my seat and continued eating.

I heard outrageous laughter getting louder, coming my way. As a politician, Iverson had something superfluous to say to most who were seated. I didn't look up.

A Willie Nelson recording, *Slow Movin' Outlaw,* quietly played in the background,

Without invitation, Iverson slid into my booth. I continued finger-eating French fry by French fry, not looking up. The hot breath of liquor blew my way. "I see things are movin' and shakin' at my place." He forced a laugh. "What's up?"

I sipped my coffee and met his eyes. Eyes that bulged watery on a round face—cherry red at the cheekbones. "Yeah, movin' and shakin'. But big changes have got to be made."

"Sure." Iverson rested his arms on the table. "Like what?"

"Sell your cattle." I stared at this pathetic man.

The demand led into a long silence.

Iverson's head swayed to attention. "Sell?" He ran a hand over his slick gray hair. "Sell…why?"

"Your herd's worthless." I waited.

His blurry eyes closed as if he hadn't heard right. "Worthless?"

"That's right! You must have known your cows were loaded with mastitis." I looked at him while feeling for another French fry.

"Well…well some…maybe some details may have gotten by me…." He cleared his throat, pausing, slowly rotating an empty Forget Me Not creamer that rested on the table. "You…you see, I'm on an important legislative committee in Montpelier, studying public safety."

I stared at him and held a steady gaze. "Your cows have got to go." I took another sip of coffee. "For beef."

"Beef!" Iverson raised his voice and leaned toward me. "Look, you wise bastard." His puffy fist pounded the table. "That'd wipe me out."

"Sorry." I took another sip. "Your cows are loaded." I continued holding a steady gaze at him. "There's no choice! They've got to go. Even if I leave, they should go!"

"Bullshit, they aren't that bad!" Iverson squeezed the creamer in his hand.

"It's bad." I picked up a fried clam and munched.

Iverson groaned. "The bank owns them at twelve hundred apiece. I can't sell."

"Cows are leaving tomorrow." I set my jaw. "Either yours or mine."

"I need a drink!" Iverson slouched. "I think you're full of shit!"

I held steady, not reacting to his anger. "Believe what you want, but they'll have to go."

He huffed. "Huh…what's beef worth?"

"Two hundred cows, they're small and thin, maybe four hundred average, if you're lucky." I chewed on another fried clam. "Some won't pass federal inspection.

"No cows!" Iverson blew a big sigh. "I can't live!"

"That's your problem!" I raised my voice. "I won't chance infecting my herd!"

"Shit, if you knew anything, I mean anything at all, you'd medicate my cows and get me shipping milk again!" Iverson yelled, "I need another drink!"

A waitress shoved a full glass in front of him.

While Iverson sat in shock, drinking his beer, I finished my plate and got up to go. "I'm calling Jacques Bassett. He'll buy your cows or mine." I stood by the table, looking down at him. "Be at the house by eight o'clock tomorrow morning, and we'll make a decision."

When I left Gilda's, I bought our local newspaper, folded it, and stuck it in my back pocket. I headed toward the farm in the cool night, wondering over the events of the next morning. I decided to call Fred Watkins, my vet. I thought Fred could confirm my fear of commingling the two herds. He would also give assurance to Iverson and Emily Ann at the bank that the Iverson herd was no longer fit for milk production.

Since our vet, Doc Chambers, died, Fred had come out of retirement as the Vermont State Veterinarian and taken over Doc Chamber's large animal practice. When Fred was employed by the State, he worked in the field of improving milk quality, especially in the control and treatment of mastitis. He was highly respected for his achievements. His presence was enhanced by his looks—a head of snow-white hair and a glass eye from an injury he'd gotten during the Korean Conflict. As a kid, I felt intimidated by Fred because I could never figure which eye was looking at me.

At first when coming to the farm, he was gruff with me. But eventually he mellowed, when he realized I had the knack to become a good cowman.

I picked up my speed, wanting to make it to the kitchen phone before it was too late, and before the folks I wanted at the meeting would have gone to bed. I knew Jacques Bassett could be at the meeting unless he was out of town. Dad and I had sold cattle to him over the years—cows that had gone to Canada for handsome prices. As a dealer, he had a sound reputation for being honest and sticking by his word. He always wore a felt hat, a V-neck sweater over a white shirt, and dress pants. With his thick French accent and good manners, he looked and acted the part of a country gentleman.

I was sure Emily Ann Gray could be at the meeting to get Iverson's account in order. However, since she had a close family connection to Iverson, the dynamics of the meeting could be interesting.

I felt uptight, thinking about my cows. If Iverson didn't sell his herd, I'd have to sell animals I cherished, such as Precious and her daughters plus five milking granddaughters. I knew I'd feel devastated if they went; however, the thought of my herd getting an epidemic was downright scary.

In the entryway, I hung my coat and glanced to see that all the lights were on in the kitchen. Rosita sat, in a white terrycloth robe, bent over with her back turned, hand-stitching pieces of cloth spread on the table. Her jet-black hair flowed down her back. She stood up and rested her hands on her work when I entered. "¡Hola, Señor Jason."

"Hi, Rosita." I pointed toward the table. "You sew a dress?"

"Sí, una falda." She motioned from her waist to the floor.

"Oh, a skirt." I lifted the wall phone and dialed the vet.

"Sí." Rosita resumed her sewing.

I managed to reach all the people I needed to and was relieved that they all could come to the meeting.

I pulled out a chair at the opposite end of the table from Rosita. An old newspaper lay in the seat, one apparently left when our belongings were stored. A news story concerning Iverson caught my eye.

The Huntersville Weekly
June 15, 1995

Huntersville's representative to the Vermont State Legislature, Steven Iverson, will run unopposed in the upcoming November election. He has been Huntersville's representative for twenty years, exerting his influence on many issues. He's been instrumental in acquiring funding for roads, bridges, and education, plus being a backer of Act 250, Vermont's development law.

O.J. Simpson, awaiting trial, has been charged with the brutal knifing murder of his former wife, Nicole Brown Simpson, and her companion, Ronald Goldman...

I finished the article, sitting in disbelief that such a crime of passion could be committed. I realized that I was pretty innocent of what's out there in the world. My problem with mastitis seemed tame. I closed the paper.

I looked across the table at Rosita, intrigued as I watched her hands move, joining two pieces of fabric along a seam. She bent closely to the material, continually smoothing the cloth. She stitched quickly, occasionally holding up her work for inspection. The seam was perfect and straight as if stitched by a sewing machine.

I continued to be amazed at how easily she moved—perfectly coordinated, with little effort. It was obvious by her looks and household activity that she was from another culture. I sat thinking about her ancestry, maybe Indian, maybe Spanish, early settlers of the Mexican territory. I wondered if she even knew who her great-grandparents were as I did, able to trace my ancestral roots back to England.

After minutes passed, I left my chair, throwing the newspaper in the waste basket. "Good night, Rosita."

"Buenas noches, Señor Jason."

I went to my room and sat on my bed in the dark. I stopped worrying over the upcoming meeting, deciding I'd done all that I could to deal with the situation.

Since the fire, my world had flipped to another universe. Just days ago, I'd dreamed of taking a rare picture of a bobcat. Now, that goal was all but forgotten—heavy stuff, my future and disease, had pushed aside what seemed like an exciting adventure— a dream flitted away by change.

My thoughts turned to Ellen. Dreaming of my love was something I often did at night in my room before going to sleep. Four more days and she'd be home. Maybe by late afternoon, we'd shop for a diamond. Then we'd go to the Hideaway, start a fire, cook our meal, and cuddle on the couch in the warmth of a sleeping bag. The thought of her brought on my manly excitement. I rubbed my hands, thinking how she'd feel as I gently pulled her body next to mine. The scent of her sweetness would put me into a swoon. I gulped hard just imagining it.

I slowly took off my shoes, then stopped. My stocking feet rested on the braided rug. I'd like to be holding Ellen on this very bed, telling her how much I missed her—how much I loved her.

Suddenly, my fantasy world stopped as I heard footsteps in the hall. The chapel door opened and shut. It slammed a couple of times but didn't latch. I listened. In moments the walls became alive with Rosita's singing and guitar-playing.

As before, I didn't understand the lyrics being sung as a chant. But I was mesmerized by the sound of her voice, again reminding me of the white-throated sparrow and how its sound affected me. For some reason, I couldn't explain why the music filled me with warmth and, for the moment, disconnected me from all my worries and cares. I wanted to go in their chapel to just sit and listen; however, I felt it best not to invade their privacy.

While I sat on my bed, the walls seemed to shake from the high-penetrating notes. After a while I stood, pulled the newspaper from my pocket, the one that I'd just bought at Gilda's, and laid it on my bureau, then headed for the bathroom. On the way, I stopped by the slightly opened door. I couldn't resist watching.

The candles flickered deep in the three jars—the only light in the room. José sat on a bench, holding a string of beads—his head bent, mumbling repetitive words. Rosita, on the other bench, faced the likeness of the crucified Christ. She cradled the guitar, and her long hair draped over her far shoulder as she sang the chant. Candlelight danced shadows on her face. Multi-colored earrings, connected in segments, dangled when she turned and sang a high note—her bottom lip slightly quivered with emotion.

After leaving the bathroom, I returned to my room with my door ajar so I could get the full effect of the music. I didn't turn on my light but stretched out listening. I fell into a deep sleep.

Some distance away, I heard an alarm clock ring. I opened my eyes and blinked, realizing the sound came from José's room. It was four-thirty.

I jumped up, turned on the light, yanked off my street clothes and threw them on the bed. I grabbed barn jeans, a flannel shirt, and changed my socks.

In the kitchen, Rosita made the coffee. "Buenos dìas, Señor Jason."

"Good morning, Rosita." I took my usual chair. "Beautiful...let's see." I motioned with my hand at my wide-open mouth. "Sing...singing... comprender?"

"Sí...noche." Rosita shook her head. "No inglés."

"Yes, but beautiful." I didn't know if she understood. I started drinking my coffee.

"Sí, cantar bonito." She smiled.

"Yes." I nodded. "Your singing *is* beautiful."

She smiled and began to hum as she served the coffee.

José came to the table. "Buenos días."

"Morning, José." My thoughts were on the upcoming meeting as the three of us sat in silence, drinking our coffee and snacking on jelly-filled tortillas.

Vehicle lights came in the yard and flashed across the kitchen windows. I wondered who would be out at this hour, but I didn't move from my chair. Soon there was a knock. I got up and went to the door. "Come in, Sheriff." I looked closely at Krads. "What's up?"

He reached in his vest pocket and thrust a folded paper at me. "The district attorney, Sean Cook, has signed an order impounding your computer." Krads enunciated his words slowly and clearly, injecting his full authority as Sheriff.

"Our computer?" Wide-eyed, I held the paper in my hand. "Strange. Don't you think?"

"The Vermont State Fire Marshal wants it." Krads reached for the paper. "Whitaker...Stanley Whitaker is the guy's name."

I stared at the legal document. "What's with the computer?"

Krads, wearing a stern expression, adjusted his pants beneath his pistol, bullet pouch, and handcuff case. "I have no idea, but I have the authority to search the premises."

"Oh, I'm sure you do!" I said with sarcasm. "I'll see if I can find it in among all of our stuff."

Heading down the hallway toward the rooms with Murray belongings, I shook my head, wondering. I found the computer setting on a table. I reached over chairs and knelt on the couch to retrieve the computer tower. I returned, handing it to Krads. "You don't need the screen?"

"No. I'm sure the crime lab has a screen." Krads turned, holding the tower while I opened the door.

The image of Ruth struck me—a victim, innocent of any crime, recovering from painful burns. Meanwhile, the fire marshal and the insurance company dig for reasons not to pay the claim. As I left the house, the charge of arson occurred to me, but Ruth...no way!

At seven with the morning chores finished, José, Rosita, and I were back at the house for breakfast. Two double-decker cattle trucks rumbled into the yard, their all-steel bodies making plenty of racket. I surmised each could fit thirty-five cows. The cattle trailers were built low to the ground with slits along the side for ventilation. The drivers got out and talked among themselves, waiting for directions from Jacques Bassett.

The dealer followed the trucks and parked near me. He got out and said, "I want to look over Iverson's cows before our meeting."

"Sure." I put aside thoughts of breakfast.

Leaving his car, Jacques pulled on light-blue coveralls and slipped into some boots. "I can find a home for your herd, but Iverson's...it's a big question." We headed toward the barn. "Mastitis pretty bad?"

"Yeah, for sure." I adjusted my cap. "The creamery shut him off because of it, besides the place being nasty dirty."

After looking over the cows, Jacques scratched his chin. "You say the bank owns Iverson's cows at twelve hundred?"

I nodded. "That's the word."

He scowled. "The bank's taking one big bath." He glanced toward the section in the barn holding my cows. "How did your herd adjust?"

"Okay, so far." I pointed out Penny and her two sisters, Posey and Poppy. "I just hope none of them get this mastitis."

"How about selling?"

"If Iverson sells, I'm staying."

Jacques looked closely at the three mostly black daughters of Precious. "You'd better sell these three at least."

"Gee, they're my best! Besides, Penny has a red and white bull calf. The bull stud will want to pass on her before they take the calf."

"It's your call, but it's months before you can collect on the calf."

"Yeah, I know." I paused. "There're a bunch of contingencies that have to be met."

"I'll take the three today and the calf for ten thousand." He looked the heifers over again. "Eighty percent of these bull contracts never come through."

"Yeah, I've heard."

"I'll stable these three and the calf in my barn on the border for testing. In a few months, if the calf makes it, I'll owe you three thousand more."

"Sounds fair." I passed my hand across my forehead. "Let me think about it."

When Fred Watkins walked in the barn, Jacques continued looking over my cows.

Fred came carrying a bottle of purple fluid and a four-section paddle. "Morning, Jason and Jacques. We moving cows today?"

"Definitely." I glanced at the kit. "You want to check through a bunch of cows?"

"Yup—confirm that the Iverson cows are as bad off as suspected." Fred, a slender guy, moved into a group. His glass eye didn't focus when he turned toward me. "You hold this cow in her stall and I'll draw milk."

"Okay." I leaned on the butt of the thin cow. She was listless, standing still was no problem.

The vet bent down, drawing milk from each quarter into the four-sectioned paddle. A squirt of fluid mixed with the milk immediately coagulated, looking like thick mucus. "No question but what she's infected." He passed me a paint stick. "Mark her." Fred looked at his watch. "To save time, I'll take milk from just one quarter. We'll randomly select cows from the group that you didn't find signs of mastitis. We'll have time to check on a bunch."

I nodded. "Sounds reasonable."

Fred rapidly moved through the cows. Nearly every one checked showed the thick slimy reaction to the testing fluid. "I'm guessing this may be mycoplasma. It could also be staph, strep, or an E. coli infection, but it's only a guess. We'd have to send samples to the lab to really know."

I drew a red paint mark on the last cow. "Is there a cure?"

"Not really, not for mycoplasma. It doesn't respond to drug therapy. A lot of these cows look depressed, with droopy ears, showing they have abscess—an indication of mycoplasma.

"Why so widespread?"

"Ignoring the problem, dirty equipment, lack of interest, you name it." Fred had emptied the bottle of testing fluid. "We've checked about thirty cows. I've seen enough." He stood in the feed alley. "I know you don't want to hear this, but your cows are exposed." He looked at me with his good eye. "I'd completely empty this barn—wash down, disinfect, idle it for a while and start over."

My eyes widened. "Gee, isn't that being overly cautious?" Fred was right. I didn't want to hear it.

"No, not with mycoplasma." He headed out of the barn. "That's my recommendation."

Emily Ann Gray drove in the yard. She wore a black pantsuit, white shirt, and a maroon ribbon tie. She was carrying a briefcase as she left her car. Her straight, salt-and-pepper hair hung evenly at shoulder length. With steel-rim glasses set on a pale complexion, she certainly looked the part as president of the Huntersville Bank.

The four of us went to the house and took chairs around the kitchen table. Rosita and José left for the barn.

Iverson walked through the door, disheveled with his slick hair uncombed, bags beneath his eyes, and the tails of his wrinkled dress shirt hanging. He looked at me. "Goddamn, you're causin' a hell of a stir!" He managed a weak laugh. "Pullin' all your guns on me!"

I snapped. "Not really!"

Iverson adjusted his belt and sat down while looking at the faces around the table. He nervously laughed again. "This looks goddamned serious." His belly rubbed the table as he hunched forward.

"It is, Steven." Emily Ann held a print-out sheet. Her demeanor of an all-business attitude held everyone's attention. "I need to satisfy our loan for your cows at two hundred and forty thousand."

Jacques coughed and rubbed his chin.

Fred's one good eye turned her way. "Emily Ann, Steven's cows have a major problem."

"What is it?" Not looking up, she continued reviewing Iverson's loan portfolio.

"Steven's herd is unfit for milk sales." Fred held his attention on her, waiting for a reaction.

"What?" She dropped the spreadsheet and turned toward Iverson. "You can't ship milk?"

"This is a bunch of shit!" Iverson grumbled. "I was shipping milk last month." He whined, "Milk inspectors have been riding me for years."

Emily Ann shoved her paperwork. "No income?"

"I...I was hoping the kid could get me back to shipping again." Iverson looked my way.

"Not with your cows." I paused. "They're radioactive with disease."

Iverson pounded the table. "Bullshit!"

Fred snapped at Iverson, "Your herd has a hot bug."

Iverson yelled back, "I don't believe it."

Emily Ann broke in, "Okay, okay." She turned to Jacques. "What are our options?"

Jacques' felt fedora rested on his knee. He ran his fingers between the two ridges. "I can't sell any to another farmer." He looked at Iverson. "I'll charge for trucking to the slaughterhouse. That's the best I can do. Even at that, a lot of cows won't pass inspection."

Iverson shook his head. "I just don't believe this!"

Emily Ann looked toward Fred. "Do they have value for meat?"

"Depends on what type of mastitis it is. Some forms are okay for beef." Fred looked at Iverson. "But his cows are small and thin."

"All of you just love this!" Iverson yelled. "Seeing a poor guy squirm. Puttin' the old screws right to me!"

Emily Ann didn't listen to Iverson. "Start moving the herd out today and send the check to the Huntersville Bank in my name, Emily Ann Gray."

"What!" Iverson cried. "But...but you can't."

Emily Ann coldly looked at the man she'd practically raised as a boy. "But I can."

Iverson pleaded. "I'm broke. I'll be out on the street!"

She scanned his asset sheet. "Do you have any of the young cattle as listed here?"

Iverson slouched, resigned. "Yeah, a few."

She placed papers into her briefcase. "Find a buyer for them and the bank will share a part of the sale with you until you can find work."

She got up, headed for the door, looking at me. "I need to talk with your folks."

Iverson yelled, "Hey, what going on?"

Emily Ann turned to look at him. "I want to see you at the bank immediately!"

The next morning Emily Ann called Dad and Mom. She wanted them to come to the bank for a hastily arranged meeting. Buddy Silver was applying pressure to settle the Iverson account. Emily Ann suggested a plan for Dad and Mom to buy the whole farm for the amount due on the Iverson real estate note which amounted to five hundred thousand. The amount seemed reasonable, but I was the catch. They signed a purchase and sales agreement for five thousand dollars to hold the deal for me, depending if I decided to stay at Iverson's. Emily Ann asked for closure within ninety days

In the negotiation, an agreement was reached that Iverson could stay in his house until April 1, 1996. However, the bank took a huge loss on the cows.

twenty-six

Ruth

I'd been home from the hospital for a day. The burns on my hands still gave me plenty of pain. It helped if I stayed quiet; I didn't feel the terrible throbbing as much. Mom put the white facial cream only on my nose to heal the deep redness. She used a soothing lanolin cream on my lips and the rest of my face.

I was totally helpless. Mom had to feed me and take care of all my needs. I hoped that within a few days I could begin to manage somewhat on my own.

After lunch, she came to my room in the front corner of the house. She stood looking out a window. "I wonder what's going on down at the farm?" She went to another window. "The standing corn Cooner and you planted this spring blocks the view of most of the farmyard."

"What do you see?" I didn't want to leave my bed and move my hands.

"Cars and people are in the drive. I can't see any more." Mom continued her curiosity. "Jason told me the district attorney impounded our computer."

"Our computer?" My hands lay flat on the sheet. Although I didn't move, a feeling of alarm started a deep wrenching pain. "The district attorney has our computer?" I drew a deep breath to hold off taking a pain pill. "They'll know all our business. Read all the letters. Letters I've sent to Frieda and others."

Mom continued to look toward the farm. "So?"

"My inquiries for the Center." I hadn't told Mom or Dad about the results of my New York trip. I wanted to wait for a good time to ask for their support. I'd told Cooner, but I was sure he hadn't mentioned it to my folks. Now, the fire—everything had changed.

"Inquiries...like what?" Mom left the window. She slid her finger feeling for a curl of her hair. "Why...what were you asking?"

"For funding. That's why I had to go to New York." The throbbing was building. "I had to ask for support for the Center from the Elias M. Cole Foundation."

"How much support?"

"I don't know. Thirty to forty thousand a year."

"Oh my God!" She stood by my bed, winding her hair. "It's up to you to find the support?"

"Yeah, there's no one else." I gritted my teeth in pain. "Mom, I need a pill!"

"Ruth!" She pulled her finger from her hair. "God!" She hurried from the room, mumbling. "So many problems!" She returned. "You haven't told us any of this!"

"I have, but you didn't listen. You knew I went to New York."

"The funding of that place is all on your shoulders?" She bent over me—a pill in one hand and a glass of water in the other.

"Yeah, that's why I've been searching on the internet."

Mom held the glass close to my mouth. "Show me your tongue for this pill...here's the straw."

I sucked down the water.

Mom's face drew taut. "Maybe they'll just keep our computer for a day or so."

She went back to the window, continuing to wind her hair. "I wonder what's going on down there?"

twenty-seven

Jason

Ruth was on my mind most of the morning. I needed to see how she was doing, but I had to stay at the farm to help load Iverson's cattle. The loading of over two hundred head lasted into the afternoon. We'd just finished when Jacques pulled into the yard with a trailer behind his truck. He rolled down his window. "You going to sell those three heifers and the red and white bull?"

For most of the day, I'd mulled over the warning in regard to the spread of disease. I remembered Ellen telling me about the Kokopelli with his flute and wares, traveling from Indian tribe to Indian tribe, presumably spreading disease. My situation was similar, unprotected cows with no immunity being exposed to diseases. While Iverson's cows were somewhat able to cope with their infection, mine might die from a case of a not-so-common strain of mastitis. How could I deny that Fred Watkins had a wealth of experience regarding animal health, especially involving the spread of mastitis. It pained me to sell, skimming the best from the top of my herd. But at the moment, I decided to err on the side of caution. "Okay, I guess I'll sell for ten thousand."

Jacques wrote the check and passed it to me.

"Thanks." I folded it and slipped it in my pocket. I vowed that this money was going to be for a special purpose. I didn't know what, but it was going to be saved for something memorable—something out of the ordinary.

My herd of nearly eighty cows, heifers, and calves appeared to be a scant number for a barn with a four-hundred- head capacity. But that was okay with me. With the Iverson cattle gone, I now had time to clean the remaining barn and make sound decisions without the fear of contamination.

Before I left the barn, I checked on Precious. She looked great—due to calve right away.

After dealing with the cattle, I was in my room sitting on my unmade bed. My pants, shirts, and socks had been thrown in disarray. While dressing for town, my thoughts went to the weekend. I was struck by a strong desire to have Ellen at my side: to feel her in my arms, and feel the willowy curves of her slender body. On Friday, we'd make it official, buy a ring, and become engaged.

Late afternoon, I headed toward town to locate a frame for the enlarged picture of Ellen wearing the butterfly shirt. Chub's Variety carried frames, but Bubble's tattooed Tree of Life and come-on style turned me off. Abe's, three doors down from the Huntersville Bank, also carried frames.

Abraham Goldstein, in his eighties, was an immigrant from Germany, a survivor of the Holocaust.

A huge electric clock, about two feet in diameter, hung in the store window. Since Abe was by trade a watch repairman, everyone in town set their time by his blue and red neon clock. The earth could be off its axis, and no one in Huntersville would know because for years Abe's clock had kept perfect time.

I parked at the curb where I saw him through the store window. He was sitting near the door on a high stool at his watch repair bench. However, now, since most of his former patrons had digital and battery-powered watches, Abe passed his time reading paperbacks and waiting for customers. He wore a green celluloid visor held by a leather strap—something left over from his watch-repair days. He lived alone since his wife had died. They had led private lives, never circulating much, so he didn't know many in town.

I entered to the sound of a bell. Abe lifted his head out of his book. He had little brown eyes with a face reminding me of a shriveled apple.

He shut his book. "Can I help you?" He spoke in a thick German accent.

"Yeah, I need a frame to fit this picture." I inhaled a stale dusty smell. Most of the merchandise on the shelves had aged along with its owner.

"Well, follow me." Abe, terribly bent, scuffed in baby steps toward the back of the store. The wooden floor creaked as we went. "I have a couple that will work." He stepped on a stool and reached for the frames, blowing the dust off before passing them to me. "The gold tin for three dollars and the mahogany for seven."

"I'll take the mahogany." I stood beside a hip-high display case. It was wooden with inlaid glass for a top. Valuables, such as rings, necklaces, watches, and silverware, were kept in the case. I casually looked through the dust at several rings. They rested on a felt pad that had faded to a pea-green.

Abe wiped the glass with a dust-rag. He flicked on a display light. "Interested?"

I detected hope in the old man's voice. "Maybe."

I wanted Ellen to have the ring of her choice. Looking down through the glass, I saw most of Abe's were silver with a diamond no bigger than a tiny pebble. He only had a half dozen in the case. Of course, I realized he hadn't restocked in years—running out his inventory until the day he closed the door. I was about to leave and settle up when I noticed a gold ring in an ivory-colored ring box with a sparkling diamond, or it could be sparkling if it wasn't in the case. It was the only gold ring and it was set off by itself.

I stared through the glass. "Gosh, what's this ring?"

Abe shrugged, disappointed in my lack of interest in any of the silver rings. "Oh, that's an antique, the von Friesian diamond."

"It's huge!" Even my untrained eye could see it was valuable. "Can I look at it?"

"Sure." Abe reached in the case. "This is a perfect diamond, flawless in every way." He handed it to me. "The band is twenty-four carat gold."

"Gosh, it's beautiful!"

"One of a kind." He leaned on the case, supporting himself by his elbows. "That ring came from the Lady von Friesian estate." He looked fondly at the diamond. "In the mid-nineteen thirties, my father was her Ladyship's closest confidant and estate manager. I was ten when Hitler rounded up my parents along with all their valuables. But before that happened, my father, fearing the worst, hid this ring in the heel of my shoe. He cut a slot and covered the ring with a thick patch of leather."

"What a story!" I slipped the ring past the first joint of my little finger.

"My father sent me to roam the streets with a fake identification and a name change. I spent the war years as a house boy for a German general." Abe took the ring. He held it up with his thumb and forefinger. "This ring stayed in my shoe long after I needed a new pair." His voice broke. "My soles were worn through but the thick heel still hid the ring. I went barefoot to save the shoes, especially when they started pinching my feet." His eyes became misty. "My wife, until her death, wore it our entire married lives."

"Is it for sale?"

Abe nodded. "Yes. You see I have no family, no one to pass it on to."

"What's a diamond like this worth?"

"Priceless." He placed it back under the glass. "This ring deserves a special lady."

"I want to give it to a special lady." I felt for Jacques' check. "How much are you asking?"

The old man looked me up and down. "Well...well." His eyelids lifted. "Five thousand would be a bargain."

"Phew...that's a bargain?"

"Yes, it's worth that." In deep thought, he climbed back on his stool and opened his book. "I guess I could sell it for five."

"I might be back. I'll be thinking of the ring and your story." I turned and left.

On my way to the bank to deposit my check, I wondered if I should part with such a sum for a ring. And anyway, what did a beautiful ring have to do with true love...nothing. On the other hand, Ellen liked nice things. A gift of the ring would show her that I was capable of going to great lengths for her. The gift would certainly outclass any worn in Huntersville. I had promised that we both would go shopping for one, but wouldn't it be nice if I absolutely stunned her with a ring that was one-of-a-kind? I smiled. "Yes... nice."

Knowing Abe would wonder about accepting a check, I cashed half of the ten thousand and deposited the other five in a separate account. I went back to Abe's.

He hadn't left his stool. "You're back so soon?"

I passed him a bulging envelope. "Here's five thousand in cash."

His little brown eyes widened. His face brightened. "Well...well. I...I really didn't..."

While reacting, he spread the unsealed envelope and counted five bundles, taking one out to check the amount. His bony thumb flipped through ten hundred-dollar bills. "You're a wise young man."

I smiled. "I guess."

He scuffed back to the display case. I followed. The bulging envelope stuck out of his coat pocket. He nodded, handing me the ring. "Such a fine bargain."

"If you say so." I really didn't know or care; this was for Ellen.

I left Abe's with the ring box in my pocket, feeling on a high, knowing I was going to blow Ellen away with this ring. I rubbed the fuzz of the box, imagining the look on her face.

I pulled into the Iverson yard near five. When I left my truck, I heard the milker pump running. José was milking. I needed to change my clothes and feed the cows and young cattle. I passed through the entry and kitchen, past the bathroom. The washer and dryer were running, and the door to my bedroom was swung open. A clean pine smell filled the air. Rosita was scrubbing the floor on her hands and knees. My bed had been neatly made, and all of my dirty clothes were nowhere to be seen.

Surprised and flustered, I'd never expected her to be my maid, on the floor of all places. "Rosita!"

"No vacas. Rosita limpia." She came to her feet motioning toward the floor and the walls, showing the entire room scrubbed and freshened.

"Oh, no cows, so you cleaned the house." I realized that this girl had to be working at something all the time.

"Sí." She smiled. "Mi padre ordeña."

"I heard the milker pump."

"Sí." She left my room and carried the scrub pail into their chapel.

I shut my door, took the frame from the bag, and mounted the enlarged picture of Ellen. I placed it on a red woven placemat Rosita had just put on my bureau. The picture was next to a freshly picked wild aster in a Forget Me Not creamer. I stepped back, beaming with joy while looking at my beautiful blond in her butterfly shirt. The purple aster added a pleasing touch. Rosita liked flowers.

I changed and headed toward the barn. After checking on Precious, feeding my cattle, and seeing José, I got in my truck to visit Ruth. I also wanted to check the corn to see how it was maturing. Driving along Murray's Flat, I looked over and noticed activity at the burn site. As I came closer there were several cars parked in the yard near the farm sign.

Yellow tape surrounded the charred heap of what was once the barn. As I drove into the yard, Sheriff Krads bounded out of his police car, waving his arms, "No one's allowed."

I sat in my truck with the window rolled down. "What's going on?" I felt my anger build.

"Crime scene, no one's allowed." Krads stood by my truck door with his hand resting on his revolver.

"Crime scene!" I felt struck like a flash of lightening. "Geez, Sheriff, don't be so goddamned dramatic." I started to open my door.

Krads pushed it shut. "Suspicious fire. Stay in the truck!"

"What do you mean?" I pulled on my cap. "This is my property!"

"You forego property rights in the face of crime." Krads adjusted his pants, bringing attention to his weapon.

"Oh, bullshit!" I could feel my head throb. "Is Stanley Whitaker here?"

"I'll get him." Krads strutted away.

I fumed, dumbfounded, but on the edge of my anger, fear crept in. I sat looking at a heap of barn ash. It was still smoldering, sending off thin ripples of smoke that rose only a few feet high from the black and gray mound. A crew circled the remains of the hay dryer.

Whitaker came to my truck.

I asked in a demanding tone, "What's going on?"

He didn't answer me. "How's your sister doing? Is she able to withstand intense questioning?"

"I don't know. I was about to check on her." My anger began to fade. "The District Attorney and I need to see her in his office."

"Why? Why Ruth?" My voice pushed the words through a sudden chill. "About what?"

"Suspected arson."

twenty-eight

Ruth

I was a prime suspect in a case of arson. Fire Marshal Whitaker sent me a formal request signed by District Attorney Sean Cook and delivered by Sheriff Krads to appear in his office at ten o'clock, Friday morning. The news struck my family as unreal.

Dad said it was the insurance company's ploy to get out of paying the coverage of $630,000. In quiet moments when Mom's hands weren't busy, she nervously worked her ringlets.

Jason was angry. "They're a bunch of badge-happy sons-a-bitches."

I was uneasy, but I had nothing to hide. I felt they could question me endlessly and it wouldn't matter. It almost seemed like a joke.

However, by Friday morning my self-assured attitude started to wither. My nervousness was intensifying. After Mom tended to my hands, I decided I wanted to see Cooner and get his take on the situation. Before leaving the house, I took some Extra-Strength Tylenol. Outside in the yard, the sun shone through the fresh morning air.

Cooner was sitting on his newly located bench. A path leading to the seat was lined with pink and white impatiens. Mom had had her workers transplant taller white and pink phlox in back of the shorter flowers.

His leverwood cane was at his side. He was rubbing the knob of the stick with his big hand. "Well, well, look who's up and at it this mornin'."

"Morning, Cooner." I sat next to him as he automatically slid over. "Mom's made a great place for your bench."

"Ain't it, though? She placed it so I can look off and see the mountain." He glanced at my hands. "How ya doing?"

"Healing nicely." I adjusted my wig with my wrists. "You'd never know I didn't have hair." It had been five days since the fire. My face was healing nicely. Since I had a fair complexion, I had blotches of red where new skin had started to grown back. My hands were different. There were still areas on the top, from my fingers to my wrist, that were open wounds.

Cooner closely checked me out. "You're lookin' good—hair could be the real thing."

"I know I'm lucky to be as well off as I am." I paused. "Except…"

"Yeah, except. Bringin' ya in…" He rapped his cane. "That's…that's hogwash!"

"I wonder why? I think I've already cleared most points with Whitaker."

"Bertha says Whitaker's been talkin' to Scoop." Cooner held his handkerchief about to wipe his mouth. "Those wires jumpin' the fuses. What about them?"

"Jason took care of that." I felt the pain creeping into my hands. "He disconnected them."

"Threw them away of course?"

"No. He left them in the bottom of the fuse box."

"No foolin'!" He tapped his cane.

"Jason said we might use them again… just in case."

Sheriff Krad's car drove in the yard at nine forty-five.

I turned to Cooner. "Oh, no! What's he doing here?"

Krads rolled down his window. "Ready to go to the District Attorney's office?"

Mom was furious. She ran out the back door. "This is ridiculous!" She went to the sheriff's car. "I'm taking Ruth in for the appointment!"

Krads nodded, backed around, and left.

Mom fumed all the way into town. "District Attorney Cook is behind all this hoopla!" Her eyes darted my way. "Being elected right out of law school, he's trying to make a name for himself!" She stopped abruptly in the Huntersville County Court House parking lot and helped me out of the car.

District Attorney Sean Cook's office was in the Court House building. Mom held my arm as we climbed the gray granite steps. Four white Grecian columns supported the front of the building, seeming like guardians of justice. We passed between two of them. The columns cast a dark shadow. Pressing a huge thumb latch, Mom opened the tall heavy door. Inside, our shoes clicked on the polished granite floor, echoing off the high ceiling and wide hallway. The place sent a chill through me. I'd never been here before.

Glossy paintings of century-old judges lined the walls. They were dressed in stiff collars and eighteen hundreds' attire. I felt that their stern expressions and beady eyes were staring at me. I calmed, reassuring myself as we walked that the scales of justice would certainly balance in my favor.

Down the hall, Mom opened the door to Cook's office. A middle-aged receptionist, wearing steel-rimmed glasses, brought us to his office. She was somber, showing no emotion as she tapped on Cook's door.

"Come in." Both Cook and Whitaker were huddled, no doubt discussing my case.

We faced a wall of books behind Cook's desk. The furnishings were unpretentious, even common.

Whitaker took a chair and Cook turned to meet us. He was about my height, dark features, black hair, well-groomed, probably just a few years older than I was.

After introductions were made, Cook said, "Ruth, we want to question you privately."

Whitaker opened the door. "Mrs. Murray, please wait in the outer office."

Mom scowled. "Okay." She walked out, reaching for strands of hair.

The three of us sat in a semicircle. I faced Cook and Whitaker.

Cook began: "Ms. Murray, you have the right to ask for council. In fact I would recommend it."

"I don't feel the need." My hands started a dull pain but I tried to force myself to stay calm.

"Okay. This questioning will be recorded." Cook flicked a switch. "You are Ruth Murray?"

"Yes." I sat, resting my hands on the arms of my chair.

"Just prior to the fire that destroyed your house and barn your insurance coverage was increased by two hundred thousand."

"Yes. This has already been discussed with Mr. Whitaker."

Cook nodded. "I want it recorded." He cleared his throat. "Again, tell me why your insurance coverage was just recently increased?"

"In an audit of our coverage by the Eagle Insurance Company, I was asked by our agent, Judge Crabtree, to increase the coverage."

Cook looked at his notes. "Did you in any way prompt this audit?"

"No." I looked directly at Cook. "I'd just recently come home from Georgia. Fire insurance was the furthest thing from my mind."

"Is Georgia connected to the Elias M. Cole Foundation?"

"No connection if they don't continue to fund the Piedmont Center."

"Do you think they will?"

"No." I answered calmly. "If they do, it will be a minimal amount."

Cook raised his voice in a pressing tone. "Weren't you trying to find substitute funding?" He leaned forward. "Telling the director of the Center," he checked his notes, "a Ms. Angrish, that you would somehow locate funding?"

"Yes." My hands were beginning to throb. My throat tightened, knowing he had my computer with a quantity of information.

"You've had no luck in finding a source of nearly forty thousand dollars...right?"

"Yes, you're right."

Cook lowered his voice. "Am I correct in saying you feel passionate over the work at the Center, helping disadvantaged children?"

"Yes."

Cook stared at me with a stern look. "You'd do most anything to locate funding?"

"I didn't start our fire if that's what you're implying." I needed more pain meds.

"Someone started the fire." There was a long pause. Both men looked at me with dour expressions.

"And you think I did it?" I was angry. "What proof do you have?"

Cook calmly asked, "Have you done electrical wiring?"

"Yes, however, I'm not an electrician."

"I'm going to show you some pictures. Tell me if you recognize them." Cook reached into his briefcase for a manila folder, holding up a picture. "Are you familiar with this fuse box?" He looked at it. "Of course it's been through the fire, charred and blackened."

"Yes." I nodded.

Cook looked at me. "Tell me what you know about it?"

"It's similar to the fuse box that went to our hay dryer."

"Right." He reached for another picture. "This is the same box with the cover open."

I studied the picture. I saw charred bypass wires connected over the remains of two blackened fuses, a broken Forget Me Not creamer, and what looked like a power drill attachment were in the bottom of the box. The attachment looked like a buffer of some sort.

A sick feeling caused me to go limp. My hands were on fire. I was the hunted, felled by a fatal blow. "Yes…the…the same box. But…but what…what is that creamer and drill thing doing there?"

Cook and Whitaker were silent. They moved to the edge of their chairs. "We want you to tell us."

"I…I *don't* know."

Cook was in my face with a steely glace and a raised voice. "You've admitted to being the last to leave the barn. Yet, you have no idea how the fire started?"

"I…I have no idea." I wanted to cry. I now knew the meaning of being framed—a pile of circumstantial evidence against me.

Cook read from a briefing pad. "We have testimony under oath that you, on two occasions, connected the wires to start the dryer motor. You knew that if the fuse box cover was shut the wires would arc against the metal—the creamer filled with fuel and a saturated felt drill buffer would burst into flames. Flames so intense the fuse box wouldn't hold them." Cook lowered the pad. "You knew that!"

"My…my brother disconnected the wires."

"You!"He raised his voice. "You, in a matter of minutes, reconnected them." He paused. "Your creamer!" He held another picture. "Your fuel can!" He reached for one more." "Your felt buffer!"

"Mine?" I stared at the unusual tool, the size and shape of a rose bud. "I...I've never seen that thing." My lips quivered as tears streamed down my face.

Cook gathered his papers. "That's enough for today. You're to stay at your home until our investigation is complete."

I stood with my throbbing hands held to my breast. Whitaker opened the office door. I ran to Mom.

I was distraught. Riding home, all I could do was sob. My hands hurt like never before, but the evidence shown hurt me even more. I was not guilty of arson. I wondered how I could prove it.

Mom wasn't in much better shape. "Being charged with arson is totally unbelievable." When she drove in, Jason was waiting to hear the news.

twenty-nine

Jason

"Ruth an arsonist! No way!" When Mom told me the news, I felt an overwhelming rage. My thoughts immediately went to Iverson as the culprit.

It was at his place that I'd seen a buffer set of three. I had a hunch that if his apartment was searched, the tool set could be found. Knowing Iverson's housekeeping habits, it would be an easy search. They wouldn't have been moved since I'd been there. If there were only three remaining buffers, he'd have to explain the whereabouts of the missing fourth.

I had to get to Whitaker and Sean Cook. I raced across town, parked, and leaped up the courthouse steps, taking two at a time.

Cook and Whitaker had left. I told Cook's secretary I needed to see them right away. As I drove back to the Iverson farm, I tried to make sense of it all. He hated the Murrays. He also was desperate for me to take over the farm. So desperate he figured he could burn us out with no one knowing who did it—except for the buffer.

Driving into the yard, I noticed his car parked by his door. While mulling over the crime, I went to my room to change for chores. I was sure Iverson was the scum-bag who started the fire. I sat on my bed with my head in my hands, gripped with anger and the overwhelming urge to run to his apartment to locate the felt buffers. But I couldn't. I needed Cook and Whitaker as witnesses to the fact that the buffer came from Iverson.

To cool my anger, I welcomed a distraction. I felt in my pocket for the fuzz-covered ring box. I put it on the bureau and opened it to admire the ring one more time. The big diamond sparkled even in the dim light that came through my window. Ellen would love it.

I couldn't wait. I flushed with excitement, thinking of seeing her. She'd run to me. I'd run to her. We'd leap into each other's arms. I could feel her slender body—our curves pressed tightly as hairs in a braid. I rubbed my finger over the diamond, rehearsing my plan. With Ellen's help, we'd make up a bed roll, pack a lunch and a bottle of wine, hike to the Hideaway, light the candles, start a fire in the stove, and eat. The wine would give us a warm relaxed feeling. After some intimate smooching and the exchange of how we would love each other forever, we'd lay out the bedroll and snuggle. This time I'd be prepared. I pulled open the top drawer of my bureau, saw the small bag, and smiled. Our time together would be fantastic.

I took a deep breath and brought myself back to reality. I shut the cover of the ring box and closed the drawer. I noticed the newspaper I'd put on the bureau earlier. I opened it and glanced as I reached for a clean pair of socks in the next drawer down. The Murrays dominated the front page:

The Huntersville Weekly
July 20, 1995

Gigantic Fire Destroys Murray Farm

In less than an hour fire ripped through the house and barn…

O.J. Simpson Trial Captivates The Country

The trial of the decade continues as evidence mounts that it was a crime of passion…two murders with a knife…

The Good Shepherd Window Restored

The beautiful multi-colored window was dedicated to Capt. Ezekial Murray, killed in the Civil War battle at Gettysburg on July 3, 1863.

Many were present for the unveiling of the refurbished window, The Good Shepherd. It was rededicated at the close of the Sunday service.

Cooner Clapton, long-time Huntersville resident and integral member of the Murray family, was also present. He provided much of the biographical information to honor the fallen hero. Capt. Murray was a highly respected Morgan horse breeder.

He enlisted in the Civil War with his prize stallion, Star. Both were killed at the Battle of Gettysburg.

I left the house around five with my thoughts on the fire.

The restoration of *The Good Shepherd* window was a big deal around town. Iverson was there for the rededication. Eve and he came only for the unveiling of the window at the conclusion of the service. He knew Cooner and all of us would be at church. He had plenty of time to connect the dryer wires and place the creamer and buffer in the fuse box.

Using fuel oil instead of gas, he also knew that, when the sparks flew, the combustibility of fuel oil would be less than gas. This fact would give him time to get back to town before the fire was noticed. Apparently, it was just starting at the time we came home.

When I was about to start chores, Whitaker's car came into the yard. Cook was with him. The District Attorney met me. "You wanted us?"

"Yes. I'm quite sure who started our fire." Both men stepped closer.

"Who?" Cook asked in an eager tone.

"Steven Iverson."

Whitaker shook his head. "I've already questioned him. He stayed the night at Eve Hebert's. He arrived at the church just in time for the dedication of the window. He wasn't at your place when you came home, was he?"

"No." I questioned sharply, "Did you search his apartment?"

"No." Whitaker straightened his shoulders in an assured manner. "There was no need."

"There is!" I pressed. "Let's go." I started toward Iverson's apartment. "Where did the drill buffer come from?"

"The buffer?" Whitaker held back. "We can't search without a warrant."

"You two watch while I search."

Cook and Whitaker followed me. Cook carried his briefcase. "This is highly unusual."

Although there was plenty of daylight, Iverson's apartment was dark. As I looked in, it reminded me of a cave. I knocked.

No answer. I opened the useless storm door and then the next. A nasty stink hit me. "Steven!" I felt for the light switch. "You've got company."

I quickly scanned the filthy place. Few things had changed since my visit, except clothes of all descriptions had been piled in the chair I'd sat in earlier.

Iverson, who had been asleep, came from a back bedroom. "What the hell are you doing in here?" He was zipping up his pants over the bottom edges of a dirty gray undershirt. His silver gray hair stood off his head as if it had been hit by a gust of wind.

"You've got company." I stood by the table where I'd sat. "You know Stanley Whitaker and Sean Cook?"

"Yeah, goddammit, Murray, get out of here!" He motioned with his arms.

I stepped closer to the table. Clothes of all sorts, cereal boxes, milk cartons, and empty bean cans filled one side of the table where I had sat. Cook and Whitaker were in back of me, not saying a word.

"Get." He came at me. I looked into his puffy red face and huge eyes. "Get your ass out of here!"

Before he could reach me, I scooped the pile of stuff off the table. The combination of junk and tools landed at his feet. I saw three various-size felt buffers. Four concave sections in the clear plastic case had been molded for four drill buffers. "Where's the fourth buffer?"

He looked down so as not to fall over his junk. "I never had four."

"You liar!" I stepped closer, the pile on the floor separating us. "You had four the night I sat in that chair!"

"Bullshit!" He roared. "Don't try and pin that fire…"

"Ah…" Cook interrupted. "We'll be back with a warrant to seize the package and three buffers,"

Iverson bent over with a grunt, picking up the package. "Here, take the goddamned things. Since the Murrays stole my farm, I ain't needing them."

The three of us left. Whitaker looked at the closed plastic case. "Since Iverson said he never had the fourth buffer, how can we prove he did?"

"It's his word against mine." I adjusted my cap. "He had four. I know he did!"

Whitaker and Cook started for the car. "We need to prove it."

After they left, hearing the milker pump, I headed toward the barn. José was milking and Rosita was cleaning stalls in the vacant part of the barn. When I checked on Precious, I was alarmed. She lay flat out in her bed with her head and neck resting, pressed against the wall. In a comatose condition, she moaned with every breath—way too out of it to stand. A calf's nose was showing at her spread vulva. My quick diagnosis told me she needed calcium. She showed the classic symptoms of milk fever. I ran to the milk house for warm water, an IV tube, a needle, and two 500cc bottles of calcium-dextrose that had been put in Iverson's cabinet from my supplies.

After I gave her the injection, there was no change. I tried to get her to stand but she made almost no effort. I cleaned her backend with soap and water, afterward slipping on a plastic sleeve. Her rump hung slightly over the curb, causing her to lie on a downward slope.

Entering the birthing canal with my gloved hand, I felt a head and neck but no feet. She couldn't calve without the feet and legs presented next to the calf's head. That meant I had to push the head and neck uphill because of the downward slant of her body. I tried but she was with it enough to continue to have contractions. Finally, even with her straining against me, I managed to push the calf's head back through the cervix into the uterus. However, with one hand, I couldn't hold the head in place and search for the feet and legs. Rosita by this time had left her cleaning and was watching my effort.

The birth canal was big and broad enough, so I thought Rosita could keep the head back while I brought the feet into place.

I motioned, "Help."

"Sí." Her coveralls were baggy with an excess of pant leg gathering at the top of her pack boots, and her sleeves were folded up a couple of times.

She unzipped the top of her coveralls. I reached for her left arm. She slipped on the plastic sleeve. Her arm was way too small for the sleeve. She held up her hand with her fingers half way filling the plastic hand. The tips of the fingers flopped over.

We both knelt behind Precious. Entering her, I could feel that the head had already returned. We pushed the calf back in place. Rosita had the strength to hold the head. Her short arm required that her shoulder partially enter the canal. I searched for the legs through a pond of fluid. I was extending my arm full length to find a leg. Once found, I reached for the calf's shin and hoof, pulling it next to the head. My shoulder and upper arm were being squeezed next to Rosita's in the canal as tightly as a bear hug.

I finally found the second hoof, pulling it in place with the head. "She's ready to calve."

Rosita pulled her arm out. We both took a hoof and pulled. The calf came easily along with a gush of uterine fluid.

The heifer calf was cold and dead. Although I felt a sinking feeling of disappointment, I checked Precious's milk. I was shocked. The same watery, stringy fluid came from each teat that I'd seen in many of Iverson's cows. I felt devastated. Our efforts at isolation from infected cows had obviously failed.

Precious continued to moan and had not moved. I felt her ear. I looked at Rosita. "Cold."

She put her hand on the cow's flank. "Sí, frío."

I went to the medicine cabinet, really knowing there was no cure for Precious. She had come around some but still couldn't stand. I was falling into a deep depression. This was hopeless.

I needed José's help. He stopped milking. Rosita, José, and I tucked her feet and legs near her body and rolled her to her opposite side to prevent prolonged weight from deadening her leg muscles.

As a last-ditch effort, I returned to Iverson's medicine cabinet and looked for medication from supplies brought from my barn. I found a bottle of tetracycline. I slowly administered a heavy dose into her bloodstream. I pumped her stomach with five gallons of warm water to keep her hydrated.

I didn't bother to call Fred Watkins, because I knew from what he had told me that there was no cure for mycoplasma mastitis and probably little hope if it was an E. coli infection. I, of course, didn't know what type of mastitis she had, but I knew if there was no improvement by morning, the case was hopeless. I'd never seen one of my cows so knocked out by an infection.

I fed the herd and mulled over the plan moving forward. I decided I wouldn't allow outstanding cows to be picked off by disease. Even though I couldn't afford to pay José and Rosita with the current numbers of milkers, I sure wasn't going to buy animals until I was confident that I'd rid the place of potential infections.

I finished feeding long after José and Rosita had left for the house. As I came to the kitchen, Rosita was solemn. "Señor Jason." Her voice was soft. "Lo siento."

"Thanks, Rosita. I'm sorry too." I was caught off guard by her tone. She knew my grief. Without a lot of words she realized how much Precious meant to me. Somehow in an unusual happenstance when we were pressed arm and arm in the birth canal, we were united in our feelings to help my favorite cow—joined in a deep meaningful way I couldn't explain.

As she hummed a tune, I watched her with renewed appreciation as she made her tortillas.

I was determined that my day would end on an up-beat note. I changed and tried to regenerate my excitement. I was about to go across the road to see Ellen, but once outside the house, I passed the barn. A terrible sinking feeling filled my thoughts. Precious was near death.

thirty

Ruth

After Jason left on Friday with the bad news of arson, Chris came to see me. I was resting, waiting for the pain to calm down. I heard him talking to Mom. Soon he came to my room and stood by my bed. "How are you doing?"

"The pain is letting up." I looked at him. "You heard?"

"Yeah." He squeezed my forearm. "So they think you set the fire?"

"Of course I denied it." I rolled to my side to face him. "I think they believed me."

"I would hope so." He paced toward the window, looking out. "Eve Hebert just drove in the yard."

We heard wild banging on the back door. Mom let her in.

Eve was hysterical. I could hear her high-pitched voice. "What's going on?" She barged into my room. "Cook and Whitaker want me at the courthouse in a half hour. I don't know why."

Quietly I told her, "The fire was set."

She turned ashen. Her hair looked scattered to the winds and she wore no makeup. She seemed on the verge of a total breakdown. "Oh, no!" She plunked into a chair and threw her head back with her hand on her forehead. "I sure as hell didn't do it! Those guys already questioned me once!"

Chris went to her and put his hand on her. "If you told them all you know, there's nothing to worry about."

Eve started sobbing. "I...I...I."

Glancing at her, I wondered. "Did Iverson stay with you the night before the fire?" I paused. "He brought you to church."

"Yeah, I...I already told them that!"

"Did he leave your place before church?"

"We partied the night before." Eve continued sobbing. "I needed some Alka Selzer."

I questioned sharply, "How long was he gone?"

"I don't know. Less than an hour."

I sat on the edge of my bed. "What's wrong? Why so upset?"

"I...I told Cook that Steven never left my apartment before he took me to church."

"Geez, Eve, you lied!" I glared at her. "Why?"

"I...I wondered why...why he was gone so long. He hated you guys so much. He was capable... I wondered if..." She continued sobbing.

Chris gently shook her. "Tell them the truth."

"You'd better come clean on this." I edged closer. "You could be in trouble."

"I know...I know!" Her hand was still on her forehead.

"They'll charge you!" I bent near her. "You could be fired!"

"I...I know. I know." She cried.

Chris quietly listened. "Eve, do you want me to go with you?"

She wiped her tears. "Would you?"

"Sure." He stood. "Just tell them the truth."

"But Steven!" Eve whined as they left.

I went to the window and watched the two. I shook my head in amazement. Chris's compassion was beyond belief.

thirty-one

Jason

Friday evening was a warm summer night when I walked past the barn, considering what I could or should do regarding Precious. A wave of sadness hit me. She was gravely ill.

I shoved that thought aside because I was headed to see Ellen— scrubbed as never before. I had on a light blue sports shirt and a new pair of khakis with a crease down the leg as sharp as a blade of grass. I felt in my pocket. I was all set for a great reuniting of two lovers—a scene I'd rehearsed many times.

In the parking lot, I passed a shiny jet-black BMW with Massachusetts plates. "Huh, that's odd."

When I opened the door, I met Gilda. Her mouth was pressed tightly—no smile. She glanced down and said in a sullen voice, "Hi, Jason."

"Ellen?" I asked.

Gilda tipped her head, motioning toward a booth in back of the restaurant. I went by the lunch counter in that direction.

Scoop turned on his counter seat but quickly looked away. Sheriff Krads acted as if I wasn't there. He shifted on his stool, adjusting himself. Iverson placed a mug of beer on the counter, wiping over his smirk. A smirk that didn't fade. Gilda's "Counter Intelligence" gave me a sinking feeling.

Bertha slid from her seat. "You'd best go home."

"Why?"

"You'll see." She lifted the end of her nose with her finger. "Doctor Peter Reed, professor of gynecology." She sneered. "So he claims."

"Huh, Ellen has mentioned him." With shaky feelings, I continued on.

My stomach suddenly knotted in a deep, all-encompassing pain. Ellen's back was to me. She was full of talk, chattering an octave higher than normal. I looked straight at the professor. He wore a light blue corduroy suit with a dark blue tie. He had a toothy smile showing a dazzling set of teeth, hair slightly gray at the temples, brown eyes, and a clean, flawless face with a prominent chin. I glared at him. He was definitely a handsome guy.

Ellen turned. "Oh, hi, Jason!"

I stared, dumbfounded.

Blushing, she said, "I'd like you to meet Doctor Peter Reed."

He slid out of the booth and shook my hand. "Ellen's been telling me all about your quaint little town."

"Quaint?" I scowled.

"Sure—dinner's at noon, and everyone's in bed by nine." He mockingly laughed and sat down.

I didn't like him. I felt he was pegging me as a country-clod. I quickly glanced at Ellen. "I...I thought...you... you and I... tonight!"

"Jason, I can't" She reached for the doctor's hand. "Peter's visiting for the weekend."

Reed smiled. "Isn't she the sweetest?"

She glowed. "Sorry, Jason."

I turned to leave, filled with anger. "So this is it?"

Ellen grabbed my arm. "Don't you understand?"

"I sure do!" I pulled away and left.

There wasn't a muscle in my body but what it was on fire, yet I felt limp. I left with my head down. I went out the door into the night—not seeing, smelling, hearing, only feeling a wrenching anger that turned to thoughts of destruction. In less than ten minutes, I'd lost all sense of self-worth. I had been totally rejected and thrown on a trash heap.

I climbed the slope into the Iverson yard. It took all the energy I had.

In my bedroom, I emptied my pocket and threw the ring and condoms into the top drawer of my bureau. I smashed the picture of Ellen on the floor, crushing the butterfly shirt with the heel of my shoe—opened another drawer and sorted through my photos. I ripped every one of Ellen into pieces. I had to destroy her. She had slammed the door on my hopes, my dreams. Ellen was gone.

I glanced at pictures of birds and wildlife, plus the first taken when my camera was new. I put them back and slammed the drawer shut.

Rosita and José were in their chapel. I sat in the kitchen, seething, but hurting at the same time.

O. J. Simpson's suspected murders now made sense—crimes of passion. I could go back to Gilda's and smash the shiny black BMW with a sledge hammer—break every window in his car—go and punch in the doctor's pearly-white teeth. I knew he'd had his way with her. At least it was satisfying to grovel in the assumption—piling the thought onto the heap of hate I had for the guy. In a strange way, taking on the role of a crazed maniac was satisfying. I pondered my thoughts of destruction for quite a while. Finally, I broke down in tears. I told myself that Jason Murray couldn't do any of what I was thinking. I felt split in half over feelings of hate and feelings of rejection.

The fact remained that everything was against me: a sinister cattle disease was in my midst, a suspected arsonist lived next door, and a guy with status had taken my girl. My girl whom I loved an hour ago—how depressing! I felt like shit.

José went to his room, and Rosita came to the kitchen to continue work on her skirt. I was bent over in my chair, looking at the floor. "Hi." My voice was glum. I must have sounded and looked on the outside how I felt on the inside—shattered.

She searched me for eye contact. "Hola." She tilted her head with a frown of concern.

I flung back in the chair, causing the ladder-back to squawk.

With hands resting on her sides, she paused. "Señor Jason, triste."

"Yes, very sad." I turned the chair, resting my elbows on the table with my head nearly resting on the white oilcloth.

"Rosita, cantar." She left and brought back her guitar. She sat next to me, playing and singing what I thought was a love song. I caught the words amor and señorita several times. She softly sang with tenderness and feeling, causing me to feel limp while tears rolled down as if cleansing my bitterness, pulling me back from my dark side.

After a half hour or so, I stood. "Thanks, Rosita. That was beautiful."

Looking at me, she scowled with concern as I left.

I went to the barn to see Precious. Earlier we'd removed a stall divider and swung her around to give her more room. We had tried several times to get her to stand. The meds I'd given her and the water pumped into her stomach didn't help. She lay flat-out. It was hopeless. She was so weak she couldn't lift her head. She was moaning with each breath.

I felt her ear. It was ice cold. While sitting on the curb next to her, I wiped tears with my sleeve.

I thought as I sat next to her. As a young heifer, you showed all the makings of being a great cow, you've given me several beautiful off-spring, you never disappointed me. All...all... I...I can do is give you peace. You...you deserve it.

I went to the medicine cabinet for my twenty-two pistol and shells. I held the weapon and pulled one bullet from the box. While walking back to Precious, the cure for her pain turned warm in my hand. I slipped the bullet into the chamber and pulled the firing pin. This was the end.

I pressed the pistol to her head and pulled the trigger. She instantly went limp. Blood trickled out the side of her slackened jaw and open mouth.

Overcome, I sat and sobbed.

thirty-two

Ruth

Jason called Mom on Monday morning to say he could get me off the hook regarding the charge of arson. Sounding glum, he was short on words. He told Mom that he and I had to be at the District Attorney's office by ten that morning, and that he'd give me a ride.

As far as I knew, the question as to who started the fire came down to the number of drill buffers in a plastic case. I knew I wasn't guilty, so I sure wanted the issue settled and soon.

The Piedmont Center had been neglected since the fire. I very much wanted to get back on track to find funding for my most pressing cause. I also wanted to stay in touch with Anadeepa—let her know that I was there for her.

My hands were healing. I could see some improvement in the eight days since the fire but I still couldn't use them to any degree. Mom had to change my dressings and tend to most all I needed. I felt badly for her, but she never complained. I was becoming creative in how to do some things without her help. With my little finger and the side of my bandaged hand, I could turn a doorknob and shove it open with my shoulder.

It had been a while since I'd talked with Cooner. I decided to go and visit him on his bench until Jason came.

July had given us some great weather. It had been dry but we had lots of sun. That morning was no exception.

Cooner saw me. "Hi, beautiful, you comin' ta tell this old man some things about life I ain't knowin' already."

I laughed. "Hardly, Cooner. You've taught me plenty."

Cooner tapped his cane. "You heard from Jason?"

"Yeah. He's picking me up this morning." I sat down. "He'll be here in a few minutes."

"Well, I know that boy better than most. He's keepin' a lot ta himself and that ain't good."

"Like what?"

"Well, the news coming out of Gilda's is that Ellen dumped him."

"Dumped—oh, my gosh!" I touched Cooner with my bandaged hand. "Why hasn't he told us?"

"Pride." He paused. "Remember that big homecoming football game when he threw an interception and Huntersville lost?"

"Yeah, vaguely."

Cooner spat. "Remember, he was down in the dumps for days, blamin' himself."

I shrugged. "Gosh, that was years ago."

"Well, the boy ain't changed." He rattled his cane. "He's never liked bein' on the losin' end. And Ellen was a lot for him ta lose." He paused and turned to me. "That ain't all."

"Oh, no. What else?"

"He had ta shoot Precious."

"Shoot Precious!" I stared at Cooner in disbelief. "How could he do that? This is terrible!"

"You ain't kiddin'. It's terrible." He pounded his cane on the earthen path. "Saturday mornin', Scoop says he got a call to bring his old man's backhoe." He sighed. "They had to bury Precious and her dead calf out in back of the barn."

"Poor Jason!" I was stunned.

He spat again. "With Iverson next door and all of this. That boy's gotta be ready ta break."

"I guess." I held my head.

"Scoop says Jason's sold his herd. They're leavin' today."

I grimaced in disbelief. "He's selling his cows, too!" I cried. "The bad news keeps coming. How come we haven't heard any of this?"

"Well, we've lost touch. Your dad's out straight at the shop and your mom's been tied carin' for you." He turned to me. "You've got ta talk ta that boy."

"I know—first Ellen, then Precious. Say nothing about arson, and now you tell me the cows have left."

Cooner leaned forward, supporting himself on his cane. "I ain't surprised he's selling the herd. He ain't wantin' ta shoot any more of his good cows."

"Oh God! Poor Jason!" I stood when I saw his truck coming. "I'll see you, Cooner."

He waved with his cane. "I hope it goes okay. I've been a worryin' over these goin's on."

Jason jumped out to open my door. "How you doing?"

I looked at him. "More to the point, how are *you* doing?" I slid in and he shut my door.

He got in and we left the yard with the tires squealing slightly when we hit the pavement, racing his truck in second gear. His jaw muscle flexed on a mouth clamped hard. He didn't look my way but was bent forward, concentrating on the road. He mumbled, "I'm getting sick of this shit." He shifted into third. "I feel like puking, having to face Whitaker and Cook one more time." He gunned his truck.

"Geez, Jason, slow down!" I glanced at him. "Cooner's been telling me what's been going on with you." I slid over and placed my bandaged hand on his arm. "I'm worried about you."

He eased off the pedal. "I'll be okay." His voice broke. "I've just got to get away."

"Cooner told me about Precious." I pressed my forearm on him. "I'm sorry."

"I am too. I had to sell the cows—no choice. Just had to sell."

"Jason, so much bad news!"

He choked back his emotion. "It's… it's just as well I…I don't have to watch my cows leave."

In a few minutes, he brought the truck to a halt in the courthouse parking lot.

"Maybe so." I turned to him. It was no surprise that his demeanor had changed. His confidence had vanished, leaving him sunken and slumped. His singed hair was growing back, looking darker and patchy. That didn't improve his looks.

His eyes filled with tears as he sniffed and wiped his nose.

I softly asked, "Tell me about Ellen?"

"She's history," he said in a strained voice. There was hurt in his eyes.

"Why…what happened?" I paused for an answer.

"Don't grill me!" He slumped. "I'm not up for it!"

"Jason, let's spend some time together and talk."

"Yeah, I'd like to." He stared off into space. "I really want to get away."

"Well, you'll have time after this arson thing is settled."

"Yeah, and I can forget it all." He reached in his back pocket, pulling out pictures for me to see. "Anything familiar?"

"What are these?" I looked briefly at three pictures, showing a heap of junk.

Jason looked my way. "They were on the roll when you bought Iverson's camera—pictures taken last Christmas."

"Really!" I examined them more closely. "I can barely see the plastic case of buffers."

"They need enlarging or examined under a microscope." He took one from me and looked closely. He held it up for more light. "It's not clear that there are four buffers in that package." He looked at another. "This picture shows the four the best."

We left the truck, surprised to see Scoop, Eve, and Iverson heading up the courthouse steps, probably going to the same place we were. None of us spoke. We all, no doubt, wondered what was about to happen. Jason held me by the arm, helping me through the door. I glanced back, having heard Sheriff Krad's boot heels ring on the hard floor. We were ushered into District Attorney Cook's office. Cook and Fire Marshal Whitaker met us.

Since the day I'd been in his office for questioning, Cook had added a circular table with seven chairs.

Iverson stood, looking neater than I'd seen him in recent memory: clean shirt with tails tucked under dress pants. His silver hair was slicked into place.

Scoop had trimmed his beard. He wore a clean western-style shirt, jeans, and cowboy boots. He stood erect and confident. I realized his self-assured manner was a cover for how he really felt—nervous.

Eve was wearing plenty of make-up, including blue eye shadow and deep red lipstick. Her blouse was low cut, revealing her ample cleavage. From her puffy face, I thought she looked on the verge of tears. I knew her well enough to realize that she was worried to death.

I must have looked pretty plain. I hadn't used make-up, so my facial burns showed various shades of red. I'd dressed simply in a white blouse and slacks.

I glanced at Jason. He wore his usual, a sport shirt and khakis. Sheriff Krads, in his law-enforcement paraphernalia, stood by the door.

As expected, Cook took the lead. "Please, everyone take a seat."

With my little finger and the side of my hand I straightened my blouse and sat between Jason and Eve. I felt sorry for Scoop. He was hesitant as to where to sit. His self-assured front was breaking down. He started chewing the mustache hair at the edge of his mouth. He avoided Iverson and ended up sitting between Whitaker and Cook. Iverson sat with plenty of space on either side of him. He leaned back in his chair as if he were conducting the meeting.

Cook began. "It's unusual for me to call all of you to this meeting." He laid his hands on a manila folder. "However, I would like to solve this case simply, without sending it to a grand jury for investigation." He opened the folder. "Since none of you have asked for counsel, I think the case can be solved with testimony from all parties involved. This meeting will be recorded." He flicked a switch in back of where he sat.

"Let's review what we've learned about the fire." He looked at us around the table.

"Theodore 'Scoop' LaQuine, let's start with you." Cook settled himself in his chair. "You've testified that you watched Ruth Murray connect wires bypassing fuses on two different occasions."

Scoop jerked to attention. "I did." He nervously stroked his beard. "I ain't sayin' she started the fire."

"However, as an electrician, you knew that if the cover closed on the metal fuse box with the wires connected that sparks would fly."

"Yup, I told Ruth that I ain't havin' nothin' to do with such a deal."

"But you watched it being done."

"Yup."

Cook held an enlarged picture for all of us to see. "Are you familiar with the objects in this picture—namely the blackened fuse box, the jumper wires connected, the Forget Me Not creamer, and the drill buffer?"

"Yup."

"Scoop, you've testified that you can't remember where you were prior to the fire."

"Yup."

Cook, sounding stern, asked, "Do you realize your lack of memory, in all probability, leads to an admission of guilt?"

"I...I ain't guilty." Scoop shook his head. "I...I remember where I was, but I...I ain't tellin'."

Cook pressed, "In your previous statement, you lied to us, saying you *didn't* remember where you were."

"Yup, I did. But it ain't anyone's business where I was."

I looked at Scoop and cleared my throat, hoping to get his attention, urging him to talk. I just knew he wasn't guilty.

Cook firmly continued, "Okay, so you're choosing not to talk." Cook reached in back for a thick folder. "Arson, added to your record for which you are now on probation, could incarcerate you for years."

"But, I...I ain't guilty."

Cook pointed to the buffer in the picture. "You're a handyman."

"Yup."

"How would you use a tool like this?"

Scoop's voice rose, pleading, "That ain't my buffer!"

Exasperated, Cook demanded, "Just answer my question! How would you use this buffer?"

"Oh, okay." Scoop shrugged. "Polishing the sharp edge of a piece of wood or plastic, cleanin' a copper pipe before solderin' a connection." He stuck his chin forward, speaking in a confirming voice, "I told you it ain't mine!"

I got Scoop's attention and said in a soft voice, "I know the buffer might not be yours, but you need to tell Attorney Cook where you were on the day of the fire." I nudged Jason with my elbow, hoping he would encourage Scoop.

Jason, sitting across from him, quietly said in a near whisper, "Tell Attorney Cook where you were."

Scoop's voice started to break. "I...I was at...the...the Hideaway."

Cook frowned. "Hideaway... Hideaway, where in the world is that?"

Iverson blurted, "Up in back of the Murray barn, or it was a barn until Scoop torched it!"

Cook snapped, "Mr. Iverson, that was uncalled for." He looked at his folder and asked quietly, "Theodore, or Scoop, what were you doing at the Hideaway?"

"Well...well...if I tell, Bubbles Chub and me will be in big trouble."

Cook asked, "Bubbles Chub?" He paused. "What's her given name?"

Scoop mumbled, "Evangeline."

Cook nodded. "Give us some details. When did you go to the Hideaway?"

"Sunday morning, we snuck up the trail to the Hideaway." Scoop nervously fidgeted in his chair. "Even though it was a windy day, we... we walked about a mile from her apartment."

"What time was that?" Cook asked.

"After I knew the Murrays went to church, and Bubbles' old man had gone fishin'." Scoop paused. "About eleven."

"Did you see or hear anyone at the farm?"

"Nope." Scoop's shaky hand stroked his beard again. "I...I promised Bubbles I'd never tell."

Jason scowled at me then asked Attorney Cook, "Have we got to hear all this stuff?"

I chimed in. "What has this got to do with the fire?"

Cook glared at us and continued. "Vital information."

Scoop pleaded, "But I ain't done nothin' wrong."

"I'm not accusing you. Just tell us in detail about your stay at the Hideaway."

"Well, Bubbles' old man hates my guts. He said if he saw me with Bubbles, he'd beat the shit outta me. He's big—twice my size."

Cook nodded. "Go on."

"Bubbles said when she saw my HIV test and it was okay, she'd let me take her to the Hideaway."

Cook looked at his notes. "And."

"Well, we went. Everybody thinks Bubbles is...you know... that...that kinda girl." He fidgeted with his hands. "Well, she ain't!" He swallowed hard. "She...she's very religious. She...she's not a bad girl."

Iverson laughed. "Bubbles Chub. She's a slut!"

Scoop turned toward Iverson and insisted, "That ain't so!"

Cook showed the flat of his hands. "Stop!" He glared at Iverson. "That's enough from you!" He turned toward Scoop. "Continue."

"Well, we just visited, on the couch, listenin' to the wind."

"Did you hear anything at the farm?"

"No! The wind was howlin' like a bastard. And anyway, I was gawkin' at Bubbles, lying next to me. You see, she has a full-body tattoo called the Tree of Life—green leaves and red apples on her shoulders and a tree trunk running up her front and brown roots running down her legs. A copper-headed snake, she calls it her serpent, is wrapped around the tree. The serpent has a long waggin' red tongue. Me lyin' next to her felt just like I was facin' The Garden of Eden. The serpent showin' his forked tongue was lookin' real."

I could see that Scoop was beginning to enjoy his audience. He scanned everyone at the table. He sat tall, waved his hands, and raised his voice.

Iverson groaned, "This is disgusting."

Cook gave Iverson a sour look and then turned to Scoop. "Continue if it's pertinent to this case."

"Okay." Scoop licked his lips. "With me lyin' next to her, Bubbles was gettin' excited. Her belly started rollin' in and out. The snake looked all the world like he was climbin' the tree. I lost my head. I thought Bubbles was a miracle. The blood from her belly had somehow given life to that serpent. All of a sudden his copper head glowed a bright orange. The serpent's blazing eyes were lookin' right at me. He was ready to strike. I was wallowin' in fear. If that waggin' red tongue struck me, I knew I'd be as dead as a day old stiff. I jumped up off the couch and looked out the window. This ball of orange rose between the trees up into the sky. I yelled, 'The barn's on fire!'

"Bubbles screamed and started yankin' on her clothes and I pulled on my pants, yellin', 'I've gotta help!' I turned to Bubbles. 'You beat it for home!'"

Iverson leaned back and fingered the loose skin under his chin. "Everyone knows Scoop's a phony. He's as crooked as that snake he's telling us about."

I broke in. "Can I be excused for a minute?"

Cook snapped the switch on the recorder. "Okay, ten minutes."

I glanced Jason's way. He jumped up to help me with the door. Out in the hall, I held him with my forearm. "Let's look closely at the three pictures."

Jason stepped toward the light and pulled them from his pockets, "They don't clearly show the four buffers."

I looked them over as he held them. I pointed with my little finger "This one shows the buffers the best."

He examined them closely. "Yeah, this one's the best." He slipped the picture in his right-hand pocket.

"All three pictures have the date on the edge, December 24, 1994." I looked at the remaining two. "Show these first."

"Why?" Jason looked at me.

I frowned. "You never know what Iverson will do in the face of evidence."

We went back to Cook's office and took our places.

Cook flicked the switch. "Theodore, during your time with Evangeline Chub, you've testified that you heard nothing at the farm."

"Yup, like I said, I...I was like in another world, facin' the Tree of Life, watchin' that serpent wiggle, waggin' his red tongue at me."

A big sigh came from Iverson.

Cook rested his hands on Scoop's file. "I might have some further questions for you."

Scoop sat back in his chair.

Up to this point Eve had been sitting quietly.

Cook continued, "Eve Hebert, I have a few questions for you."

Eve's eyes widened as she jerked to attention.

"Ms. Hebert, I have testimony from you that Mr. Iverson left your apartment for about an hour before he brought you to church on Sunday, July 16."

"Ya...yes." Eve nervously whimpered.

"This is bogus!" Iverson roared, "I wasn't gone for any hour."

"How long?" Cook asked.

"Well...er...I...I don't know?" Iverson sat up. "Ten minutes... maybe."

Eve gasped and put her hand on her mouth.

Cook looked at her. "You don't agree?"

Eve looked at Iverson. "Maybe...maybe it was...was just ten minutes." Her voice broke. "I...I was awful sick."

Iverson looked at Eve and smiled.

At that moment, I knew Eve was lying.

Cook held the picture of the electrical box and its contents. "As you all know, this case revolves around who connected the jumper wires. Fire Marshal Whitaker suspects that a flammable soaked felt buffer and a Forget Me Not creamer filled with fuel oil were placed in this fuse box. Then the fuse box cover was shut, and the power was turned on." He scanned the table at all of us. "Who did it? No one here has agreed to owning the drill buffer, but I think everyone here has a Forget Me Not creamer."

Cook looked at me. "Ruth Murray, you testified that you were the last to leave the barn on the day of the fire."

"Yes." I flushed.

"Yet you didn't see or hear anyone?"

"Right." I nodded. "No one."

I noticed that Iverson was getting fidgety, wanting to say something. He turned to Cook. "I can solve this case." He confidently leaned back with his hands resting on his paunch. "You fellows took a case of three drill buffers from my apartment the other day. I borrowed them from Scoop when I was fixing a leak in a copper pipe."

"You're a liar!" Scoop fumed. "I ain't never owned no drill buffers."

Iverson continued, "He loaned the three to me and held the fourth back for his own use."

"Liar!" Scoop yelled.

All of our attention was focused on Iverson, expecting some sort of revelation. I held my breath.

Iverson rambled on, "Who are you going to believe, a jail bird or me, Huntersville's town representative?" He smiled. "This case is simple. Scoop didn't tell you where he was on that Sunday morning because he connected the wires and set the stuff in the fuse box, shut the cover, turned on the power, and went with Bubbles up to the Hideaway to watch the fireworks."

Fire Marshal Whitaker scowled at Iverson. "Attorney Cook and I are very capable of drawing our own conclusions."

Jason broke in, "I think I have evidence that earlier there were four drill buffers in that case."

"Oh, yeah?" Iverson sneered. "You might know a Murray's trying to nail me."

"I have two pictures of interest." Jason reached in his pocket. "I think these faintly show four buffers."

"This is a set-up!" Iverson roared. "Where did you get them?"

Jason calmly said, "From your camera. They were taken last Christmas Eve in your kitchen."

Iverson jumped up and snatched them from Jason's hand, then studied them. "They don't show a thing!"

Cook demanded, "Give them here!" He examined the pictures closely. "Yes, I can barely make out four buffers in that case, lying with a pile of other things around it." He turned to Iverson. "Were these pictures taken in your kitchen?"

"Yes, goddamnit, but they don't show a thing!"

I nudged Jason. He pulled the most revealing photo from his pocket. "This picture may show the buffer case more clearly."

Cook held the picture under his desk lamp. "Yes, there are four buffers in that case." He glanced at Iverson." This is surely incriminating evidence."

Iverson shouted, "Incriminating!" He jumped up. "This is coming from a Murray! I'm not putting up with this bullshit!"

Cook motioned for Sheriff Krads. "Steven Iverson, you're being held on the suspicion of arson." Cook stood. "This picture shows there were four buffers in the case."

Iverson exploded in anger. He came swinging at Jason. Jason backed away and helped Krads handcuff the madman.

Iverson bellowed, "Those Murrays deserved everything I gave them. They stole my meadow. They're about to steal my farm, even my house. I have nothing! But I feel good! I burned them out!" With his hands held in cuffs behind his back, he turned, yelling at Jason and me. "Yeah, I burned you guys out, but good!"

thirty-three

Jason

All of us, except for Iverson, slowly left the courthouse emotionally drained. I carried the computer tower under my arm. I mumbled in disbelief. "I can't believe Iverson hated us enough to start the fire."

"I agree." Ruth said, carefully watching for the next step, "I wonder what will happen to him?"

Scoop, still nerved-up, was biting hair at the corner of his mouth. "That son-of-a-bitch. They'll throw him in the poky."

Eve was crying. "I just can't believe it!"

We didn't comment.

I reached for Eve's arm. "Do you want a ride?"

She got in my truck and sobbed, "I'm going to miss him." Neither I nor Ruth said anything. I was thinking that she deserved a better man. Arriving at Eve's apartment, I pulled the truck to the curb. She thanked me and left.

While riding home, Ruth glanced my way. "I feel sorry for Eve."

I passively nodded in agreement, since I was absorbed in thinking about the immediate future. I wanted out of Huntersville. Truthfully, I was mourning the fire, the loss of Ellen, the loss of Precious, and the loss of my herd. But there wasn't a thing I could do about it, except to leave and try and forget it all.

I pulled into the yard with Ruth. She went to see Cooner who was sitting on his bench, waiting for the news.

In the house, after I told Mom and Dad what had happened, Dad shook his head. "I can't believe he'd stoop that low."

Mom agreed. "He's lost everything." She paused. "Poor Shirley and Joe."

"I want to get away for a while." I sat at the kitchen table. "We'll spend some time cleaning up the place, and then I'll give the barn a rest until spring."

Dad looked at me. "So you want to carry through with our purchase and sales agreement and buy the place?

"Let me think this through and make a final decision when I return in a few weeks."

Mom placed a cup of coffee in front of me and a cup for Dad. "Thanks, Mom." I looked at Dad. "Maybe I'll track that bobcat and get a good picture."

Dad nodded, "You need a break. You've been through a lot."

"I'll have time to locate breeding stock when I come back." I drank some coffee. "I want animals with potential."

Dad glanced up. "What about your labor?"

"Rosita has told me that she and her dad are going to Florida to pick oranges." I placed my cup on the table. "One of their friends is taking them."

"Oh." Dad drained his cup. "Sounds all settled."

"It is." I got up. "I want to see Cooner."

Mom sat with her cup in hand. "You should. He's been worried for you and Ruth."

As I went out the door, he was on his bench talking to Ruth. He turned my way. "Ain't ya feelin' good the case is settled?"

"Yeah." I walked toward him. "But I've got lots of other things to think about." I reset my cap. "I want to leave for a while."

Cooner spat. "Where ya headed?"

"Hardhack Mountain to track a bobcat." I stood in deep thought. "Take my time—a good long time—six weeks."

Cooner scratched his head. "You're serious?"

"Darn right! It's something I've always wanted to do."

Cooner tapped his cane. "Why don't you camp at Wunderland, the headwaters of the Blue?"

"Wunderland?" I looked toward the mountain. "You've mentioned it before."

"Yup, a German settlement abandoned in the late thirties—small place." He pointed with his cane. "Folks say only a stone buildin' stands. It don't look far from here, but it'll be a rugged climb."

"Sounds interesting."

"Jason?" Ruth frowned. "How are we going to know you're okay?"

"Start a campfire in the mornin'." Cooner pointed with his cane. "From where I'm sittin', I'll be able to see the smoke ripple up through the trees right at that spot in the mountain."

I nodded. "That should work."

"Gosh, six weeks!" Ruth turned to me. "Hope you'll bring plenty of supplies."

"I plan to." I gave Ruth a hug and left.

That night Mom invited me to supper for one last good meal before my trip. Shirley Iverson came to the house. Her white hair was held in place by the same silver barrette she always wore. In her mid-sixties, she still stood erect, but her face had a frown of grief. "I'm here to apologize for the horrible crime Steven has committed against you folks," she said, barely holding back tears.

Dad stood and went to her. "Steven acted on his own." Dad shook her hand. "We know this wasn't like you."

"Well, I personally want to express our deep regrets. Joe and I have tried, over the years, to lead Steven in the right direction, but after a while we had to let him be who he is." She wiped her nose with a Kleenex. "I'm so sorry. Joe and I both feel sick for your loss."

I felt sorry for the poor woman. "Where's Steven?"

"He's with...with us until...until sentencing." She wiped tears again.

Dad motioned toward the table. "Have a seat."

"No, I need to run along." She looked at Ruth. "How are you doing?"

"I'm okay, almost completely healed." Ruth held up her hands.

"Thank goodness." Shirley sniffed again. "I don't know what I'd have done if the fire had taken your life."

"Well, it didn't." Ruth went to her. "I'm nearly all healed."
"Thanks for being so understanding." She left.

I said my goodbyes that night and left for the farm. Alone in my truck, I consoled myself as to why in the last few weeks I'd been apart from my family.

While Mom was caring for Ruth, Dad was doing double-duty at the florist shop, preparing sets of mums, geraniums, Christmas cactus, and poinsettias for the months ahead. Consequently, as the days whizzed by in our busy lives, no one was aware of my arrangements while living with the Mexicans. They knew, of course, I was staying at the farmhouse, but none of my family realized how I willingly ate Mexican food, sharing meals with Rosita and her dad, that she washed my clothes, and cleaned my room. No one knew how her singing calmed my turmoil, taking the edge off the pain of loss. I hadn't shared with anyone that Rosita had lifted me from the depths of my darkest desperation. She was my invisible crutch that helped me to keep going.

I found myself comparing the feelings I had toward Ellen to those for Rosita. Ellen had stirred a passion in me that I'd never felt before. I had been star-struck in love with her, experiencing a heady infatuation, a feeling so strong, I hadn't yet recovered from losing her. I compared the situation to a house. Ellen had entered my front door, filling my rooms with thoughts of love, while Rosita came through the back door, laboring in a quiet way while singing her heart out, calming my troubled spirit. Without my realizing, she had become a part of me. Even she didn't know how much she meant to me. But I needed to end my attachment—one more reason to get away. She was of another culture, another world, and I was a Murray born of New England stock. She would leave to pick oranges in Florida, and I'd head for Hardhack Mountain. I was surely going to miss her.

I hoped to forget her, as well as all my other losses, by starting a new life. I wanted to begin by being close to the land, to fill myself with the smell of the woods, while hearing the songs of birds and seeing animals in the wild. I also yearned for the feel of rain on my face and the warmth of sun on my back. Being away, I hoped my roar of grief would calm and I could be once again at peace.

In school, I learned of Henry David Thoreau and John Muir, both naturalists. Their lives intrigued me. It would be fun to be by myself in the wild for a few weeks, as they once were, then maybe I could feel strong again. The past would never change, but I hoped that I could come home and start a brighter future.

That night as I lay in bed, making a mental list of all the things I needed to bring on my trip, Rosita started singing, *Ky-ri-e e-le-i-son...*

With her previous help, I'd translated the opening phrase: *Lord have mercy...*

Maybe the time off I was planning was a mercy trip. Time away from civilization would be like a salve covering an open wound. As I listened that night to Rosita, every ache, every nerve, every troubled thought was soothed, relaxed and laid to rest by the soft sound of her voice.

The next night after a day of pressure-washing the barn with a strong disinfectant, I once again sat in the evening, watching Rosita sew her skirt.

I was working on my list of things for the trip: a frame backpack, a feather-weight tent, axe, sleeping bag, compass, camera, a quantity of dried food...

Rosita hummed a tune I thought was a Spanish ballad. She cut a red piece of fabric about three feet long and twelve inches wide that would be the waist-band of her skirt. She was distracting me as I listened to her hum.

I looked down at my list, remembering the ring. At this point, I wished I hadn't bought it. What in the world would I ever do with it? I couldn't leave it unprotected in the old farmhouse. On the other hand, I felt that at five thousand dollars, I'd gotten a deal and could sell it at an auction house someday and realize a handsome profit. Heck, it was no big deal. It didn't take much room; I'd bring it with me.

Rosita began humming *Secret Love*. The tune rang in my ears. I didn't look at her, and as far as I know, she never looked up at me, but I wondered if she was sending me a message. Maybe we both had thoughts for one another—feelings we held tightly to ourselves, feelings like I had toward Ruth, like sisterly love. But I wasn't sure about Rosita, what her thoughts were toward me.

Whatever the case, I was aware that my being drawn to her was beginning to mean something—an emotional connection that could run deep and be lasting. But she was going away that next night. I felt an overwhelming need to give her some security in appreciation for what she meant to me.

I'd asked in the past for José's and Rosita's immigration papers. They had none. Knowing that they had no legal identity, I realized Rosita could face dangerous times when money might be needed to pay her way to freedom, but money could also be stolen. Since I assumed she was undocumented and had no way to establish her identity, she couldn't open a savings or checking account in this country.

The strip of red cloth she was working with gave me an idea. The next morning I went to the bank and drew out the five thousand dollars I'd deposited from the sale of Rover Red and the three daughters of Precious. I'd promised myself the money would be used for a special purpose, and Rosita was that special purpose. Besides, I had so much and I knew she had so little. I put the fifty crisp hundred-dollar bills in an envelope. I also stopped at the book store and bought a Spanish and English dictionary.

When I got to the farm before noon, José and Rosita were getting ready for a late night departure. I figured that illegal immigrants, as some called them, or undocumented workers traveled in the dead of night in order to be undetected.

After lunch, I asked José to tend to the final wrap-up of the cleaning process in the barn. Rosita was standing at the sink washing dishes. "Rosita." I pointed to my waist and then at her. "Your falda."

She smiled. "Sí." She wiped her hands, and left for her room, returning with the nearly completed skirt.

I passed the envelope to her. She opened it. Her face flushed. "Mucho dólar."

"Yes." I pointed. "For you."

She closed her eyes. Tears rolled down her face. She threw her arms around me. "Gracias! Gracias!"

Her hug warmed me, but I quickly pulled away. She laid out her sewing. We measured her waist for length and placed the bills for equal thickness on the flat cloth. She quickly got the idea that the money would be hidden in a belt or her waistband. She pulled the remaining cloth over the bills and started stitching to firmly hold the money. I think she got the idea that her father was at the barn for a reason. This was to be her money. She worked fast, cutting a second layer of cloth to act as a cover for the belt. Within a short time she had it completed with buttons and buttonholes sewn. All she had left to do was to sew the waistband to her skirt.

She packed the belt and skirt in a canvas bag as I watched while holding the dictionary. She saw me and again flung herself into my arms. "Gracias."

I backed away and passed her the dictionary. "I want you to have this." She smiled. "Gracias."

Later that night, Rosita sang in their chapel. I wanted to get out of bed and say goodbye, but I didn't want to show any emotion and give her a hint of my deep feelings for her. I fell asleep and woke, hearing the door shut and a car drive away. I got out of bed and went to their chapel. The room was empty. The voice I'd come to love was gone. I leaned against the empty wall while a desperate loneliness came over me. A torrent of tears rolled down as pain washed through me. My life was filled with loss. I shook with grief.

The next morning, I called Scoop to tell him where I was going, and that I wanted him to check the farm now and then.

"Sure, I'll swing into the yard on my way to Gilda's" He laughed. "If Iverson's snoopin' around, I'll kick him in the ass."

I chuckled. "He won't be there. He's on Pine Mountain."

"Yup, right." He paused. "It would just feel good to show him who's boss."

After talking to Scoop, I left in my truck and parked it at the homestead.

I said goodbye to my family, then Dad gave me a ride to the ridge where I planned to pick up a trail to Wunderland. The sun was just coming up behind Hardhack Mountain when I looked off toward the peak. Strapping on my backpack, I waved goodbye. Although it was heavy, I felt like a true adventurer. I know Dad didn't understand me, but I accepted the fact that Dad was Dad. I had my own mission.

Before starting, I set my compass for a southeast direction so that I would bisect the Blue at some point. By heading high across the mountain, I hoped I'd selected a direction that would avoid the cliff that I, an inexperienced hiker, would find impossible to climb. Cooner told me that in his hunting days, he found the rock formation stretched for more than a mile north to south across the mountain. Vermont's Long Trail was on the other side of the Hardhack peak, bypassing Wunderland. The inaccessibility of the former settlement was, no doubt, the reason the small group of German immigrants chose the location.

I quickly came to the place where Ellen and I had picnicked earlier that summer. I stood on the very spot where we'd rolled and both nearly lost our virginity. I reminded myself that I wouldn't be standing where I was if I'd gotten her pregnant. Thank God that never happened. I was free and surprised to find that my grief from losing her was easing. One thing for sure, she wouldn't care to go to Wunderland with me and fight the bugs and the sweat. She definitely fit the hygienic setting of a hospital.

Before leaving the area, I sat and took off my cap that Ellen gave me and wiped my face and arms with bug repellant. I looked at the logo of a chicken's head embossed *Lay Or Bust,* in white lettering, and chuckled. I got the cap, and the professor got the girl.

When I left, I started looking for the tracks and trails of animals, knowing they'd have to go for water. I found the cloven-hoof signs of a whitetail deer path but soon encountered blow-downs and ledges, forcing detours. I kept checking my compass and checking for animal tracks. I was traveling in uncharted territory with no distinct trail, stepping over and around any number of obstructions. I hadn't seen any wildlife all morning but continued to look for animal signs. The noise caused by stepping on rotted branches and twigs probably had spooked woodland creatures. A red squirrel scolded me, but I didn't take the time to actually see it.

Although my compass pointed southeast, I was climbing on steep terrain. Near noon, I felt I'd put in a full day. My shoulders and back ached. In spite of the high altitude and cool air, I was sweaty hot. I drained my water jug while stopping for a rest. I knew if I ate any dried food, it would make me even thirstier. So, after a rest, I chose to go hungry until reaching the Blue River for a drink.

After three more hours of picking my way, searching for tracks, I heard splashing water up ahead. Since the short drought just weeks ago, we'd gotten some generous amounts of rain, rejuvenating the river. I was excited to hear the water. When I reached the Blue, I looked up. A waterfall was coming from the top of a sheer wall of rock that rose at least two hundred feet above me. Water splashed over the rock formation, causing a spectacular show as it fell through the air, landing near where I stood to form the Blue River.

I slipped off my pack. Kneeling, I thirstily drank from the cool stream and filled my water bottle. The cold spray on my face and shoulders felt good.

The waterfall caused a transparent mist resulting in mini-rainbows. The natural phenomenon was beautiful to see, but I felt an urgency to press onward to reach my destination before dark. Wunderland was above and beyond the cliff.

I estimated that I had to backtrack along the sharp incline of stone for at least a half mile before I could continue climbing in a southeast direction. The steepness of the ledge underfoot was treacherous, causing me to crawl in places. To my left, I was looking at the tops of trees, which told me if I slipped I'd be a goner, landing among the treetops.

Finally, by four o'clock, I was once again headed in my desired direction, but it was steep. I was getting above the tree-line, depending on shrubs, cracks, and crevices in the ledge for handholds to help me make the climb.

I could feel coolness as the sun neared the horizon. It was getting late. I started doubting myself, thinking my time away was a bad idea. I was exhausted—in no shape for the demanding climb. Wunderland sounded like a neat place to camp, but was it really worth it? I knew the folks back home were depending on smoke from my fire, so I had to press onward and reach the site before dark. A picture of a bobcat was beginning to sound ridiculous. My fantasy of being some great wildlife photographer was making me feel stupid. Here I was on a slope so steep, I had to hang on with both hands or fall off into space.

Finally, by six o'clock I was in view of Wunderland. Up ahead I saw the remnants of an old building. I dropped flat on my face and lay lifeless from exhaustion.

After a short while, I caught my breath, slipped off my pack, and stood on the upper side of the waterfalls, watching the river flow westward until it was hidden below in the low shrubs and overhanging trees.

I looked down shivering at the distance below then I backed away from the edge.

Following the stream up the mountain, I came to a small plateau with a pond that was about a half-acre in size. The water was so clear I could see fish, mostly brook trout. Apparently, the pool was deep enough for them to have survived the variable temperatures and seasons. I surmised the fish had been stocked, a clue that probably some back-to-earth folks had been at Wunderland, trying to live off the land. Also, the brush growing around the pool looked to have sprung up in just a short time. Perhaps the inhabitants left a year ago when winter set in.

Beyond the pool, the remains of a fireplace stood. Old timbers and rusty tin still hung attached to the stone—the remains of a roof.

I decided to camp under the roof and set up my small tent on the flooring. I sat, planning, while chewing on some beef jerky. The only thing I had to do was to lay out my bedroll in the tent and start a fire for the folks back home—like a telephone call: *I made it!* However, the fire could wait until morning.

I couldn't see the valley below because of the brush, so decided that in the morning, I'd cut most of it with my ax, and also chop down a nearly dead white birch, cutting pieces for the fireplace. I'd also use two solid pieces to build a crude latrine not far from the campsite.

Looking toward the west, watching the sun disappear beyond the horizon, it was exhilarating to be free without a single thing to do, with absolutely no responsibilities. I'd brought along several books to read, but even that seemed unimportant. As it turned out, Iverson had changed my life maybe for the better, removing all my responsibilities of the farm. I even had enough food for six weeks. I was going to enjoy my stay—maybe even luck out and get a picture of a bobcat. Mom and Dad could work in their business, Ruth could pursue her Piedmont cause, and after I sent my smoke signal, Cooner could rest easy, knowing I was okay. Building a fire each morning, making lots of smoke, was all I had to do.

I set up my single-burner propane stove and heated water for a cup of coffee. Coffee, trail-mix, and banana chips were enough for supper. After the quick bite, I crawled into my sleeping bag and fell dead asleep.

I woke around five a.m. to the familiar sound of chickadees flitting in the nearby shrubs. I lay for a while, very comfortable in my sleeping bag. After a while I got up to start a fire in the fireplace. Once it was burning, I threw on a few soggy birch logs to cause a lot of smoke. My one and only job completed for the day, I started my propane burner, heated some water, and sat with a cup of coffee in hand. I located my binoculars and watched an occasional car traveling along Murray's Flats. It looked like an ant. The green meadow and corn with brown tassels made for an attractive patchwork. I slipped the binocular's strap over my head and stood up, deciding to take a walk and explore my new home.

thirty-four

Ruth

Jason left on his trek to Wunderland on the 28th of July. I had a lump in my throat seeing him go. Cooner said it would take most of the day to reach his destination. After going to bed, I didn't sleep well, thinking about him, worrying if he made the hike, and if he was okay. I got up at a little after five to go out and check for his smoke signal.

Cooner was already on his bench, looking off toward the mountain. "Morning, Ruth."

"Good morning, Cooner. I can see you were thinking the same as I, hoping to see some smoke."

Golly, I've been sittin' here since the crack of dawn and I ain't seen any yet."

I sat flexing my bandaged hands. "Maybe we're rushing him too much. We should give him a chance to get up and have some breakfast."

"That boy's an independent cuss." Cooner rapped his cane on the path. "He's prob'ly forgotten he's got folks back home waitin' on his smoke signal."

"No, he'll start a fire. Let's give him some time."

We were both seated, straining to look toward Wunderland. Sure enough! In minutes we could barely see a thin line of gray curl into the sky. We both excitedly said, "There it is!"

What a relief! I tore into the kitchen where Mom and Dad were eating breakfast. "Jason just sent us his smoke signal!"

Both smiled. Dad rested his cup on the table. "Well, he's doing something I'd never do, but I guess he had to get it out of his system."

Mom, sounding relieved, said, "Thanks for the good news!" She looked up at me. "How are your hands feeling?"

"Much better." I held them out for her to remove the bandaging.

She examined them closely. "Gee, the open sores are covered with new skin. I think you could go without bandages."

"Super!" I sat at the table. "Chris called. He's stopping by soon."

Mom started clearing dishes. "If that's the case, there's no need for me. I'll go to the shop this morning."

As Mom and Dad went across the street to work, I rejoined Cooner, who hadn't left for Butson's. He was enjoying watching Jason's smoke while he basked in the early morning sun. "Well, well, nothin' on your hands." He looked up at me before I sat. "Let me see your hair."

"Sure." I slipped off my wig.

"Looks like ya just had a buzz-cut."

"Isn't that great!" I sat next to him. "Soon I'll be able to throw this wig away."

Suddenly, I noticed in the distance what looked like a young kid walking on the side of the road toward us. He or she was bent over, carrying a heavy load of something covered by black plastic. All that could be seen were swinging arms and short legs. It looked like a fast-moving turtle with its head looking out from under its shell. The homemade covering had tails that were tied at the mid-section.

Cooner spat. "Golly, I ain't believin' what I'm seein'."

"Who is it?"

The morning sun was getting hot. As the kid came closer, I could see a face sweaty-red from the heat.

Cooner leaned forward, squinting. "It's Rosita, the Mexican gal that worked for Jason."

"Rosita? I've never met her." I stood and waved. "Hi."

"Señor Jason." She pointed toward his red truck in the yard.

With the help of his cane, Cooner stood. He motioned for her and pointed. "See the smoke?"

"Smook?" She nodded. "Sí."

"That's Jason. I wish I could give you a ride." Cooner sat with a thud. "With that load, well…well…" He shook his head.

Rosita had a blank expression. She turned to me. "Cantar…Señor Jason."

I nodded. "Oh, you want to sing to Jason."

"Sí, sí…cantar."

"I'm Ruth, Jason's sister." I vaguely remembered some of my Spanish from school. "His hermana."

"Sí, sí." She smiled, pulling a dictionary from her pack. "I no speaka bueno inglés."

Her pack looked to weigh a ton. I motioned next to Cooner. "Sit and rest."

"No…no. I cantar Señor Jason." She wiped her sweaty face. "He triste, cantar bueno."

In an instant it all made sense to me, what beautiful sounds meant to Jason. Living with him in the same house, Rosita had seen him during his toughest moments. Knowing Jason and his self-assured demeanor, he wouldn't easily share how important Rosita had been to him. I realized that this Mexican girl might have been the source of Jason's strength.

Rosita looked in the direction of the smoke and started to leave.

I glanced at her load, then at the smoke, realizing she didn't have a clue as to how to reach Wunderland.

"We'll take you part way to find Jason." I motioned for Cooner. "Let's get in your truck. We can at least take her to the heifer pasture and show her the trail."

Cooner again looked at what she was carrying. He went toward his truck continuing to shake his head.

Rosita obviously did not understand us. I pointed toward Cooner's truck. "A ride."

"Sí, sí paseo." She headed toward the truck.

Cooner followed. "I'll bet our boy ain't expectin' company."

"Maybe so. Just the same, I have a feeling he'll be excited to see her."

The use of my hands was limited, so Cooner helped her lift her pack into the back of his truck.

I slid in next to him and she hopped up and shut the door. I glanced her way, trying not to stare. Her hair was covered by a brightly colored bandana. Her hands were small compared to mine, but they looked rough and muscled. It seemed odd that she wore a red cloth belt above a pair of denim pants. The belt covered the bottom of a long-sleeve work shirt. She made no effort to talk to me or Cooner, no doubt because of the language barrier. With a look of determination, her alert brown eyes focused on the road ahead.

We reached the burn site and crossed the bridge. In first gear, the truck groaned its way to the ridge. I showed her the trail as best I could, hoping she'd reach Jason by nightfall.

Before she left, I tried to explain that she needed to follow the river to find Jason. We stood on the ridge, looking down at the Blue. I pointed toward the Hardhack peak. "Follow the agua."

Cooner raised his voice from the truck. "She'll have to hike around the cliff."

How could I explain that she'd have to take a detour? I couldn't. Her common sense would have to prevail.

"Sí, agua." She looked toward the direction of the peak.

I worried, wondering if Rosita could make the climb. I got a scrap of paper and a pencil stub from the truck and, with my stiff fingers, wrote a note:

> *Jason, start a fire as soon as Rosita finds you.*
> *We'll want to know if she's okay. Love, Ruth*

I tucked it in her backpack. "For Jason."

"Sí."

I wasn't sure she understood the difficulty in reaching him. Cooner helped her with her pack, covering it with the plastic. She tied the tails around her waist and headed toward the path. She waved. "Gracias."

I did have the consoling realization that Rosita was no ordinary girl. She seemed full of grit and determination. If anyone could make the hike to Wunderland, Rosita surely would. Especially considering that the last we were told, she was in Florida. She had to have had a lot of spunk, returning to Huntersville from God knows where. "Wow, there must have been something special between her and Jason."

Cooner nodded in agreement. He didn't go to Butson's after Rosita left but came back to the homestead with me. He got out of his truck and hobbled to his bench. "I might's well stick around and wait for the smoke."

I chuckled. "Aren't you being a little impatient?"

"I know, I know." He tapped the end of his cane. "Wonderin' about that poor girl findin' Jason has got me all worked up."

"Don't even think about seeing Jason's signal until late today." I went to him. "Go to Butson's and ease your mind."

"I might's well. Sitting here waiting for smoke is like watchin' corn grow."

thirty-five

Jason

On my second morning at Wunderland, after starting a fire, I left my campsite to continue exploring the area. I looked for bobcat signs and found a tree near a trail with claw marks about three feet off the ground. The discovery excited me, realizing that my years of wanting to see a bobcat might actually become a reality. Back a distance from the trail near my camp, I found a place to stake out, giving a clear view of the tree.

By mid-afternoon I returned to camp for something to eat. It was about three o'clock. The sun still hung high in a cloudless sky. The shaded platform felt good away from the incredible heat. The temperature felt like it was near ninety degrees.

I was drinking water and nibbling on a granola bar when I heard a faint call that sounded like my name. It was difficult to tell because of the waterfall. I tipped my head and held my breath to be sure I wasn't imagining things. It sounded familiar, although I couldn't catch the first word. I grabbed my binoculars and hurried toward the cliff.

The calls stopped. I lay on my stomach, hidden by a young gray birch that hung out over the edge. Its lower leaves gave me some cover. Adjusting my binoculars, I searched the sheer wall. Irregular footholds had been formed over the years by chunks of shale breaking away. I spotted what at first looked like a bear, but it wasn't. It was a person carrying a load covered in black plastic. The person didn't make a sound while creeping over the steep lichen-covered rock, searching for something to hold on to. I couldn't see a face. He or she had climbed about a third of the way up the cliff and apparently had decided to turn back. In a moment, the person knelt, looking around, seemingly trapped, trying to decide what to do next.

Putting aside the binoculars, I rested my eyes. A wave of disappointment struck me. I could be having company. If this hiker joined me, my time alone would be short-lived. Looking again, I saw a face—stunned, I mumbled in amazement, "Rosita!" I checked again. "What is she doing? She was supposed to be in Florida."

My attitude suddenly changed to excitement. She's coming to see me! What for? Why? She was in danger, walking and crawling on steep rock, carrying what looked like a huge load. If she slipped and lost her footing, she could fall to her death.

How could I tell her I'd meet her down the mountain? If she saw me, she would no doubt ignore all danger and turn around. The language barrier was too great to be able to reason the fine points of a critical decision. Pushing back from the edge, considering options, I felt helpless. On hands and knees, I went back to the edge, looking through the birch leaves again. She was crawling away. Maybe she'd given up. I had no idea how long she'd been calling my name.

I grabbed my empty backpack to help with her load and started down the mountain, hoping to meet her beyond the cliff. I kept calling, "Rosita. Rosita." Maybe at some point she would hear me.

Carefully inching down the steepness of the bare rock north of the cliff, I continued calling. After traveling some distance, I faintly heard what I thought was "Señor Jason!" I kept sliding downward on the rock and walking when I could, coming closer to the sound of her voice. We finally met where the incline was less severe. "Rosita!" I hurried to her. "Rosita!"

She fell forward, crying. "Señor Jason!" Her voice was muffled. The black plastic had slid forward, covering her head.

The poor girl sounded exhausted from the hike. It seemed like a miracle that we had finally found each other. I pulled back the plastic and helped her stand. Her face was a brilliant red, wet with sweat and tears. From beneath her load, she reached for me and squeezed my hand.

She continued crying as I lightened her load, removing her guitar, several five pound bags of white corn, a tortilla maker, a pack of spices, sleeping bag, bed roll, and bags of her belongings. Ruth's note was sticking out of Rosita's backpack. The smoke signal had to wait until we reached camp.

"Gracias!" She continued, clinging to my hand.

I worried that she had no water. I didn't bring any, being in such a hurry to reach her. She kept repeating, "Gracias, mi ángulo."

"Angel?" She obviously believed in an angel, which at the moment seemed appropriate.

"Sí, sí." She pressed her hands as if sending up a prayer. "Gracias, mi ángulo."

She began to relax and looked up. Streams of sweat ran from her forehead. She smiled tiredly.

With most of the weight of Rosita's things in my backpack, I held her firm hand, helping her to resume our climb. At some points, we crawled up the face of steeper rock to reach a more reasonable incline leading to the campsite. We got there about an hour before sunset.

After removing my load, I helped her with her belongings plus her makeshift plastic pack frame. Her red belt was soaked, but nearly all the money was still bound by the cloth. I hung it on a nail under the shelter. Her shirt was drenched.

She stood on the floor of the shelter. I was a foot below on the ground. She threw her arms around me and uncontrollably cried. "Florida." She sniffed. "No Señor Jason."

I hugged her.

She smiled and nodded, removing her bandana, shirt, shoes, socks, and pants, and laid them on the floor. Holding a clean change of clothes, she ran in her panties and t-shirt for the pond, plunging into the water.

While she swam, I began the fire for the folks back home. After getting a good flame, I threw on all sorts of damp rotted sticks I'd gathered from the wood's floor for my morning smoke signal. Slabs of half dried moss worked the best in sending up the most smoke.

Next, I rolled out her bedroll and sleeping bag next to mine in the tent. With some adjusting for width, the two just fit. She had an extra flannel blanket for a pillow or for more warmth in case it got really cold.

From three hundred feet away, I saw Rosita's head bobbing above the water. Soon she came ashore, spreading her wet clothes out to dry and dressing in her clean ones.

I noticed her dangling silver chain and crucifix when she came back for a comb. Out in the sun, she sat combing her wet hair that reached to the small of her back. She spread it in the shape of a fan and rested face down.

I decided right then that we were going to start communicating with each other by both learning the other's language. I spent the next hour or more printing sentences in my log book, double-spacing so I could print the same in Spanish words that I took from her dictionary.

Rosita hadn't moved. It was still a warm evening although the sun was much lower. It was obvious that she was exhausted because, by nature, she was always busy. Before the sun disappeared behind the horizon, she woke and fixed her hair in a knot above her head, holding it in place with a fresh bandana.

I continued printing practice sentences that we could learn together.

Using the supplies and tortilla press, she quickly made our meal on my camp burner. We shared our food and finished an early supper. Afterward, I showed her the sentences I'd written.

I explained to her that I was going to hike to my outpost in hopes of seeing some wildlife and maybe a bobcat. When I left with my camera, she started studying what I had written.

The place I'd chosen to wait and watch the trail gave me good cover in low shrubs, mostly juniper and scrub cedar. Although hidden, I had a clear view of the small tree that had the bobcat scratch marks. As I waited that night, I realized right off that the life of a wildlife photographer was solitary and could easily be boring. On the other hand, I had time to think. I wouldn't stay long; darkness was quickly coming on. The sounds of the summer night had started—mostly crickets. The temperature was rapidly falling.

As I waited, I mulled over my thoughts of Rosita. How long will she stay? What would we do? We had to be able to talk and understand each other, which at this point was minimal. We were going to have to spend lots of time learning our languages. I really didn't know much about her. From her personal belongings, she'd never shown me an ID or birth certificate. Was she a U.S. citizen? I didn't know. How old was she? Of course, I didn't know that either.

Our relationship to this point was that of boss and employee. However, I did love her singing, her pleasant personality, and her work ethic. I was drawn to her qualities and respected her for them.

What did she see in me? Why didn't she go to Florida but turned around instead? The reason had to be more than the fact that I liked her singing. Maybe I represented stability to her, something she'd never had. Then there was the money belt, but I didn't have the feeling that money was the reason she came back. These questions sparked my curiosity.

Our relationship was such that I felt we connected very nicely as friends. I didn't feel attracted to her as I was toward Ellen. Her non-descript figure was made up of mostly muscle and bone with no luscious curves to admire. She didn't weigh much over a hundred pounds. But her personality—yes, her personality was special. Her broad, ready smile and pleasant demeanor made it easy to be with her. A long-lasting relationship couldn't be based on the love of her singing. The attraction had to be something more. Spending time together might allow us to find qualities in each other that we could grow to love.

On my return to camp, I could feel a gentle westerly breeze. Rosita was singing. The sound of her voice was riding on the waves of the warm summer night.

At the campsite, she had a candle glowing in front of her crucifix that leaned against a post. She was wearing her white robe as she played the guitar. In only shorts and a t-shirt, I pulled her flannel sheet around me and sat listening to her sing a familiar series of Latin chants. She seemed unaware that I was waiting for her.

After several minutes, she turned back in surprise. "Señor Jason!"

"Yes." By candlelight, she could see me pointing toward the tent. "Sleep?"

She smiled. Her soft brown eyes brightened. "It...is...time...to sleep."

"Good for you!" I nodded.

After going to the latrine across the yard, I crawled in the tent. The insulated lining of the sleeping bag gave me plenty of warmth. She crawled in behind me, and I pulled up the zipper closing the tent.

Rosita, in her sleeping bag on the foam cushion, hummed a barely audible tune, probably an evening prayer. The sound was relaxing and quickly lulled me to sleep.

thirty-six

Ruth

After Cooner left for Butson's, I went to the house. I took some time over a cup of coffee to think through my situation. With the charge of arson settled, Jason gone, and no farm responsibilities, I once again returned to my pressing problem. So much had happened since my visit to New York and the board meeting. As I sat flexing my hands in between sips, I decided that my best approach would be to return to Piedmont for a visit, and reconnect with the Center, Frieda, Sara, Anadeepa, and the other children, and put all my energy into finding a solution for funding.

While at the table, I watched Chris drive into the yard. I smiled and felt a twinge of excitement, seeing his fuzzy hair and gawky appearance as he walked toward the house. He had a bounce to his step as he met me at the door. He came in the house and pulled me into his arms, planting a big kiss on my lips. "Wow, what's this all about!"

He chuckled. "Did I scare you?"

"Well, yes." I straightened my wig. "Some change for the Reverend Christopher Ball."

"It is. I have some good news." He gave me a flirting look with his eyes dancing in excitement. "The Executive Board has voted to change my contract. I'm now free to date anyone I want to."

"That's great news!" I kissed him back. "So they agreed to your terms."

"Yeah, Bertha was cleaning my office, and I mentioned to her that I was going to ask for the change.

"She nodded, agreeing. 'I'll take care of it. I always thought your contract was ridiculous'.

"Last night at our Executive Board meeting, Bertha, right out of the blue, opened the subject under *New Business*. She cleared her throat and, I think, caught most members off guard. 'I move we make a change in Chris's contract. Let him date the gal of his choice'.

"Judge Crabtree seconded the motion. There was no discussion. Mildred Butson, the chair, might have opposed, but she didn't say a word. The motion passed unanimously."

I jumped. "Yay, for Bertha!" I pulled on Chris's hand. "Let's go to the front room and sit on the couch."

"Hey, your hand!" He held it up. "It looks nearly healed."

I showed him. "They both are."

"They look kind of tender."

"Well, I'm not ready to swing a nail hammer." I laughed. "But I'm ready to jump on a plane for Georgia. Do you want to come?"

"Whoa, not so fast!" We sat down. "What's this all about?"

"I think it's time I launched an all-out effort to solve the problem of funding for the Center. I want to begin by visiting Piedmont."

He pushed his glasses into place. "How long would we be gone?"

"We could get a flight on Sunday after church and be back by Friday."

"Sounds doable." He smiled. "I'll have to readjust my schedule."

"Do it!" I gently shook his forearm. "Let's go."

He held me tightly. "I'll talk to Mildred and get her okay for a few days' vacation." We kissed and he got up to leave.

Early that afternoon after lunch, I spent some time in the new office Mom had built just off the kitchen. There were lots to do, reorganizing the space and filing. After a couple of hours, I set office work aside, knowing Cooner was on his bench, looking toward Hardhack Mountain, waiting for a smoke signal. It was going to be a long vigil before seeing smoke, since Cooner himself said it would be a tough hike for Rosita.

I went out to keep him company. "You must be getting tired." I rested my hand on his shoulder and sat.

"Well, I ain't thinkin' about bein' tired. I jest wanna see smoke."

"I'll watch the mountain while you take a rest."

He didn't resist. Soon, he slumped into a deep sleep. His hand lost grip on his cane. The shiny knob-end rested in his lap.

After my vigil at supper time, I brought Cooner a sandwich and a glass of iced tea. He thanked me, while reaching for the food. "I'm gettin' a mite worried that we ain't seein' smoke."

Just as he spoke, I saw a ripple of gray, darker than a cloud, rise above the Wunderland site. "There it is, Cooner!" I jumped up from the bench. "Rosita made it!"

The old man chuckled. "By golly, she did!"

The next day, after Chris got approval for vacation time, I called Frieda, telling her we'd arrive at the Center on Monday afternoon.

Her voice rose over the phone. "Well, I'll be. We sure will be happy to see y'all!"

Sunday night we were on a flight taking us to JFK. We connected in New York with a flight to Atlanta. After we rented a car, it was ten p.m. We stopped at a Red Roof Motel. The young attendant behind the counter barely looked at us as he glanced at his list of available rooms. "What do you want, a king or two queen-size beds?"

Chris paused. "Two...two queen-size."

A part of me was relieved. I was hoping our new-found relationship wouldn't move too quickly. As it was, we went to our room and sat for a while eating snacks. We both were tired. We hugged and kissed, and I could feel our emotions heating up. I looked at a bed. It would easily hold the both of us. My breasts were pressed tightly to him, giving me a shiver of passion. But I pulled back. "Let's get some sleep in our own beds."

He quickly kissed me. "I agree."

Monday morning after breakfast it was already hot outside. We turned the car's air conditioner on full bore. We took Route 19 south through Griffin, Thomaston, Americus, Albany, Camilla, onto Route 37 toward Piedmont. When we pulled in the Center's yard around one o'clock, the kids poured out of the building. Some kids came running from the playground.

Frieda had her arms out for a hug. "Hallelujah, look at ya all!" Her round face had a big smile. "And this is the Reverend." She shook Chris's hand.

The kids crowded in with a chorus of "Hi, Ms. Murray."

I knelt and Anadeepa came toward me. We hugged for several moments. She whispered, "I miss you a lot!"

"Well, honey, I miss you." I could feel my emotions taking over and sniffed. "Kids, this is Chris." He bent down and Anadeepa went to him. She hesitantly reached for his fuzzy hair—then she touched her own. "Just like me."

All the kids laughed.

I glanced up and saw Sara standing in the background. I went to her. "How are you?"

"I'm fine." She frowned. "Anadeepa cries a lot at night. She sure misses you."

"I feel the same. I miss her."

I saw Chris already playing low-net volley ball with the kids—most ranged in ages from six to ten.

Anadeepa left the group and came to hold my hand. Her squeeze was tight. My hand was still tender but I didn't say anything.

"Ya all gonna stay?" she asked.

I hated to tell her. "For a few days."

"Oh." She hung her head.

She was growing tall and slender with delicate long fingers. I glanced at the top of her head that was level with my mid-section. I admired her two tight braids, tied with red ribbons. She was fine-featured with light black coloring, slender, and her complexion had a smooth glow. She looked much healthier since living at the Center.

It pained me to see her reaction to the fact that we weren't staying longer. On impulse, I asked, "Would you like to visit Vermont and come home with Chris and me?"

She jumped. "Yippee!"

"Maybe you could stay for a month or so." I hugged her. "We'll ask Frieda."

Of course, Frieda agreed to let Anadeepa leave.

I looked toward the playground. "How will the other kids take this?"

Frieda thought for a minute. "We'll plan a trip and they'll be okay."

In the next few days, Chris connected with the kids. He read to them, told stories and, amazingly, could call all thirty kids by their first names. The group swelled to forty when the day kids were dropped off in the late afternoon.

Sara had her hands full tutoring, trying to get children ready for the first grade, plus helping those who were already struggling in school, but I could see progress. Since I'd been away the kids' reading and writing skills had improved.

Friday came quickly. We left at four in the morning to make our flight out of Atlanta. The kids were still sleeping, making it easier to leave without a lot of tears. Since Chris had connected with the kids, even he was saddened to leave. In the car, we were sleepy and didn't talk much. I sat with Anadeepa cuddling next to me. While driving, Chris kept repeating to himself in a whisper, "Such needy kids!"

We arrived in Huntersville at the homestead Friday night around ten. Chris carried Anadeepa to a daybed placed next to mine. Mom had rearranged my room after I let her know Anadeepa was coming for a visit.

At breakfast she was wide-eyed in shock, looking at three strangers. She didn't say or eat much but spent her time staring at Mom, Cooner, and then Dad.

Cooner was in a hurry to check on Jason's morning smoke signal, something that had become a daily routine.

Dad was taken by our guest. He winked at her, and she tried to wink, shutting both eyes. This little game relaxed her. They continued through most of breakfast. In a total surprise to me, she left her seat and motioned to sit in Dad's lap. He glowed with a broad smile. She was as fascinated by his hair as she was with Chris's, reaching, running her fingers through his short cut. She giggled. Then she felt the bristles on his chin and again giggled. "You feel funny."

Dad laughed. I don't think he ever held a child Anadeepa's age that much. She left his lap and ran for one of her books that we'd brought along. She returned, holding it up and placing it in his lap before she climbed on his knee. Mom and I sat in surprise as Dad read to her, letting her turn the pages.

The little girl had brought out a different side of Dad, who was always in a dash to go to work. Mom and I cleared the table and did the dishes while he continued reading. Finally, he announced, "I've got to go to the greenhouse."

"Me, too." She grabbed his hand.

Dad looked a little surprised, lifting his brow. "Okay."

They left holding hands. We watched as the two crossed the street. Mom smiled. "This is something else!" She pushed back her hair. "Your father has a new buddy."

As the days passed, Dad didn't tire having Anadeepa as a sidekick. If he was watering plants, she had her own child's watering can. If he was transplanting, she transplanted with him. If he was driving the forklift, she sat in his lap. On trips to the hardware store, she tagged along. At noon, she didn't want to take a nap, but he insisted, promising he'd return in an hour and take her for an ice-cream. At night I'd spend time reading to her, but make no mistake, she was Dad's girl.

The month of August flew by. Chris told me he needed some clerical help, so I bought a laptop and volunteered to be church secretary. I also did some of the Murray financial work, paying bills at Chris's office. I had plenty of time to do church clerical work and answer the phone. Chris and I made a good team.

Over the summer, I felt that we really got to know each other, coming to appreciate our similar values. We had to be discreet in acting on our love, as church members visited quite regularly. However, we had terrific moments in his apartment.

At the end of August, it was time for Anadeepa to go home and back to school. I was surprised when Dad announced that he and Mom were taking her back to Piedmont. I was pleased he was getting more and more invested in the welfare of what was now *our* little friend.

While they were gone, a letter came from the Eagle Fire Insurance Company explaining their payment of the claim. They had deducted thirty-thousand dollars because the cement silo didn't burn. The amount of six hundred thousand dollars had been transferred into the account of Marcus and Margaret Murray.

When Mom and Dad came back from Piedmont, I showed them the deposit notice. For a few days, Dad seemed especially quiet. At meals, Mom looked at him with concern. I know he missed his side-kick. No words were spoken, something had changed with Dad.

He had always been a man of few words but now he acted detached. Several days after they returned from Georgia, I left the house to see Cooner. I sat, waiting for Jason's smoke signal. "Nothing, yet?"

"No, it's a might early." He reached for a pinch of Beechnut.

I turned to him. "What do you make of Dad lately?"

He spat and wiped his mouth. "'Course, he misses that little girl."

"I know, but it seems to be more."

"He's...he's at war with himself. You know, he wants to help her."

"You think so?" I shrugged, feeling mystified. "Maybe?"

"Yup." He sniffed. "His old ways have given way ta new ways. That little girl has poured oil on his tight squeaky thinkin'.

"Thinking?"

"Well, all of his life he's traveled a narrow little path." Cooner spat again. "Now, he's been thrown off track...havin' a hard time to handle it."

Several days passed. Dad hadn't changed. Meals continued to be quiet. I tried drawing him into a conversation.

"Dad, what's wrong? What are you thinking?"

"Huh...oh..." He stared across the table. "Those kids...those kids."

"Yeah, what about them?"

He shook his head. "I...I just don't...don't know." He got up and left the house.

Mom and I watch him head to work. His shoulders were bent as he walked dejectedly toward the florist shop.

"Mom, you're with him more than anyone. What's wrong?"

"I really don't know. Last night I woke and he was sitting on the edge of the bed."

"What did he say?"

"Nothing. I pulled on his arm and asked, 'What is it, dear'? He told me he was dreaming about Anadeepa and kids."

Mom moved over to the sink. "I assured him, 'She'll do just fine where she is'."

I started clearing the table. "Do you think I should talk to Dad about the Center?"

Mom drew a blank. "You could try, but he's a private man."

He continued to be depressed. One morning I was with Cooner on his bench when Dad called from the house, asking me to come to the kitchen.

He shut the door behind me. "Let's sit."

I looked at Mom and Dad, thinking the worst: a terminal illness, a separation, Dad leaving for Georgia. But I doubted my thoughts as they both were all smiles, relieved and relaxed.

Dad looked up at me. "We've always, up until recent days, lived and worked for ourselves, even allowing Cooner to raise you and Jason."

I caught my breath. "What's up?"

"Well, we need to change and your mom agrees. With the insurance money we are starting a trust fund for the Piedmont Center."

I couldn't believe it. "Oh my gosh! This is wonderful!" I jumped up and hugged them. "I can't believe your generosity. This is much more than I could ever have expected!"

Dad smiled. "We want you to manage the fund."

I cried with my arms spread. "Out of the fire, a rose has bloomed!"

After Dad made the decision to secure a future for Anadeepa and the kids, he seemed to be a completely different person—a load of worry had been lifted.

thirty-seven

Jason

It was five o'clock in the morning. As I lay in my sleeping bag, I could hear rain hitting the tin roof and splattering on the ground next to our tent. Rosita had already gotten up. I could hear her mixing the dough for the tortillas.

I got up, pulled on my pants, yawning while stretching my arms. "Good morning, Rosita."

She was rolling the golf-ball-size tortilla dough in her hands. "Buenos días, Señor Jason."

I started the fire while she continued making breakfast. This was the beginning of what was to become a daily routine. On that morning, the rain kept us undercover for most of the day, giving plenty of time to work on our language skills. We enjoyed ourselves as we laughed at each other's pronunciation of words. I pointed at the flame. "Fire."

"Fiure."

I laughed. "No, fire—i—i—fire."

She smiled. "Oh, fuego."

"Fugo." I repeated.

Then she laughed. "No, fuego."

We continued naming all the items and articles in our campsite. It was a slow and laborious process, but there was no urgency in learning. We had as much time as we wanted to spend, a freedom that was new to me. I was no longer controlled by a rigid routine.

Most of our time was spent learning languages, collecting firewood, and keeping our clothes washed. Tracking a bobcat and getting a good picture was not uppermost in my mind anymore, although we often sat in the evening to watch the trail. Sometimes we'd go to the pond, swim, and feed the fish small bits of beef jerky. We loved to see them swim to the surface and grab food.

We tried to catch some to eat, but they always slipped through our hands. Rosita was the quickest and caught the most, but she couldn't hold them from slipping away.

I had lots of film and took many pictures of the valley, Rosita, wildlife, and the birds.

As the days passed and we moved toward the first of September, the nights became colder, and Rosita and I became closer and understood each other better. I began to see her as a beautiful woman. She liked to flirt with her funny laugh and the twinkle in her brown eyes. She became sexy to me. We often smooched in the tent. I loved her kisses and the feel of her sleek body and the nipples of her small breasts. But we stayed in our own sleeping bags—going further was out of the question.

One morning as we were eating breakfast, I asked, "Where were you born?"

"Las Cruces."

"Mexico?" I munched on granola.

"No, New Mexico."

"Oh. In this country?" I'd always assumed she was an undocumented worker, instead she was a legal citizen.

"Sí. In Padre's casa."

"A church?" I tried to imagine her background as I sat watching her. She had eaten and was sewing her skirt.

"No, mission. Me padre and madre work at mission. Holy Padre's mucho pray. I sing and play guitar." She glanced at me with her warm eyes. "Sí, I sing mucho prayer for Padre."

"You sing to yourself." I looked in the dictionary. "Zumbido—hum." I pointed. "You hum a lot."

"Sí. I hum mucho: Praise you my angel. You never forget me."

Remembering her difficult time to reach me, I asked, "Your angel's always at your side?"

"Sí, my angel." She smiled, looking up from her sewing. "You comprender. Padre say angel always with me."

"How long were you at the mission?" I asked, as she hung her finished skirt on a nail.

"I born—eighteen years."

When I went to stand beside her, her brown eyes caught mine. I saw into the looking glass of a beautiful soul. We warmly kissed. At that moment, I realized that my feelings for her had grown deeper.

She continued. "My padre hear about wonderful Señor Iverson in Vermont— not so wonderful." She opened her mouth and pressed for a wet kiss. "Oh, but Señor Jason, wonderful!"

"And Señorita Rosita's wonderful!" I held her by the waist and swung her around. Later, she played the guitar while teaching me a song. I never thought that I could feel so contented. Near the end of the day, we walked to the hiding place off the trail.

We held hands through the low bushes. Her firm hand was something I admired. As we waited and watched, she'd quietly sit in my lap with her head resting on my chest. I loved inhaling deeply, smelling the pleasing scent of her hair. I could feel myself yearning for her, having her by my side. I wanted it to continue even after we left Wunderland. So what if she was from the Mexican culture and I was a native Vermonter? That shouldn't matter. Maybe folks would talk, but people can change and grow to like her as I had been growing to love her. Mom and Dad would gulp a little, I knew that, but they'd change to love her as I do.

As we sat near the trail, we often saw a deer and her fawn, and once a coyote, but that was all. I figured the bobcat knew where we were. Just to satisfy myself that I'd seen something in our hours of solitude, I took pictures of the other animals.

Before dark, when leaving our hiding place, I enjoyed sweeping Rosita off her feet, holding her in my arms as if she was my bride and I was carrying her over the threshold. She usually let out something between a scream and a giggle, but I knew she liked it. If there was ever a bobcat in the area, it would have been frightened by our noisy encroachment into its territory.

One cool morning as we sat next to each other with our jackets on, drinking hot coffee, I asked, "How did you find me? The last I knew, you were headed to Florida."

"I miss you! Don't you know?" She turned to me with an incredulous look. "I say in car—'stop! I go to Señor Jason'."

I thought in amazement. "Right in the middle of the night?"

"Sí. My father say, 'No!'"

"I say, 'Sí!' I cry and the car stops." She held her arms in circular fashion, showing quantity. "Mucho stuff. Es night, es dark." She finished her coffee. "I have bag, corn for tortilla, my guitar, coffee pot, and tortilla pan. I look. Lights come. Maybe my angel."

"Weren't you scared?"

"No. Why?" She shrugged. "No worry."

Shaking my head in disbelief, "Wow! Really?"

"Old truck come and stop. Door open. Señor Scoop."

"Oh, my gosh, Scoop!" I nodded in amazement. "How lucky!"

"Scoop run to me. I no comprender. I say, 'Señor Jason!'

He look at me... then all my stuff. He say, 'Jesus Christ!'" She shrugged. "I no comprender Señor Scoop."

I laughed.

"Señor Scoop take me Señorita Bubbles. Bubbles say, 'Jason?' She point high. 'Up Mountain!' "I no comprender. Señor Scoop make my back to hold all stuff and black plastic for rain. Señor Scoop go."

"Good ole Scoop." I smiled. "It didn't hurt that you're a pretty girl."

"What? Me no comprender."

"Never mind."

"Bubbles give sleeping bag, blanket. It mucho late. I sleep at Señorita Bubbles. I hum prayer. Find Señor Jason."

I kissed her. "And you did."

"Sí, Bubbles say go to Señor Cooner." Rosita jumped up. "I forget. Señorita Bubbles give little bag. I no need." She searched among her things, finding what looked like toiletries. She unzipped the bag, showing me the items, while trying and doing well reading the labels. "*Lip*

Balm, Gin…ger's Eye Sha…dow, Beige Fac…ial Powder, Lilac Per…fume, Gloria's Eye Liner, and Tro…jan…Trojans." She held the box of condoms for a moment and started to zip up the bag. "No need."

I reached. "I'll take the Trojans." Immediately, my face felt hot.

She looked at me with a blank expression and shrugged.

I stepped by the tent and threw the box in a far corner. Flustered, I blurted. "Let's go for a walk."

She smiled. "Oh, today uno September, sí."

"Yes, let me look in my log book." I opened it where it rested on a timber. "Yes, September 1, 1995."

"My birthday. I nineteen." She jumped, grabbing me by the waist. "Esta noche, grande party."

She swung me as if to dance as I awkwardly stumbled. I looked around at what we had, and it wasn't much for a celebration.

"Yes, we eat fish!"

"Fish?" I thought, doubting. "How?"

"Sí." She jumped up on the platform and tore a strip of beef jerky into small pieces—then reached inside the tent and brought out her flannel sheet. "Come!" She pulled me along with the sheet toward the pond. At the edge, we took off our pants, shoes, and socks.

Rosita was all business, holding the sheet at two corners. I did the same with my end as she motioned with her head to lower the sheet as we walked into the water. She let go of a corner and threw the beef jerky pieces onto the water. The trout came for the food. She quickly grabbed her corner, and we raised the sheet. It was heavy with water. A few escaped, but we had a good catch. With our arms high, we walked to the pond's edge and dumped the fish onto the shore.

I counted five big ones as they flopped on dry land. We slipped on our pants and shoes, collected the fish, and began preparing them for our feast. It would be a feast, too, since all we had lived on for four weeks was tortillas, beef jerky, dried fruit, and granola.

That night as Rosita fried the fish, I got the fire roaring. There was a spectacular sunset, sending shades of red and orange over the valley below. I was dizzy with anticipation. The smell wafting from the pan was like a feast for kings. The taste matched my expectation.

Shortly after the meal, I sat leaning up against a post, watching Rosita twirling, wearing her new skirt as it flared above her knees with her long hair flying. Her many-layered, white-ruffled blouse and long segmented earrings made a perfect picture of a Spanish dancer. I used a whole roll of film during her performance.

She sang beautifully of a discovered lover as she spun. The glowing fire sent shadows across her full lips and deep smiling eyes. I was mesmerized as I remembered something special, the ring—the von Friesian diamond.

My impulse buying had been foolish. Especially now, the ring's size would look ridiculous on a small hand. Besides, the lavish thing didn't remotely fit Rosita's nature.

When the evening ended, I had the ring in hand. I went to her, held her in my arms and looked into her brown eyes. "Will you stay with me, always?"

With her arms around my neck she jumped and cried, "Sí, Señor Jason!"

I unclipped her silver chain and slipped on the ring. "Now, and forever more, I'm Jason to you."

She held out the crucifix with the large diamond resting on the head of the crucified Christ. The light from the fireplace made it dazzle. Rosita cried, "Es bonito!"

In the tent later that night, I held her hand and invited her into my sleeping bag. She smiled and with no hesitation, she crawled in beside me. With the feel of her body next to me, I was delirious. We discovered ourselves in a new and beautiful way.

The next morning on September 2nd, I glanced outside our tent. The world looked pure, dressed in white frosting. Even though it was cold outside, we were in each other's arms, warm and content to stay under the covers. The folks at home would have to wait for their daily smoke signal.

thirty-eight

Ruth

On September 2nd I was with Cooner on his bench waiting for the smoke signal from Jason. It was cold, our first killing frost of the season. He and I sat with our winter jackets on, since the sun hadn't yet warmed up the land.

He nervously rattled his cane. "I ain't seen any smoke yet."

I looked off at the peak. "Maybe they've overslept."

The old man chuckled. "Wouldn't ya like ta be a set of eyes at Wunderland?"

"I wonder what's going on up there?"

He smiled. "We'll just have ta wait and see."

Cooner Clapton

Well, I ain't moved from this bench, rememberin' Ruth and Jason's story of what took place in the summer of '95. I'm sorta outta breath just thinkin' about it.

Ain't it nice, Ruth and that minister, Chris, appear to have teamed up. There ain't been no announcements or rings, but the two are darn serious. Watchin' them, you can tell they're in love. Ruth's a different girl since she has Chris and since solvin' the problem of supportin' her kids in Georgia—thanks to Marcus and Maggie.

Speakin' of Georgia, Anadeepa is due ta spend Thanksgivin' here and Christmas vacation, too. It's kinda special ta see her and Marcus together. That little girl has found a place in his heart. And because Marcus has changed, Maggie ain't playin' with her hair like she used ta.

Word has it that Eve goes ta visit Iverson every weekend. He's servin' out his five years at Rutland's Correctional. Golly, why do the most promisin' women seem ta sometimes get hooked up with the biggest losers? Well, the answer is way beyond me.

Golly, it was good ta see Jason back from Wunderland. Ruth said, and I agreed, that his time away was worth it. 'Course we all knew Rosita brought Jason back ta life. He wears a big smile and stands as straight as a freshly sawed timber. He's lookin' like he can take on the world. Everyone was wonderin' about his picture of a bobcat. When asked, he turned red-faced, admittin', "I never saw hide nor hair of one."

Meetin' Rosita, I realized she came in a dynamite package, small and burstin' with life. Her warm smile's won the hearts of us all. With her at

his side, Jason acts as if he just found a diamond in a haystack. Speakin'
of a diamond, the von Friesian diamond didn't stay around Rosita's neck
long, because it covered too much of the crucifix. Ruth told me that
even if Rosita thought the precious stone was beautiful, she didn't like
the huge thing on her neck coverin' Christ's crown of thorns. Rosita
said, "Jesus born in manger. He no like diamonds."

Jason agreed ta take it back. So he sent it ta London to be auctioned
off. No one, not even Ruth, was ever told what the diamond sold for.
The "Counter Intelligence" sure talked plenty, and the boys at Butson's
asked me about every day what I thought it brought at auction. I wan't
never told. Not even Bertha could find the answer. Clyde Shanks sneered
that he bet the rock sold for a million bucks. 'Course he was jealous.
No way could a five-thousand-dollar diamond bring any such money as
Clyde claimed, but some folks around Huntersville think they have all
the answers.

The town was abuzz with the news that Jason was goin' ta marry a
Mexican. With Rosita in charge and plenty of cash plus diamond money,
we all learnt pretty quick that this gal was no shrinkin' violet. Their
weddin' was goin' ta be the likes that Huntersville had never seen.